I0822363

Stars and Other Monsters

cassandra celia

STARS AND OTHER MONSTERS

CASSANDRA CELIA

Stars and Other Monsters

First Edition Hardcover | Publication Date: August 11th, 2023

ISBN-13 (Hardcover): 979-8-9858659-2-9

ISBN-13 (Paperback): 979-8-9858659-0-5

ISBN (EBook): 979-8-9858659-1-2

Cover Design © Dani Figueroa @danisaur.art

Edited by Alexis Aumagamanaia @littlelionslibrary

Interior Formatting by Cassandra Celia @authorcassandracelia

CONTENTS

Also by Cassandra Celia

Sugarcane

The Elric Undoing

CAUTION!

By reading past this point, you are recognizing that STARS AND OTHER MONSTERS is an adult book that features mature and at times triggering themes and material. For a complete list of relevant content warnings, please visit my landing page located at the end of this book.

We are all in control of our own content consumption.

Thank you, and I hope you enjoy!

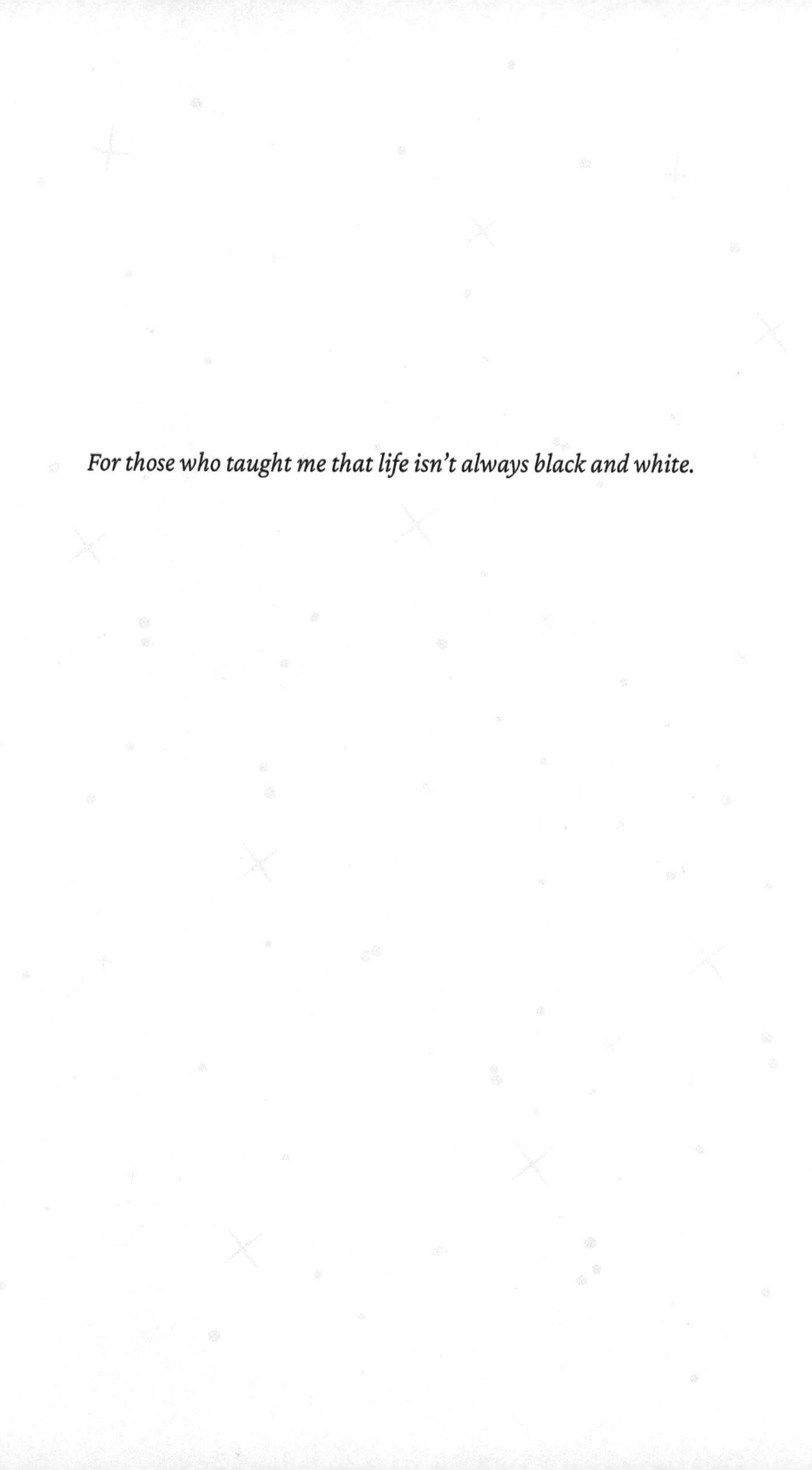

For those who taught me that life isn't always black and white.

PART ONE
STARS

"Heaven has no rage like love to hatred turned, nor Hell a fury like a woman scorned."

-William Congreve

I

Day 99

The sun wavered high in the sky, its rays glittering across the unknown city below. It was surely given a name at one point in time- though no one could remember it. There wasn't much this town *could* remember now. Even just past daybreak, there was a never-ending loop of reds and purples, never higher than just over the horizon. It was beautiful in its haze, if not the most beautiful sight anyone had ever seen. That was, if they could remember it. The people of this unnamed city were unremarkable, unworthy of sharing the golden light ricocheting off of the building walls. Their faces were blank, sullen, and empty. There was something about this place, and even its residents weren't able to pinpoint the source of its oddity.

Luci looked towards the sun, her hair billowing across her olive-toned shoulders. A brushed finger across her collarbone, a hand running down to the frills of her dress. Her dress was befitting of her remarkable appearance, with intricate beading and lace more regal than any garment in the city. Her movements were smooth and gentle, contrary to the shape of her face and the point of her joints. She was out of this world.

Far too peculiar for this unremarkable place.

When Luci walked across the Earth, people stopped to stare. It had been this way for years and every day was the same; she slid past each face, awed with silent appreciation. Her eyes stayed forward, her determination set towards her destination. There was something special about this place, certainly by design, and she would have it no other way. She waited, here at the center of the universe.

People often did their best to avoid places like this; they would step around it if they could, their blood rushing if they came too close. The people in this town were unwelcome trespassers at the center of the universe, and she was the only one invited here. There Luci stood, dead center, her eyes closed and hands draped down her sides. She was waiting for something here, *someone*.

When Icarus looked out towards the horizon, his eyes glazed over like the evening glow. His bones creaked in anticipation as he floated through the city. He, too, was remarkable with his dark complexion that complimented the pink of his lips. The people of this city never remembered him, and though they seemed familiar, he couldn't place a face either. He watched silently as they turned to him, like baubles fixated with interest. It felt as though something might be following Icarus, and with a quick turn of his head, he noticed a dark mist that snaked near his ankles.

The feeling of unease flowed through him, and he hastened his pace.

His eyes glazed over with emotion when he saw Luci standing there. The gazebo was tall and pointed, quaint but distinguished. It was porcelain white with accents of yellows and purples to match the sky. From sunrise to sunset, she waited for him there.

He straightened his suit, tightly fitted around his tensing muscles. He, too, moved gracefully, powerfully. When Icarus saw her, the corners of his mouth twitched upward, despite his reluctance, and he stepped towards the graceful figure in the clearing. With her eyes closed as they were, Luci looked as though she could be a ghost- she might as well have been. The draw to her was pulling on him so hard he could hardly stand it. In no time at all, Icarus was at the center of the universe, and his mist faded away. It was what he had called it once before- the only time they had spoken. What else could it have been when it was the place he first saw her? Luci was there, and so, it had become the center of his world and beyond. Gods, he hated it.

Icarus reached out and touched her hands briefly, watching the intake of her breath. She opened her eyes to look at him and said nothing at all, instead falling into him. Together they took a deep step, their hearts clapping together in a similar beat. Where there was nothing before, now there was music pumping into the night. It was slow and deliberate. After an easy count of one, two, and three, he took a step back and held out a hand.

They moved with the beat; the music refusing to stop while they danced. Passersby seemed to disappear into their buildings and they were lost in each other. Luci reveled in this memory of dance; there was no space left at this moment when their bodies moved so close together, something to remember in a way no other person could in this unnamed city.

Icarus caught fire in front of her, and her eyes widened as they twirled. Smooth and sticky caramel flames traveled up her arm, golden strands wrapping around her. He spun her then, another breath of one, two, three. Luci's body twirled as the sun drowned them and the wind lifted her dress up around her. The world followed her on her 360 to reveal a deep blue sky, littered with falling stars. If he was fire, then she was pure light, a spark to the night.

As stars glittered around them, the world emptied. There were no longer any blank faces, nothing keeping them from remembering. It was just enough time to let their bodies be. And it hurt, far worse than the fire licking at their arms. Luci caught a star in her palm then, lifting it to her face and blowing softly, causing it to streak across the street; she had created a star chaser in Icarus, and he twirled her relentlessly. They spun and spun together until they could no longer. They danced through the night, stars falling around them, and the music so loud it shattered eardrums. No one noticed but them.

When day broke, he let go of her hand and the music faded into nothing. Luci looked down at her feet, tiptoeing away from his embrace. There was something special about that sunrise, so hazy and purple. She looked at Icarus, taking in every feature of his face, determined to capture the way his eyebrows arched and the way the skin pulled at the corners of his eyes. They both stood, staring at each other for just a moment too long. Longing for more but getting nothing but a memory. She disappeared with the music in the wind and he fell to his knees. The hurt of abandonment filled his chest.

2

Day 100

Luci moved her hands down her sides, smoothing out the frills of her dress. The sunrise was beautiful, she thought. It was just high enough in the sky to say that it wasn't far past daybreak. She couldn't think of anything more beautiful than this city. It was surely named something at one point in time, though no one could remember it. All she knew was a face. Long and handsome, striking. There was an urge Luci couldn't describe, pulling her towards something. She needed to get to the center of the universe.

Icarus walked downtown, purpose driving his steps. His suit was painted across his skin, the faces of people around him staring with lifeless eyes. There was something different about him, but he couldn't quite place it. Each time he tried, the ribbon of memory unraveled from his fingertips, evading him. Tendrils of smoky darkness followed him where he went.

Sometimes he tried to ignore them, they never harmed him, but the desire to run was almost impossible to withstand. If only his feet could take him there quick enough. If only he wasn't stuck in this limbo, this place after life. It wasn't much longer now; the sun was dripping by the second, stars threatening in the distance. He quit his worrying, keeping his walk steady and easily paced even though it pained him. When Icarus stepped out into the clearing he saw her in the middle of the gazebo, hands resting patiently at her sides.

Luci didn't seem to know who he was, her expression was too serene for her to have remembered anything that happened between them, right?

Icarus could remember it all. He remembered the day he died, he remembered the monster who put him here...her. He remembered the way her face would twitch in the same way each time he saw her, not a second off. He remembered that there was no way out of here, that he would spend each day dancing, remembering.

If there was nothing else in the world but this, he knew they would always find each other at the center of the universe, if only for a moment.

They created magic together. They created destruction.

They danced ninety-nine dances and then one more, and the stars fell all around them.

PART TWO
DEATH AT A FUNERAL

"The death of a beautiful woman is, unquestionably, the most poetical topic in the world."

-Edgar Allen Poe

I

Unlike most stories, Lola Duvall's opens at a funeral. The circle of life had, once again, brought her face to face with the beauty of Death. Her jaguar eyes crawled across the scene, making note of every face in attendance. She was there looking for someone, though not the dead type you would expect in a place like this. This someone was very much alive. Lola popped her lips, taking in a breath of cool air; the wind whipped around her body and she almost laughed at the cruelty of it. The funeral nor the weather could ruin her purpose today. She had been called here, and Lola would finish the job that needed to be done.

"I am here, and you cannot stop me," She murmured, watching as the wind took her words and warped them into nonexistence. The weather seemed to fight back, the wind twisting her words and pulling at them until there was nothing left. Strips of dark shadowed tendrils, invisible to most, found her then and pushed her forward to the sea of black-clad bodies; Lola tried hard to focus on the task at hand

and less on the elements surrounding her. Threads of dark magic moved around her, so much like the wind but more menacing. Lola ground her teeth together silently, for once wishing for the gritty sounds of wet bone against wet bone, but the wind took that sound away too. She snarled like an animal as she fought against the elements. Lola and the wind had a relationship built on mutual hatred, but she was far too afraid of its power to dismiss it completely. She scowled, ignoring the breeze, and sauntered down into the crowd, an obvious air of disrespect laced in her movements. The gown flowed behind her, catching fallen leaves that clung to the bottom of the fabric as she walked. The wind, leaves, and tendrils followed her every step.

There was so much magic in the air, but those who were unwilling to believe it would only see darkness in the periphery of their vision or serendipitous wind gusts. Human minds were so naive, so easy to manipulate. They would always make excuses for what was right in front of them to try and rationalize what they were seeing. Humans were so undeserving of the life they were given. Lola wrapped her arms around her torso to shield herself from the cold, wondering if anyone else on the cemetery grounds felt it too. The sky overhead was cloudy and threatening rainfall, but she doubted it would get in the way of her mission; Mother Nature herself would not interfere with this. Lola looked towards the sky in a challenge, descending further into the ocean of somber faces before her.

Her dress wasn't tight or formfitting, not like what she would wear on another day; instead, it was loose on her body, cinching her ribs comfortably and coming up into a gentle "V". The sleeves fell gracefully across her upper arms, leaving her shoulders and collarbone exposed. This dress was a mournful one, not a smoldering one. It was meant for nice girls, not

Devils like Lola. She swallowed, the air catching in her throat as saliva slid down. Lola's mouth moved into a cocky smile as she weaved her way in and out of the crowd. Although she was cloaked in the same dull black as everyone else, she stood out. She would always stand out.

Why was everyone always so sad during a funeral? Lola was taught that the most beautiful part of life was death. It was when your body decided you had learned all there was to learn and it would return to the place it came from. It was when we were no longer servants of the wind and Mother Nature, and we could become night itself again. Death was not weakness, it was strength. She scowled. These people mocked death by trying to escape it; it was their fear that made them weak. She cast disdainful glances around her and the people all looked the same. The women were swathed in shades of black, lace covering their faces. The men were much more uniform, their suits tucked in nice and tidy. Lola wondered how many of them actually knew the deceased and how many came looking for a score. Be it sex, food, or companionship, funerals made everyone hungry for it. It was eerie, the way they all talked in hushed voices and moved around in unison. Her movements were far less gentle and hurried. Many people noticed but none dared approach the woman who descended upon them with leaves trailing her every step. She found herself in the middle of the audience, ignoring stares and trying desperately to find the one she was searching for.

The hearse came forward, and Lola felt when they all looked away from her and towards it instead. She trained her eyes forward, grazing over the crowd like a predator. Her focus wavered only slightly as the hearse rolled closer. The air smelled so much of death, and Lola's nostrils flared. The tendrils wrapped around her leg, and the wind blew cool air that caused goose bumps to freckle across her skin. Her scowl deepened, refocusing. She was looking for a face, a particular one with a deep pink scar running from his temple to his jaw. It was new, still stitched together by feeble medical floss. He told everyone that he had been attacked by a jaguar. Lola's lip twitched at the memory. He either blended in with the crowd well or had not yet made his appearance. Each face was hard to tell apart she noticed with a disgruntled huff, and the consistent pull of the tendrils must have meant she was not close enough. She *needed* to be close. This was not the first time the uncomfortable pull had brought her this close to death. Lola was married to it, she devoured every moment, and stood on the line between life and after-life. This adrenaline-inducing feeling overwhelmed her like a rolling force, and she settled into it. She could feel the spirit moving within the hearse, and the tendrils slithered from her legs and returned to the crowd eagerly awaiting its fill.

This mission was both given to and requested by her. He was now marked for death- how fitting in a place like this. Lola volunteered to take his life and was more than happy to watch the last light leave his eyes for good. They'd met only briefly before today; there were moments, nothing of significance, at least not to her. It took one look, and she had him wrapped around her finger. She moved onward in her search, her eyes burning like the pits of Hell. She was like a distant cousin to Medusa, without the petrifying stone stare. Instead, she burned them up from the inside. For her, just one look was like a match, and Lola could incinerate them all.

Her emerald eyes continued to scan, each new face giving her glimpses of the lives of the people in mourning. She felt like she needed to take their broken hearts and set fire to them with her gaze, that would be the only way to relieve them of this unhappiness, to erase the heartache completely. Their grief stained the air with a pressure that was so similar to that in her own chest. She let loose a breath, releasing her tension and relaxing the muscles in her face. Her jaw stretched, aching from the hold she had on it. Lola would not allow herself to feel sorry for these people. Humans were nasty creatures. They might have thought she was malice, but they would prove to always be far worse than she could ever conjure.

"Is she in that car, momma?" Lola's head snapped towards a young boy and his mother standing just a few feet to her right. The mother looked familiar to Lola, but she blinked the deja vu away and cocked her head. Not everything she saw and remembered was her own memory, Lola unwillingly let the thoughts and lives of everyone here infiltrate her body, and the tendrils swirled around her unhappily. They couldn't spend much more time up here, she had overstayed her welcome and needed to move quicker. The woman knelt onto one knee, wiping at her tear-stained face beneath the lace covering. She cradled her son's small face in her hands.

"Yes," she whispered. Lola had to take a step forward to hear her. The wind rattled around them in warning, but she paid it no mind. The hearse came to a stop, its brakes roaring loudly. Death was like a virus, something to be caught. She could see the fear in their bodies as they parted for the long black van, not wanting to be the first ones to catch it. The mother let go of her child, shoving her face into her now open palms, crying. "Yes, she's there," she managed.

"Will I be able to see her?" he whimpered. The boy danced on tiptoes, trying to see over the heads of those who loomed above him. The woman shook her head fiercely, dabbing at her tears and containing her grief, hugging him close as if trying to shield him from the realities of this harsh world. Lola wanted to spit at them.

"I'm afraid not, son. It's for the grown-ups only," she lifted herself from her knees and looked Lola right in the eyes.

Humans and their grief. It fed her and gave her the energy she needed to complete her task. Lola smirked, turning her head and moving on. She walked up the stairs to the Cathedral, away from the collection of sheep, the hearse, and the person inside it.

2

She was seated in the upper pews with a clear view of the altar. Lola was intrigued by the sterility of the Cathedral, white from top to bottom and far too clean for death. Stained glass sent ribbons of rainbows to ricochet off the walls and her eyes narrowed at the *brightness* of it all. Lola rested her head on crossed arms across the railing and watched as people filed in. Guests parted naturally as they entered, the waves of black suits and lace dresses opening up for the pall-bearers to move forward. The difference was striking, their black ensemble against the white walls and floors made for a compelling visual from up this high. Each step the pallbearers took was matched by their partners, and together they brought the opalescent casket in through the large doors and up towards the altar. Lola stood, catching no attention from below as the casket was rested on a bier and the room quieted around them.

The service was long and mundane. Humans didn't even know how to throw a decent party, Lola was bored with it only five minutes in. The speakers were hard to understand past their gasping sobs and they spoke in such quiet voices it was a wonder they could even be heard from the upper level. Time passed too slowly, and the tendrils were tugging on her arm; wrapping up across her ghostly skin, tightening like an anaconda preparing for its meal. Lola felt the hard tug, threatening to bring her down the stairs headfirst. Nevertheless, she persisted. This was a favorite game of hers and the shadows, a version of hot and cold that she never grew tired of playing. She sought and they guided, albeit aggressive when the game didn't move along fast enough. Which was certainly the case for them today.

She tapped her fingers against her sides as she slid through the growing collection of grieving bodies. She felt her instincts bring her closer and closer to the casket as if the being inside is what wanted her, what called to her. The tendrils didn't try to stop her this time, they were just as curious, just as hungry for it as she was. Lola bumped into someone on her journey, hearing a quiet but painful exclamation. She looked down at the source of the noise, and, while she would typically ignore the call of dismay, what stopped her was its familiar face. It was not the one she sought out, no, this face was clear of any scars and as pure as they come. While it disgusted her, she felt a strange pang of interest for the small child at her feet. It was the same one she saw before the service. More curious than before, she noticed his round red cheeks and platinum curls that fell over his dark skin. She reached instinctively to touch his face, the shadows pulling in the opposite direction, back towards the original destination. Lola stopped and opted instead to pull on a strand of his blonde hair. Her tendrils hardened their pressure on her arm, trying to tear her away. She whipped her head around and snapped her teeth, though to anyone watching, it would look as though she was talking to herself.

When she turned back around she noticed that tears stained those rosy cheeks, and wondered briefly if it was her or the funeral bringing him such sadness. Lola didn't apologize, instead bending over to see him at eye level. The boy looked away awkwardly. She remembered why she didn't often seek out the company of children; they would always know what she was. Adults rationalized away the truth, children were not yet taught to do so. He looked like he wanted to run. It made her thin black lips curl upwards in a cruel-looking smile.

"Would you like to see it, boy?" She asked, laying a delicate hand on his arm. The shadows released their grip, content with this lost battle for the time being. His skin was beautiful mahogany and Lola could feel the dainty bones underneath his flesh. She looked for his mother, finding her several yards over speaking to another mourner. The boy looked her way too, then back to Lola.

"See what?" He asked, interest evident in his expression. Despite his fear, he was curious, and while in this situation it wasn't smart to do so, she realized she appreciated children much more than their adult companions, if only for entertainment.

"What's in the casket, of course," she answered, her voice layered with amusement. The boy shifted from foot to foot.

"Momma says I can't see, it's for grown-ups," he was only about seven years old and full of life. She could smell the years he had left on him and wanted so badly to swallow him whole. She wanted to take those years for herself. Lola pulled on the strand of hair again, watching the curl bounce while her other hand lay comfortably on his arm. She tightened her grip and pulled him forward, using as little pressure as possible. She couldn't break those dainty bones.

"She won't mind," Lola cooed, "Don't you want to say goodbye?" The boy kept shifting, and she could tell his restraint was wavering. His mother was doing him a disservice in not allowing him to see life for what it truly was. If she wouldn't do it, Lola was more than happy to take on the job herself. The boy gave in then, chubby legs following Lola through the crowd. Further, they moved away from his mother, and up towards the dead on the steps. They were so close to the altar now, and she felt her mouth salivating at the proximity.

"I miss my aunt," he said sadly, tearing his arm from her grip and grabbing onto her hand instead. Lola felt his tiny fingers interlace with hers, seeking comfort. She looked down and frowned. Grief made even children blind to the horror that she was. And this child, no longer curious, made her pull harder on his hand. She was not here to console him and offered him no reply. When they reached the casket, he was too short to look into it. Lola looked up to see the disapproval stamped across the faces of onlookers; she bared her teeth at them and lifted the small child by his waist to offer him a closer look. She heard a quiet gasp and his breathing quickened. When she peaked in herself, the shadows rumbled in satisfaction.

The woman in the tomb had the same long onyx hair, the same reddened circles around her eyes, and the same sunken cheeks. It was almost as if she was looking back at herself, and while she entertained the idea for a moment, she tore away her gaze. Lola set the boy down and he turned to look her in the eyes.

"Will I look like that?" he asked. There was a new quiver to his lip and fear in his voice. Lola narrowed her eyes. She would not let him grow up with fear, not like the rest of the sheep that meandered around the room like zombies.

"We all will," she said, honestly. Lola made sure not to break their eye contact. She was no liar. "It's what happens with your lot in life. You are born, you make bad decisions, and you die."

"Is that what you did?" He asked. The question shocked her. Lola couldn't imagine being rocked by a simple question from a child, but she stared at him, frowning so low that it touched her jaw.

"How do you mean, child?" She hissed, voice low and dangerous, challenging. The boy's eyes widened in horror, taking a hesitant step back. His back bumped into the casket and it wiggled, threatening to collapse. His doe eyes made it seem as though he was getting ready to run, but she watched as he squared his shoulders. Children were so entertaining.

"You made bad choices," he said. His voice was breaking. She didn't expect him to be confident, not in front of a dead body, not in front of her. The dark tendrils swirled around her curiously, detaching from her and tentatively wrapping around the legs of the boy in front of her. Lola watched as it slithered around his tiny body. Her eyebrows raised and she smiled-trying to ignore the dread that filled her with each word he spoke. The boy stared at her, oblivious to the tendrils as they slid up his arms and lingered around his head. It found nothing interesting there, which didn't surprise her. Children's minds were as empty as a wheat field.

"Stop staring at me," he complained. Lola blinked out of her trance and smiled. Her hand raised to touch the curl of his hair again, touching the tendril instead. She held out a finger, willing it to roll back up her hand and down to where it belonged.

"I did make bad decisions," she said slowly. The boy looked at her with shock in his expression. Humans hated being right. He stepped casually to the side of the casket, casting a quick glance out into the crowd, looking for his mother. Lola had forgotten about the human beast and did the same. She could spot her easy enough, and when she'd broken away from the moment she had with the child she could see that there was quite a bit of commotion.

People were running around frantically, looking around pillars and screaming a name.

"Henry!" They shouted, "Henry!" The boy shook his head, as if he also hadn't heard them until this moment, and pointed.

"That's me," he said, turning away from her. Lola grabbed for his hand, closing her nails into his skin and causing him to yelp. She didn't apologize, instead, pulled him close so that her breath tickled his ear. She watched him shiver, delighting in the fear she could create in him.

"If you make bad decisions too, you'll end up just like me," she said, her smile curving upwards in a cruel grin. She let him go, leaving nail marks on his skin. They were red around the edges and left deep crescent indentations. Lola looked up and found the bobbing blonde head of a mother heading towards him. She had an angry walk about her, with a red face and glazed-over eyes.

"I sort of hope you grow up bad, Henry. It's fun on this side," Henry turned his head and started running. Lola watched his shoelaces trailing behind him. The kid had some magic working for him, allowing him to run without the fear of tripping. She laughed, a sound that ricocheted off the walls. People turned her way, their faces masking horror. She followed the boy and his mother, who was screaming obscenities at her and weaving through the crowd. Trying their hardest to get away from Lola.

She looked back towards the casket, watching for a sign of movement from the body inside it. The tendrils wrapped around her arm, tugging lightly. She had her fun, and now it was time to go. Her jobs didn't normally take as long as this one had, and the darkness was getting restless. Lola sighed heavily, reluctantly moving away from the white, shiny box. She stepped down the alter steps and made her way back into the sea of people. They parted ways for her, wary, with suspicious looks in their eyes. She might have overstayed her welcome.

"How could you show a child that?" Someone spat in her direction. Lola's eyes raged, the fire igniting with just a flip of a switch. She turned her gaze to the sound of the voice, staring deep into the soul of the person who dared confront her. Lola didn't even have the time to know who it was that said anything, the minute she turned her eyes to the man, no, the woman who'd spoken, she was on the floor. The woman rolled around in agony. She tore the black laced hat away from her face and threw it hard. Lola laughed as the wind caught it, shooting it against the wall. Everyone stopped to look at the two of them. None dared to help. The room was silent save for the howls of pain from the woman on the floor. The leaves danced around Lola, and the tendrils pulled her forward once more. She walked carefully towards the center of the room, daring another soul to stare at her.

Lola laughed, savoring the sound against the silence. Once she was in the center, she heard him. It must have been him, he had the same throaty laugh and the same deep bravado. He didn't say her name, wouldn't dare, but he spoke with dark confidence that made her toes curl in with delight. The first thing she noticed was a scar that ran from his temple down to his jaw. It was beautifully raw, the pink blisters and inflamed skin crying out with each twitch of his muscle. He was perfect.

"This is a day of mourning," he said, in a commanding tone. Lola looked at him, amusement filling out her face. "No human, or creature, will ruin it."

She almost laughed again, but her throat ran dry. The

tendrils seemed to hiss for her, rumbling in displeasure. They had caught the mark of their target, and it would take the forces of heaven and hell to keep them from devouring him whole. She recognized his inclusion of the word creature, though no one else seemed to mind, or had paid any attention to it.

She enjoyed this dance that they had, weaving this web of lies they created. And while he strode towards her, each foot planted firmly in front of the other, the rest of the world around them disappeared. *Poor, poor humans,* Lola thought as she followed suit. She was determined to meet him in the middle as if there was a center to this universe that they were in and they desperately needed to get to it. It seemed the closer she got, the further she was from him. The crowd grew thicker, the distance farther. She felt a push of the wind and the pull of the tendrils, and without the help of either, she might not have made it that far. The man in the blue suit took the last feeble steps towards her. She so enjoyed the blue against his white skin. She enjoyed the sickly color as much as she enjoyed the expression on his face. He looked shocked, the bravado gone now as he entered her circle of acquaintance.

Had he seen the dead yet? He must not of, since the look of shock so outweighed the grief that should be there. Lola should have worn blue too, but the black dress seemed to rumble with displeasure at the thought. She smoothed out the edges to calm it down; the dress was an extension of where she had come from, a place of magic and monsters. She couldn't wait until he was ready to see it with her.

3

Lola looked at him, a predatory look clouding her green eyes. She grabbed onto the lapels of his suit, pulling him close to her. The pull from the tendrils was gone and she felt the pressure release in her chest. He was who she had been looking for. She would have been able to pick him out anywhere, and not because of the color of his suit. She would have walked and destroyed the world to find him again.

"I found you," she growled.

"We should probably move this elsewhere," he said roughly. He sounded like he was out of breath. She only nodded. He tried grabbing for her hand but Lola pulled it away before he could touch her. They walked through the maze of hallways, was this building always this big? The walls seemed to expand, propelling them into a world unlike their own. Lola stopped, waiting for him to turn to face her. He took a few steps more before stopping himself, taking his time before he looked at her again.

She was here to kill him, she had no time for anything else.

He finally looked at her, and Lola wished he would have

looked shocked. Instead, he stared, soft and gentle in his gaze. He reached out for her, and Lola took a step back; her retreat made him shake his head as if he snapped out of whatever trance he was trapped in. She yearned for him; to hold him close to her, to feel the heat between them catch fire, while simultaneously wanting to grab for the heart inside his chest and crumble it with her own two hands.

"You're here," he said simply. His voice didn't sound remorseful or guilty. He just was, as if he'd always been that way. It made Lola curious. He was so unlike those others she'd met before. He must have known his end was coming so soon, they all did in the end. Lola watched him slide his clammy hands down his lapels, his eyes darting to either side of her. She followed his gaze curiously, masking the shock on her own face when she realized he had been watching the tendrils. They stayed by her side like a quiet dog, flicking towards him aggressively, weaving through her legs and wrapping around her ankles waiting for their command. Although their relationship was strained at best, they would always wait for her call. Lola never disappointed them on the job. His eyes darted to and fro, wary of the dark shadows. Not many were able to see them- even the child hadn't recognized the darkness. Who was this man that killed his own wife?

"I'm here," she replied. They looked at each other for what seemed like days, though only mere minutes passed. Lola couldn't help but focus on the intense attraction that sat between them. Her shadows were getting more and more restless, taking daring charges towards the man in the blue suit, and it made her hesitate, just for a moment. It was the first time in her life that she'd second-guessed a job, and it made her uncomfortable.

"You don't seem to be the grieving husband I'd expect you'd be," her voice was cold and distant.

"I thought you weren't going to come," he said instead, ignoring her question and moving on with one of his own. She would have chastised him. Should have chastised him. There was hardly a person in this world that could talk to her that way, as if they were old friends. If it had been anyone else they'd have already been dead by now. Lola put her hands out in front of her, watching in horror as they shook from apprehension. The wind blew past her, ruffling the black of her hair and sending shivers up her spine. The tendrils were aggressive now, charging against him with all their might. If she waited any longer, they might both be dead.

"You know why I came."

"I did this for you."

"The hell you did!" She screeched. Her palms were now shaking terribly and it rumbled through her entire body, "You did this for *you*. You're a mortal, and the only thing you ever cared about was yourself."

Lola put her head in her hands, feeling the razor-sharp talons crawl out of her nail beds. She fisted her hands together, inhaling sharply as she pinched the skin there, and blood leaked down her hands. His eyes shot to the blood now dripping onto the ground, but came immediately back to her lips. She licked them, the dry cracks splitting at the touch. He took another step toward her, and this time, Lola didn't step away.

"It's you," he whispered. He was so close now that they were almost touching. Lola looked up, hating that he was so much taller than her. He put out his hand hesitantly, lifting her head from her hands and tilting her chin up to make her meet his eyes. The tendrils roar in disapproval, whipping back and forth. The wind wasn't much help either, wrapping them tightly in a tornado. Leaves from her dress blew around them, trapping them together. Lola needed to do it. Her nails longed to drag across his throat. She hungered for it as much as she hungered for him.

Lola closed her eyes and her fingers twitched. This was going to be the end of him.

"Say my name," he said then, knocking her out of her trance. Did he know how close he was to dying? He wasn't safe with her because it was his time. He did this to himself.

"I ca-"

"Say it," he commanded.

"Why?" She relented, panting heavily. Lola was sweating from the effort it took to keep the magic at bay. Her resistance was waning and the air dripped with a feeling she couldn't describe. He closed his eyes and breathed in deeply.

"Because you're here to kill me," he said. She didn't want to tell him yes. If she didn't speak at all, maybe it would make this less difficult. "If you say my name, I know it would change your mind."

"I don't really have a choice," she said finally, grinding her teeth together.

"I don't believe you. You feel this?" He lifted his hand and placed it against her chest. Lola felt the hard pressure and breathed in deep. He wouldn't be able to feel the beating of her heart because her heart was no longer there. She couldn't remember the last time she heard her own heartbeat. "You know you feel this too. I don't know what it is, but it feels like love." *It's not love*, she thought to herself. Because Lola never did know the feeling. She might have, once, in a previous life. But, if Lola did, she could no longer remember. She was a creature that completed jobs, she was one of the grim reapers that serviced the world.

"I have a job to do," she said. "This cannot be love. The air stinks of lust, and I am not a part of your world. I can't feel, not in the way you humans can."

"Just say my name, I know you'll feel it then," He pleaded. The blue of his suit really complimented him, it contorted around his muscles and cut in at all the right places. It took Lola a great deal of effort to not look him up and down. She could feel it press against the back of her lips, ready to escape her body. The tendrils hissed, and she watched his eyes flick back down to them. Lola could sense his immediate discomfort as if he'd forgotten that they were even there in the first place.

"Evra," she said. The v was soft sounding, and her bottom lip pushed against her teeth so lightly that it didn't feel like she said his name at all. He sighed in contentment, his eyes fluttering at the release. He was right, the name did change things. Lola barred her teeth, the feeling of pain cracking in her chest. It couldn't change anything. She felt the nails grow from the bed again, sharpening to the touch. She grabbed his hand to remove it and the touch set them on fire.

4

Instead of seeming pleased with himself, Lola noticed the darkness in his eyes that clouded his entire expression. Evra took a step back from her and she noticed how graceful it seemed despite him being too large and too stocky to create such a motion. There was a sharp intake of breath and neither of them could determine who had emitted it. The tendrils wrapped around Lola's legs, tightening so hard that she grumbled in pain. His eyes dipped down to the darkness once again. Lola shifted the weight from one foot to the other, the tickle rushed through her and made her nervous. When had she ever been nervous?

"Did that change anything?" The sound of his voice brought her back to reality.

She didn't want to answer, but it was hard to ignore the flames licking the space between them. She wondered if that was visible to him, too. He noticed the tentacles tightening themselves around her, and he was terrified of them. Did he notice the flames, a delightful black, and blue color so very reminiscent of what death might look like? Lola sighed, sucking in her cheeks and biting the insides of her mouth. At one point you might have thought her dark and dangerous. Who would have known that all it took was a man in a blue suit to bring her to her knees? Her eyes drifted down his body, disobeying the logic and the magic that wanted her to be done with this job and back where she belonged.

The blue suit really did fit him nicely, much to her dismay.

It was difficult to not notice how it hugged his body perfectly, accentuated every curve, and loosed around his waist. Fuck, when would she stop noticing? He was a model, maybe not in the profession, but in the way he carried himself. Evra's face dimpled, softening his expression even further and she wanted so badly to touch his face. Even his walk was model-esque. He pushed away from her then, moving further into the maze of hallways that she was still unconvinced was real. There was nothing real in this room anymore. He moved his hips like he was walking a runway show, and without question, Lola followed him deeper in. She didn't really have a choice.

"It changes nothing," she said confidently. When Evra wasn't looking at her it was easier to shake off the way he was making her feel. She snapped her fingers gently and the black flames disappeared, sinking into the tile floor. Lola stomped on the rest to smother them, walking over the now-burned marble. The black markings looked wonderful against the whiteness of the floor. Lola stopped after about twenty feet, ready to end this once and for all.

"You don't look frightened," she was speaking at his back, it was easier this way. Either Evra knew that, or he wasn't turning around because it was easier for him this way, too.

"Why should I be?" He was disgruntled, she could hear it in

the rumbling growl that emitted from his throat. Lola wondered if he always sounded this inhuman. She must have missed it, there was no way a simple mortal could be standing in the same room as her, not sweating or leaving as those in the large, open room of the cathedral did.

"You know I'm here to kill you. So save the pretending."

"I'm not pretending,"

"You're not scared of me?" She said the words in a purr, though it came off as more like a threat. Good. Evra needed to know how much she would enjoy killing him.

"Did it ever occur to you that this has nothing to do with you, Lola?" His harsh tone caught her off guard. Did he think she was some sorry, mortal girl? Did he know who he was talking to? Lola barred her teeth at him, letting loose a hiss that bounced off the marble tiles, echoing around them. The long hallways seemed to amplify the noise. Her neck snapped around, forgetting where they were momentarily. She needed to be quick before someone would come looking for him. Quick as a flash Lola was flat up against his backside, nails wrapped around his neck, threatening to slice through it and unload everything that was inside of it. She could feel Evra's heavy breathing. She was smaller than he was in size, but he wouldn't dare underestimate her. He knew what she could do.

"I am at my wife's funeral. I took a disruptive guest from the service. I am mourning," Evra was too calm with her fingers poised at the end of his throat, nails threatening to puncture his thin skin. Lola hissed again, her dress billowing with rage beneath her. The tendrils were quiet for once. They watched her with hunger and satisfaction, making her anxious to finish the task. Each time she tried to do it, though, she stopped. Lola waited for him to say something, anything that would make her stop. It was so unlike her that it made her wobble. Her fingers shook delicately, and she felt him place a hand over the top of hers. The sharpness of her teeth dulled and her eyes narrowed.

"The wife that *you* killed." He didn't disagree.

"Is that all you came here for?" He asked in a whisper. As if there was more that needed to be done than killing him and leaving his body to be found by mourning onlookers.

"I'm here to mourn too, of course," she mocked. Lola could feel him tighten beneath her grip. She released the pressure against his neck and walked fingertips up his sleeve. If she didn't know any better, she would have thought he didn't want her here, not with the way he pulled away from her. The tendrils roared with aggression. He was right there beneath her fingertips and she didn't do it. They were getting too restless, too dangerous.

"Don't disrespect her," Evra growled. Lola only smiled. It was more menacing than it was apologetic. She continued playing with his sleeve but he didn't pull away. Lola didn't believe the faux anger or the face he put on for everyone else. And even though her nerves tickled with the harshness of his words, Lola felt herself wanting to laugh, not slice through him. It was an odd sensation. This back and forth, hot and cold was taking a toll on her psyche. She couldn't keep up with her emotions as much as she could keep up with his thoughts. It was all so unpredictable.

"You're wearing blue," she deadpanned, "...To your own wife's funeral." His mouth twitched. It was the way they continued saying the word, *wife*. It rolled off the tongue well, but sounded funny every time. Lola could tell it felt the same to Evra, too. She thought that maybe that twitch was a smile, but she couldn't tell for sure. All she knew was that Evra was the man she was searching for. "I feel as though that might have been a bit too much, don't you think? Every funeral I've been to, the spouse has always at least had the decency to wear black. Even if they despised the one in the coffin."

Evra relaxed some, and Lola could tell it took a lot of effort. He was used to playing the part, it was about time he let the front down.

"I said, don't disrespect her." The tone wasn't as harsh as the first time, but Lola still raised her eyebrows in confusion. Evra walked to the wall and leaned up against it. He played with the cuffs of his suit, pinching the sleeves and swallowing hard. She noticed the way his adam's apple bobbed, and it was like the fire erupted all over again. Lola shook her head to snap herself out of it. When he looked at her, she disguised any emotion that might have crossed her face. She didn't want him to know what it was she might have been thinking about.

"What do you want, Lola?" He said finally, exasperated. She could have laughed. He wasn't dumb, but he was trying her patience.

"I told you what I was here for. To kill you."

"Ah, yeah. That and mourning. You know I'm sick and tired of games. If you really wanted to kill me, I feel like I would have been dead a long time ago. Either you don't want to, or you're just bad at your job," her eyes narrowed again.

"Watch yourself, human," she said.

"Don't disrespect me by calling me human. Especially when we both know you've said my name many times over."

"Are you that ready to die?" Lola spat, "That you keep insulting an immortal?"

Evra rolled up his sleeves, staring at her. They were several feet apart again, but they always felt so much closer. "You think I mean to insult you? My apologies, Lola. I speak freely because of our acquaintance." His eyes twinkled with humor, and the smile she wasn't sure was there earlier appeared again.

Lola should have been angry, but instead, she laughed. What was it about Evra that made her this way?

"We are not acquainted. We hardly know each other. I am here for a job, and that is it."

"You wound me," he said, the twinkle died a little, but not enough to chase his spirits.

"I am not playing any games," Lola said slowly. "Your time is up, and I gave you more time than you deserved. If it was discovered that you were still alive past your death day, I don't know what would be done to me. You spent your week of grace..." Lola looked around them, "rather differently than I suspect someone else in your position might've." She expected to see guilt in his expression, instead finding a smile on his face.

"I killed her," Evra said. There was a flash of red that flooded his cheeks, the color was so pretty against his pale skin. Lola wondered if it was the first time he said it out loud. He looked around frantically as if someone was there that could hear him, other than Lola. *Too bad*, she thought, when he confirmed that there was no one else in sight.

"Of course you did," she said softly, almost endearing in her caress of those words. Lola moved towards him in a graceful movement, almost floating above the ground, tendrils following her. She stood in front of him, with a wicked gleam in her eyes. Evra at least had the decency to look nervous. With his back flush against the wall, he was trapped by her. His hands raised in an almost warning, knowing full well it wouldn't do much of anything with Lola.

"Tell me, Evra, why did you kill her? Did you truly believe that you couldn't live without her? Or was it fear that she could live without *you*?"

She watched his adam's apple bob. It bounced up and down on his neck, settling with a rattle at the center of his throat. He swallowed, sitting in silence for a second before responding. She appreciated that about him at the very least. He had always been someone who was intentional about his words.

"I did it for you," He said softly, finally. He'd said it before, but it was this time, against the wall with her chest up close to his, that she really believed him.

5

"That's not very smart," Lola said sweetly, tracing her finger along the outlines of his suit. "Because you know it would never work between us, Evra. It couldn't." She made a mistake when she stayed with him. She made a mistake when she took his hand and allowed him to take her to their bedroom when his wife was out. She made a mistake when she bedded him, and it was a mistake Lola would live with for the rest of her eternal life.

"It could," he counterargued, "With Luara, gone, we can start over. Run away with me, Lola, and we can be together."

If she had a heart, it might have twisted in her chest. *Luara*, the name rolled off her tongue smooth like chocolate. It was the name of a woman that looked so much like her, the woman that had stolen Evra's heart first. All of this was a mistake, and a job was still needing to be done.

"And go where?" Lola pressured, leaning forward and taking in a large whiff of him. He smelled of forest, pine, and wood chips, and it sent her back home, for just a second.

"Go, somewhere. Lola, take me with you." Could it work?

Would Lola be able to live without the darkness of the tendrils or wrestling the wind? Her long black waves rustled past her ears as if in a warning. Evra shivered with the cool air, and she snapped back to his face. Unconsciously, Lola pulled her hand to touch him. Even though his hair was cut shorter than the last time she saw it, the pretty dirty blonde color made it look messy no matter how short it was. She missed its bouncy curls, and her fingertips traced the hairlines, bringing her nails down to the soft flesh of his face. His cheeks were pink, wind brushed, and his chest was heaving in big gulps of air. The tension between them sparked like electricity.

"Go with me," Evra said again, brushing his lips against her hand. The warm heat of him made her breath hitch. She wasn't allowed to *want* him.

"Tell me one thing," Lola said, panting. He didn't say a word, waiting for her to mark him. She traced the curve of his sharp chin with a long nail. Evra winced in pain, and Lola noticed the red line of blood that followed the movement. She leaned in, taking her slick tongue and running over the cut to lick the blood clean off. She could have sworn Evra stopped breathing completely. "Why did you kill her?" It was the only question she couldn't get a real answer to, so she would keep asking until she got it from him.

His mouth opened in answer, but she shushed him with her finger. "No," she commanded. The tip of her nail, sharp as a pin needle, threatened to puncture his lip. "Not for me. That's not a proper answer. *Why* did you kill her, Evra?" He swallowed hard again. Lola was content knowing he was being intentional once more. His eyes flicked down her body, and if she had been any closer she'd have been able to feel the hardness under his trousers.

"She found out," he said simply, finally. There was no hurt or remorse in his voice, only a hint of satisfaction. She smiled, and this time with little cruelty in it. Lola would be lying if she didn't say it was everything she wanted to hear, that he had killed her, that he had killed *for* her. To hear that she found out, however, now that was *everything*. She only wished she had been there to see the sadness, hurt, and betrayal in that woman's eyes. She may have been his wife, but Lola was his in every meaning of the word. She felt, then, that she was chosen for him. This job to take the life of Evra Mekabre was one written in the books for much longer than either of them had been alive.

Lola didn't say anything in return, didn't give him what he needed to hear back. Instead, her lips smashed into his. She kissed him long and deep, and there was no intention of breaking it off. There was a fierce impatience and hunger that surprised him. She'd never kissed him like this before, without abandon. Where she had been holding back before, she unleashed the terrible beauty in her now. Her tendrils hissed again in impatience, sliding between them and flattening themselves until they disappeared. Lola couldn't be bothered with their lack of presence. She pressed her body fully against his now, biting his lip as she felt the swelling in his pants sliding up her stomach. The dress hitched higher as his arms wrapped around her, lifting her until she could comfortably wrap her legs around him.

There had always been a familiarity about him, as if she was circling the world, waiting for him. This great and terrible beauty, succumbing to the poison of a married man. Lola was just as intoxicated with him as he had been with her, and she would always find him. It wasn't love, but it was something that ran much deeper than a mere acquaintance, or an intense attraction. This was a deep ache that rattled her to her core. It had only been once, *one time*, and yet she was so taken by his darkness. Her sharp teeth bit the inside of her mouth, trying to convince herself to regain control. She moved her hands from him, curling her fingertips upwards in a gesture meant to summon the darkness back to her. She snapped her thumb against her index finger, but nothing came. The tendrils abandoned her. Lola was sent to destroy him, but in the process, she was starting to destroy herself.

She didn't want to think about it, nothing but the softness of Evra's lips, morphing around the sharpness of all of her. He was so warm, and he was the one starting the fire again between them. Lola really wished he could see the magic he was creating with the friction between their bodies, the flames bright and black around them. This certainly wasn't the first kiss they'd shared, but it was easily the most damning. Lola broke away and she noticed the flash of hurt that crossed Evra's expression. His hand caressed the side of her face. When he was with her, Evra was so soft, and she winced at the delicate touch. It was the first time she had ever allowed it. He leaned further into her, dipping his nose into her raven hair, taking a deep breath, and sighing against her.

Lola needed to stop. She needed to descend back into the deep pits of hell that she had come from. She didn't need, couldn't afford this lapse in judgment. What was it about him?

"What is it?" he asked, his breath coming in and out quickly. "Why did you stop?"

"I'm here to kill you," she whispered against his chest. The tension in the air fluttered around them, and the wind howled angrily. He stared at her, his diamond blue eyes penetrating a part of her soul that hadn't been touched in so long, if ever at all. She shook her head and frowned, narrowing her eyes.

"You don't get the luxury of saying nothing," she growled. He was seeing a far more dangerous side of her now, one that had very little control over the hunger for intimacy. Lola was done trying to pretend that she didn't want him as badly as she did.

"Yes, you are," he murmured. The sound was barely audible, and she could hear the darkness flicker as the tension shifted around them.

"So why are we doing this?"

"Because if I must die, then you must as well. We will destroy each other."

That should have been the end of their wicked dance. Instead, Evra grabbed her chin and raised it slightly, returning his mouth to hers. This kiss was far more impatient than the others. It wasn't careful or crafted, there was no question or probing as they discovered just how well fitted they were for one another. Evra bit her lip and ran a finger into the blacks of her hair again. It felt good, so good.

"Now," Lola growled again, and Evra was all too eager to oblige. It made heat swell between her legs. Evra's voice turned predatory and it made her cheeks flush with color. It complemented the red rings around her eyes and the blood that dripped from his chin. His hair showed the wear of ragged passion. They were still out in the open, waiting for a passerby from the service to catch them in the middle of this infidelity. Evra noticed this the same time she did, opening his mouth and looking around them. They were brought back to the present moment, no longer in their own world.

"Shouldn't we-?" He laughed. The sound was foreign to her, and her face betrayed the bare of her teeth.

"We don't follow the rules, Evra," Lola said simply. If he cared about the admittance to their sins, he didn't say. Instead, he ground his body into her with more urgency. It was like he knew they were running out of time, and this was all that they had left. Evra didn't want to think about that. He fumbled around with the lace of her dress, ripping the black dyed leaves from the seams. Lola could hear their screams as he tore them to shreds, now desperate to undress her. She had only known this desperate feeling, only kissing with abandon and not the slow, achy kiss he was trying to give her now.

She couldn't admit that they fit together, more than she would have liked. It was so wrong to be here with him, not with what she knew would have to be completed before nightfall. Lola couldn't say no though, she couldn't fall out of whatever this was with Evra. She wasn't sure if it was love anymore, or maybe it was. There were no questions, instead, she tore the top of her dress off her body, revealing her beautiful, polished chest. Evra moved away from her lips and started trailing kisses down her neck and across her collarbone. He was being far too gentle with her, caressing her body as he worshiped her. She was sure he did.

"Stop comparing me to her," Lola growled under her breath, heaving as she took in his scent again. She wanted his touch all over her body, but only if he was thinking about her. There was no room for Luara here between them, and she wouldn't let him think of her. Not when she was here, lying with him in the building where her dead body rested. There was no room for the both of them in this world. Somehow it would always end up this way.

She could feel him tighten his grip on either side of her. He moved with newfound aggression, and Lola found herself moaning as she felt the dullness of his teeth sink into the skin just above her breast. He let go and let his instincts take over. Lola recognized the movement and hissed happily, tearing her dress off completely now, revealing the slickness of her body. It was all fake, delicate looking like porcelain as if she would break at his touch. Looks were so deceiving. His eyes glazed over at every new spot he'd discovered. Evra did in fact, worship her body. Her belly wasn't completely flat, and the padding of her hips rolled over each other as the last of the dress disintegrated, as if it had been burned off. He lowered his mouth to taste the curve of her breast, and sighed as he took her nipple into his mouth to suck lightly. Lola jolted upwards, her back curving at the sensation rocking her to her core.

She lost control, grabbing onto either side of his face and letting him take her in whatever way he could. Evra moaned loudly, the sounds crashing into the walls and engulfing them in a wave of desire.

It all happened in a moment. It was a slip of the wrist, a glitch in the matrix. Lola let go for just a moment too long, and Evra had no time to stop it. A long nail sliced through the paper-thin skin that wrapped around his throat. She watched as his eyes went wide in surprise, and his mouth left her bust. Evra spasmed next to her, his royal blue suit drenched in a ruby pool of ichor. Lola leaned back and closed her eyes, reveling in the ecstasy that erupted from her. She lifted her finger to her mouth and licked the blood clean.

She sat up at once, content at feeling the returning presence of her dark shadow tendrils. They slivered around her body, disguising her figure in a new wrap of garments. As Lola rose to her feet she glanced down at the body now convulsing before her. Evra's eyes seemed hazy, not quite as blue as they were when they met. She had no guilt that laced her expression, nor fear for that matter. She could feel the moment when his life left his body, when the man whose attention she craved was just another tally to add to her list. The wind rustled around her and the tension released. She took a big breath of air. The pressure that laid dormant inside of her was now gone, and she wondered, briefly, why it was he felt like he was the center of the universe. There was a new draw, a new point in the ether that called to her, and Lola knew this to be the call of another job.

She had fulfilled her task as a reaper of souls, sending his soul down under to where it belonged. Lola wiped her hands on the sides of her newly painted dress, content with the tiny leaves that littered the bottom, flowing around her. The fabric hardly covered a thing in the condition it was in, and so she shimmied it up to cover the parts of her that mattered. She glanced back up at the sound of sneakers against the marble and jumped back in physical shock.

The boy with the bouncy blonde curls, curls much like Evra's, looked at the body in front of her, eyes wide and expression locked in a permanent scream, but no sound came out. He looked from the body to her, trying to comprehend what was right in front of him. Lola took one last look at Evra, no longer feeling the unbearable lust towards that body- as if it was not the vessel, but the soul inside of it that she would follow anywhere.

Lola glanced at the boy, locking eyes with him and bringing her fingers to her lips in a shushing movement. She smiled, snapped the fingers on her other hand, and the tendrils helped her vanish into the darkness.

PART THREE
THE DRINK

"Oh pity the poor glutton, whose troubles all began, in struggling on and on to turn, what's out into what's in."

-Walter de la Mare

I

The deepest parts of hell were underwater.

It was the furthest south they could go before crossing over into the Underworld, which was probably why the Life Drinkers lived down there. It was easy when they didn't need to breathe, and didn't need to eat or drink. All they needed was the salty sweetness of the blood coursing through the veins of mortals walking on dry land, and they could get that whenever they wanted. Gerre pushed forward through the water, his feet kicking out like a frog. When Gerre looked up he saw sunlight still beaming through a pocket of clear water and he avoided it as he delved deeper. There were millions of fish down here, and as he fluttered his feet, they scattered. He felt more comfortable the deeper he went and as the light disappeared while he sliced through the darkness. Gerre dug into the pocket of his wetsuit, pulling out a tiny sphere. He clicked it with his thumb and a fluorescent light lit up the depths. It was like a glowing pearl when he held it between his thumb and index finger. Gerre flicked it out into the deep and watched it fall, its weight pulling it downward;

following it with a quick gracefulness he sunk deeper, and deeper still until it seemed he could not go much further.

Of course, that was just a trick of the water, the Ocean loved to play tricks. Some believed it was ruled by the Father, Poseidon, but Gerre always thought it was a lie. Poseidon would never desire to travel this deep, not unless he too, wanted to die. As Gerre looked down, he could see the layers of ocean that still stretched before him, and although this had been his destination, he assumed it might have gone on forever with no definite end. The Ocean and its tricks, he would never understand them.

Gerre felt the awful popping in his ears, and just this once he was grateful for his superhuman capabilities. Humans would never be able to catapult this low into the sea without the risk of rupturing a lung from the pressure changes. Even man-made machines could be thwarted by the water around him. However, a Life Drinker himself, the magic that held him together blessed him with more ability than he knew what to do with. There was no need for air in his body to begin with, and if the uncomfortable popping of his ears was the only thing he'd have to put up with down here, then Gerre would have said he'd had worse. The further down he drifted in the water, the better he felt. For years this was home to Drinkers. It was a preferable alternative to their previous lives on dry land with the mortals. Without the worry of water pressure, the lack of a traditional appetite, and the ability to hold their breath for an infinite amount of time, life Underwater was a peaceful existence for them.

He held out his arm and waved it in front of him, enjoying the resistance against his skin. Without the sunlight above him, he felt free to move around openly. His powerful muscles hidden behind lean, lanky limbs gave him the push he needed to propel through the water. Sometimes he hated being a Drinker, but being down here, it didn't seem so bad.

The tiny ball of light was slowing its fall, as it was trained to do. He kept up with it easily, until it hit a glass ceiling. Gerre landed lightly on the glass, careful to watch his strength so he didn't punch a hole through it with his legs. It wouldn't be the first time some bloodsucker didn't pay attention. Their strength was a huge asset when hunting prey, but it could also be their weakness if they couldn't control it. He gripped as best as he could with his nails, maneuvering until he was upside down, flat against the pane. Their cave was close, and he would have to feel around in the dark to find it.

The tiny light pearl fizzled out, disappearing like a lightning bug in a thunderstorm. Even without it, he could see fairly easily. His ruby red eyes were much like a cat, taking in the available light- however slim- and he prowled around with little difficulty. Drinkers were the world's best predators. They were faster, stronger, and more agile. Gerre could glamour his features, hide his long fangs, and had the ability to live for many years. He wasn't immortal, but as close to it as it comes. Down here in his element, he was absolutely lethal. They'd almost become too dangerous, handpicking their human meals so often that they worried the mortal lands would find themselves endangered in the next hundred years if they kept doing so.

It was too bad hunting was Gerre's favorite activity. The long swim wasn't just an elaborate exercise, but a means to a very delicious end. In their little corner of the world, "shark attacks" had accounted for more than several dozen ocean disappearances a month. Mortals were always blaming others for their wrongdoings; they'd been warned that the waters weren't their own for many years, so it should come as no shock that the hunters found their meals close to the surface, if and when, they ignored that knowledge.

They'd catch surfers or those that got caught in a current. Most were easy, like plucking a feather from a bird's back. Once underwater, no one heard their screams. Gerre smiled at the thought. Shark attacks were a great way to shield yourself from reality. He bit his lip and let the water infiltrate his lungs. Although it wasn't painful, it was an unwelcome guest. The water invaded his throat and expanded into his lungs, filling up the entire space and sloshing around uncomfortably. He pushed it back out in a long exhale before continuing his search.

Within minutes Gerre came across an imperfection on the dome. A very large, defined crack split the glass in two, zig-zagging across for five meters. Those unfamiliar with the structure would believe it to be a flaw in the creation itself or a product of a capricious Drinker. Though unsightly and disrespectful to the mastery of the architecture, it actually aided in keeping their fortress impenetrable. He followed the crack with his claw, guiding him towards the entrance only those with blood staining their teeth could find, much less enter.

2

Deep-set within a coral reef cave, just off the glass, was a small hole where the glass parted just wide enough to fit a small creature. Logically, there was no way that Gerre could fit through such a hole. He smiled wickedly. Snapping his fingers underwater didn't have quite the same flair that it had when he was above ground. Instead, Gerre flicked his wrist and in a moment he was no longer Gerre at all. He morphed into something resembling a tiny bat, its sticky smooth wings flapping helplessly in the water. As he transformed, his body shifted to accommodate. The wings that were so used to flying stretched wider and webbing formed between the bones. His tiny nose flattened against his skull and several small gills erupted from both sides of his neck. There was nothing more beautiful, or magical, than a bat in the sea.

In his new form, Gerre squeezed through the parted glass and fell face first down a waterfall. The water fell quickly towards the bottom, and Gerre squealed in excitement as his blood rushed to his head. When he landed in the body of shallow water, he emerged as a man once more, suit and all.

"Welcome," someone hissed from afar. He went to nod in their direction, but when he turned his head there was no one there. The underwater darkness was amplified in this dome, casting shadows and eerie quiet around them. The bloodsuckers weren't interested in the man-made items that their mortal counterparts had chosen to peruse. Instead, the sandy ground was covered in waxy candles that lit a path from the site of the waterfall and into the world of the bloodsuckers themselves. Looking up, he could make out the flurry of fish and creatures just outside, relieved that the Life Drinker in their midst was gone, for now.

Wiping his hands on the sides of his suit, Gerre looked up towards the chasm once more. The water cascaded down so elegantly as if it were at the top of a large cliff and not the bottom of the ocean. He admired again the sheer strength of the dome that surrounded him, awed at the size. It spanned about a mile in either direction. Not big in retrospect, but enough to house the hundreds of Life Drinkers across the world. Gerre had always wondered how many of them there were out there. He was still young, only 159 years into his servitude himself, and had never found someone to walk along the tightrope of this life with him.

He started along the path and weaved in and out of the reef. The Life Drinkers who created this place chose well; while the mortals killed off the reefs closer to the surface, down here the coral was flourishing. The stories they told about the Drinkers and their damnation, as if they were any worse than the mortals who killed just by breathing, made him prickle with loathing. Gerre was a killer because he needed to survive. Mortals? Mortals killed because it was in their blood.

The farther he walked through the seabed, the tighter his

chest became. He'd gone an extra week without feeding, and the desire shot through him. He could smell the blood thick in the stale air and shut his mouth against it. From just a whiff, his mouth salivated, his upper lip catching on the enlarged fangs. They had mortals here to feast on. Gerre's pace quickened. He neared a large structure at the center of the dome, covered in algae and water kelp. Once in front of the blocked entrance, he knelt. Below him were the markings and indentations of those that have kneeled before him; there must have been hundreds, thousands of them. As for Gerre, he had knelt seventy-two times.

"Speak brother," the voice came from inside the cave-like structure. The sheer volume of it was enough to rock him side to side. He bowed his head in deep respect. "What is it you desire?"

In the seventy-two times he'd been here, he's discovered that whoever was inside had never once ventured out. It was said that inside held the world's oldest Life Drinker. But to all of those that come to him, he was known only as the Oracle.

"I come seeking your guidance," Gerre answered quickly, and his stomach gave an uncomfortable rumble. He waited in silence for a moment, expecting a reply. When none came, he continued. "I am looking for a meal."

The voice was so loud it shook the building itself. "Your name, Drinker," It said. The voice was powerful, it had the raspiness of someone who had spoken many times in their long life. What Gerre wouldn't give to see its face. Would it be dead and wrinkled? Or would it be full of life and youth?

"Gerre Babs, resident of Region Five, Drinker in the North American cluster," he said as he had countless times before. Did the Oracle not know who he was, truly?

"And you are incapable of finding your own sustenance?" its voice wasn't menacing, or accusatory like he'd expected. It just sounded tired, and maybe a bit confused. Gerre had never learned the art of tracking, not like Drinkers before him. He'd fed from mortals walking on dry land before, but it always caused him deep discomfort. He was never a wolf in sheep's clothing. Gerre wasn't subtle. He relied heavily on the prey in the waters since his last public burning, surviving every few months on those that ventured into the ocean. Never too close to the surface, Gerre was too intimidated to risk his exposure there. Who knew what they might have done to him? He enjoyed hunting the deep water game, the divers, and the vacationers. The ones that expected to be safe in waters this big.

"So...you are not looking for assistance," the voice murmured. It echoed his thoughts, predicting his intentions accurately. Had the Old One been a mind reader, too? "You look for permissions to hunt again."

Gerre shifted his weight onto both of his knees, holding his breath tightly, he stayed that way for what seemed to be hours.

"Very well, the waters are filthy today. There may be enough to spare."

Gerre bowed his head deeper in appreciation, "Thank you, Oracle-"

"This is your last time, Gerre Babs."

His eyes widened in exclamation. In his time as a Drinker, he had never heard of the Oracle denying a request prematurely, even with the decreasing human population. He bared his teeth, though he resisted the urge to hiss at the large fortress in front of him. "I don't understand," he let out. His voice was barely more than a whisper. Gerre had to tread lightly in order to not disrespect the Oracle, who had granted him access to his meal this week.

"You have taken advantage of my hospitality, Gerre. Have you not noticed the amount of time you spend here? Have you once met another soul while you've delved to these depths?" Gerre looked around. He'd noticed the lack of Drinkers, even if he could feel their presence. Now that he thought about it clearly, he missed the night flyers whenever he was this far under, only seeing vague shapeless figures and hearing low hisses nearby. He'd always expected that to be because of their nature, not because they hardly visited this place at all. He looked all around him. The candle-lit path flickered and the shadows ricocheted off the dome exterior, but there was no other Drinker in sight.

He twitched nervously. He wanted to admit that he didn't know how he wasn't as accustomed to this life as the others who lived it. Gerre was a coward, and that was worse than a sin to his kind. Would he be judged for admitting it, or had the Oracle already known? "You cannot be a Drinker if you do not know how to feast on land." It spoke again.

"I did not choose this life."

"And you've chosen not to acclimate to your...rather unfortunate predicament. Tell me, have you always been this weak?"

Gerre liked the hunt. He had long since accepted himself and his lot in life 159 years ago, a year after he had been damned by the person who hunted *him*. Being a Life Drinker was what Gerre was built for. The problem was that he couldn't control himself after he hunted. The rage boiled deep in his core, and he lusted for more of it. The authorities caught him the first time after he lay naked and full on the belly of a street that everyone knew. Her name was Lindin Doyle, and she was everything he knew he'd ever love. She was pretty, thick, and confident, her swaying hips enough to drive Gerre mad with desire.

Had he been a mortal, he may have tried to court her as he would a bride. Alas, she was not destined to be his companion, and he was not destined to court. He followed her from the theater, from a film they both had seen. She was watching the moving pictures, laughing at all the right parts, crying when she was meant to. Gerre couldn't focus on the film, as he was only ever interested in her. It was dark outside when they left, and when she dropped her bags, being the gentleman that he was, Gerre rushed over to pick them up for her.

"Apologies, mister," she curtsied and blushed. He watched the blood rush to her cheeks and he felt the inside of his mouth dampening. The tips of his canines pricked with anticipation. Gerre covered his mouth and coughed. He bowed to her slightly.

"There's no need to apologize," he said quickly. "May I seek the pleasure of your company and walk you home? The dark is no place for a lady to be on her own." Gerre almost wished she would have said no. Had she carried on with her night and not taken his lead, she might still be alive. He could just picture how beautiful and bright she would be now if he hadn't drained her dry. She was so clumsy, tripping over herself and giggling profusely. She had such terrible taste in men, such terrible instincts. Gerre could tell she felt comfortable around him. He was never as strong looking as some of his brothers. Standing at 5'7 in his boots, with stringy black locks and a thin body, no one would have suspected poor Gerre Babs as being a murderer. A Drinker.

She tasted deliciously sweet. Her blood was warm as he sunk two perfectly shaped, sharp canines into her open neck. She didn't even scream, instead, moaning as if he was pleasuring her. Gerre was a quick hunter, and quickly drained every last drop from her beautiful body. He left her, lying with her back to the floor and still smiling as if he had said something funny, stroking her hand, and to this day, Gerre couldn't tell anyone why. He felt sorry for her, felt something stronger tugging at the pit of his chest where his heart might have been.

He could have loved her, had this been a different life. Temptress, she was, and, ultimately, his demise. She could have been the center of his universe.

When the morning woke and the sun rose high in the sky, they found them. His eyes were closed when he heard the first screams, and when the authorities showed up and cuffed his hands behind his back, Gerre snapped out of his trance. He kicked and screamed, tearing the cuffs open with a pull and snarling at the gathered police before taking off into the city. People moved out of his way as he ran, and he could hear the distant sounds of his enemies catching up to him. Gerre outran them easily, and it was the first time he jumped in the ocean and swam to the very bottom.

He heard about the underwater Atlantis for the Life Drinkers. And when he was greeted not like an unwelcome monster but a beloved brother, he returned, and then returned again. Each time Gerre came up for air the world was different. Styles changed and cities grew. He asked permission to drink from the people in the ocean, and he once thought he'd grown close to this city underwater. It wasn't until this moment when he was sitting on his knees and listening to Oracle chastise him, that he realized he had never been close to this place at all.

“I know how to feast,” he snarled.

“Mortals have tiny minds, Gerre Babs. They don't keep memories as long as you and I. I know you've been hiding in the waters, and it is time you live amongst the other Life Drinkers in the mortal lands again. This place is sacred, meant as a haven for traveling blood thieves. If you continue using it as a permanent residence, you will be no better than the mortals we drink from.”

Gerre hissed. Had they told him earlier that he overstayed his welcome, he would have left a long time ago. He rose to his feet. "They will not remember you, Babs. Enjoy your life, and hunt to your heart's desire. Be the Drinker we know you can be. This will be your last hunt in these waters for decades to come. Use it well."

He kicked his feet, hissing loudly and snapping his fingers. He shifted back into his bat form, his wings gloriously large and his nose catching all the ocean's scents. Gerre circled Atlantis, his eyes soaking in the world around him. The city was always quiet, its ruins undisturbed under the dome of glass. He thought again of what the Oracle said. This was a place for travelers, meant as a waypoint for other Life Drinkers like him. Not meant for long-term use. Why had he been able to feast in these waters for so many years? He screeched, the tiny body incapable of wreaking havoc like he wanted to. When he followed the waterfall back up to its entrance, he dove into the water, his features morphing again.

When he exited and rose higher still, his body was wrapped in a slick black wet suit that tightened around all of his joints and creases. At once Gerre felt relief. He needed to be in the water. It was where he was the most comfortable, and he couldn't imagine his life outside of it. Would he truly be unwelcome in the ocean after today? Could he be a trespasser in this place he had called home for so long?

3

His legs kicked out and shot him through the water once more. He was quick as lightning, flying through the water much faster than any other living mammal. Gerre passed fish of all shapes and sizes, escaping him frantically. The only creatures that didn't part were his shark companions. They were so much like him, almost as if they were brothers too. One dared so much as to get close to him and Gerre smiled, reaching out a hand and stroking its backside and tail fin. He was not afraid of sharks, and the shark was not afraid of him. He leaned into his touch, and Gerre felt it slide past his fingertips. These predators and he were one and the same.

The shark opened its mouth as if testing the waters for prey. He could see the rows and rows of tiny sharp teeth, much like his own. *What do you sense, friend?* Gerre thought, trying desperately to make it see what he wanted from it without having to say a word. Talking underwater was not the easiest, and communicating with a species outside his own, even despite the water surrounding them, was a task in itself.

Although it didn't seem to understand *him*, it moved forward in the water and Gerre followed its lead, determined it would lead him to prey worthy of his last meal.

They did come upon it in the end, and Gerre could smell the blood as they neared. In the dark waters they waded, and the shark looked at him before scurrying off in another direction. Gerre watched him disappear into the darkness before turning to eye his prey. He sent a quiet prayer of thanks, wondering still just how close they were in relation. The animal led him here in silent camaraderie, a gesture of goodwill- if sharks had any sort of goodwill in them. He was still several hundred yards away, but his eyes filtered through the murky ocean to see a single figure sinking further and further into his home. They looked similar, with the same shade of wet suit and ocean salted hair in their face. This woman had long red hair that struck him in his heart and stopped him in his swim. She looked so much like Lindin that it punched him in the gut. This was a trick of the gods and the devils themselves. She had the same sort of innocence about her face, eyes wide in awe as she looked around her. There were heavy amounts of gear weighing her down and covering her features, but Gerre was sure it was her. The center of his universe had returned to him.

He looked around, curious at the lack of other bodies present. He was used to mortals traveling in packs, especially in places like this, too far and out of their depth. A long tube connected her to the surface, and he recognized it as her lifeline. There must have been someone hovering near the top. His eyes glazed over in that predatory way of his, mouth dripping with saliva and chest heaving with desire. He dipped deeper in the water, staying just out of reach until the very last moment. His hunger was unmanageable. It rumbled in his core, speaking to him in a delicate purr that was hard to ignore. It rattled through his body, making it difficult, if not impossible to think of anything else besides it. It scorched the blood in his dead heart, raking across his lungs and holding on for dear life. Gerre couldn't ever forget who he was, he couldn't forgive what he was made to be, and he couldn't deserve her.

It was all too easy. When Gerre grabbed her from behind she couldn't even scream. He wrapped his strong hands around her figure, feeling her body tighten and resist, kicking her legs and arms out. It was no use. The resistance of the water against her bones affected her ability far more than it did him, and he tightened his grip like an anaconda. When he lowered his mouth to her neck, stretching the skin until he was able to puncture the wet suit, he felt a tug on the line. Transfixed, they both looked up. He wasn't curious about what was on the other side of the line, only annoyed. Gerre dove deeper, pulling until her oxygen line was taut. With a quick movement, he snapped the line that held her life and dug his teeth into her skin, and soon her body was limp.

He whispered something unintelligible to her, but her consciousness was long gone, so she hadn't heard him before passing. It was for the best, she wasn't who he so desperately wanted her to be. He sucked harder against her neck, rougher than he usually would. The wound in his heart made him angry, and with his emotions amplified, he couldn't control the speed with which he drank the life from her. Gerre was clean at the very least, he learned his lesson. This might have been the cleanest hunt he's had in his 159 years as a Drinker. No drop of blood escaped her and he sucked until he felt nothing but dry air. The heat in his throat subsided, though the ache still sat at the back of his throat. The hunger never went away completely. Gerre swallowed hard, his body shaking in contentment. No matter the dread he was feeling in his soul, he couldn't help but feel satisfaction fill him up, sharing the same space. He released his hold on the woman who was begrudgingly, not Lindin, but as close as he could ever get to her again, and he watched her body sink down to the ocean floor.

"The water is no place for a lady to be on her own," he said, smiling as the deja vu surrounded him. Gerre had finished too fast, and though his hunger was quieted for a few weeks, months if he could stretch it out some, he was frustrated with his lack of emotional control. The Oracle promised him one more hunt, and he had wasted it. There was no savoring of his last meal in the water, he fell for the girl underneath instead, and he wanted to tear something apart to rid himself of the dread that overtook him.

4

The tubing that supplied her oxygen slowly rose to the surface, and Gerre watched. The energy tightened around him and he watched as it disappeared from his immediate periphery, rising with quick intensity. He turned away from it, wanting to vanish down to the seafloor to find the shiver of sharks his new friend might have come from. As he took his first strokes downward, something sharp sliced past him. Gerre turned in shock, wincing at the pain that stroked his ear. His hand immediately raised, catching the blood that webbed through the water. A throbbing pain emanated from his earlobe. When the momentary paralysis released its grip on him, his hand moved to touch the lobe, and his scowl deepened in horror. He couldn't remember the last time he'd been injured.

The pain that accompanied the injury was also new. He hissed, letting the water fill his airways once more. The ocean slurred around inside him, and he desperately tried to expel it with a long exhale. He pressed his lips tightly together to not let one more ounce of water in again and turned his head towards the direction of the incoming shrapnel. It had to have been from the surface, there was nothing down here in the water that would have attempted to injure him- not with permission from the Oracle to hunt. They were the predators down here, not the prey.

The pain throbbed heavily, and he groaned in hunger at the scent of blood leaking out of his system. *Her blood.* What left his body now was the blood that he stole from her, and he wasn't interested in letting someone steal it back. There was a comfort in knowing that her blood, maybe not Lindin's, but *hers* was the blood making its course through his system, keeping him alive for the weeks to come. Hunting was a sensual and intimate act for Life Drinkers, and his last meal was draining from him with each second he wasted in shock.

Gerre licked his palm, sealing the wound with his saliva. Aconite was a tricky poison, one he was taught to fear. It was the only thing that could truly wound him, and kill him. Their weapon was laced with it, the bastards. The bleeding ceased quickly, leaving only ruby red traces disintegrating in the salty water. Any other, more rational Drinker would have disappeared and gone far away from this place with the aconite-laced metals. He was no ordinary, rational Drinker, though. Gerre was a proud creature, and the anger that flooded through him was unmanageable.

He kicked his legs out behind him and wrapped his arms close to his sides, shooting up through the water and up towards the surface. The closer he got, the hotter his skin became. It burned from the rays of the sun, and though he could tell it was setting by the warm orange glow around him, it still wasn't comfortable. Gerre rose anyway, ignoring the blistering of his skin. What was left of the cool blood circulating in his veins boiled inside of him. He cried out in pain.

He was so close to the surface now, and Gerre could make

out the shapes above the water, a blurry but tangible threat. He would drain them dry. They were not technically off-limits, and while he wasn't hungry, he wouldn't waste a second in draining whoever was on that boat. They were going to pay for the pain they caused him. If he could see past the rage and the anguish, he would have seen it coming. He might have seen the way the figures raised their arms in threat, might have seen the sharp metal that gleamed in the setting sun.

It all happened so quickly. The aconite-laced shrapnel sliced through the water cleanly, stabbing him right in the shoulder. Gerre howled in agony, breaking the surface like a whale breaching for air. The water rose around them in large waves, and the boat moved further into the distance at a speed he wasn't sure he could match in this condition. The sun was close to setting, though not hidden completely. The fire still burned within him, masking the throb in his shoulder with an even greater sensation of death and doom. Gerre saw the boat fade into thin air, and he could have sworn he heard mortal screams around him before he closed his eyes, and dreamed of death.

Anyone who would have seen him would assume him to be dead. Gerre was floating back up in the ocean, his eyes closed and his body paralyzed; he thought he was dead, too. He wasn't well versed in the lives of Life Drinkers. As a loner for most of his life, he didn't feel it was necessary to seek out companionship from one of his kind. So he didn't know what death looked like for someone like him. Would it mean he would be like this, sitting out here paralyzed in the water for the rest of eternity? Or would the final death come far quieter, but much quicker? He would never know, and so Gerre was trapped in this body, moving with the waves.

It seems fitting that he was to die here in the open water, in the place he called home for so long. It was fitting that the last thing he would remember was this, his body on fire from the burning rays of the setting sun, and the sting of aconite. It reminded him so much of the day of his burning, and the moment he gave in to the hunger and feasted, truly feasted. That was the real beginning of his life. In fact, if there was one thing about this life that Gerre didn't absolutely detest, it was the act of feeding itself. He didn't necessarily like having to find his prey within the mortal population- as he was once one and the idea was uncomfortable in his pre-death life. But once he caught a whiff of the blood, once the scent filled his nostrils and traveled down to his throat to where the dormant hunger pounded there was nothing he could do. He would submit to it every time because he loved it.

The morning he was found with Lindin was when he made a run for it. He jumped into the water, determined to never be seen again. Gerre swam down to the bottom of the ocean and found the dome where the Oracle lived, but soon discovered that he couldn't live there permanently. The Oracle was never displeased to see him, not like he was today, but he had always made one thing clear. Gerre could come and go as often as he wished, he could ask permission to feast in the waters, with the caveat that he was not allowed to rest there. This was fine, as he didn't find that he needed to sleep.

During periods of his life when he *was* required to sleep on land, he would stray into the dark parts of town, feasting on drunken merry men from pubs or mortals with no sense to avoid him. Since mourning the death of the love he would never have, Gerre was moved by the emotional attachment he could have to the blood of the deceased. He could still feel

Lindin in his veins weeks after she had died in his arms, and he was hungry for more of it. Each time he feasted on land was dirtier and messier than the last. Gerre didn't want to be careful, he didn't want to hide what it was he was doing. He just wanted to feel.

Maybe it wasn't that Gerre didn't look for companionship, maybe it was that the other Life Drinkers that didn't want to look for *him*. Each time he was caught with the still body of another mortal walker, he would disappear to the sea. His crime counts rose higher and higher still, and on the 54th week since drinking Lindin, he was caught once again. Gerre wasn't very selective about his kills since he tasted her. He enjoyed the hunger, and he delighted in the ability to gorge himself on the blood that made him feel invincible. No other Drinkers would come here because Gerre made it difficult to live discreetly. The day he took it too far was a day he would never forget, though. He was drunk on blood if there ever was such a thing.

Gerre stumbled around, the body of a bulky 30-year-old man hanging off of his hands. Although he looked lanky, the strength behind his skin was enough to lug around 230 pounds of literal dead weight. He walked along the cobbled street, stumbling out of the alleyway just before sunrise. This was always his favorite time of night when it was the most dangerous. He had roughly twenty minutes until sunrise, but without a proper place to retire to before the sun was high in the sky, most Drinkers wouldn't ever come out this late into the evening. He was caught. It was the only time Gerre had ever been captured after a hunt since her. Even with his strength, they had the numbers to throw him to the floor.

The townsfolk had watched him all of these months, and they were prepared for him to make a mistake. They were on him quick, strapping ropes around his torso and arms, causing him to drop the man he'd drained. Gerre could hear the small gasps as the commotion brought out more and more residents. He was no use this disoriented, and he felt worse when the sun split through the mountains and lit him on fire. The flames licked his skin, and Gerre couldn't make it stop. He yowled in pain, screaming so loud he could be heard across the plaza. The townspeople roared back defiantly, tying him to a metal figure in the middle of the clearing closest to the water. It was old and rusting, but he could see from his squinting eyes the slickness of it too.

"Finally, we created something to kill you bloodsuckers for good," someone hissed in his ear. Gerre doubled over in agony. Aconite, Vervain, Monkshood, it was all the same, and it all burned like Hell.

Gerre was strapped to the rotted green metal, and if he wasn't already numb from the fire engulfing him, he would have cried out in something worse than pain from the stickiness of what was layered on the statue. It poisoned his skin, creating dark purple welts from prolonged exposure. Or that could have been the way the sun burned holes through him. Gerre was oblivious to everything else around him except for the realization of what he was and what he did. He was a monster who fed. Gerre was created by the demons housed in hell, and it was time for him to return home.

But he didn't die. He briefly removed himself from the recollection, his back was still up against the sun which now rose high in the sky. It burned just as hot as it did that day he was tied to that statue, and he felt just as paralyzed. Gerre remembered the strength that surged through him then, before falling back into the memory.

Gerre waited until they moved away from him, content to watch him burn at the stake like some sort of witch. His focus would waver if he didn't do it quickly enough. Pushing his arms against the ropes was a fate worse than death. He could feel the burning ripple across his arms, yet he persisted until he could feel the ropes taut against his skin. The strings pulled until they couldn't any longer, and they released, flying in either direction, now frayed at the edges. Gerre moved before he could think twice about it, sprinting out towards the water once more. He could hear the angry mob behind him, but all of that was a blur.

Gerre put his arms out in front of him, diving into the ocean and swimming as far away from land as he could. There was no more hunting on the land, Gerre promised himself that he would never go back. If they remembered him, if they even caught a glimpse of who he was, he worried fate might catch back up to him and they would keep him tied to that statue for as long as it took to die, to really die this time.

If he survived then, he needed to survive this. Gerre had always found a way to be strong enough.

He opened his eyes, grinding his teeth and pushing against his insides until he could move again. Gerre looked side to side, looking for a way to relieve himself of the sun that beat against his exposed skin. He narrowed his eyes, feeling a rush of adrenaline when he recognized the shark circling with his shiver meters below him. His mouth opened slowly, and Gerre felt his throat rumble in fury, pain, grief, and for the first time since that day, fear. The shark looked at him with his beady black eyes, and Gerre breathed evenly, ready to die knowing there were other predators that could call the ocean their home, too. He remembered feeling the shark tooth closing around his arm. If he could smile he would have, knowing that his life might truly be ended by the shark that had shown him his last meal.

That wasn't what happened, though. As sharp as its teeth were, he could feel himself sink deep into the sea again, and the relief that filled him as he was underwater once more. The sun finally dipped below the horizon, and Gerre could feel the power of the moon. The feeling of the shark's teeth was nothing like the release he felt when there was no laser penetrating his skin any longer. He smiled something wicked, tearing his hand away from the now open-mouthed shark, who scurried away.

"Thank you, friend," Gerre whispered to the water. He could feel the burns on his back, knowing relief was not a prolonged feeling. He would feel pain again soon enough, but it was a pain that he could manage. Gerre did not die that day against the statue, and he would not die here. Someone knew what he was, or who he was, or both. He licked his palm and moved it to the wound in his shoulder, wincing as the poison burned. He moved his arm tentatively, tensing his muscles at the stiffness that lingered. Gerre blew out the last of the air that hid in his lungs and took one big kick forward through the water.

He was starting to feel hungry.

PART FOUR
A TASTE OF SOUR

"The first and worst of all frauds is to cheat one's self. All sin is easy after that."

- Pearl Bailey

I

He was a fraud, a cheat, and a liar, the whole package. There was not one person in this god-forsaken city that trusted Tristan Cohen, even himself, but that was because he planned it that way. Tristan unraveled the blue wrapping and cracked a piece of peppermint-flavored gum into his mouth. The smell of mint burned his nostrils, the feel of crisp cool delight flowed through him and made Tristan shiver in contentment. If there was one thing he could trust about his life- and believe me there weren't many- it was the dependability of a stupid stick of gum.

"The fuck do you think you're doing?" He growled, scratching at the designer stubble across his sharp jawline. Tristan tried hard to nail the 5 o'clock shadow that freckled his chin, making it just so that he could pass off older than he was. Thirty-one was not young, but it wasn't old enough to be hanging with this crowd and earning a wrinkle of respect. There was a reputation he needed to uphold, and any misstep would be scrutinized- Tristan could not afford to be scrutinized. He was handsome, but not exceptional. His saving grace was the sharpness of his features, high cheekbones, and the cruelty in his expressions. Pretty enough to get his way, rugged enough to be taken seriously amidst these dumb, bulky thugs. His lip curled in contempt and he threw the cards in his empty hand to the green felt table in front of him. He won, of course. He always won, even if he didn't. The rat man looking at him obviously did not get the deal here. He was staring at Tristan with a shocked expression, hands already outstretched towards the pile of chips in the center of the table. Those were his chips. His winnings. Everything in this fucking world was his.

"Sorry Tristan," the man panicked, folding his own cards face down on the table. Tristan looked upon him with every ounce of condescending pity he could muster, and he watched as the man folded just like his cards, curling inward on himself.

"You don't call me that," he snapped, cinching his teeth together so quickly and so tight that those around the tables could hear the bones crashing together.

"Sorry, Mr. Cohen! I'm sorry!" the rat man said in that terrible high-pitched tone again. Tristan turned to his right, where a large beefy man in dark shades stood, rigid and uncaring. He only needed to nod once and the man moved, bending to his every will and command. He liked having control over such a large piece of muscle. The big man grabbed onto Rat Man's shoulders roughly, pulling him from his chair and dragging him by the arm out the door. The minute the heavy door shut, the screams began.

The poker table stayed silent, each face wincing with every whine and every thump. Tristan laughed.

"Does anyone else want to treat me like we're friends?" The room waited patiently, fearfully. They didn't shake their heads, but no one said a word, either. Tristan grunted in approval. He pushed his chair back, the legs screeching as it skids across the floor, and pulled the chips to his seat.

The trials and tribulations of this city's most feared boss.

"Don't test your luck boys," he taunted, flicking his wadded-up gum wrapper towards the table on top of the cards he'd folded earlier. No one looked him in the eyes as he departed. Good. He didn't need his muscle to kill any more guys today, no matter how good at it he was.

Tristan scuffed the bottom of his boots on the floor and frowned before he headed to the door, that frown deepening the closer he got. He'd waited long enough for his guy to dispose of the Rat Man, but he could still hear the pathetic whimpers from behind the wood. When he opened the door he saw the Rat Man, his tears staining the pink of his cheeks as he curled on the floor. The bones of his arms were broken in several places, and blood coated his face. His nose was cracked, protruding at a terrible angle. But he wasn't dead. He should be dead.

It wasn't an explicit order, but the implication was clear. He and his guy had been working together for too long for him to not know when he needed someone killed. Rat Man deserved it, anyway.

"Is there a reason why you're still alive, boy?" He asked curiously. The door closed behind him, but he was sure he could hear the gasps of his companions in the poker room. Tristan ran a calloused hand, the hands that proved he was willing to put in the hard work, through his dusty brown hair. His nails were clipped close to the nail bed but the edges still caught as he dragged his hand through the strands. Tristan was used to pain much worse than that, and so the pull was nothing short of an annoyance. The boy just sat there, his little whines enough to tell him that he was very much alive.

"Fuck, I guess that's my bad luck, then," he said, cracking

his knuckles as he walked away, leaving the boy a crumpled mess on the floor. "Win a game of pool, lose my best fucking muscle. This deal gets more fucking unfair by the day."

Their home was nothing special, small, but quaint, more so the old lady's taste than his. It backed a large forest, perfectly quiet and hidden. Very few knew where he lived, and he liked it that way. In contrast, Tristan's office was large, and expensive, and fell in line with his reputation- a more adequate fit, which was probably why he found himself there more often than he found himself here. Here, he was just "husband" and "father". The latter was still strange to say on his lips, even after a few years of practice.

Jameson was about ten now, old enough to keep his mouth shut and stay out of the way when told. He was always the best kid, if there was such thing as good kids. If it was just James and the old lady, he might have stayed at the office a bit longer tonight. Now that he was in the market for new muscle he needed to interview and promote right away- someone like Tristan couldn't afford to be unprotected for too long. There were too many people in this world that wanted him dead. And, with his luck, he would be dead by morning. As it was, however, his youngest Norman, just days old, was wailing loud enough that he could hear him before he opened the front door.

The whole house shook as he slammed it closed and latched the seven separate locks tight. Tristan didn't call out, instead, he moved silently through the halls of his quaint little house. He could still hear Nor screaming from his upstairs nursery. It was far too late for their sitter to still be here and he could imagine his wife was rocking him senseless, desperate to make him fall back asleep. Tristan wasn't cut out for this life.

He slunk through the house, sneaking into his office. This room was the largest in the house, even larger than the master bedroom. In the center of the room sat a large oak desk. It was empty, save for the desktop monitor and keyboard that rested unused in the corner. Tristan sighed, raking his hands through his hair once more. It had become something of a nervous tick. Just another sign of the humanity that was left in him. Some days he saw it more than others, and each time he did there was a deep seeded rage that burned in the pit of his stomach. He hated this mortal life he lived more than he cared to admit.

Of course, it was good to be feared, good to be revered, even if it was false idolization.

Tristan sat at his desk. The baby seemed to stop crying now, and he could feel the breath of relief riding up through him as his headache subsided. The feeling, however fleeting, scared him. Relief was never something he wanted, he'd much rather live a life of perpetual disgruntlement.

It was a give and take, this world. No matter what good came from his deal with the Devil, because certainly, that was what *she* was. Equilibrium she called it once. When he was young and dumb, it seemed to have been the obvious choice, to trade happiness for luck. Of course, that trade was easy to make when you thought you had nothing left to give; had he been where he was now, had he known a child like him, he would have had them killed.

Tristan should have died.

Instead, he took her word. *You will be great*, she whispered in his ear. Her voice was velvet smooth. It was dangerous but sultry. And even though he knew he shouldn't, Tristan had the urge to follow every direction she might give him. The devil, she was. Gorgeous as ever, and ready to raise hell.

Tristan begged for the relief to leave him and was once again filled with anticipation of the sorrowful sort. It didn't matter how small his happiness was, that relief would cost him something. It could be as inconsequential as a stubbed toe, or an earthquake-sized catastrophe. He never knew what the equilibrium would take from him, or what *she* could take from him.

He leaned forward, placing his hands across his knees, and stared intently at the drawers. There was something askew that caught his eye; a beautiful fountain pen, one of those that were specially made and expensive, nothing like the ones you could find at the store. The hilt was a gorgeous marbled emerald green with flecks of gold that caught the light. It was passed onto him by his father, and his father's father before that. A beautiful thing, really, and never used. Tristan refused to touch it, and instead, it sat as a piece of decor.

The pen had been moved. It was no longer in its usual spot, the same place it had been day after day. A different sort of person would miss it, but for someone like Tristan Cohen, it was something he couldn't stop staring at it.

Someone had been in this room.

What were the odds that his luck would be as backward as it was today? He won a poker game, his baby wasn't crying. There was no way that awarded him both a dead muscle man and a thief in his own home.

"Lena!" He called from his office. His voice was loud and in charge, bouncing off the walls of this tiny house but no answer came. Had she fallen asleep with the baby in her arms again? Grunting in frustration, Tristan turned back to the crooked pen, narrowing his eyes as if it would be able to tell him exactly whose hands had touched it.

2

"Fuck me," he whispered, opening his drawers and pulling out file after file. They were smart coming here, whoever they were.

"Lena!" He screamed louder now, his frustration ringing throughout the house. If she was sleeping, she wouldn't be anymore. Who cared if the neighbors heard him? It didn't matter- no one would think twice to cross Tristan unless they were very, very stupid. Lena was too smart to disobey him a second time. His head turned after a few moments when he finally heard the quiet shuffling of his wife coming down the stairs. His body could feel her presence as she hovered near the door. Good girl.

"You may enter," he said.

She hesitated a second longer, waiting as if he didn't know what he was saying. She was not allowed in this room. It was man's business, and as much as she might hate him for it- it was safer for her that way. He was a monster, but he wasn't the worst there was. At least not to the people who mattered.

Unfortunately, that list was growing shorter and shorter by the day.

Lena cracked the door tentatively, her eyes seeking his for a moment, forgetting her place before she flicked them back to the floor again. She was still beautiful, especially in the darkness of night. When they were young her light was so bright you could see it from her eyes. Nowadays, they were duller, far less appealing than in her youth, but Tristan would take responsibility for that. It took guts to be the wife of a feared celebrity. You know, Lena Cohen could hang with the best of them. Her black hair fell past her shoulders in waves, and that beautiful tan skin of hers was delicious.

"Lena, were you in my room tonight?" His voice was calm enough, it could have been accused of being polite, but she knew better.

"No, dear," she said quickly. After the babies, her anxiety was at an all-time high. He couldn't blame her.

"Head up," he snapped, teeth grinding together in an awful way. She was obedient, her chin tilting towards him, her eyes slower but compliant anyway. He loved looking into those green eyes. They used to be sharp as a jaguar's, but in recent years they'd dulled like the rest of her. Tristan was almost sad that she wasn't the same feisty, sarcastic woman he'd fallen in love with. It was for the best, anyway. Being anything other than a quiet wife would get her into trouble. With him or otherwise.

"I'm going to ask again, and please remember, Lena, that I don't like liars." She shook her head fervently.

"I didn't, I promise. I would never go in without being explicitly told to do so, like right now," she was genuine. She wouldn't be here if he couldn't trust her, however, the skewed pen made him waver. He should have known better, the deal was going to ruin him, in the end.

"Did you let anyone back here?" He pressed, met with the continued shaking of her head. That wasn't the only thing shaking, though. He could see her arms vibrating harshly against her sides. "Did you see anyone leave?!"

"No Tristan, no. No one was in the house, Genevieve left after she fed Norman. Jameson has been in his bed since seven, poor thing. I haven't heard a peep from him."

Tristan narrowed his eyes and let out an impatient hiss. Here it was, it was never the pen at all. The relief he felt earlier, just barely, he couldn't squash it fast enough. Something had happened, and the pit that settled deep in his belly sprouted roots that anchored him to the floor as he started swaying.

"Why are you asking?" His voice was growing panicked.

"Someone's been in this room," his voice had grown deeper by the sentence, and this one was so low it sounded like a predatory growl. She looked at him dumbfounded, and he hadn't ever wanted to slap her more than he did at this moment. Tristan would never lay a finger on his wife, despite how terrified of him she was, and so his fists just clenched together tightly at his own sides.

"Are you sure?"

"Quite positive," he grumbled, pointing to the pen that sat at that awkward angle. Looking at it made him want to vomit. Her eyes flicked to the pen and back to him. She didn't ask any questions, instead narrowed her own eyes. That's his girl.

"I need to check on Jameson," she hissed. The green in her eyes peaked again, glowing dangerously. He nodded once, curtly, giving her permission. Lena moved like lightning, tearing down the hall as if her life, or her son's life, depended on it. Tristan followed.

When they both crashed against the door to their eldest son's room, he heard Lena screech in anger. Tristan was desperate to look around her, to reach his arms out to his wife and throw her to the side like a rag doll. The moment he saw what had caused his wife's distress, he roared. The sound rattled the walls of their quaint little house. It could collapse around him and he wouldn't care. Because in that bed, where Jameson should be sleeping, was nothing but a faint imprint of where his body had been. There had been no fight, no struggle. It was as if his son vanished into thin air. The only indication that he hadn't done just that were the tiny marks across his window sill. They dug into the white clay, and he almost had the nerve to be impressed with his boy. Because he had left them a clue. It was nothing, just fingernails embedded into the drywall.

It was enough for him to know that Jameson didn't leave, he was taken. It didn't matter what they might have found in his study- which, after his digging, he didn't notice a thing missing, everything worth anything was too well hidden. They took his son, and they were going to die because of it. He would find them, and he didn't need the muscle to do so.

Because he was going to fucking kill them himself.

3

Tristan didn't do birthdays. He knew how old he was, knew the day his mother gave birth to him- and the rest of the world cried in horror- but the day itself was something he avoided at all costs. When he turned ten years old, Jameson's age, in fact, his mother tried throwing him a birthday party. The word try is used loosely because the day was filled with empty promises and too much cake. There wasn't a birthday at all when no one showed up. That must have been the day Tristan stopped believing in birthdays, stopped believing in people, period.

He often wondered now in his adulthood, what those children did that day. What their parents thought when they saw the cardstock invitation that his mother insisted he fill out by hand. Did they squirm when they saw his name? Did they feel the presence of evil dormant inside of him long before he did? It was the only plausible reason he could imagine for no one coming. Tristan grew up feeling the rage and the monster running laps inside of him, waiting until he could let it out. His mother, father, and everyone he came into contact with saw it.

So it should come as no surprise, but something like that could scar a child. When he was ten years old, he could go through anything and come out stronger. Could the same be said for Jameson?

He was so different than his son, who got his softness from his mother. His cheeks were round and pink, and instead of anger, he saw curiosity and joy. Jameson didn't care that Tristan was never there, or at least it never seemed that way. He was a bright light, and now that brightness was gone, taken from him in a single moment. For Jameson, he was sure it would destroy him, smother what light was left, and he would reemerge with the same dark tendrils that followed Tristan everywhere. Darkness reincarnate. Lena was heaving heavy sobs on his bed, the sound ragged and sharp. He resisted the immediate urge to go to her side and console her- that was not his place here. He paced back and forth instead, and for so long he was sure the soft carpet would bare the marks of erosion.

"Close the window. Lock the doors," he said to her, letting out a quick breath before holding it in again. She looked at him, a tear-stained face, hand moving instinctively to her belly. She'd been doing it a lot lately- he figured so soon after the birth of Norman it was a comfort to her. A harsh determination laced with fierce protection over what was hers took over her expression. He felt it was an inappropriate time to chastise her- because Jameson and Norman were his- and so he watched with narrowed eyes as she gave him a nod and ran out of the room to secure their home. Tristan would take care of this, he gave her no reason to mistrust his ability.

He had almost forgotten about his phone in his back pocket until the sound made him jump. The ring pierced through the dead silence, it was an ugly sound. He reached his hand down his pocket and retrieved the sleek black thing, raising it to his ear.

"Hello," he breathed into the receiver.

"I expected something a bit harsher out of you," a sultry voice came from the other end. His breath hitched. He would know the voice from anywhere. It was a voice he'd race to the ends of the Earth for. It was the voice of the only woman in the world that could make him abandon his home, his family, Jameson. "For the big ol' scary crime boss, you need a harsher phone voice."

He should have known she would call. She was always just a small itch in the back of his heart. The tendrils swirled around him in excitement, the darkness coming out to play. He needed to stay focused. He needed to find Jameson.

"I don't have the time,"

"You will make the time for me dear, I am sure," she said in response. If he was scary she was worse, a terror. The threat sent shivers down the bones in his back. Tristan looked towards the door as if he was expecting Lena there. Not like he would care, even if she was. She'd caught him a few times with other women- and after the last time, he made sure she would turn a blind eye if it ever happened again.

"My child is missing," he snapped, urgent and impatient with her. "I don't have time for games. I need to find him, you know as well as I do that my time is precious. I don't have much of it before whoever took him figures out that they're dead. You know they'll kill them, just because they can."

"Oh Tristy," she cooed. He felt as if her breaths were there against his skin. Black tendrils coiled around him, anticipating her, they would welcome her just as easily as his body did. He could feel his pants tighten around the crotch, and the muscles in his thighs tense. Only a few people on this planet were allowed to call him by his name, and it always shocked him how easily she was able to say it, and how often he wanted her to. "I think you're going to want to hear what I have to say. You see, I know where your son is."

Tristan's breath caught in his throat. "You know where Jameson is?"

"I was going to say Norman, wouldn't that have been funny if I had? Since you are a father to two boys now?" She laughed, and the sound echoed off Jameson's walls. He stood, rigid, feet planted firmly in place. "Of course *Jameson*. He's the one missing, isn't he?"

"Where is he?" Tristan roared. He would get his son back. That child would have a better life than the one his father forced on him, he would make sure of it.

"You know I don't just give away my information,"

"What do you want from me that you haven't already taken?" he would beg her for this. While she had made him feel a desire he'd never felt before, she ruined him.

"I want you to tell me *the* story," his face dropped its rage for one of confusion.

"You will hold my son's life in your hands over a story?" His voice was a low and predatory growl.

"No, Tristan Cohen. *You* hold your son's life in your hands. Tell me the story and you will know where your son is."

"What story do you want?" He was not used to being told what to do, he was used to being the enforcer. Tristan was the man that had it all, but only because of her.

"I feel like I don't need to answer that," her laugh rang through the receiver again. "You know which one I want."

"But why do you want it?"

"My motives are of no concern of yours," she snapped. "And I would hurry, your son's life hangs in the balance, after all."

"Lessa," her name tasted delightful on his tongue. Tristan walked to the door, shutting it with all his strength. He could hear the walls rattle. Lena would not bother him in here. She would go lock up as she was told, and spend her night with Norman. Tristan doubted she would let their baby out of her sight now. She trusted him to find Jameson, and he would not let her down.

"Oh, please tell me about the day we met, Tristan."

He started pacing the room again, the soles of his shoes worn from doing only that. Finally, Tristan sighed and sat on the bed, rolling the phone in his hand and pressing his head down towards his knees. His plea was no more than a whisper.

"Okay, but not over the phone. I need you here. And when I am done, you will tell me where Jameson is. Am I clear?"

He felt her cool breath on his neck again. Tristan turned around and came face to face with her. He almost fell to the floor right then and there, staring as she manifested herself into Jameson's room. The tendrils were on her instantly, wrapping themselves around her legs as a cat might. Instinctively his eyes flickered to the door again, as if Lena could hear him, *them*.

"She won't be here," Lessa smirked, the tips of her mouth curling up to touch her eyes. Her delicate hand rose to his chest, feeling her way across his torso and back over his pectorals. "I'm sure we could finish before she would even hear a peep."

He pushed her away with the palms of his hands. But even Tristan wasn't immune to the way his body responded whenever he was around her. If he had been aroused by the mere sound of her voice, then he was powerless when she stood in front of him. She was beautiful, of course, with piercing eyes that seemed to change color as often as her moods. They were green most of the time, but a piercing shade- nothing like that of his wife. He felt as if Lessa changed into what he liked as if she was here to please *him*. He liked it when she took control, and even though he didn't own her, she let him play the role.

She hissed under her breath at the feel of his hands on her. "Don't we like it rough tonight," the menacing tone her voice took sent a chord of fear radiating through him.

"My son," was all Tristan had been able to say.

"Fine," she sighed in disappointment, sitting on Jameson's bed, crossing her legs and petting one of the tendrils softly. She was capable of delicate movements, but he knew she was as sharp as a razor blade. Lessa looked up at him and patted the spot next to her.

"Come join me," she said. He had no choice but to agree. There was never any choice when it came to her. He sighed, ran a hand through his hair, and shifted closer to her, sitting hesitantly. Her hand went straight to the cock in his jeans. Tristan fought the urge to not forget about his problems right then and there and take her. This amount of self-restraint was legendary.

"Can we get this over with?" he snapped.

"Oh, you're not fun tonight."

"You promised me my son."

"And you promised me a story. So get to it."

"Why are you making me do this?" He didn't want to relive that day, didn't want to remember the reason why his son was taken. Because no matter what, this was all his fault. Directly, certainly, but even indirectly. Tristan wanted nothing more than to forget that fact, and he was running out of time. Jameson would always be the child he was not- he was the one with friends, with a future that didn't seem as dark as his had been. Jameson had people that wanted to come to his birthday parties (if they would ever throw one). Because of Tristan, he wouldn't have that. She just looked at him, a serene expression on her face laced with irritation. "You needed to remember where we came from. And honestly...I just wanted to make you sweat a little. It's fun."

Fuck he was a terrible father. It was because of her, of course. Tristan might have been raised in darkness, but Lessa was the reason he let it all out. Their story was one he would pay the consequences for over and over again.

She would never stop being the center of his universe.

4

There was something about being a teenager that made you feel like you could get away with anything. When you were a teenager like Tristan, who didn't give a fuck about what he was doing, where he was going, or what people thought of him, you were absolutely invincible.

When Lessa found him, smoking a long, thin cigarette in the alleyway near his home, he fell in love. She was absolutely stunning, with long onyx-colored hair that fell the length of her backside. It was straight as a board and unmoving even in the harshest winds. Her body was tight with curves, and every time his eyes laid upon her he feasted, taking in everything she wanted to give. She looked the same now as she did then-but every now and then Tristan saw something about her features change. Once in a while he saw past the mask she put on for everyone else, and it was terrifying. Lessa glided through this world, stealthy and graceful, and lethal. He knew, even then, that she was something not of this world. There was no way someone could be this beautiful, but so frightening at once. Lessa owned her otherworldliness, flaunting the magic she possessed in her veins. Tristan was in awe of her.

"I know how beautiful I am," she purred, running her hand up his chest again, grabbing onto a pinch of hair above his shirt and tugging gently. Tristan felt the red creep into his cheeks before shaking his head. He had gotten caught up in her, as he always did. The time slipped away from them, and he almost completely forgot the reason for this story, the reason she was sitting next to him on his son's bed. The bed of his missing son. Tristan's eyes widened in realization and promptly blinked several times. This witch, though enchanting as she may be, would need to be watched. Jameson's life was at stake.

"I'm sure you know exactly the kind of effect you have on people," he said to her softly.

"Not everyone," she argued. "Only the ones I like the most."

"You mean the bad ones."

"Of course, those are the only fun ones around." Her jeweled eye winked at him, causing him to ruffle his feathers once more.

He was a bad one. As he grew into his adulthood, Tristan was a thief. He was a liar. He was everything you always kept away from, the one you'd never bring home. That was part of the reason why Lessa was so much fun. She didn't have any family, no morals or expectations, and it *was* fun. She'd egg him on, would teach him more than he could ever learn on his own. He couldn't imagine not loving her.

Until he didn't anymore.

"I remember the first time you told me you hated me," Lessa sighed next to him. He turned to her and frowned. He wasn't so much telling her the story as he was showing her. In his many years of knowing her, Tristan never once asked about the magic. He accepted it as he did the sun setting or the moon rising. She was always in his head.

“Can you fucking stop?” He pushed himself off the bed and raked his nails down the sides of his scalp. Tristan could feel the blood well before droplets slid down his neck. Lessa looked at it hungrily.

“You’re the one telling the story. You do know your son is about to die, don’t you?”

He wanted to scream in frustration. What did he do to deserve all the evil this life had given him? “Of course, I know that,” he spat.

“Then get on with it.”

Tristan thought hard about the events that followed, and the years that passed after meeting her. Nothing important to note, other than the copious amounts of trouble he’d gotten into. He didn’t even remember that night clearly, the one she was so keen on making him relive. His body repelled the memory like the plague, and although at the time it wasn’t a terrible, hurtful experience, it was difficult to look back on it and not see it as one of the biggest mistakes of his life. He wasn’t sure if it was him trying to keep that memory at bay, or her trying to smother it. It could have been a little bit of both.

When Tristan was twenty-five, his father committed suicide. It wasn’t a somber event for him, in fact, it wasn’t something that made him feel much at all. Tristan had moved out at eighteen and had very little contact with his parents through those formative years. His father was an addict, and a dangerous one at that. He was the kind to take it out on his mother, the kind to inflict his horror on other people. This was where the evil had come from, he was sure. When you lived with a monster for most of your life, it was hard not to see the same in yourself.

“I don’t remember you being quite so bad,” she mused,

sifting through his thoughts. He could feel her probing each memory, just strands attached to the place his soul stayed. Her fingers curled around each string, tugging on it, testing them to see if they would break. They might have, back then. She didn't know him now, though. Tristan changed in those years they were apart, he'd grown as hard as she was, as vile, as cruel. He was an embodiment of her, to her chagrin. It was a weird feeling, having someone else inside your head, plucking at each memory you had. There was no way to keep her out, either, Tristan had stopped so long ago now. She knew every inch of him, every thought, and every wicked thing he did. She reveled in it.

"Because you are far crueler," he snapped, his teeth clamping hard together. Tristan could hear her tut. He was never good at hiding and rationalizing his emotions around her.

"I am what you are," Lessa said. Her voice was quickly becoming short and curt with him. "I am here because your soul called to me. Do you think I come to bother just anyone, Tristy? I am here because you have asked for me."

"I never asked for you to be in my life," he snarled. They were running out of time.

"You didn't have to ask verbally. It was the darkness in you. That is why you made the deal is it not?"

The deal. The fucking deal. The reason why he was sitting here with the devil and his son missing.

"I made the deal because I had no other options." The words slid between his teeth. Somehow his body was holding it in like it knew it was a lie before it came out. Or she was still in there, keeping him from believing that it was true.

"Oh, you had options. You just chose wrong. That is not my fault, my sweet Tristan. You could have lived the rest of your life, in jail...or dead, even. Probably. That is the road you were leading in your life. I offered you salvation. I gave you everything!" Her voice raised. It whistled into the silence, deafening.

She wasn't wrong. He would have been dead, if she hadn't found him, hadn't offered him the deal. That was what made it worse, that he knew she was right, and that he took it willingly.

"Tell me," she said, voice eerily calm once more. "Is your son dying because of you? Because you were so afraid of being a nobody, that you sacrificed everything to be a somebody?"

Tristan exploded. He jumped off the bed, face red with anger. His foot hit the first thing it came across, sending a tiny toy airplane across the room. It hit the other side of the wall and shattered.

"Fuck you!" he screamed. "I was losing her. I was losing my wife!"

There it was, the reason why he was here. It wasn't him at all, it was Lena.

She was dying. Her body sat unmoving on a hospital bed, vitals looking grim. Her face was pale and her hands cold to the touch. He was here to say goodbye, that was what the specialist told him. She had only a few breaths left in her and he would never see those eyes, or that beautiful smile again.

Lessa walked in then, not in the sort of uniform one might expect from a medical staff member.

"Is it time?" he asked her, tears staining his face. He cringed as she touched his chin, as she tilted it up to meet her face. Her eyes were a similar shade to his wife's. It was like he was looking at her, what she could be again. His soul called to her like she was the center of the universe.

"It doesn't have to be," Lessa whispered, her lips lingering so close to his. "Follow me, and I can bring her back."

He was stupid to follow her outside of that room, but he was desperate to save the life of this woman. The woman that would soon birth his children, because he would marry her and he would grow old with her. Nothing would change that, nothing at all.

"Ah," I remember that," Lessa laughed, looking at him with another cruel smile on her face. Tristan's rage had quieted, the tears welling in his eyes. He hadn't cried since that day, and the life he lived was so different now. "You thought it would just bring her back. You didn't think of the consequences,"

"I didn't know," he sobbed into his hands. She got up to comfort him, reaching her hand out to touch his face. Tristan shied away from it.

"You didn't ask," she corrected him, "I do want to know though, what your little victory was? What was the one good thing that caused your boy to go missing tonight?"

A long sigh escaped his throat, hitching with his breath.

"Norman," He said, "It was Norman's fault."

5

Resentment flooded through him, filling each crevasse in his head until he was sure there was no space left for anything else. He was right, it was Norman's fault Jameson was gone. His son was the one good thing in his life, and it was likely he would never return.

"There he is, I thought you left me," Lessa reached out to touch him again, and this time he didn't move away from her. He let her hand glide across his cheek, down to his chin. Her hands were soft, with an almost slimy texture that you couldn't describe. "Let the rage fuel you."

"You tricked me," he said softly. There was no hurt in his tone, just a simple fact. She did not disagree.

"It is my way," she replied, heaving her shoulders into a light sigh. "I was built to make deals, or at least, that was the life that I chose. It's a long story, not one that I want to get into. But you, you needed to make the deal, you needed to save your poor wife from dying and I gave you that opportunity, you should be thanking me."

She was alive because of Lessa, but Tristan would rather her dead.

"Your magic. You could save Jameson if you wanted to. You're a witch, I can make another deal."

"Are you so sure that your son is dead?"

He looked her straight in the eyes. Of course, he thought he was dead. If Tristan had any hope of Jameson being alive he wouldn't be standing here talking to Lessa. He would be tearing this world apart for him. Tristan hung his head down in guilt.

"That's what I thought," she mused curiously, "I am not a witch by the way, and to be frank, I'm offended you even keep me in the same company. Why is it that humans always try to rationalize what's around them? There is magic all around you, and yet you see the need to contain it. That box you keep yourself in will be the death of you, Tristan. You and everyone else on this wretched planet." He couldn't find it in him to say another word, what was the point?

"You are right in your assumption that I could feasibly do something about it, however," His head tilted to her in curiosity, "There are limits though, I cannot just snap my fingers and magically bring a boy back to life."

"Are you saying that he's really dead?"

"He is, of course," she didn't care that his face contorted into pain. Lessa's cavalier response was intentioned to be full of malice. She wanted him to suffer. "But you know that. Jameson was dead before you noticed him missing. I could tell you where the body is, but I'm not sure that's the body you want to go looking for right now, is it?"

His fists clenched tightly together. She was right, again. They tensed, hanging at his sides and wanting to punch something. He didn't want to caress the face of his son. He was angry, and he wanted to wrap his hands around the neck of something much younger than that. He made steps towards the door, and Lessa didn't stop him. Instead, she just followed him, disappearing from the world, residing in the corner that belonged to her in his head.

"Did you find him?" The voice startled Tristan because it wasn't the one he was anticipating. Lena came rushing down the hallway, almost slipping on the tile. She skidded to a halt as she approached him, and Tristan looked back as if he expected to see Lessa standing there, too.

"I'm still here," she whispered in his thoughts, "But Lena doesn't know."

"Find who?" It was discombobulating, not really knowing where Lessa stopped and Lena started. He looked at his wife, whose forehead wrinkled in concern, but also in question. Frustration.

"Jameson!" she practically screeched, "Did you find him?!"

Lena was used to Tristan fixing her problems. Granted they usually started off because of him anyway, but he could see the worry cross her face when she realized he hadn't found their son yet. He wondered how she might look at him when she finds out that the only way they would see Jameson again was when they visited his grave.

"Lena," he started slowly, reaching out to her. As he had with Lessa, she took a step away from him. She brought her hands to her chest in defense.

"*You like the fighters,*" Lessa confirmed, smirking. He wanted to tell her to shut her mouth, to leave them alone, to let them mourn. "*You gave up that right when you made that deal. The deal was binding. I couldn't leave you alone even if I wanted to. Oh but trust me, Tristy, you've always been so much fun, I would never want to leave you.*" He growled under his breath.

"Lena, Jameson isn't coming back to us." The wrinkled worry turned into familiar hatred.

"It's been less than an hour! We will find him, we can't give up!"

"It's been longer than an hour," he corrected, "We don't know how long he'd been missing. You didn't check on him, he could have been taken the second you left him alone in his room." Her mouth hung agape, her eyes welling up with tears.

"It—you're saying it's my fault?"

"It was her fault she birthed another joy. Had she not, you both wouldn't be in this situation right now, would you?"

SHUT UP! He screamed internally, so loud he couldn't hear the words coming from Lena's mouth.

"*She's not weak,*" Lessa whispered, "*She can take it.*"

It was difficult to shut her out. He couldn't separate her thoughts from his own, he wasn't sure what he believed anymore. Tristan grabbed ahold of Lena's shoulder and yanked her towards him. His empty hand grasped her chin roughly, drawing it so that her eyes were looking up at him.

"Is Norman in his crib?" He was not gentle with her. It was like Lessa was truly becoming a part of him now, able to control his movements. His grip hardened as if to prove to him that he was right. Tristan watched as Lena winced. She tried nodding, but his grip was too hard.

"Yes," she whined, closing her eyes. Tristan, or rather, Lessa, let go of her face and shoved her harshly to the side.

"Where are you going?" She asked, panic leaking into every word. He strode past her, not daring to look back. If Tristan looked into her eyes, he would stop, and he could not afford to do so. Norman's life needed to end, he was the reason for this loss.

"Don't hurt him!" Lena was crying now, her sobs echoing off the walls, each sound piercing what was left of his black heart. He ignored her, walking up the stairs, hesitating enough on each step that there was an awful creaking sound. Lena was right behind him, pulling on his arms, his clothing, every single inch of him that she could get her hands on.

"What happened, why are you going to hurt my baby?!"

He whirled on her, the fire in his eyes tangible. "He is the reason why Jameson is gone! He took our son away from us!" He could see the confusion in her eyes, but the fight was still there. It was what he admired most about her.

"Norman is just a baby! He couldn't do anything! Jameson is not his fault, Tristan what's going on?"

Tristan kept walking up the stairs at Lessa's silent nudge. He let her take over, let her flow through him. He could feel her flexing his fingers, relishing in control. Lena slumped onto the bottom step, he could feel her under him as her body hit the floor with a silent thump.

"I know you think the deal has control over you, but it doesn't," she said in a silent plea. Her bright green eyes looked at him warily, unsure of the person he had become. This was unlike the roughness he let out each day. This was a wickedness that even Lena was afraid of. His neck twisted so far around, that it was almost unnatural. The minute the words escaped her lips, he was on top of her, quick as lightning. Lessa grasped her chin once more, watching with delight as Lena winced in pain.

"What did you say, human?" She said, her voice sounding so much like his that Tristan didn't realize it was his hands on her cheeks until he blinked.

"I know about the deal," she said, strength flowing back through her, defiance flashing across those emerald eyes. Lessa's own flashed, predatory. There was a sense of familiarity between the two, but the moment passed before Tristan could comprehend it.

"...and I know about the witch, too."

6

Lessa hissed under her breath, snapping her teeth at the words.

"I am not a witch, human."

Lena's gaze held firm. She pushed Lessa's hand away from her face, wrapping her own around his temples.

"Tristan, I know you're in there," she searched for him, not knowing where to look. He tried to reach out to her, but he couldn't find his way back either. It was Lessa in control now, and even he wasn't strong enough to take his body back. Tristan should have known it would come to this. He knew he would never be able to leave her all those years ago, not fully.

The deal was struck the minute they shook hands. He laughed at the formality of it once, and he would regret the indifferent attitude he had. He never took her seriously, and that was a mistake. Lessa promised him a fortune.

"You will become wealthy, powerful. Everything you want to be, Tristan Cohen. I know that's what you want."

He pleaded with her in return. Of course, it was what he wanted, to not feel unwanted, useless. He did not want to be the man they thought he was.

"My magic will bring you not just luck. It will let you earn it. Of course, you might want to get a couple of lottery tickets. But it will give you the work ethic to succeed. It will bring you the knowledge you need to make a name for yourself. Be warned, it will certainly not be the path you envisioned for yourself. Those who use magic to succeed aren't blessed with kosher lives. But it will be enough for you to feel the importance and the power that you crave so deeply, and it will keep Lena alive."

He asked her for the caveat. Surely a woman like herself would not give him everything he wanted without something in return? He would give her his body. He would give her his mind, letting her make a home in the deepest corner she could find. He would trade his soul, his happiness, giving up what little of it was left to be the man he wanted to be. At the time it seemed a fair trade. Lena was worth it, at the time.

"A caveat, Tristan? See, I knew you deserved this. You're smarter than all the rest of them. Of course, magic comes at a price. There is a balance to the world, you must give in order to succeed, even that of success instead of material is no exception." Lessa always talked in riddles when it came to her magic. She wasn't clear on the boundaries or the extent of her reach. There was only ever talk about the balance.

"For every good thing that happens to you, Tristan Cohen, the world will need something in return. It will need a bad moment, too."

"Do you mean that I will be stealing happy moments from someone else?"

She laughed and the sound was melodic even in its threat. "Wicked and cruel, just like me. No, not from someone else. For every good thing that you receive, no matter how small, you will get its opposite. Say you win the lottery one day, the next you might stub your toe. Do you get what I'm trying to say?" It seemed like a fair trade. She didn't promise him when it would happen, or the severity or magnitude of the events, just that there was a give and take. He was young and dumb, and of course, he took it. Now, because of the silent reprieve he had from the wails of his days-old child, his other boy was taken from him. That relief killed him. This deal was not balanced, it was anything but.

* * *

"How do you know about that?" He asked Lena, narrowing his eyes at her.

"I am a wife. I am a mother. Nothing happens in this house without me knowing about it." Her gaze was steely.

"This wasn't your fault Tristan. You're not a fraud like you think you are. Those good things, your successes. They happened because of her, maybe, but you are the person that still experienced them. You made the decisions, you got where you are now because of *you*. And whatever you think happened to Jameson, we will find him. He is not gone because of you."

"Jameson is dead!" he screamed at her, but this time, she didn't wince. Lena stood her ground. Lessa hissed at her from the back of Tristan's brain. He used the moment to push his way forward, retaking control of his limbs and moving his face from her grip. Looking at her clearly now, he could see the deep purples and blues, the shadow of his fingerprints freckling her skin.

"Don't let her win, Tristan. You are a wicked man, but you will not hurt Norman," Tristan staggered back a few steps, unsure of what to do. Lessa was pulling on each string in his brain, egging him to walk up the steps and find Norman, to strangle the life out of him, as his wailing had done to Jameson. But Tristan, held together by Lena's willpower, stayed right where he was. He fell to his bottom, resting his head between his knees and rocking back and forth. This was not the Tristan Cohen everyone knew him as, this was someone else entirely. He was completely broken.

Lessa pulled herself away from him, materializing beside them both. Lena didn't even flinch, instead, she glared at the woman, hate and mistrust beaming from her eyes like lasers.

"You made a deal, Tristan," Lessa spat, "a deal is binding. No matter what you do in your life, luck will be there. And with every moment you feel joy, just know something terrible is coming along with it. And one day I will see you again. You cannot rid yourself of me, not for long. And soon I will find your son, I will make him suffer just as I will make you suffer."

"Get away from here, witch." He said through gritted teeth.

Lessa tutted. She was disappointed in him. Because of course, he was just as awful as she was, even if he didn't want to admit it. "I promise you, one day you will be crying for me, you will wish me back. You will have wished you killed your youngest tonight."

Lessa cackled before disappearing into thin air again. Lena and Tristan looked at one another, exhaustion ringing into the air. He fell back on his tailbone, his back arching off the steps of the stairs. And in that moment of relief, a feeling he knew the moment it hit him that he would regret it, a piercing sound barreled into their eardrums.

Norman was crying. Tristan brought his hands to his face and groaned into them, letting go of all the frustration, the fear, the sorrow out in a single noise. Nothing could give him the satisfaction he needed and craved. He would have to promise to no longer feel a moment of happiness again. He couldn't afford to cost his family any more than what he already had.

"I'll get him," Lena whispered, patting his knee with a tentative touch and getting up, running up the stairs. It was like she was afraid he would change his mind, that he would come after her and finish what he started. Tristan wasn't that confident in himself either. Was it all Lessa moving him and making him feel the darkness wrap around his heart? The rage that flowed through him was a product of her, but it certainly wasn't all of her. She was right, he was too much like her to be naive enough to think that he couldn't house some of the blame and the pain.

Lena returned a moment later with Norman in her arms. Tristan couldn't look at him without feeling disgust. He wondered if that feeling would ever go away.

"I don't know how to act, or what to do," she said honestly, and the thought hurt him. The mistrust was blatant in her expressions and he couldn't find it in himself to tell her that it was going to be okay. He was who he would always be, and that wasn't anything he could change, especially if he wanted to.

"Let's go find our son's body," he said solemnly, instead. He was not prepared for her reaction. Lena nodded, not challenging his words with her own. There was surprise on his face and a terrible amount of sadness on hers. He knew there was no use in hoping. Jameson was as good as gone, and Lessa hadn't told them where to go looking. He was not prepared to handle that death, but he was never really given a choice...

maybe once, but not now. Tristan was nothing but a fraud, he was a cheater, and worse of all he was a liar. There was not one person in this god-forsaken city that trusted him, even himself.

Nobody ever will.

PART FIVE
NYCTOPHOBIA

"Stare at the dark too long and you will eventually see what isn't there."

- Cameron Jace

I

The sun dipped below the horizon so quickly in the wintertime, covering the trees in shadow and night. Lorena looked out at the skyline and could see very little except for two lone birds flying south towards the sunset. She rubbed her shoulders with both of her arms, feeling the crisp night air settle around her. Normally she was more careful than this, but time got away from her today. She was so stupid. It was one of the things Lorena didn't like about this new ballet studio, no windows, just walls of mirrors. It was hard to gauge the time when there wasn't an easily accessible source of light. The sun dipped so early in the evening now in the later months of the year, too. The stars just didn't align for Lorena tonight. It seemed like this was a reoccurring theme in her life.

"Need a ride home?" The voice shook her out of her trance. She flinched at the touch to her shoulder. The hand that'd accompanied the touch was owned by a beautiful petite woman in her forties. Despite her non-threatening appearance, Lorena couldn't calm the shot of adrenaline that coursed through her veins. She shivered and looked back. The woman was easily a decade older than Lorena but looked like she was still in her early thirties. Dance would do that to you if you were talented enough. This woman could run circles around almost everyone she knew. Lorena shook her head, trying to hide her flinch. She didn't do a very good job, she could see the frown cross the woman's face, just for a moment.

"No, I drove tonight."

"I can walk you to your car if it helps."

Lorena shook her head again. Her therapist said specifically that she needed to do this on her own. It had gotten better these last few months, but while she desperately wanted to take the old woman's offer, she knew she couldn't. Not if she wanted to get over this silly fear of the dark.

"I can't," she stuttered. The old woman patted her shoulder again in understanding. Unlike before, this touch calmed Lorena. It was a touch that conveyed understanding, not pity like she had been used to from others. It was as if she was just as normal as this woman was. She was lying of course, but the sentiment was nice. Lorena was tempted to change her mind and take the help after all, if it wasn't for her therapist's insistence, and her mother's threats, she might have. But she was feeling extra brave tonight, believe it or not. Lorena watched as her eyes crinkled in displeasure, but the old woman didn't stop her.

"Very well. I knew we should have stopped. I didn't catch the time, and with the new studio-"

"It's fine, Maria," Lorena soothed, "We're all having to transition to the new studio. It's just different, that's all. I'll get used to it. I'll make sure it doesn't happen again. You're not supposed to take care of me." Maria pursed her lips as if she thought otherwise. Lorena was a thirty-year-old woman, she should be able to take care of herself.

"Do you need the keys? You can hang out here until you're ready."

Her head was going to break from shaking it too hard. Lorena tried to smile, but it didn't quite meet her eyes.

"It's okay. I was just about ready to go. I'll just wait until you leave." Another phrase of her therapist. Though, he didn't quite say "walk to your car alone" exactly. Lorena had a hard time having other people watch her fail and break down, and took his "work this through on your own" comments a little too seriously.

Maria didn't seem to like that, but she didn't say anything. Instead, she shrugged and grunted in displeasure. Lorena didn't tell her that it was scarier to be inside the locked building than outside of it anyway. Pair that with responsibility over a set of keys to the said building? No, she had far too many other anxieties. It was best to say no to one more, at least for tonight.

"Well, okay then. Have a good night," she leaned forward to give Lorena a hug but thought better of it when she watched her body physically recoil from the touch. There was a flash of pain across her eyes, but she smiled lightly and started walking towards her car instead. Lorena wasn't her daughter, but she was as close to it as it comes. Maria's daughter was a dancer too, ballet, specifically. She died tragically several years back. Lorena spent most of her time around Maria now, keeping her company. It helped that she was one of the state's best teachers.

They were parked next to one another, and Lorena was starting to see how silly it was for her to reject Maria's offer. She waved loftily as she watched her turn the key in the ignition and the small, rust-colored car roared to life. For a little old woman, she had a heavy foot, and Lorena was close to laughing as she watched the car speed off into the distance.

The sounds echoed in the night air, dying far quicker than she wanted them to. She could hear the trails of her laughter dying as it met the edge of the concrete, dissolving into the asphalt.

She bit her lip and could feel her body quiver, knowing the time for procrastination was coming to a close. As soon as the sound of Maria's car died, the night settled around her once more. Away from the building were two lone stop lights. They each flickered as if complimenting one another. It was eerie, and the more she looked out the more her blood raced. She could feel the coolness wrapping around her and she tightened her grip on her arms.

Lorena needed to take one step, that was the hardest part. She needed to put one foot in front of the other and walk straight to her car. But something wouldn't let her do it. Something inside of her refused to let the muscles move freely. It was like she was one of the trees she could see in the distance. She was planted firmly to the ground, the roots threatening to keep her there forever. All around her the shadows danced in the dark. She bent over, throwing her head into her hands. Lorena shook her head and closed her eyes, desperate to keep the demons of the night at bay.

No one would ever believe her, no matter how hard she tried. The monsters were dancing at the edge of her vision, taunting her. Lorena took a deep breath.

One, two, three, four, five, si-

She counted, slow and steady. They weren't real, nothing about this was real. She counted until she reached seventy-five before she couldn't go on anymore. Soon her heart did slow, and her breaths did even. Soon she tore her face from her hands and straightened herself out. She could have been home by now, she could have been comfy on her couch, watching another rerun of a stupid comedy. She needed to snap out of it.

The dark reminded her of those days, and maybe that was

why she couldn't function like a proper adult any longer. The night reminded her of *him*, and while there was a lot of rage that built up inside of her; more often than not the fear consumed her instead. She'd been going to her therapist for years now, but even still they've only just barely scratched the surface. Realistically, Lorena was convinced she would spend the rest of her sad life living in perpetual fear of the night.

She flinched again, aching from the guilt that rumbled in her stomach. She moved her watch to check the time. Seven forty-five in the evening. Why had the night draped over them so quickly? She took another hesitant breath, breathing out an exhale so cool you could see it in the air. Her feet were heavy as lead, but Lorena moved one in front of the other. Her eyes were partially closed again, and she waved her arms out in front of her in case she hit something.

Slowly she made her way down from the studio until her feet were about to touch the asphalt. She stopped then, making sure to take deep breaths and focus on the car in front of her.

Focusing was easier said than done, her eyes kept snapping to various pits of darkness. Her mind was playing tricks on her. In her peripherals she could have sworn she saw the demons crawling around the trees, waiting for the perfect moment to take her. Lorena fisted her palms together, digging her nails into the soft skin. She was sure she would start bleeding, and Lorena bit her lip from the pain. There was someone watching her. She could feel it on her back, on either side of her, everywhere around her. She should have had Maria walk her to her car. None of this was a good idea, Lorena couldn't do this alone.

The feeling worsened the further she trekked into the darkness. The light posts did very little in giving off ample amounts of light. They did more harm than good and added to the ambiance of totally, fucking, creepy. The night wrapped around the light, and Lorena felt like she was suffocating. Did everyone else feel this way when they were wandering around in the dark? She was halfway there now, even if it felt like she had been walking for hours. Each step was tormenting, and Lorena licked her lips in anticipation. The warmth of her car was so close now, and soon she'd be locked in, cozy.

The eyes that penetrated her back made her more nervous now. Lorena couldn't shake the feeling that something darker was waiting for her. This was different than the demons at play. It was different than the nightmares that hung around in the shadows. This felt real. It was as if there was someone out there waiting for her, wanting to rip her limb from limb. Her brain played dirty tricks on her, and the feeling in her gut made it feel so real. Lorena hated this, the weakness that took over her body. She was a successful professional dancer. She was lithe, strong, and solid. She had a daughter at home and a husband that loved her so aggressively that she knew she didn't deserve them. She planned everything in her life, was controlled and organized, and was meticulous about the path that had been laid out for her by whatever holy force created her. There was no reason why she should feel so utterly weak at this moment.

The darkness overwhelmed her. None of the good things in her life were worth this absolute terror. Her breathing stayed a quick, raspy rhythm and Lorena continued to take the walk one step at a time. There was a pressure surrounding her, but she ignored it willfully, focusing instead back onto the two fluorescent yellow bulbs in the lamps, pulsating to a beat only they knew. The wind nipped at her ankles, rushing Lorena along, and when she finally looked up, eyes wide as they ever had been, it seemed like her car kept going further, and further away.

Something that sounded like the crackle of fall leaves being stepped on snapped her attention to the right. Her entire body froze, and she could feel the chill run up her bones again. It was threatening to freeze her in place, to strong-arm her into not moving one more inch. Lorena could see the progress she'd made run right out from under her again. Her heartbeat pulsed faster and faster, and she blinked once hard, willing herself to move forward.

He was going to get her, he was going to get her he...was... going...to...get...her!

Lorena ran.

2

He watched her as she ran. She was so beautiful, so perfect and lithe. The body of a dancer. He watched her often, just as he was right now. There were ample amounts of space here to hide between the leaves and branches. The trees were used to hiding demons after dark. It was what they were built for, their lanky forms shifting as the moonlight touched it. If ever there was an enemy to the darkness, it was the moon.

He molded himself to the darkness well, it was almost as if he was born in it. The news had called him sin incarnate. Fitting, for a man that had murdered 20 women in his lifetime. The memory of all his women made him shiver in anticipation. He was certainly past due for another adventure. Lorena was close to her car now, and he knew he would get no other chance than this moment. He slunk out from behind the trees, hissing slightly as the light from the moon wrapped around him and exposed his dark-colored long sleeve, hiding a fragile sheet of white skin. Across his hands were silky blue nitrile gloves, his jeans a dirty denim. He was fit for a job tonight, and would not let the light distract him. He reveled in the moonlight, there was a certain glory to being unapologetically who you were born to be.

The man sprinted from between the trees, saddling close to her, and bringing Lorena into a large bear hug. It might have looked like a lover's embrace, if not for the deafening scream she let out. He brought his hand up to her mouth and covered it with his palm, feeling the isolated warmth of her breath against his skin.

"Don't you dare do that again," he snarled lightly in her ear. To his delight and surprise, she loosened in his grip so much that he almost dropped her. Lorena put up no fight for him. She didn't kick or scream, she didn't try to bite the hand firmly locked over her mouth. She just stood there, so still that she could be praying.

He felt her head nod once at his command, and the man readjusted himself. She was so unlike any of the others, even if she looked identical. Lorena had long black hair that ran down her back and settled at her waistline. The man frowned, that pretty long hair was tied tightly in a bun, and he was so close to pulling the tie out of it and letting it fall. She was tall, but not quite as tall as he was. Good thing, too, he never would have been able to tighten his arms around her if she was. He'd studied her from a distance for several weeks, cataloging her features. They were the ones he looked for every time- he was convinced she was the one. The center of his universe.

She was the woman that ruined his life, time and time again. And so the man would find her, and he would kill her, just as he would kill her again in the next life. He would not stop, not while she continued coming back to this world. The man sighed in contentment, having felt victorious after finding her once again. Soon this would all be over, at least for a little while. He slid his hand between his jeans and his back, gripping the handle of something solid and heavy. When he slipped it out of his waistband, the moonlight ricocheted off of a used steel blade. The edges were dull- he hadn't changed his blade since his first kill. He would have to soon, the edge made it difficult to slice through anything of substance. It would catch on a thread, and require a heavy hand to guide it. Her breathing quickened, and he shivered beneath it.

It was still so bizarre, standing with her like this in the middle of a parking lot. They both knew their fates, he would kill her- as he had so many other times before. Although the man knew this was the right one, it pained him to notice that she was so unlike all the others. Why hadn't she fought? Why was she so quick to assume that there was no way she would get away? He almost laughed, even though it was surprising to him, wasn't it still the correct reaction for this moment? To accept your cards, to lean so hard into the fates that you trusted their judgment when it came? He brought the knife to her throat, relishing in the way her breath hitched. It would be too easy now, he would slide the dull blade through her skin and let her blood run dry. He would see the light in those emerald eyes fade, and he would enjoy it. The man put slight pressure on his grip, pushing hard against her skin, though not hard enough to puncture yet. He wasn't sure why he hadn't done it already. His muscles didn't move a single inch.

"What's your name?" She asked quietly. Confusion was taut on his lips as he pursed, pulling them to a tilt on the side of his mouth. Not one of his women had ever asked him that. It made him anxious- not as it should have. She wasn't going to live to see another day. She wouldn't breathe long enough to be able to tell anyone the sins that would occur here tonight. Would it be such a bad thing? He breathed out. Her backside was still flesh against his and she hadn't caught a glimpse of his face. He could credit that to the two-dollar pair of stockings he'd stolen from a department store a few weeks back.

Her calmness was unsettling. He had expected much more of a fight, he wanted it. It was more fun when he felt like he had to conquer a challenge and this seemed far too easy. The man's mouth watered and he opened his mouth in a pant. He hungered for her fear, for her screams. Instead, he sat, a knife at her throat, coming up empty. Her breaths, though once rapid and shallow, evened out. Long and deep, he could feel her inhaling the night air around them, and letting it go into the wind. She was so unlike what he had expected her to be.

"Kill," he whispered, finally, almost cradling her neck with the long blade. He still wasn't harsh enough to puncture the skin, not yet. He could feel Lorena deflate in front of him. Any hope she might have had was gone -was there any?- and he could tell she didn't understand what it was he had said.

"I know," her voice caught in her throat. There was the fear he wanted so badly. It tasted wonderful on his tongue.

"No," his voice was deeper than he remembered it. He wasn't one to talk often, so when he did it unsettled him. This was the voice of a killer, someone who had slain many women in parking lots so similar to this one they stood in now. The fluorescent lights above them flickered eerily. He was lucky it had grown so late in the evening. It was unlikely people would drive by and witness them, and if they had they'd probably just assume they were two lovers finding privacy where they could.

The man liked that more than he wanted to admit.

"I don't think you do." He finished, purring in her ear. A shiver shot up her spine, and he reveled in feeling her all wound up against him the way she was.

"Kill," he said again. "My name is Killian." Lorena didn't relax- although that didn't surprise him. This was uncharted territory. Kill's blood sped through his veins in anticipation, his fingers making the knife bobble back and forth in his hand. He wasn't anxious, the nerves died away with her body's acceptance of her fate. But it was thrilling watching her tremble in his arms, knowing the name of the man that was going to run this smooth blade across her throat.

Lorena's muscles twitched, her hand jerking ever so slightly. Killian shifted his weight, guiding her back further towards him. They couldn't get any closer if they tried, save for removing their clothes. He'd never killed a dancer before, but Kill wouldn't take the chance. As docile as she had been, she had a fire in her, he could see it. He was lucky she hadn't seen it herself. She was plagued by fear and self-loathing and he was drinking in every moment of it. There was a reason he had chosen her.

"My name is Lorena," she replied finally. Did she know it was the last words she would ever utter? Was she sure this was what she wanted to say?

"I know," He whispered. It almost pained him to say the words. She didn't need to know that he had planned this, that this moment was mapped out for months. Lorena wasn't crazy, she was far from it, and Killian was sad he was taking that moment away from her. But it couldn't be helped. He couldn't stop, no matter how hard he tried.

Killian smiled then and leaned over to kiss the side of her neck with chapped lips. He inhaled a quick, sharp breath, and steadied his features.

Killian's arm moved quickly, a professional at his work. Her skin was butter, so soft and malleable. It took one moment, the adrenaline shot through his veins, and a hit of dopamine assaulted his system. He sighed happily, feeling her body drop to the floor. Even in death, she was graceful. He would expect nothing less from the body of a dancer.

As she sagged against him, Killian let her lay on her back,

careful to not touch her body with anything but gloved hands. He stepped away and stared at her, he really needed to get away from this place now.

He wanted to stay with her, to worship that beautiful soul. Lorena felt so familiar to him as if they'd known each other for several lifetimes. And while she was someone that he cared about so deeply, he couldn't help but feel a similar rage when he looked at her. Killian couldn't separate the feelings inside of him; so really she was the bane of his existence, she was the one who made him this way.

Killian was a killer because of Lorena. She ruined him, and so he decided it was time to ruin her in return. Until she came back to another body, another life, and he would have to do it all over again.

"Goodbye, Lorena," He said softly, though the words barely left his mouth before they were taken by the wind. His blood chilled, gone was the high that he chased after so often. Killian slid the knife back into the waist of his jeans and stepped away.

He didn't give her one last look, she didn't deserve that.

He walked away.

PART SIX
IN BETWEEN

"It is not death, but dying, which is terrible."
- Henry Fielding

I

She didn't remember dying.

Well, Layla remembered what *happened*. It was more like she didn't remember what it *felt* like to die.

One minute she was drowning and the next, she was here. In this place, not quite limbo, not quite the land of the living. It was a place in between those two worlds. Odder, eerier and stranger. It was all that she knew now, and a place she was desperate to get out of.

The crunch of bones and dead, rotting things shifted under her bare feet. She hissed at the stench that reeked from them as they moved and her nostrils expanded as the smell settled around her. The sharp, white shards of the tree roots protruded from the ground, dropping tiny teeth when the world shook above them. Layla crouched low, curling her toes over the debris and stepping slowly, careful to not make a sound.

Souls of the recently deceased did pass through this place, the in-between. Layla had wandered since death, she was quick and stealthy, not easily seen, the only person she knew of that stayed. Her home was the forest of teeth, though she was tired of taking shelter in the bruised blacks and blues of the foliage. Layla wasn't staring at the trees any longer though, now her gaze was focused on the place just outside of the tree line, the place where those that died passed through. It was an arch carved from roots, and it was the only place in this world that seemed to be held in as much esteem as those that shepherd it. Her close proximity made living on disjointed bones and flaking foliage worth the struggle, even if it did make her want to vomit. It was where the Kharon guided those lost souls to their new resting place, whether it be down in the deepest pits of the underworld, the warrior fields of Elysium, or whatever it was that lay beyond this place. It wasn't that she was wanting to find her way back to living. Layla just felt closer to...*something* when she was around it. It felt like an itch she couldn't scratch. The center of the universe.

There was a point when Layla *did* want to go back to the land of the living. She yearned for the sun that beat hard on her back and the beauty of that world. That desire didn't last long. Death would be so much easier if she didn't have to remember what she was like when she was living. There was a particular brand of beauty in life, but it was not her. The ugliness of her soul tarnished everything she touched. Layla was a touch of something unholy. They danced on her grave, she was sure, celebrating the day of her death like it was the Danse Macabre.

Her breath hitched as a shard of fresh bone sliced through the rough calluses of her foot. There was no blood, though a slow queasy looking puss erupted as if she was a balloon that had just been popped. Layla didn't feel the pain, the other benefit of her soul being trapped here. Her body could sense the intrusion, but no hurt came along with it. Just an uncomfortable pulsing of puss leaving her body. She grabbed a shred of fabric from her back pocket stash, winding it tightly around her foot to stop the leak. Her body shifted again, her hips dipping lower to the filthy undergrowth. Beyond the roots of the tooth forest were dark cloaked figures hovering near the shore. Layla felt the shiver roll up her spine.

The Kharon had been looking for her since her escape those years ago, and had she not been good at evasion in her previous life, she would most certainly be facing their judgment and an inevitable placement in hell. The reminder made her shrink back into the cover of the forest. Rule number one of the in-between? Never be seen. Even from a distance, they were striking to look at, intimidating. Their bodies were tall, long, and slender, baggy robes draped over them like fine antique furniture. They didn't quite walk but hovered over the ground by several inches. From their sleeves hung rotted flesh. The skin was torn at the seams, hanging by strings at the joints. Their presence brought a familiar tendril of darkness wherever they went, and as she watched the tendrils coil around them like dogs, Layla felt fear latch onto her heart. They followed them everywhere- it always seemed as though they found her, too. The tendrils weren't communicative, to Layla's limited knowledge, they'd snaked through her legs so many times, and yet she'd never been seen by a Kharon. It seemed to her that they were nothing of a threat, their only purpose was to feed off of the dead. There was a lot of it here, and so the tendrils were everywhere. Maybe too satisfied to alert their masters of her presence.

Layla felt a tug, a suspicion that they were far more than they appeared to be. The tendrils were biding their time until something suited their needs, and until then they would wander this world, all-seeing but never interfering, sticky in the air and clinging to every surface they touched. Layla sucked in a breath, narrowing her eyes and squinting to get a better look. The most frightening things about the Kharon weren't their tendrils or their flesh. It was the large thing that sat on the top of their heads.

It was the shape of a large bird's head, like that of a plague doctor's mask in the mid-1300s. They varied in size and shape, sometimes manifesting as a finch, a vulture, or the classic interpretation. Its color and texture were closest to bone, though Layla was not brave enough to get close to one to verify. The beak was long, white, and curved, opening only when their herbs and dried flowers needed replacing. The eyes were hollow holes of black, and the more Layla looked at them the harder it was to stay hidden.

They were the shepherds of this world, big and terrifying, and she could not be caught. Layla blinked hard, shaking her head to rid herself of the fuzziness that was infiltrating it. If you didn't keep your wits about you, this world will ruin you. The shore they circled around reminded Layla of her last days on earth. The sand was coarser, rougher, and jagged. It circled a large body of water, though it was very different than any bay or lake she was familiar with. The water was dark and murky and Layla blinked away illusions of the monsters and demons that made their home there. The Kharon's boat conjured out of thin air, creating rippling waves in the otherwise calm lake. She watched as they sailed across it at least seventy feet in until they hit the solid mass of an island.

Layla had seen the island a dozen times before, and every time her eyes laid upon it she was taken aback with awe. It was small in size, only about ten feet across in either direction. The sandy floor looked to be rugged, with sharp textures like it was littered with sea glass. Two dark black roots emerged from the ground, tangling in each other and meeting in the middle, curling into a beautiful, intricate knot at the center. She could see through to both ends, and had she not remembered stepping through it herself when she watched the Kharon dip into a respectful bow and a figure crossed through it, she might have fainted. This was why she looked into it longingly from the forest, the sight was mesmerizing.

The body that emerged from the altar was thick and meaty. It fell through easily and Layla winced as it hit the ground. It collapsed to the floor and she realized it was not so much the body of a person, but their soul. There was a ring of tousled hair on its head, and when it looked up to the Kharon, their hands outstretched in a semi-circle around him, he screamed.

Layla had done the exact same thing.

I.5

Her last day alive was on a beach. It was the best sort of last day, if you asked her. The sky was overcast, but she could still feel the sun attacking her skin. By midday she was already pink to the touch, no matter the amount of sunscreen she put on. Layla woke up not knowing she was going to die, and maybe it was for the best. She lived each day like it was her last anyway, and that was the way she wanted to go out. She was single at twenty-four, living in Orange County. She worked a shitty job at a souvenir shop on the boardwalk, and she would chew gum and get high on the pier.

Some would have said she leaned too far over the edge but Layla was sure someone had pushed her. She felt the pressure on her back and fell right over the side railing. Had she not been so far out, so far gone, she could have caught herself. But she flipped over, the feeling of weightlessness taking over as she descended into the ocean below. She was a great swimmer, first in her school's swim team and second in the county. But even her skill could not beat the wooden post, and the searing pain as her head smashed against it.

She remembered her head dipping underwater, she remembered the waves crashing around her. She remembered opening her mouth and gasping for air, catching nothing but a lung full of water. The pain roared in her ears, an aching throb pounded in her chest. Layla wished the pain would leave. She wished to never feel the water lapping at her skin ever again.

The memories faded from her body and she felt no peace, but no malice either. It was as if the string had been cut, her chord sliced into a million pieces. Layla remembered crying out in fear, in utter agony. It was the last thing she was allowed to feel until death took her completely.

And soon she couldn't remember feeling anything at all.

2

It took her a second to snap back to reality, and her eyes focused once more as the glaze faded. Layla shook her mess of hair and stared at the group in the clearing, knowing each move that would happen before it was happening. She hissed under her breath as the Kharon lifted their bird heads, reaching out for the man on the floor as they had every other lost soul. Layla wasn't sure where it was they judged him, she didn't know if there was a protocol or an order in the in-between. Were all the dead the same down here? Layla dared to move closer now that they were so far away from the shoreline. She took quick, silent steps out into the open, feeling the crisp coolness of the air hit her skin. It felt neither pleasant nor uncomfortable, the pressure across her skin just was. No longer protected by the coverage of the forest, she needed to be extra careful, and Layla took each step with care despite the speed of her walk.

Being out in the in-between was an incredibly unsettling experience. Despite not being a fully corporeal being in a place that reeked of loss and death, the world around them rumbled with life. She glanced up towards the sky, constantly startled by the sight. Layla had to remember that this world was so very different than the one she was used to. These worlds were full of trees littered with teeth, with silent soul guides. And as Layla's eyes grazed the ceiling above them, she almost let out a gasp, as she had almost every time she looked up at it. Although she could see no further than the immediate surface she still could have sworn they were underwater.

Sea life was rampant above them. Layla could see whales as large as the lake itself, she could see sharks and something else shoot deeper into the water. They were not only the place between life and death, but the place between the bottom of the sea, and the hell that flourished beneath them. The shadow cast by the whale spanned the entire lake, and the bodies on the island looked up in unison, too. She didn't have much time before they would return.

Forcing her eyes to desert their current fixation, Layla ran towards the lake. She gagged the closer she got to the scent of the Kharon, but shifted through the gravel as quickly as she could. One by one she grabbed pieces of herbs, dried flowers, and old leaves. Everything she had seen them dump from their masks and onto the floor, she sought. She looked for anything that her soul might be able to inhale. Her body did not need food in this state, but it needed something, and in a place like this food was scarce. This was the only source she could find, without going into the depths of the hell demon's lair herself. Layla grabbed what she was able, stuffing them into the pocket of her jacket and sprinting back towards the forest of teeth before the Kharon could miss her.

There was a screech that echoed through the world, an earth-shattering, bone-chilling noise that wasn't meant to exist. Layla turned her head just as she breached the cover of the forest, her feet cut up from the teeth that were scattered across the forest floor. The Kharon were in the same boat, guiding the boy across the lake. She sprinted further into the forest, desperate to escape the sound of the dead man. She didn't want to know what was going to happen to him, she didn't want to watch as they damned him to his eternal hell. Layla didn't want to see where it was she belonged.

Something collided with her, hard. Her head snapped around, and the tiny figure that was heavy as lead stood firmly planted in front of her. Layla tumbled over, rolling over the bones and debris. She lay there for a few moments, her heart pounding outside of her chest. When she had caught her breath, Layla scrambled to sit up, her face a mixture of confusion and fear. Her wide eyes focused on the figure in front of her, though her peripherals were searching for a way to escape. The outline of a bird skull made her breath hitch, but it only took a second for her face to fall from worried desperation to a frustrated suspicion.

"Bird, it's you," she said. Layla's voice croaked, the strings of her voice not accustomed to speaking any longer. The words hung in the air for a second, and the figure, Bird, looked at her curiously.

It was hard to look at. The skull was that of a tiny finch, the beak short and stout and not quite as menacing as the others she had seen. The mask was new, with barely any scratches or gaping holes. The flesh that hung at its sides wasn't so rotted either. The smell was subdued, and it didn't quite tickle the insides of her nose as much. She wriggled it anyway. It looked like the Kharon was looking straight at her, the hollow black of its eyes full of question. Layla narrowed her eyes, scooting further back on her butt, reluctant to get up, but ready to run if need be.

"What are you doing here, Bird?" She asked it. The dryness of her throat had her coughing mid-sentence, but she sucked in her breath, careful to keep her voice low in case there were other eavesdroppers nearby. Layla knew better than to lose her guard in this forest. The trees heard every secret in this world. The thing made a small squeak. She'd learned in the few months following her death that the companionship of Bird was not a bad one to have. Though they showed up at the most inconvenient of times, they never gave her cause to be alarmed. At first, maybe. The newly dead, evading the clutches of the Kharon to only come face to face with one? Once the immediate sense of danger disappeared, Layla was almost happy to have the thing around, sometimes.

Bird was a small creature, about half the size of its brothers. She looked at it warily as its tiny hand reached up to its beak. Bird pried it open with one hand, careful to turn their face away. They didn't say a word as they reached far back into the blackness beyond the white bird's skull. Bird held out their hand, and Layla widened her eyes at the sight of a fresh bundle of herbs and flowers. Nothing like the dry ones she now carried in her pockets

"Where did you-" she reached out, her mouth salivating at the sight. She'd met Bird almost a week after her death, and her escape. They watched as she crawled across the floor of the forest of teeth, long pointed finger lifting in the direction of the lake. When she watched the Kharon dump the content of their masks onto the floor, fill the tiny wooden boar, and sail across the lake to the center island, it took a moment before she realized what they were saying.

"Food?" Layla had asked. Tiny Bird didn't have to say a word, continuing to point in the direction of the lake.

Maybe it was a bad decision to listen to Bird, but who else could Layla trust? Everything here was meant to be a nightmare, everything here wasn't meant for souls like hers to wander it; and yet Layla had done just that. She would always bring her shitty life into her death, no one would have been surprised about that. The minute the herbs touched her lips, Layla felt a burst of life rush through her. It wasn't like what it was before. She was a shadow of her old, living self. But it was enough to get her off the floor, to walk among them once more. Bird saved her from a second death, and Layla- for better or worse- owed them something she could not give. They had come a long way.

Bird wasn't around often. She could go days or weeks before seeing them again, but they would always find her, in the end. They were the only Kharon that could, for whatever reasons the universe had. Bird never said a word, making Layla wonder if it wasn't a matter of them wanting to talk so much as it was the ability to. They had spoken to her only once before, and nothing since. They would usually stand there ominously, looming over her as she did numerous, mundane tasks. Bathing, fetching herbs, and making a nest to sleep in.

This was the first time Bird had ever offered her herbs from its own beak, however. Like she'd expected, they refused to say a word, but their hand stayed outstretched, waiting patiently. Layla was wary to take it, but the hunger won out. The rumble started in her stomach and expanded into her limbs. Her body felt deteriorated every moment she went without the herbs as if her body couldn't survive without them. It was a peculiar sensation, to not feel hunger but know your body needs it like humans need to breathe air. She grasped hungrily at Bird's hand, careful not to touch it, but rather pick the items out of their opened, rotted palm.

She'd never noticed before that Bird had worn a pair of thick black gloves over their hands. Was that something she overlooked before? Layla squinted her eyes, tearing them from Bird and focusing on the herbs in her possession. She placed a flower petal on her outstretched tongue and sighed in contentment. The effect was immediate, she could no longer feel the prickles under her skin. Relief flooded through her, and she shoved the rest into her last empty pocket. Layla would need to unload when she got back to her nest.

"Thank you," she said earnestly. It might have been the first time she ever thanked anyone. This gift that Bird had given her, well, it was more than she deserved. The Kharon dipped their head in answer, taking a step back. They didn't leave, but they didn't make a move towards her, either.

"Can I ask you something, Bird-o?" Layla said, looking at them curiously. Bird just stared right through her. She'd tried making them talk before, saying random antagonistic things that might have scared them into talking. Nothing worked. And every time Layla failed, she was reminded of how alone she was in this world full of souls. At least when she was living she had the bodies to fill up the space. Here, Layla only had her thoughts- and that was not a fun place to be.

"How come you've never turned me in?"

She'd never asked the question explicitly. Truth be told, she'd always been frightened. Did Bird even know that she wasn't supposed to be here? Layla moved her hand from her mouth, the fingers playing with the last of the petals. She wanted to savor every moment of this fresh flower- who knew when she would ever get the chance at them again?

"I suppose it's the wrong question, innit?" She sighed, the energy in her palpable again. She was exhausted and could feel the light running through her veins drain even as she sucked down the rest of that fresh floral. This world was tiring, and just the simplest of tasks- like fetching dropped herbs- was enough to make her want to sleep for an eternity. She let it slide, as she usually did, opting to roll her shoulders back and change course. It was probably best to not give her silent friend any more reason to turn her in anyway. Layla sat up properly and brushed herself off.

"Have you ever been so tired that you can't even sleep properly?" Layla looked at Bird and cocked her head, hoping just for a second that she might have gotten a head nod or something. Grunting when the physical confirmation didn't come, she lifted her foot to inspect the new cuts that materialized across them. The forest murdered the soles- it was this one time that she was grateful for the lack of feeling in them. It would be pointless to use the rest of her fabric, so Layla let it be, heaving a heavy sigh and wiping at them with her hand. The puss smeared across the bones, the contrast of tainted yellow and sharp white making her wince in discomfort. When she glanced up at a still staring Bird, she rolled her eyes. Layla didn't need the validation. Sometimes it was clear they understood her words and her thoughts, or maybe that was just Layla's wishful thinking.

"It's getting dark soon, you should probably go." Just past the tree line, she could see darkness cross over the world once more. The sea creatures swimming above them layered the ocean floor and covered their sky. It was less gray and more black- darker than any night above ground. It was a dangerous place for her to be, Layla would need to turn in soon, too.

At this point, she was rewarded by Bird turning their head to gaze out at the setting light. It was the most she would get from her friend. Then, like the light itself, Bird disappeared. They faded quickly, and once again Layla was alone.

It was what she deserved.

2.5

She fell face-first into the gravel, but it didn't hurt as it should have. Her fists grabbed the rough ground beneath her, and she felt the pinpricks of something sharp. Layla winced, closing her eyes tight and waiting for the pain, but none came. It was more uncomfortable than anything, odd, but not the most unusual thing to have happened to her today. She extended out her arms, grabbing handfuls of the hard dirt. Layla struggled to get up, pulling her stretched muscles back towards her to position them at either side when she was ready to sit upright. When she opened her eyes, Layla went rigid. She wasn't in water any longer, she realized, and wasn't that the last thing she remembered? Quickly her fingers flexed, forcing her eyes to look at them.

Those weren't rocks. They were bones.

Layla crawled onto all fours, shoving her body back and releasing her grip on the bones she'd been holding onto so tightly a minute before. Her eyes widened in shock and Layla felt her head flick up to seek help from someone nearby. She must be dreaming. She must be dreaming. She must be dreaming.

Her eyes met the hollows of a crow-shaped skull.

Layla screamed as loud as her lungs were able, letting out every ounce of breath that she'd been holding. She was surprised there was any left, wincing once more as flashes of water infiltrating her insides, drowning her from the inside out blurred at the seams of her memories. The scream echoed through this small land, bouncing off of the invisible walls that entombed them here.

Layla tried to stand up, her legs like that of a newborn fawn, wobbling as they tried to support her weight. She fell once more to the ground. Layla glanced around helplessly, her body shaking violently as the skulled figures in robes approached her. They cornered her from all sides, trapping her, suffocating her. When one held out its hand gently, though she thrashed below them, Layla could hear a voice echo through her thoughts.

"Come with us, small one," it said. The voice was omnipresent, everywhere at once and yet she knew exactly who it came from. She looked at them, fear smeared across her vision, and shook her head. They would not take her, not today. The figures leaned closer, allowing her to see the rotting flesh. Its finger was hanging on by a thread, the skin a green color that made her want to vomit. Layla didn't reach for it.

"I...will...not!" She gasped. Why did it still feel like her lungs were full of water? Layla brought her hands to her head and shoved three fingers down her mouth, begging herself to throw up the last of the salty ocean that coated her throat.

"We have come to guide you to your home," they said in unison. Their voices were one and the same. Though she could not distinguish one from them all in her head, her eyes settled on the one in the center. It was the tallest of the three, and she noticed its beak was particularly longer than the others.

"I am home!" She hissed, though not in fury or in rage. A beautiful shade of confusion clouded her vision instead, the arch of her brow and the twitch of her freckled nose reminding her of who she was, really. She was not this scared, tiny person who stood before

them but someone strong, someone brave, someone reckless. Her hands left her mouth though the taste of salt was almost too overbearing as she looked from side to side. This was not home, there was no warm sun or calming splashing of the waves. There were no rumbles of traffic or chatter of tourists. This was not her home, although all parties involved seemed to be heavily aware of that already. Layla allowed her lie to weave into the air around them, refusing to correct herself.

"You have passed on, Layla Laurent. Life is no longer yours to keep. We are here to guide you home, to the place for your soul to rest eternally." Their voices were soothing, despite their frightening exterior. She could not see under their masks, or the robes that cloaked them, but she sensed the doom that surrounded them, and even worse, the death. Layla's nose crinkled in discomfort at the smell, a sweet sickly thing.

Their hands stayed open, palm up in her direction. She would not take it. Instead, Layla's hands grabbed another fistful of scattered bones from the floor.

"And what will happen if I decline?" She asked sharply. Layla surveyed their surroundings through her peripherals, gently lifting herself off the ground. This time her legs obeyed her, and though she struggled, the cloaked skulled creatures did not disturb her as she stood on her feet. She found herself on a small island, surrounded by a large body of water. The trees to her right looked promising. She was a swimmer, and the lake was not too long of a trek for someone of her talents. She could make it to the trees quickly, she could evade them if she needed to.

They either chose to ignore her curiosity or didn't notice it, their stares focused on the place where her heart should be instead of her wildly searching eyes. Layla wished she could tell what they were thinking or what they were feeling, their gaze was too unsettling. There seemed to be a peacefulness that washed over them all here, but the looming sense of dread stilled her shallow breaths; it kept her on her toes, her senses sharp and her will strong as ever. The silence filled the space they occupied, and Layla was sure they wouldn't answer her at all until the familiar presence crawled into a small corner of her mind once more.

"Then your soul will be doomed to Hell," they said grimly. Even she could not mistake the shivers that rumbled through the air as they spoke it- it was as if the word was forbidden. "Come," they insisted, their hands flexing to punctuate the request.

"So I am dead," she mused. They refused to answer again, either they said all that they needed to say or they would not give her the benefit of hearing them say it out loud.

The pieces slowly fell into place, like a jigsaw puzzle she spent far too long on. Were these the long foretold Kharon, the shepherds to the underworld? These monsters from her textbooks that she'd so dubiously ignored, karma had an odd way of kicking her in the ass. "Kharon," she whispered. What did she remember about Hades' ferryman? "I have no payments," Layla's voice was still hoarse, and the backs of her hands grazed against her pockets. Were those who died simply given a token to cross over, or were they expected to carry coins with them wherever they went, a grim reminder of the payment they'd have to make if they died? She narrowed her eyes and glared at them.

She hadn't expected them to answer, Layla wasn't daft enough to not catch onto their game. One of the cloaked figures took a step closer, and that was all it took. Layla burst to life, she threw her hands in the direction of the Kharon. The bones she had been holding onto scattered towards them. If it affected them any she had no idea, Layla was already running in the opposite direction. The lake that surrounded her seemed deep enough, and she said a silent prayer, despite her aversion to the church she came from, and the religion she refused to believe in, and swan dived into it.

The water was cold against her skin, her body - or soul?- could register the chill that assaulted it, but it didn't bother her any. The gap between her and the shoreline was closing. Layla didn't take any time to stop and see if her captors we chasing after her, instead, her strokes became long and deep. She lifted her head for air, and as the water shallowed and the shore closed in on her, Layla felt a tug on her legs. And another gut-wrenching scream escaped her.

Layla didn't notice the bodies upon bodies of souls that littered the lake. Their faces were distorted, their bodies wispy and transparent. They were unlike anything she'd ever seen before. And they pulled her farther and farther down into their depths.

"Help!" She screamed. Layla looked frightfully in the direction in which she swam. The Kharon looked down on her, expressionless. They would not interfere. It seemed to enrage her further, and Layla kicked her legs out underneath her as she tried desperately to escape the grip of souls. They grabbed at her arms, her legs, her body, clinging to her like they had nothing else to hold onto. She needed to get out of here. Layla flailed her arms wildly, screaming and kicking and tearing herself away from the souls in the lake. When at last she freed herself from their clutches, Layla swan to the shore. She scrambled out of the water, wiping at her clothes and tearing off into the direction of the forest.

Her clothes were dry, a type of magic from the lake she would not care to think about at this moment. The Kharon didn't seem to be following her, but maybe it was because they couldn't swim. She was determined to believe that she had made it out of their clutches all by herself. Layla raced to the forest, relief flooding her when she crossed the threshold of the trees.

A loony, deranged cackle escaped her. Layla didn't even care about the bones she noticed littering the floor. She didn't cry when the teeth fell from the branches and hit her face as she ran. She hadn't evaded death, but she evaded whatever hell was waiting for her if the Kharon had taken her.

Layla fell further into the forest, running until her feet fell off of her. As her pace slowed she turned her head around. She could just make out the figures on a boat, streaming down a river that manifested from the lake itself like the river Styx. She was in awe of it, and with her attention turned away from the path in front of her, she was unsurprised when she hit something solid. Layla staggered and fell on her back. When she shook her head and turned to assess the wall she came face to face with another Kharon.

Layla almost screamed again, before the Kharon wrapped its rotted skin around her mouth.

"Do not scream, and they will not find you," she could hear the voice inside her head again. This one was younger, less abrasive, and more curious. She looked at them in panic, and the wildness in her eyes resulted in a tighter grip against the Kharon. It loosened its hold on her mouth after a few moments when it was certain Layla was not going to scream.

"Are you here to help me?" She thought hard. She wasn't sure if they could hear her, Layla had only spoken to them aloud before she ran. The figure shook its head, and Layla whined- it didn't want her to scream because it wanted her for itself.

"Are you here to hurt me?" Another thought shot through her with worry. Again she felt the slow shakes of their head.

"No, Layla. I am just here to observe." Her brows creased in confusion, and she looked up at the Kharon. Its beak was short and stocky, like a finch. They were shorter than their brothers, and not as intimidating to look at. Layla looked at them curiously and was beside herself with questions.

"Observing...me?" she asked. Was this something she really wanted to know?

That was the last time she's ever heard a Kharon speak.

3

When Layla was alive, daylight usually meant brightness and warmth on your skin, but that was the opposite of what this place brought. The glow shone through the ocean, but with the marine life active above them there were only flickers of the sunshine. It was barely visible this far underwater, refracted slivers of the sun almost invisible unless you were actively looking for them, and Layla would always look for those small beams of another life. All she was left with was the pale gray hue of the world around her, almost completely without light. She walked through the maze of trees with a tired pessimism, a frown forming across her lips.

She used to love the sun, and now, especially through the haze of the forest- it was likely something she would never see again. Layla had a few months of getting used to it and yet she couldn't help but feel the somber nostalgia crawl up her back. Her hands caressed the branches, following a path she'd known so well. She had only been dead for two months but there were already scuffs in the bone trees and worn trails on the paths she frequented. The in-between welcomed her existence, molding to the shape she needed it to be as she adjusted to this world of death in return. Nostalgia aside, Layla needed to create a new reality, one without the comfort of the sun.

After a few more moments of wandering the forest of teeth, Layla heard the sound of shattering bones as they fell from the trees like leaves, cracking harshly off the ground. Months ago she would have disintegrated in fear, but in that time she'd learned to distinguish the presence of her Kharon from the others. They made themselves known by shifting between the trees just so. Bird could travel this world in infinite quiet, and so Layla knew they were only doing it for her sake, in sounds that brought her comfort instead of terror. Together they walked like this for some time through the trees, with Bird floating behind her silently. It might have been uncomfortable had she not been used to the deafening stillness. As it was, Layla welcomed their presence. They spoke to her only once before and she could remember every syllable of that day, although that might have only been because they were the ones that saved her. Even though she antagonized, prodded, and tried to trick the Kharon into speaking again, her efforts were unsuccessful. There were reasons Bird would not talk to her, and she was determined to find out why. If Layla was going to spend the rest of her eternal death in the in-between, she would be incredibly lonely without it for long. Those few spoken words are what kept her from going down a spiral she could not return from.

Was it difficult for the Kharon to speak? Were they not allowed to speak? Or was it far simpler than that...what if they just didn't want to speak? The last would infuriate her. For as much time as she spent with Bird, Layla believed they were almost friends. She turned on them in haste, frowning. Bird stopped as she did, hovering just an inch above the ground. It was another thing she never thought to ask, not that she would get an answer from them. Layla spat at the ground.

"Why are you following me?" She asked, her brows furrowed and her hands grabbed a tree branch tightly. The movement made more tiny teeth fall, ricocheting off of Bird and onto the floor, rolling towards her. Layla placed a foot over them, stepping on the yellowing bones until they made a satisfying crunching sound. The patience had all but left her today, and she had just opened her eyes an hour before.

Sleep didn't work the same here as she remembered it did back home. Here, sleep was something to pass the time, it had no influence on her energy or activity. Truly, Layla didn't care to sleep at all if she could help it. She never knew if the Kharon would find her, and wanted to constantly be moving throughout the forest. Thankfully, the forest she wandered through circled the lake and River Styx, so the island that centered it was always accessible. And so, she climbed trees, she skipped rocks across the lake in late hours, and she stayed well hidden. Sleep was just another activity, and while it was not entirely restful like she wished for, it was another reminder of her life before this. Layla continued looking for those little glimpses of life whenever she could.

She felt...unfinished. Her soul went unrested here. It might have been her fault that she was trapped in the in-between, to begin with, but it was difficult not holding resentment in her heart for the Kharon, who haven't tried hard enough to find her. Because as it was, Layla wanted to be done with this. She was sick of what she had become here, sick of being forced to remember her life. Even Bird, a delight their presence had become, was only a constant reminder of what she had lost.

When expectedly they didn't respond, Layla kept talking, shaking her head in frustration. She did it often enough, guessing at what they might have said instead.

"I know you've done this since I...arrived," the wording was tricky, what if they decided against keeping her presence hidden? It was like constant eggshell walking. "And yesterday with the herbs, I guess I just can't catch your angle. You disappear at night for no reason, you hover inches off of the fucking ground. You're the creature I know most in this world and I don't know a thing about you." Bird looked at her, cocking its head to the side, but still no answer. Frustrated, Layla threw her arms in the air and turned to stalk away.

When people died they were supposed to pass on. She expected to die and move on to a better place, but she should have known that was just something else her father lied about. With all of the lies he fed to his followers, how could she think that he was able to sell a single truth? Layla officially left her father and his church well into her early teens. In every situation, you could say Layla was always her own demise. She couldn't just let herself die properly.

The boredom struck around midday. She yawned without feeling and swung her arms about. They were only just deep enough to where the lake was out of focus, but she wouldn't need to find more herbs until later that afternoon. The Kharon were consistent in that at the very least, always guiding and shepherding the recently deceased just before darkness flooded the night sky. Finding a large bone on the ground, Layla bent over and picked it up, appreciating the balance of weight as she held it in her arms. Bird looked at her curiously. Sighing heavily, Layla shook her head and swung the bone hard against the tree. The sound echoed throughout their world, startling even the swarm of fish swimming above them. Even Bird jumped in shock, stumbling a few feet backward and ruining their immortal being facade. They disappeared in a second, leaving Layla to manage on her own.

Layla cackled, a real laugh for the first time in ages. It

rumbled through her stomach and left her mouth in a sound that radiated crazy. Maybe she really was going crazy here.

And then something hit her.

Bulldozed right into her, making her cough and choke on the sounds that left her. Layla fell hard to the ground, grunting as whatever it was knocked the wind out of her.

"What the fu-"

"Shh!" The figure said, grabbing at her mouth and covering it with the palm of its hand. Layla had a moment of terrible panic. *They got me they got me they got me.* She closed her eyes and kept chanting it in her head. Something needed to be said about manifesting their destiny. She wanted to laugh but felt the tears coming instead.

"Stop heaving, don't scream," the voice was husky, out of breath itself. It sounded tired, but his hand was still planted firmly over her mouth. The voice made her hyperventilating heavier. The man- it could be nothing but a man with the deepness of his voice and the callouses on his hands- lifted and slammed her head against the ground.

"I said shut the fuck up!" he said in an angry whisper, pinning her face to the ground. He lifted his head back and she opened her eyes, finally taking him in fully. He was long and lengthy, built like a proper personal trainer. He was in a pair of baggy basketball shorts and a plain blue t-shirt. His hair was long and chocolate brown, falling over his face. He was scary and intimidating. She found it hard to stop crying, stop thrashing about. This was the end, it had to be.

The man leaned over and whispered in her ear. "If you don't stop, I'm going to have to kill you. And you don't want that, do you?" She shook her head. "Are you going to be quiet now?" A nod. "Good. I'm going to lift my hand from your mouth. Don't scream, or they're going to get us. They're going to kill us. And I don't want to die. Not again."

Layla could actually understand that one. She nodded a bit more vigorously. The man removed his hand slowly, the threat still prominent in his expression. She scrambled out from under him when she was free of his grip, grabbing for something sharp on the ground, whatever she could find. Layla raised it high in the air, ready to use it if she needed to.

"I'm sorry," he said. She looked up at him with a wild expression. The angry man that stood before her was gone, replaced by someone wide-eyed and apologetic. Who was this man? He took a step forward, and Layla mimicked the movements backward.

"My name is Killian," He said softly. He spoke to her like she was a wild animal, not the person who had her pinned and threw her head against the ground a few moments before. "I'm so sorry about that...I'm not quite myself sometimes. It's the stress, it does it to me at the most inconvenient times," He must have been crazy, the look of fear and self-loathing plastered across his face not enough to make her believe him. Everything about him was a lie.

"Ho-How are you here?" She let out, her hand still trembling above her head.

"I got away. Ran for my fucking life. I didn't know other people did too."

"No. You're wrong." They were both breathing heavily, panting like animals.

"Wrong? What do you mean?"

"It's just me. I'm the only other person who got away. I didn't know anyone else could," It was stupid to believe that. That she would be the only person in the world to have been able to escape the clutches of the Kharon. None of it made any sense. Killian deflated, his hands running through his long hair, pulling at the tangles there.

"That doesn't make sense," he said, his voice laced with accusation. Layla narrowed her eyes and snarled at him.

"None of this makes sense!" Layla wasn't sure why she was still here, arguing with the man that almost killed her, again. She turned around, determined to walk away from him. Layla didn't need any more distractions, especially from him. She started walking deeper into the forest, wiping her face. She thought she wanted company, turns out she wanted none of it at all.

"No, wait!" He screamed, running after her. Layla ignored him, pushing further and further through the forest. "Don't leave me! We're the only two people here, how in the hell are you going to leave me like this?"

Layla spun on him. "You almost killed me!" she shrieked. Killian shifted on the soles of his feet. It made him uncomfortable when she said it. Good, it should. What kind of person acted the way he did? The magic of this world was being tainted by another dark soul. At least for once, she didn't feel so alone.

"Look, I said I was sorry."

"Sorry you almost smashed my skull to pieces?" She spat. Layla didn't know why she was still indulging him. Killian was struggling, the painful expression on his face was almost believable if she didn't already feel the thumping of her brain against her skull. It wasn't painful, more annoying than anything.

"I can explain! It's not what you think."

It wasn't the first time she'd heard that. Layla sighed audibly and turned around again. She needed to leave, she needed to get away.

"Layla!" He screamed, desperate now. Her head was getting whiplash, the number of times she tried to leave, but he wouldn't let her go. But he knew her name, and he knew her name, *he knew her name.* Her face dropped, her palms were sweaty and Layla turned her face to look at him one last time.

"How do you know my name?" She asked quietly. She could feel the tension electrify the air around them. Killian shifted uncomfortably.

"Layla, please come back, I can explain everything."

"I'm not going to come back!" They needed to stop screaming, dark was upon them now - she would never get over how time worked in this place- and the Kharon were bound to be appearing at the lake soon "...not until you tell me what the hell is going on Killian!" she spat out his name like it tasted like dirt. She wouldn't be surprised if it did.

Killian looked around anxiously, but even Bird decided it was an appropriate time to disappear again. Just as quickly as they reappeared, they left her to fend for her own once more. Layla felt their absence immediately, it made all of this seem much more dangerous. He signed in resignation.

"I knew your mother, Layla. I knew Lorena."

She sucked in a breath, holding it until she felt like she could no longer keep it in.

"You knew my mother?" Her voice was only a soft whisper now. Memories flooded her, not all of them unpleasant, not all of them wonderful. All of them were painful. It was the first time since she stepped foot in this place that she could feel the pain. It throbbed in the space where her heart was, agonizing and never-ending.

"Of course I did," he said it like it was the most obvious thing in the world. "I was the one that killed her."

3.5

"Layla!" her father screamed her name over the other end of the receiver. Layla laughed wickedly, tossing her hair back over her shoulder and rolling her eyes in the direction of her partner. Being a teenager was nothing short of torture, she thought. Having to constantly be something you weren't. It was terribly exhausting, but alas, she had appearances to keep up, and acting the part of a sinful, rebellious daughter of a pastor was part of it. Her dad sounded panicky, and she knew going home now at such a late hour would have horrible consequences. It was far more dangerous in her home now than it was in the back of this old truck. Father would be waiting for her and his consequences weren't... pastor-friendly to say the least. Even if the truck was running on fumes and the smell of weed slithered out of the cracked windows, she'd rather be here. Layla opened her mouth to reply with something snarky, but only squeaked in shock instead as the boy to her right tore the phone from her hand and held it far towards the other side of the backseat. She could barely hear him anymore, save for the string of crackles that must have been father calling out obscenities. For a pastor, he was very un-pastor-like.

"Erick," she hissed through clenched teeth, but couldn't disguise the laughter that escaped her throat instead. His pants were to his ankles and she slapped at his bare stomach. He smiled, the tilt of it looking so ruggedly handsome in the street lamps that lit this abandoned road. She had half the nerve to tell him to hang up the phone so they could get back to the activities they originally planned for the night. Maybe the act of a rebellious sinner wasn't quite an act, anymore.

"Laylita!" His raised voice from her cell echoed throughout the pickup. Layla couldn't help but cringe.

"What did he call you?" the boy asked, still holding it far from her reach. Layla furrowed her brows and scowled at him.

"Nothing," she spat, all humor gone from her voice. "Give me the phone." Her tone must have done the trick, the cocky smile that sat on his face slipped away slowly. He shook his head and ran his free hand through the silvery blonde of his hair. Erick always did that when he was nervous, and she found that he was nervous a lot whenever he was around her. Layla had that way about her, a bright light in the room until she willed the darkness upon her. Erick was only here because she wanted him to be. As much as he enjoyed it, he knew that when the demon in her eyes shone bright, his feet needed to tread lightly. That coupled with his guilt of being with her in the first place- his own reputation at their Christian private school wouldn't hold up if they found out he was getting down and dirty with the sinful slut- must have done him in. He handed her the phone with more enthusiasm than he might have a few seconds before. Their fingertips touched gently, and Layla felt his heat seep back through her. Her eyes warmed again, and Layla felt the need to reassure Erick with a small smile and a quick wink.

His tension eased immediately and his hand lowered from his head, resting on the bare of his belly. He made no move to fix his pants situation, confident little fuck. Layla raised the end of the receiver to her ear. Her face slid into an easy, impassive expression.

"Hey dad," she said. Her voice was liquid honey, dripping in sweetness but with all of the bite. She could hear the hitch of his breath from the other end and could sense his panic, heavier than usual. It made her heart beat quickly in her chest, and Layla had to frantically remind herself of the horror that will await her when she got back to the house to slow it back down again. Nothing he could say would bring her home.

"Laylita," he said again, and that was all she heard. He rambled on the other end before she cut him off.

"That's not my name!" she snapped, growling into the receiver. "You might find that I listen better when I'm called the right name."

"Layla listen to me!" He was breathless. It was then that Layla noticed that she couldn't hear the familiar strand of anger in his voice, but fear instead. She quieted, the first time she actually listened to her father in several years now.

"I need you to come home."

"No."

"I'm serious, you need to come home this instant, there's some-"

"Fuck off, I'm busy." For a beat of a moment, she could hear him heave breaths to center himself. He'd given up on trying to curb her sailor vocabulary, at least in private. Layla knew he liked it, in secret, but they were always opposite sides of the same coin. Layla knew her father never really knew how to speak to her, not when she was so much like him. The thought disgusted her and she had to keep from vomiting right there in the truck. He didn't even feel the need to question her about her whereabouts. He didn't give a shit about her in the slightest.

"Layli-Layla," he spoke her name slowly and deliberately, Layla ground her teeth together tightly. She would let him say what he needed to say, just this once, she would pretend she didn't absolutely detest this man with every ounce of her soul, she would pretend...

"Layla your mother died last night," his voice was grave and solemn, and Layla could have sworn she heard regret in his tone,

too. And heaven -if it did exist- knew that there was an exuberant amount of regret that he needed to have. She wasn't sure she heard him correctly, despite the punctuality and emphasis of each word.

"Laylita did you hear me? Your mother-"

"I heard what you said!" She screeched into the phone. Erick slid back into the seat, far away from her and against the window. He looked as if he was desperate for an escape.

"She was murdered, Laylita. On her way home from the dance studio. It was after dark, yesterday. You know how she is...was. There's nothing we could have done." She was empty inside. Nothing seemed to work properly anymore, not her heart, or her breaths. She wished she could just die. Keel over, right here in this stupid, ugly fucking pickup truck. The one person who was just as afraid of her father as she was, was gone. She no longer existed in this physical world. Layla rolled her tongue in her mouth, dry as a desert in a drought.

"You must be happy she's gone." She said. All light died from within her, and Layla was consumed by the darkness. Her eyes, already striking green in color, deepened in understanding, in rage. Her father said nothing on the other end, confirming her own suspicions. "Fuck you, and get the fuck out of my life." And then she hung up. Layla rolled down the window, cranking it with already sore arms, and threw her phone out onto the asphalt. It was an invitation for it to be run over. Her hands were shaking and her heart palpated faster than she could count. He would not, could not find pleasure in her pain anymore. Layla would cut him off, not allowing him access to her, her body, her mind, ever, ever again. No matter what they called her, they could never take this away from her, because he had already taken away everything. Without her mom, who was she? Layla was alone in this world, but being alone was better than what awaited her back home.

Labels, all they were, were labels. Slut, whore, bitch, cunt. An official apostasy, how relieving it was to be free from the church they so claimed were the "purest of them all". If only they knew the man that led their brigade. It was the same that sang verses with them each Sunday, the one that kissed their children on the head, the one that raised money and paraded, talking about goodwill to all men. They would never see the darkness that haunted him, the same that now wrapped its tendrils around her. With simple words- though people would not know how hard it was to say, how it took her eighteen years to say them out loud and mean them- she let go. To be free from the man that took advantage of his privileges, who took advantage of her. Her own father, the man who swore to protect her. There was only one label she sought out now, one that she would take to her grave. Survivor.

Layla's breaths came out ragged and half-hazard. She could tell Erick didn't know what to do, and to be frank, she wasn't quite sure what she wanted either. How could she tell him all that she endured in her lifetime in just a few moments? That was not what he was here for, not what she had promised him. To Erick, Layla was just the whore that would get him off. The one that wouldn't tell, if you asked her nicely.

"A-are you okay?" He asked. Even his voice was sexy. It wasn't high-pitched like some of the boys his age, it was the voice of a man coming to fruition. Her jaguar eyes flicked to his and her mouth quirked to the side.

"My mother is dead," She said. The words tasted bitter on her lips, but not impossible like she thought they might. The ache in her heart throbbed, but it was manageable. She would be okay, she realized. Layla would get through this, scarred and broken, a fragmented piece of what she was before. But she would make it. Erick didn't know how to process that information, she could sense his discomfort as he squirmed in his seat. He didn't know what to do or say, but Layla had no desire to feel pitied. She needed to forget about it all.

"I'm er, I'm sorry, Layla," He said. The boy even had the balls to

sound earnest in his apology. It made her like him a bit more, and she smiled lightly. She said nothing back to him, instead looking at him with a desire that outmatched an alcoholic in a room full of Spirytus Vodka. She moved towards him very quickly, catching him off guard. It was nice to see, as her gaze flickered from his face to his torso, to further south. The Lord knew he was still happy to have her here. Not even the stench of death could keep a boy from arousal. Layla would reward him, she decided.

Thinking of nothing else but this singular goal, she grabbed hold of his knees and pried them open with her fingers, watching him bounce up and down in anticipation. His back was flush against the door now, his legs spread out as much as he was able in the back seat of a pickup truck. Layla licked her lips and lowered her mouth to him. She could feel Erick's restraint ease with each pump, his guilt, and apprehension disappearing as she had her way. She knew he had completely let go when his hands wrapped around her head and his fingers intertwined in her hair, pulling hard. Erick yanked her face back, that wicked gleam back in his eyes. They made eye contact for just a moment before he shoved her head back down onto him.

Thoughts of her mother, her father, and her old life faded quickly. She refused to think about it for one second longer, for the rest of her living days. Layla was no longer a victim of that world, she was not a slave any longer.

She was a survivor, and she will not be tamed.

4

"You must be fucking crazy," she gasped, the branch raising higher above her head, if she could lift it any higher. The bone rattled in her hands, following the movements of her shaking arms. He was either the person that killed her mother or a liar who knew their names. Neither of those options seemed good for Layla.

"My nickname was Kill," he continued slowly, articulating his words so that she wouldn't miss a syllable. Layla looked wildly from side to side. She didn't want to hear anything he had to say. Why the fuck would he tell her this? They sat there in silence for a few moments longer after he finished, him waiting on her to speak, her waiting on an opening to escape. Her curiosity won out before her innate desire to flee, however sick and twisted that sounded.

"Was?" she asked hesitantly. Killian smirked, recognizing the fear that shot through her. She had thrown all of her cards on the table with that one word. He had piqued her interest, they both knew she wouldn't be able to leave now. Not until she got the answers she craved so badly.

She didn't trust him. Was it even possible for her to die, twice? Layla wasn't sure if he actually did want to hurt her, but the pain that ricocheted off the walls in her head and the space under her ribs made her squirm. How was it she was able to feel these things around him? She hadn't felt physical pain in the two months since she died.

"I'm dead, aren't I?" His joke settled between them. Layla stared at him with a deadpan expression, one that betrayed none of her emotions.

"You better start talking and stop telling jokes, or I swear to god that I will leave you here for the Kharon to find you."

"I'm sorry...the what?"

"Kharon. You know, the shepherds of the underworld? The Ferryman? That's what those dead things remind me of. I don't know, it was the best I could come up with at the time." Killian's face was pensive for a moment before he nodded. Just like that, he took her word. What a weird man he was, and what a weird girl she was, for standing here still, for not running for the hills. He was the person that killed her mother, after all.

"So the...Kharon, are they after you?" he looked at her curiously, as if she was the most interesting thing in this world. Not the ocean above them or the river of the dead out beyond the forest. She didn't really think about that all too much anymore, Layla just assumed they were still looking for her. They had to have been looking for him too now, but he was far too clever to be caught, she thought.

"Of course they are. We're the only two people to have escaped their...judgment, whatever they call it. I'm sure they wouldn't be happy that we're parading around this place."

"Fair point." Layla resisted the urge to roll her eyes in his direction. She should be frightened, should be shivering in her boots at the sight of the person she's detested all these years.

But fear and rage could not find a place inside of her- each was fighting for a space that was not entirely there.

"No more jokes," She snapped again, their eyes meeting once again. Layla was thrown by the youth she found there. He was around the same age as she was, though he seemed older before. His hair was long and had a slight curl to it. He looked, not innocent, but decent. Layla shook her head, trying to ignore the overwhelming doubt creeping into her head. He was anything but decent, the tender hurt in her head should have been enough to convince her.

"Layla I don't know how to say this in a way that you'll believe me."

"Give it your best shot."

"I, uh," he looked around them, the sun was dipping over the horizon far too quick for her liking. Killian seemed thrown off by it too. It took some time to get used to the short days and nights here. Time moved so quickly in the in-between. "Kill, that guy isn't me. I mean, it is me, my body. But that guy isn't me."

"Then who was it, Killian? Who killed my mother?"

He ran his hands through his hair and tipped his head back. Layla was sure he was going to scream, and the movement made her crouch, ready to run if the sound attracted the Kharon.

"It was the demon, the mistress. I don't know what the fuck she was. But she gets into your head and she makes you do things that aren't you. I was a good person, Layla! I was good! But she made me."

"I don't understand, how did she make you do anything? Honestly, she sounds like someone you made up to make you feel better. I've read about that before, in school or something. Things like that happen to murderers. It makes you think you have a conscious, but the rest of us know better than that."

Layla was less and less afraid of the man and more irritated by the second. Watching him make excuses for the hurt and pain he's caused made her skin boil.

"I'm not lying!" He begged. As Layla narrowed her eyes she stared at him with curiosity. Was he crying? Killian wiped at his red face. There were in fact tear stains there, fresh but disturbing to look at regardless. "She...she took over my mind, my body. She made me believe it was what I wanted, and then she would do it. Oh Layla you don't know how much I punished myself after she let me have my body back." Killian hunched over and his sobs were audible from where she stood. With nightfall coming soon, and Bird nowhere in sight, they needed to find someplace to turn in for the night. This place was scary after dark.

"I don't know how to believe you. But you need to convince me quickly because it's getting dark and we shouldn't be this far out into the open. I want to believe you, Killian, but I can't do that if I want to rip your head off. You're the first person I've spoken to in a few months. And trust me, I've been waiting for the day I could kill you since the day I didn't get to say goodbye." Killian shrunk back into himself, flinching at her harsh words. It made Layla angry and made her want to throw something across the forest. How dare this weak man be the one that ruined her life? He was nothing, not worth the rage that now coursed through her veins.

"I wish I could, but I have nothing, Layla. I knew about you, but I don't know if it makes this better or worse."

She hadn't thought about how he'd seemed to know her already. Sometimes it all felt like a trick of this world, everything that had happened to her up until this point. Layla didn't answer him, instead, she lowered the bone in her hand, more from its weight than her feelings, and tossed it to the side. She waited for it to make a sound, and when nothing came she turned her head in question, jumping when she saw Bird standing there with it in hand.

"Bird what are you...?" she looked from Killian and back, and Bird took a step towards him. She could see him fluster and move in the opposite direction. The murderer was afraid of a runt. Bird dropped the bone and instead, brought their hand up towards their beak.

"Layla, you need to get away from it!"

"I'm sorry, what?" Killian looked rapidly from her to Bird, and waved his arms at them wildly.

"The Kharon, or whatever, are you crazy?" She whirled on him. It took her a second to grasp what he was saying before realization coated her expression.

"Oh, Bird is..." she didn't want to say harmless, because Layla couldn't promise that, not entirely. She settled on, "a friend." Still not completely accurate, but it was more of an answer than Killian deserved. Bird retrieved another handful of fresh herbs and flowers. The sight of it made her stomach rumble, even if she had already had some earlier. The world was going to drain every ounce of life out of her. Even just this exchange with Killian was exhausting, she felt like she could sleep for an eternity. Layla reached out her hand to take the bundle from Bird, but the Kharon shook their head. She narrowed her eyes in suspicion, mouth agape as they took another confident step towards Kill.

"Friend," Layla repeated uneasily, and to her surprise, he listened to her. He had no right to believe a word she said, Lord knew she didn't trust a single word coming out of his mouth, either. Bird hovered until they were about five feet in front of Killian and dropped the herbs at his feet. Just as quickly as they had approached him, they vanished, leaving the two together alone once more. Bird's initiative to help Killian felt like a betrayal. It wasn't like the Kharon knew why she hated this man so much, but it stung regardless.

"These are for you to eat," she said, tired. Her voice held no enthusiasm. He looked at her curiously and bent forward, grabbing the herbs and plucking a leaf from the pile. "On your tongue. In your mouth," Layla rolled her eyes. Skeptically, he placed the leaf in his mouth. Unlike her, he didn't savor it. He shoved his palm towards his mouth and Killian swallowed the thing in one gulp, looking around eagerly at the pile for more.

"What was that?" He asked in amazement. She could tell he had more energy back in his body. She hadn't gone without her own share for so long that she forgot how depleted you would feel in a place like this. This world didn't want them here.

"Herbs. The Kharon keep herbs in their beaks, I think this world deteriorates their bodies just as much as it does ours. Passing dead don't need any I don't think, because they won't be here for long, but the Kharon are here every day. I have a theory that's why their skin is so rotted. This air will kill you if you're here long enough."

"I thought the people here were already dead," he said, raising an eyebrow.

"Well, yes, but I meant it kills your body. There's something in the air here. The herbs give you energy."

"What about food, and water?"

"I haven't needed it, and I've been here for a few months. Just having the herbs has kept me...functioning."

"I believe it. I feel better already." He flexed his hands and shook his head in amazement. As if he'd never felt this type of relief in his life. She could relate to the feeling. Layla took in a deep breath, balancing herself again. They didn't have much time, they needed to find cover from the night.

"Good luck out here, Killian. Go somewhere high and somewhere hidden." She wouldn't wish the tendrils on anyone, even him. He didn't say anything in return, instead, he nodded and followed her, matching each step with the same hurried worry.

Layla didn't stop him. Killian stayed a good distance behind her, to his benefit. He had the advantage before when he ran into her harder than a truck, but when they were on level footing he wouldn't know what was coming for him. Layla hadn't gotten this far in life without knowing how to fight. She might have grown up in a church, but she only survived because she knew when to drop-kick some stupid boy wanting to take advantage of her.

Scrunching up her nose, Layla pressed forward through the trees, too cognizant of the absence of Bird and the shallow steps of her unwanted companion behind her. Even this was better to think about than the horror that was her life above ground, though. When she spotted her usual spot, a tree rotted enough for her to shimmy her way inside to the thin layer of leaves huddled together, she made a beeline to it. Layla crawled inside, curling in on herself and folding her body to fill out the hole in the nest of foliage she'd left there. Once she was sure she was out of eyesight for the night, she widened her eyes and looked out into the clearing while there was still time left. Killian had stood just ten feet away from her tree stump, staring at her. He shifted on both of his feet, watching her, but not moving. Layla thought he annoyed her as he talked to her, he was far more infuriating just standing there in silence. She waved her arms at him.

"Are you going to move? You need to get out of the open!" She hissed. It was hard not to remember her first night here, and how terrified she was. He might have deserved it, but Layla was too selfish to want to watch. Killian was a monster, a murderer, but he needed to get away, too. Layla couldn't watch him die.

"I don't expect you want me to cuddle in there with you?" Even with the looming danger, Kill had a half-cocky smile on his face. It made her snarl.

"Climb the trees. I've never seen them climb the trees. Watch for the teeth, but the leaves are enough to keep you warm for the night.

"I don't think I can,"

"What do you mean you don't think you can?!" Layla wanted to scream in frustration. She cursed to herself and crawled out of her hole and out into the open once more. The forest was dark and spooky, and the longer she was outside of the tree trunk, the more likely the tendrils would find her. She ran to Killian with her arms outstretched, grabbing hold of his arm and pulling harshly. He wouldn't move.

"C'mon!" Layla yelled at him, watching the cocky smile turn downward. For the first time, she could see fear cross his features.

"I can't climb," he said, "I can't climb." Layla looked around wildly. She pulled on his arm harder.

"Get in my trunk then!" She could see the tendrils inching closer, curling around like snakes. Although they liked the darkness, they didn't like the trees. The rotted things were eerie, and while she'd gotten used to them, Layla wasn't fond of them either. The tendril's aversion was enough of a non-endorsement.

'Go!" she hissed, pushing him towards her trunk. She expected to push harder and expected to beg, but to her surprise, he moved. The glaze was gone in his eyes, and Layla watched as her words finally registered. He shook his head and started running towards her trunk, shoving his large body inside. Layla was worried he wouldn't be able to fit in, but he managed.

She sprinted towards the tree, there was no way she would have been able to fit in with Killian, who was already too cramped. As she neared it, instead of diving down towards her safe haven she jumped as high as she could. Reaching her hands out towards one of the lowest hanging branches, Layla grabbed hold, using her feet to wrap around the trunk and shimmy her way up. It was a good thing she'd spent the first month living up there anyway, the movement felt second nature. A collection of teeth fell from the trees, the tendrils hissing as it rained around them. Layla settled in an elbow of branches, uncomfortable, but not in pain. Even as she winced from indentations of teeth, she would take that over being victim to those dark snakes in the darkness.

When over an hour had passed, Layla opened her eyes. She wouldn't be sleeping tonight, knowing her mother's killer was sitting below her. She could see the dark smoke snaking through the forest.

"They don't stop, do they?" She heard his voice, soft but loud enough to reach her from her space in the tree. He must have heard Layla moving, repositioning herself between the branches. She sighed heavily, trying to ignore him; she wouldn't dare answer him.

"I can't believe you've lived here as long as you have. It doesn't feel like a place you can survive...unless you're strong. You seem like the strong type."

She tried closing her eyes, tried desperately to fall asleep and forget about where they were for just one moment, but he would never let her do that. Someone like Killian couldn't let go.

"I know you're awake, it's stupid of you to think I don't know that."

"I'm not stupid," she snapped.

"Oh! She speaks! I knew you could."

"Keep quiet, they're going to hear you." Layla ran her hands through her hair, pulling on the strands and wincing as she plucked a few from her scalp.

"Do they?" he asked.

"Do they what?"

"Do you think they hear us?"

She was tempted not to answer, but basic human decency won out.

"I don't know," she answered honestly. "They don't answer you, they don't have any sort of response to anything you say. I think they're just drawn to death, but sometimes I think they do. Maybe they just don't want us to know that they are listening."

He was silent for a few moments. She wasn't sure he was going to say anything more.

"Layla, do you miss being alive?"

It wasn't a question she wanted to answer. She thought about it far more often than a dead person should. She couldn't find the words, because the feelings that were there were so complicated. Because she didn't miss being alive, she didn't miss a damn thing about the world above ground. But she did miss the feeling of breathing in the salty sea air in California. She missed the feeling of driving on the roads, and of swimming in chlorine pools. But she couldn't tell Killian that. None of her good memories, none of the things she missed on Earth had anything to do with her father or her dead mother. None of those things were what Killian deserved to hear. And so she said the one thing she could think of that was anything but those things.

"So, why can't you climb trees?"

5

Killian couldn't climb trees because he'd fallen out of one as a child. It wasn't very high, but falling face first out of a tree, chin striking the flagstone at just the right angle, and getting six stitches would do that to you. It wasn't a story that Layla prompted, but it was a story he shared anyway. It must have been the darkness, the loneliness that convinced her to continue talking to him; it was nice, to have someone that responded to her. Of course, Killian was nothing like the presence of Bird. Hearing his voice, the way he laughed, even though it wasn't appropriate to, the forced confidence- it was different than Bird's comforting silence, but not worse. It felt like they had known each other for their entire lives. They refused to talk about her mother, instead talking about lighter things. Where he grew up, where she went to school, the first girl he kissed, the first boy she dumped. He was surprisingly easy to talk to, and when they both drifted off to sleep, now unafraid of the darkness around them, Layla felt like he was almost human.

When the sun started flickering through the trees and the

sea above, Layla frowned and dropped from the tree, landing roughly on her feet. The impact wouldn't usually affect her, but her close proximity to Killian seemed to change a fundamental part of this world. There was pain shooting from the bottom of her foot up her spine. She was rigid in hurt for just a moment until the vibrations left her, and she looked behind her. There was no stirring from her trunk, and so she assumed Killian might have still been sleeping. She plucked a shard of bone from the ground and walked towards the tree, hovering until she saw the faint rise and fall of his chest. Layla got as close as she could, careful to tread lightly on the filthy ground. As she neared him, she raised her bone high above her head. Layla's arms wobbled, but she knew they would not fail her. She was not prepared to feel friendship and camaraderie with this man sleeping before her. She didn't want to see him as human, because if she did, she might forgive him for what he did to her mother. Killian had killed far more than the one person she would never forgive him for, he killed daughters and mothers of others, too many to count.

He couldn't take responsibility. The longer he kept blaming his dirty hands on the make-believe person in his head, the easier it would be for him to forgive himself. Layla couldn't let that happen. She sent out a silent prayer to whatever was listening- not like anything ever was- and brought her sharp bone shard down, hitting the middle of his chest.

His eyes opened in surprise, the corners crinkling in agony as the bone penetrated deeper and deeper into his chest cavity. She should have been more strategic in her placement of the bone, but Layla staggered backward as yellow puss protruded from the wound. He wheezed, coughing and spitting and... dying, she realized. It was what she wanted, what she needed. Watching Killian die was everything she needed. His body jerked a few times, the source of the wound swelling around the bone. Layla scrambled backward, eyes narrowing in, watching his eyes roam wildly until they locked onto hers. And after what seemed like too long, when they stared at each other for what seemed like hours, his eyelids shut. She watched as he stopped breathing. Layla stood up and straightened out her back, sighing in relief. She didn't know why she needed him to lie there, dead. She didn't know what was inside of her that made her wish that this was it for him, the final death; but it felt good. It felt like a large weight was lifted off of her shoulders, and even if she didn't know why she needed that from him, seeing it was a breath of fresh air. She *needed* it.

And then his chest moved.

"Fuck you Killian!" she said, shaking her head. Layla laughed, watching the steady rise and fall of his chest. Because of course, he wouldn't die, there's no way that life would give her that much. If refused to even give her an inch.

"You fucking tried to kill me!" His voice was hoarse, but it was there. Layla heard him cough and sputter, and she kicked the floor in frustration.

"Killed. I did kill you!" She screamed at him. "Why didn't you just stay fucking dead?"

Killian laughed. It was nice to hear, even if it pissed her off. "I'm already dead," he scoffed, raising his arm to pull the bone out of his chest. "You thought you could kill someone who's already dead?" His laughing bordered on hysteria. "You really thought I wouldn't leave if I could?"

"Don't lie to me," Layla snapped. "You ran from them too."

"Too. See? You know, for someone who hates me so much, you keep forgetting that you ran from the Kharon too. I know I'm not perfect, Layla. I'm damaged, and I know you think I'm crazy, but there are deep sinister things following me in my head. Things I don't think anyone in the world would be able to understand. But you? You refuse to see yourself as you are.

You're just as selfish as I am. We're too selfish for death, Layla. I think we're the same."

She looked at him with raised eyebrows and a dumbfounded expression. Her breathing hitched and she felt herself swaying. Killian watched her curiously, before recognizing the panic that flooded her eyes in that doe-like expression.

"Okay, no, not the same I'm sorry," he said, raising his hands and approaching her as if he would a frightened animal. Layla backed away and turned her back on him. Her head looked in either direction, seeking something, anything. She needed Bird, and she hadn't seen them since yesterday. It was early and she needed to be at the lake before noon high, or else they'd go a full day without herbs again. A nervous twitch started in her left leg. She needed her tiny Kharon here.

"I don't murder people," She said instead, out of breath.

Kill tried to stand, moving his body not so gracefully out of the hole in the tree. He stepped towards her and Layla couldn't stand another moment of it. She sprinted through the trees, getting as far away from him as humanly possible, no step forward was too far away. They were not the same, because every time she looked at him the only thing she could recognize was the face of her dead mother. When she was as far as her legs would take her, the world seemed small but was endless in actuality; she leaned her back against one of the trees, hung her head in her hands, and started to cry.

He found her too easily, but maybe that was because she wasn't trying too hard to hide. She didn't even flinch away when he touched her. Killian kneeled, his hand resting on the bare of her shoulder. It did nothing to stop the shaking of her chest, and the heaving of her lungs. "I'm sorry," he said, rubbing a thumb over the one, "I was out of line."

"Yeah you were," she wheezed. Her breaths rushed in and out, closing in on hyperventilating.

"I'm not going to apologize for saying that we're..." Layla lifted her finger and pressed it to his mouth.

"Don't finish, Killian. I might try to kill you again."

"And, like me, seems like you need something to happen twice before it gets through your head. You can't kill me, Layla."

"Maybe not but I wish I could."

"I wish you could, too," Layla looked up at him, watching regret pass his features. She didn't want to feel sorry for him, but he had a way of creeping up on her that she couldn't quite explain. He was starting to feel like the center of this universe.

"Can I tell you about the way I died?" he asked suddenly. Layla blinked a few times, but she didn't answer him. Instead, she just stared, desperately trying to see past and into the murder, the man with his hand on her shoulder and the sadness in his eyes. "Well?" he pressed. She nodded, finally.

"I died because someone ran me over with a car." Killian started laughing. The sound rattled her insides.

"Excuse me?"

"Not what you expected to hear was it?" Layla looked up at him curiously. She hated herself for wanting to understand this man, she should have nothing to do with him. Instead, she blinked at him, urging him to go on despite what she should be wanting.

"They labeled it suicide, which is funny. I'd been telling her that I wanted to die for a while. She knew I wouldn't do it myself though, I was far too selfish for that. So no, instead I let her kill me. She of course made it the worst possible death I could experience..." Layla recoiled from his touch. She wasn't stupid, she had no intention of believing a single word that left his mouth.

"You don't believe me." He said. It was the way that he said it as if he was living in her mind with her. Layla shook her head.

"I can't." She whispered, voice hoarse from dryness in her throat that she couldn't get rid of.

"Why?" She could feel the anger rippling off of him in waves. They breathed in the same air, the tension wrapping around them like two coiled snakes, ready to lunge. She could see the soul inside of him and wondered if he saw the same. "You can believe this?" A gesture towards the teeth scattered around them, "And you can't believe me?"

"Why do you even care?" She spat back at him. "Do you think I want to be here? That I want to believe this? You want me to believe you? There. You're right, there was a crazy lady speaking to you, telling you to kill people. Happy now? How does that help anything?"

Killian rolled his eyes and took a step back. He shook his head, his messy locks falling over his eyes. He brought his hands to his face, picking at tiny flaking pieces of skin.

"She chose to kill me because I was going to turn myself in. After your mother died," his voice faltered, knowing he made a mistake in wording but pressing forwards anyway, "when I killed her, you were next. She told me you were. But then you died, and I didn't want to do it anymore. I went to your funeral you know."

Layla turned her head. She couldn't look at him any longer.

"Seeing you in the casket. Seeing the blue on your face, they didn't even try to hide it. Your lips were a pretty shade of aqua, matching the beds of your fingernails. I thought you killed yourself, and so, I would do the same. Of course, she wasn't pleased with that. I had given her what she needed, an outlet. Sometimes I believed that what we were doing was right. I couldn't even tell you why. She was always so convincing. Layla, you have no idea what it felt like to hold the knife in my hands. To be responsible for that. I wouldn't wish it on anyone." She knew. It must have felt the same as the bone she shoved into his chest.

"What was her name?"

"What?" he looked at her with a wild expression. His eyes were wide and his mouth was pulled into a frown at the corners.

Layla didn't remember when she turned to look at him again, although it must have been the same reason why the tears started falling again. There was so much pain laced in his voice, it was unmistakably similar to her own.

"What was her name?" She watched as he winced. Even though the gears were turning in his head, the amount of resentment tensing across his muscles told her he might have actually been telling her the truth. It was hard to shake the feeling.

"Lessa," He whispered. Layla didn't want to ask him anything else, the name was like fire on his lips. His tongue might burn from saying it again.

"Layla, we're here together. I think we're here for a reason. Not destiny," he added in response to her scrunched nose, "No, more like punishment. I do think our souls found each other. But I also think it was a planned encounter. Naturally, it was her that did it for me. What better way to torment me one last time than to let me see you? But you? I don't know what you did to deserve this sort of torment. I'm sorry for that. Truly."

He rocked back on both heels. This boy was just that, a lost, tired, scared boy. He was different than the person that found her yesterday.

"Why did you bring a bone to my neck yesterday?" she asked. Killian laughed.

"Why did you stab me in the chest this morning?"

"Fair enough," For once, Layla laughed back.

"Come on, get up, we gotta get the leaves and shit." Killian reached out his hand to her. The movement was inviting, but frightening. She knew the minute she took his offer, that was it. What kind of person befriended the person who killed their mother? It took her a second, a long minute of hesitation. Killian stayed still, careful not to make any sudden movements. He waited for her to make a choice. They both knew how important it was because it could change everything. What seemed like hours only had to have been forty-five seconds. She sucked in a large breath and reached out her hand to latch with his. You could tell he was holding in his own breath, Killian let it out in a slow, quiet rush of wind.

He pulled her up and they let go quickly. Though the step was enough to let loose the harsh grip of hatred around her heart, and regret woven through his brain, it was not enough to erase the history. But it was a step, and a step was a lot further than she'd been yesterday. There was less of a heavy burden on her soul, and that was enough for now.

"Herbs, we need herbs," S\she said. He nodded. They could both feel the exhaustion rolling through them, even after a few hours of sleep. No amount was enough to live in this world.

The sun was rising, she could feel the heat through the trees. And the longer they stayed hidden, the more she longed to see the ocean above them. It was the view that kept her grounded. She started walking in the direction she learned so well in the last few months, Killian following her silently. Layla missed Bird. It was odd for them to be gone for so long. She found herself looking through the trunks, trying hard to listen. Would she be able to identify the silent sounds they made? Could she recognize the cloak she'd come to know?

"Have you seen Bird?" She asked him. Layla refused to look back, it seemed that if she did, she'd give him an opening to talk with her. She didn't want that, not really. They would never be friends, even if she was finding the road to forgiveness.

"The Kharon?" he asked. She could hear his silent, steady footsteps behind her. "No, not since last night. Why do you care? It's probably for the best. It would turn us in eventually."

Layla huffed and rolled her eyes. "Bird wouldn't do that. We've had...an arrangement for the last month." Before you showed up, she thought. The common thread was Killian, as it always would be, now. But Bird had given him herbs; it was the only reason Killian was still here. Layla would have found a way to lose him if Bird didn't trust them.

"Your attachment to that Kharon is not smart."

She whirled on him, hissing. "Neither was your attachment to your demon, Killian." Layla spat his name as hard as she could, putting the full force of the insult into it. She couldn't tell if it affected him or not. Layla was starting to panic the more they talked about her missing Kharon. She wouldn't be able to live in this world without the comfort of her bird-faced friend. They were the only reason she got away safely. And now she was just going to let their disappearance go unnoticed.

"We have to go find them. We have to."

"We need the fuel if we're going to do anything," he replied, a twinge of frustration seeping into his tone. Layla grunted and turned back around to walk towards the lake again.

"You wouldn't even have fuel if not for Bird." She reminded him, though not unkindly.

"I don't know its motives." She ignored him and continued along the path. They walked together in silence, coming up upon the lake. He must have been uncomfortable in the silence, she felt him behind her shoulder once more. Instead of wincing or flinching, however, she stayed strong in her course.

"It means that much to you?" He sounded irritated, but at

least he was finally listening. She could feel the cool breath on her neck. Layla nodded helplessly, unable to hide the panic now that he'd come this close. Killian brought his hands up to his face and sighed into it.

"Okay, we'll go find it...them." She was still apprehensive and Layla would feel better if Bird was there with them. Truthfully, she also didn't want to be alone. Killian would have to do, and now knowing they couldn't just...murder each other helped. She didn't want to be near him, and Layla didn't trust the man as far as she could throw him. Their moment had been just that, a moment. Even as she felt sympathy finding a place settle near her heart, she ignored it as best as she could. He killed someone she loved, that's the only thing she should be remembering. Not the softness, not the pain.

"You know Layla, I did some fucked up things in my life. Like your mother," he had the audacity to look at her with pain in his eyes. "A lot of it was my fault, I will never forgive what I've done...what these hands have done." Layla closed her eyes again, she didn't want to think about her mother anymore. She was so goddamn tired of being angry all the time.

"Please don't, Kill," She whispered.

"Don't call me that," Killian growled. The heat was coming back into his voice and it surprised her. The kind boy she spoke with was gone again, instead the killer, the murderer, returned. "That person is the one that used a knife to cut the throats of too many women. And I didn't like it, you hear me? I didn't like it!" He yowled it into the trees. It was weird seeing Lessa come to life in him. Even when she was no longer here, she was everywhere. She had done irreparable damage to this boy, and he was broken.

They had reached the end of the tree line, staring into the lake once more. She'd lost track of time, lost her sense of direction. Layla forgot the Kharon would be there, right on time, she turned to shush him, but the rage was leaving his body again. His eyes widened and Killian went rigid. The heads of the Kharon she'd seen every day since dying turned to face them. She stared deep into the sockets of their skulls, and real fear rumbled inside of her. They were quiet for a while, and when the Kharon finally turned their heads around to head to the lake, Layla looked at Killian expectantly. She didn't want an apology, not for this anyway.

"We need to follow them," Layla whispered. He looked at her crazed.

"You must not be talking to me," He said, incredulously. "Towards the demon crows? Yeah, I don't think so."

"You owe me, Kill," She said solemnly. There was only one time she might have been able to use it, and for it to work. Killian didn't understand, she needed Bird. The tentative truce between them was in shambles at best. He shouldn't listen to her, he should be running in the other direction.

The shambles must have been enough, because he dipped his head and placed both hands on his knees, fighting the urge to throw up.

"Okay," he said at last. The words were rushed like he had to get them out before he changed his mind. "Okay, let's go."

5.5

Laylita's mother loved it when she cried. Even if her face swelled up the size of a balloon and flooded with large red blotchy spots, she always made sure she was there when the tears started to form. She said it was because Laylita's eyes were the brightest when there were tears in them. Small, grass-green bulbs turned into large emerald jewels. It wasn't because she was much of a caring caretaker, more like she enjoyed the personified sadness. When the water welled, Laylita's first instinct was to run to the person who birthed her, but not for obvious reasons. She was the only one who cared when Laylita cried, but it wasn't even to console her.

Her head ached from a migraine and her body ached from the cold wind whipping around her jacket. Despite the school she'd gone to and the church they came from, despite what people thought of them, they weren't the richest family on the block. Her jacket was big and puffy, but it was also from the discounted section at the local Goodwill. Father made money from the church, but he never spent it on them. The wind penetrated through the material and touched her skin, turning it ice hard and fragile to the touch. Most of all, her heart ached for her mother. The fear that spread through her as they left the department store to see the sun already dipping below the horizon was evident on her face.

Nyctophobia, that's what her father told her. A very intense, irrational fear of the dark. It was a slow process, not something Laylita noticed happening overnight. At one point she would ask to race her to the car when they left with bags of groceries in the evening. Another day, when Laylita was old enough to drive, she started paying her to run her errands instead. After a while, Laylita couldn't remember when her mother left the house at all after 2:00 pm.

She'd tried a few times to coax her into it. She was a dancer for crying out loud. Her ballet studio was only a few blocks from the house, and her recitals were at night. She couldn't just stop living her life because of some fear of the dark. And yet, she did. Life changed for everyone when the paranoia took hold of her.

They'd been standing at the entrance to the department store for twenty minutes now. The longer they stood there the faster night surrounded them. It would have been different had she trusted Laylita to run to the car herself, start it up, get warm and roll around the lot to get her. She could see it now, the bright orange rust sitting alone in its spot. The parking lot emptied the longer they stayed, and soon the white snow flurries started falling from the sky.

Laylita didn't want to wait another hour to make it fifty feet from the door to their car. She wanted to be in her bed with thick socks and three dozen blankets to cover her, now.

"Mom c'mon, let's go. Nothing's out there, and it's just you and me," she didn't say anything, instead, her eyes looked back and forth to either side of the lot. It was as if she was looking for something, looking at something. Her breathing came out ragged, and Laylita could tell it wasn't exactly from the cold. Laylita took her hand and placed it on her mom's shoulder. Still no movement.

"Mom?" She asked again. Patience was wearing thin, but she had to remember what the therapist told her; gentle voices, and light touches. No sharp movements or tense accusations. That would just make her spiral, and the last thing they wanted was for her to spiral.

"Just...just," Her mom's lips quivered slightly, a mixture of the chill and the fear. "Just give me a minute."

"Mom," Laylita said it more firmly, tightening her grip on her arm. She could feel her mother tense under her. But it was so goddamn cold outside that she didn't care. She couldn't wait to move to California, where it was warmer and the sun dipped later.

"Mom. It's right there. We can see it. People are leaving. We're safe while people are still in the parking lot."

Her eyes glazed over and she could feel the panic settling in. They were further away from the car than they had been ten minutes ago. Laylita could feel the nip of the cold bite her open skin. The snow was no longer flurries, but thick white snowflakes. If they didn't want to freeze to death she needed to get them to the car, now. She moved her hand from her shoulder and instead turned her mother to face her. It was surprisingly easy to move her, despite how rigid she was.

"Mom, I'm going now. I'll bring it up and we'll be okay. We'll be home before you know it."

"NO!" Her mom screeched suddenly. The sudden movement

frightened Laylita. She wobbled on the soles of her feet before having to take a second or two to right herself again.

"They're out there," she whispered, "Waiting by the sidelines. They'll catch you if you go. We're not safe from the devil here." The shivers moved through her body. Laylita felt a tug on her heart- but it wasn't the urge to comfort.

"I'm going, I'll be right back I promise."

Laylita started to walk away. She got one step before her mother's fingers dug into the soft skin on her arm. Pain rushed through her, but it was only temporary. In fact, it was a relief as her nails drew blood. Her head snapped backward.

"But mom!" Laylita cried, her voice loud enough to attract the attention of passersby. A few heads turned, but none paid them any mind. Even if they had, her mother wouldn't pay attention to them, she never did when she was in one of these moods.

"My little raccoon," her mother cooed instead, lifting her hand to her cheek. Laylita didn't notice but her eyes were leaking again. The wetness froze as they fell onto her cheeks. She could feel the red creep up her face. "Your eyes are so pretty when you cry." She tried yanking her arm away but the grip was too tight.

"You don't understand you don't understand you don't understand," her mother kept repeating over and over again. "There are so many bad people out this in this world." Laylita had no idea what she was talking about. Her mother had officially stepped over the line, she was too far gone and Laylita didn't know what to do.

"Laylita, my little raccoon, my little girl, my little Sinner. It's like I knew what was coming for you in the end." Her blood froze as the words crawled through her ears. This was not the person that birthed her. This was no sick person. This was someone possessed by the devil.

"You're so special, Layla," she'd never been called Layla in her life. Laylita. That was her name, that was what her mother called her when she wanted a favor, it was what her friends called her

when they wanted her to hang out. It was what her father called her when he...

"Your life will not be easy. But mine will end soon. It's them, out there," One of her hands left to point out into Laylita's peripherals. "You're special to them, Layla I don't know why. But you are."

Laylita closed her eyes and willed the tears to stop. She had to remind herself to breathe in and out. Her mother was having an episode. That was all. There were no demons dancing in the dark, nobody coming to grab them. It was the fear and the paranoia. It was the visions that she could see, a sticky glaze to her eyes that Laylita couldn't shake from her.

She tore her arms away from her mother and ran towards the parking lot. She expected her mom to follow her, but she didn't turn to look. When Laylita made it to the car she was out of breath. At least the blood was pumping through her veins again. She could feel the sting from where her mother's nails dug into her, but the pain was nothing compared to the relief she felt being at the driver's door.

She dug into her pocket to retrieve her key fob and popped the door. When she finally turned on the car, cranked the heat, and leaned back into the chair, Laylita could have started crying again. She sat there for a moment, before looking back out towards the department store.

Her mother was still standing there, unaffected by the white snow that now caked the sidewalks. Laylita let out a big sigh, pulled the stick into reverse, and pulled out. It was a long, slow crawl to the front of the store. Laylita was scared to get her mom, she didn't want to drive back with her, and that was not a feeling she liked having in her body. Another quick shake released the rest of her pent-up energy, and her mom opened the passenger door.

The haziness in her eyes was now gone, replaced by the familiar warmth she was used to. This was the mother she remembered.

"Thanks, Laylita," she smiled. As if nothing had happened. As if

they didn't just stand 30 minutes in the cold. It was like her mother didn't remember the events that just occurred.

"No problem," she whispered, desperate to escape the now desolate parking lot. They sat in silence for most of the drive. Laylita grabbed at her forearms every other minute, scratching at the marks on her skin. She could have sworn she saw her mother glancing at them as she drove, too.

"I know you don't understand it, Laylita." She started. Laylita harrumphed, "But this disease, it strikes at the oddest times. I can't control myself when it happens. The doctor says-"

"Yes mom, I know," she tried to feel sympathy, but came up short, "Dad and I need to learn to be patient with you." She watched as her mom flinched at the mention of her father. It made her uncomfortable too.

"I don't want you to just be patient with me. I need you to understand me."

"That's unlikely. At least right now. I'm trying mom, I really am," her face turned downward into a frown.

"I know. This is as bad for me as it is for you. It's ruining my dancing career. Half the time, I don't even remember what I said."

Laylita tried to focus on the road in front of her. They were so close to being home.

"I know more than you think I do," she said suddenly. "I know how you call me Lorena to your friends, I know you avoid the house if it's possible for you. I know you're trying hard but sometimes it doesn't feel like it's enough." Laylita didn't want to speak. If there was anything worse than Nyctophobia, it was this. Where Lorena tried to pretend she was the mom of the year.

They rode up their small driveway, and Laylita put the car in park once they were safely inside the garage. Her mother wouldn't dream of getting out of her car if they were still out in the dark.

When she opened the door, sudden movement flashed in front of her. Her mother had grabbed for her arm again.

"I know what he does. And he will pay," S\she said in a hushed voice. "No matter what happens out there," her mother's head flicked behind them towards the darkness outside her house. "You're strong. You will make it out of here, of this world, and in any other."

"Okay, mom." Laylita just wanted to leave. She wanted to be under those covers and away from this entire experience. She didn't even want to take the time to try to understand what it was she was saying.

"You're my little Sinner, Layla. Don't you forget that," Laylita didn't turn to look at her, she tore her arm from her grasp, gasping as she slammed the door and sprinted inside. Her mother stayed sitting in the car a moment longer. She slid into her room, away from her father's grasp and her mother's harsh touches. Laylita could hear her enter the house from the garage and walk down the hall. She prayed she wouldn't come to find her.

Despite the moment of weakness, the moment of paranoia, the moment of chaos, Laylita felt herself straighten a little more as she remembered her mother's words. Maybe she was right. There were few things she wanted in this world as badly as she wanted her mom to be proud of her, to know that she was strong and that she could make it through whatever was coming her way.

Maybe she wasn't Laylita after all. She was far more than that. Her father the pastor, who "embodied all of the goodness in the world"...there was no way she wanted to be anything like him. So maybe she was a sinner after all. Maybe she was sin itself.

6

Layla couldn't do this anymore. She didn't want to be here, especially when she was so conflicted about Killian; the last thing she expected to feel was pity for him. Layla watched as he bent over a fallen branch between the trees, grabbing for a bone on the ground and twirling it between his fingers. It was something to do with his hands as they decided what they needed to do. It was difficult not to look at it as it twirled between his smooth hands, and she imagined him spinning a knife in them instead. She watched as it spun, the silver light bouncing off the tree trunks. Layla blinked once and gasped when she opened them again. The knife was red, dripping with sticky red honey. Below him was a pool of blood- her mother's she imagined- and she felt like she would drown in it if she looked at it hard enough. Kill glanced at her and she could have sworn that he was smiling. A cruel and wicked gleam in his eyes, the same that murdered her mother in the parking lot of her own dance studio only blocks away from her house.

Layla had to stifle a scream before she fell over.

"Whoa there!" She heard Killian yell, dropping the bone and rushing to her side. His eyes held so much worry as he reached out to caress her face. Layla's eyes snapped back open at the touch and she shot backward. Her hands cut from splintered fragments as she scooted across the floor and she looked frantically from side to side, trying to find a weapon to use against him if she needed to. Her own blood coated the dirty bones beneath her.

"Don't fucking touch me," she wheezed, out of breath. The worry on his face disappeared, replaced by a steely hardness. He held up his hands and took two very distinct, large steps backward.

"I'm not going to hurt you," He said again. He could say that every chance he got, and she would never fully believe him. Layla wasn't sure she ever could. Even so, the way the words left him and hung in the air struck a pang of sadness in her. She had to do what she could to rid herself of that feeling once and for all. There was no room for pity in her heart, no matter what her feelings tried to tell her otherwise.

She ignored him as she stood, wiping her hands against her legs.

"Sorry," She said gruffly, her sanity returning to her. She watched as Kill shook his head, disbelief caking his expression.

"No need," His voice was deep and velvety. Had he not been her mother's demise she could have thought him to be handsome. His hair was pulled back into a tightly woven knot, and the dirt that covered his face emphasized his rugged charm. "I deserved it."

She could feel her mouth turning up in a smirk. "Yeah, you did." Fuck her and her pity, and her morbid desire to get to know this person. He was nothing like she thought he would be. Why couldn't he just be the monster that she envisioned in her head for so long?

They continued walking along the line of trees in the forest of teeth, no longer speaking, but both highly aware of the other. Every move he made sent signals to her senses. He was within her orbit and she couldn't help but gravitate toward him. She wanted to tell him to stop following her. Layla had made it this far on her own, she could handle herself and Killian should have been able to do so on his own too. But she had told him to come with, had told him he owed her. They circled the lake a few times, keeping an eye on the Kharon, waiting for them to make their trek across the lake to welcome home new souls.

It was long, tiresome, and tedious, but there was nothing else they could do. A pit of frustration made her stomach queasy. Despite what he had told her, despite her feeling... sorry for him, instead of the rage that boiled in her belly for the last year, she wanted to comfort him instead. Who the hell was she anymore? She couldn't afford someone here to make her death any more complicated than it was. Layla turned around to tell him exactly where she wished he would go, only to come face to face with him. Kill had maneuvered through the undergrowth until he was mere inches from her face. She could feel his breath against her mouth, his breathing even and warm.

"Why do you come this way every day?" He asked her quietly. There was this charged energy in the air around them not exactly sexual tension, but more likely the lingering desire to kill one another.

She didn't have to tell him anything. She didn't need to explain to him why she was doing what she was doing...what was she doing? Layla wasn't sure herself. She'd come this way every day since she escaped the Kharon. And circling the lake was the only way to clear her head. It was much better than sitting there, waiting. Anything was better than waiting. Bird led her through this forest once, and it was the only comfort she had, but there wasn't a particular reason why she came to the island every day. If only Bird was there now to help her rid herself of him, too. Why hadn't they been there when they woke? Layla came to expect their presence, it strengthened her. Not having them was jarring, especially after waking up instead to the stressful energy that Killian radiated.

"I need the herbs," She whispered, he was close enough to her that he could hear every word no matter the level of her voice. They stopped halfway through their third circle. She could see the place they started from here. He knew the answers to his questions but he asked her anyway.

"Do you?" Killian mused, his hand came up and grazed her collarbone, across her neck. It seemed less like a sexual caress than it did a threat. Layla couldn't help but shiver.

"Yes, they give me- us- the energy. Haven't you felt the difference since Bird gave them to you?"

"Yes, your...Kharon, or whatever it is you call its flowers made me feel something. But why do we need it, anyway?"

"I think it's like hunger, our bodies need it to survive here. You felt it, you were the one that told us to come here,"

"What would happen if we didn't have it, though?"

Another cold shiver ran up her spine. She remembered what it felt like that first day when she felt like she wanted to do nothing but sleep for an eternity. This was far better than that feeling.

"I don't know. Eternal exhaustion, I guess. But it didn't last long. I found it quickly when I got here," What he didn't have to know was that it was Bird that kept her from fading away; Killian didn't need to know the extent of their relationship, Bird didn't seem to like him that much.

"Okay but let's say that you didn't meet the thing."

"Bird."

"Whatever. Let's say you never met Bird. And you would

have what? Starved yourself?" She never thought about it. Maybe she might have, curled up into a ball and stayed that way until she couldn't any longer. But Layla was strong and surprisingly self-reliant. She might have found a way to survive here without Bird's help, anyway. Killian continued to look at her with a deadly stare. She kept forgetting that he couldn't kill her here- he'd already tried once and failed. Even still she couldn't stop the fear that flooded through her. It was a weird thing, to feel again. She could only catch glimpses of it, and they weren't very pleasant feelings. Kill was the one that brought them out, and she hated him for it. Why was everything about their encounter so unlike what seemed to be normal here? Everything about this was abnormal, and yet, Layla kept finding ways to confuse even this new world she didn't fully understand.

He didn't wait for an answer. "I don't understand why you think that thing is your friend. What if you're not supposed to stay here, Lorena? You're supposed to move on to a better place, or whatever it is. You are not supposed to be here. And that, that, that thing keeps trying to keep you here. I don't understand why!"

"Lorena is my mother." She said quietly. It was the first time he'd mixed up their names since meeting her. During their first encounter, it seemed like Killian tried very hard to not call her Lorena. The mistake made red creep up his cheeks and left him speechless. Kill stuttered before finally throwing his hands up into the air and stalking back towards the opposite direction of where they came. Layla watched him carefully, he seemed more boy than man, certainly not the person capable of the heinous crimes he'd committed in his life. In fact, she almost wanted to laugh at them, had she not been furious for even daring to challenge her choice in trusting Bird.

And then they heard the scream. It was petrifying, shaking

the trees to their roots. Layla and Killian both stilled, heads turning towards the direction where the lake rested in the middle of the clearing. The sound could only be Bird. She didn't know how she knew, but she did.

That was the fastest she'd ever run in her life. Layla could hear Killian fall in behind her, and soon his stride matched hers. They didn't have that much room between the trees to run and her bare feet made her stumble a few times, but Kill was there to right her with an outstretched arm. When they reached the place closest to the Kharon, Killian grabbed her arm before they broke through the forest. They skidded to a quick stop, surprisingly silent even as their breaths heaved in and out. Layla fought the urge to slap his hand away as the scene of horror opened up before them.

Bird was there in the center of the clearing, right along the shoreline she had picked for herbs just a day before. Surrounding them were three large Kharon. How had she missed them? She'd been too preoccupied with Killian, she should have been looking for her friend. If they hadn't all looked so similar to one another, Layla would have thought they were the same ones that almost caught her that day two months ago. The reminder had her clutching at her chest, the panic pounding beneath her ribcage. She never had this kind of reaction to them. But with Bird gone, with them at the mercy of those three...it was too much to bear.

"Shh shh shh," Killian whispered in her ear. They needed to stay quiet if they wanted to stay hidden. Layla was dry heaving, she kneeled over and dipped her face into her knees.

"Do you hear that?"

She couldn't hear a thing besides the ache that rattled through her. The world was silent around them, but Layla made a point to nod and listen with intention. Their energy was chaos, and it was hard to notice anything besides that, but she tried. Her eyes stayed trained on Bird, her heart tearing at the seams. This was why Bird didn't come find her when they usually did. How long had they been here, suffering, while she was spending her time with Killian instead? Another surge of bile filled her throat and the palm of her hand hit the center of his chest hard, sending him back a few steps.

"What the fuck?" He growled, rubbing the spot where his chest was. He didn't sound in pain, but he was frustrated and the anger came off of him in waves.

"Or what, you're going to kill me?" Her sour voice was cruel, but Layla was lashing out, and the closest target was Killian. Not like he didn't deserve it.

"I should just let it die." He hissed. The humor, the sadness, and the pain that covered his face once before were gone. Killian had either given up on her or given up on himself, she could see the shift in his demeanor. It was better this way, Layla was never meant to befriend the person who killed her mom.

"Maybe you should let us both die. Go on, you already took away the one thing that mattered most to me in my life." Something flashed in his eyes but she didn't want to see it. If he was done with her, she was done with him, too.

"I thought we had an understanding," she recognized his reluctance to say it even as it came out of his mouth. Of course, she didn't understand it. Even still, the hurt slapped her in the face. She didn't want to understand, she didn't want to forgive him, but she could see the terrors that haunted him. To have been in his shoes when she was living, to have lived those horrors herself. It was near as bad as the life she lived as well. She wanted so badly to feel a sense of understanding for this man in front of her that went through so much and made the decisions he felt he had to make. Would Layla have done the same?

"I could never understand the monster in you, Kill. Just go, I made a mistake asking you to come with," she said, a sense of finality in her tone. Even as her breath hitched, Layla felt relief run through her too. It was an awful feeling, one she wanted to shove back down and never let come up again. Those days when she wished she could feel again. She was a masochist. There was no reason she should ever want to feel these things again.

Killian didn't say anything, though it seemed like he wanted to. Instead, he nodded once, curtly- reminding her so much of the deathly silence her father had when dealing with her Nyctophobic mother. She watched with disinterest and he turned around and started walking away.

7

Layla felt like she had made a mistake. In watching Kill go, she found that there was a part of her going along with him. She felt wrong, she felt pained, she felt guilty. But the further he walked away, the more those feelings left her too. And it was soon that Layla was back to where she started, where she couldn't feel anything at all anymore.

She should have felt relieved. The ache in her chest was gone, replaced by her growing concern for her Kharon friend. How could she have neglected what they came here to do, to begin with? With Kill now gone into the depths of the trees, her attention turned back to the clearing. Where it seemed like it had been hours they were standing there, only minutes might have passed. Bird was still standing there, the other Kharon looming over them threateningly.

They were saying something to Bird, but from this distance, Layla couldn't hear it, or they didn't want her to. She still had no idea how speech worked for them here in the in-between. She would have to go in, there was no other choice.

Bird had been there for her when she needed it the most, and as selfish as she was, Layla could not abandon them in return.

She ran out from the trees, careful to stay as low to the ground as she was able. Their backs were turned to her, so as long as she stayed silent she would be able to...what? Distract them, take Bird and run for the forest again? Layla sighed, this wasn't the death she had planned. Killian might have been right, not about Bird of course, but of the idea that maybe she should have let herself have that second death. The fight she put up the keep living this half-life was not worth the eternal existence without feeling and purpose

The closer she tiptoed to the Kharon the more she could hear what it was Killian was hearing back in the trees. They had the same raspy voice she remembered hearing two months before. Her veins pulsed beneath her skin, and as she inched closer the desire to run away became more and more prominent.

"You know our purpose quiet one," one of them hissed. The voice seemed old, wise, and frightening.

"Yes, and yet you disobeyed us!" another croaked.

"You know what we must do to those that break the code!" The last was high-pitched and eerier than the rest. Layla stopped, hesitant to take another step forward. She would be lying if she didn't acknowledge the curiosity that brimmed under all of that fear. The Kharon had such distinct voices, and it seemed easy for them to communicate at their will. It made Layla even more curious as to why Bird had chosen not to speak to her.

"I couldn't let her starve," a voice pleaded. Her breath caught in her throat. The voice was terribly familiar. She shook her head to break herself from the trance. It was just so nice to hear their voice after so long. Layla felt like a part of her had returned from a long journey.

"It is the natural way of things, quiet one. The girl is important to you, but you are important to this process. We cannot disrupt the natural order of things."

"But this one is special!"

"She might be," one of them agreed, "but you are not the one to facilitate it. Everyone thinks their kin is special." Kin? Layla couldn't understand what they were saying, or what it all meant.

"She is not my kin any longer," Bird said helplessly. In a moment, Layla's heart broke. It didn't matter what they meant, hearing them disown her like she was nothing, like she meant nothing...It killed her.

"Fitting though, your end in the land of the living and your end here. Your life will be taken involuntarily, you know the rules for your indiscretions."

"And where would I go?"

"To where the other lost Kharon go." Layla could feel the tension in the air. Wherever it was, it would not be a peaceful place.

There were no other words spoken, what left could be said? Layla heard something sharp slice clean through the air. The swish sound was loud, then it was gone. There was no blood, no evidence of their murder, but Layla could feel it in her soul. It hurt worse than not feeling anything at all. There was a gaping hole in her chest, and she knew Bird was gone. Not for the night, not for the meantime, Bird was gone from her life forever.

She staggered backward, her foot catching on bone and causing her to fall on her back. All three of the Kharon turned their heads, their beaks snapping shut and piercing gazes on her. She didn't have the time to be frightened by the hollows of their sockets, Layla was far more concerned with watching Bird's body fall to the ground, lifeless before her. Her gasp was audible, and time seemed to stop for a moment. She watched as the body disappeared into thin air until there was nothing remaining of the friend that she'd grown to love so much.

"She knows too much," one of them hissed.

"You monsters, you killed them!" she screamed, scooting backward, unable to find the strength to get up and run. Without herbs this morning, the exhaustion was catching up to her quickly.

"If its mother would have just let her go, we wouldn't be in this mess!" The sounds that they emitted were like tiny snakes, the voices slithering and wrapping around Layla, suffocating her. The pieces started to fall together, the hushed whispers, the gentle camaraderie. Even the way Bird always took care of her. Bird was her mother. Killian killed Bird. Killian killed her mother.

"We know what we have to do now," one stepped forward, taking out its rotted hand and tipping her chin up with a long, fragile nail. "Tell me," it spoke freely to her now, more menacing as its voice turned a torturous shade of malice, "how is it you evaded us for so long?" Layla shivered beneath the touch but glared directly into its sockets. She only had a few seconds to run, she only needed to make it to the trees again.

Layla was tired of running. She was tired of living in fear of this place, tired of not knowing her purpose. She had guilt manifesting in her heart for Bird, a renewed hurt and anger manifesting for Killian. She just wanted to escape this world, and maybe this was the time to do it.

"Kill me," she spat, "You would be doing me a favor."

"Kill you? Sweet child, we cannot kill someone who is already dead. No, someone like you should have faced judgment when you passed. Now, because of your naivety and your selfishness, you will go to where the other lost souls go. It will not be pleasant, no, but you can forget the life you lived here.

You will hurt, but you will be new. It is likely you will remember nothing else."

Anything was better than it was here. Layla said a silent prayer to her future self. *I'm so sorry I'm doing this to you*, she sobbed internally. There was nothing else she could do, she couldn't stay here, couldn't live this very sad, lonely existence any longer. Anything was better than this, even pain. Layla closed her eyes, accepting her fate. She couldn't see it, but she could feel the moment when the Kharon lifted its arms when it stretched out its long sharp nails and readied itself to slice her throat.

And then nothing came.

Instead, Killian came barreling into her again, knocking her out of the way and awaiting the fate of the Kharon himself. She watched as the nails sliced through his stomach. Kill clutched at the wound, falling to his knees and gurgling the puss that ran up his throat.

"Kill!" She screamed. The Kharon let out a hiss of disapproval, and the other two snapped their fingers, disappearing into thin air. Layla narrowed her eyes in their direction before refocusing on Killian. He was in poor shape. His face was contorted in pain, and his hands were stained with his own fluid. She looked at him in shock, unable to make a move, afraid that if she did, he too would be gone forever. The moment was coming too soon, she could feel his presence leaving his body with each waking moment. The Kharon continued to stare at them, a certain gleam in their eye and an impatience in their posture.

"Go!" Kill found her eyes and begged her to leave. But where would she go? The Kharon followed her gaze, seeming to ask itself the same question.

"I can't leave you too," she cried, reaching out for him.

Killian coughed, spitting saliva. Her hand dropped back to her side, her panic rising once more.

"Layla you have to go. I'm so sorry about your mother. This is the only way I can prove that to you. Please!" Another cough made him weaker by the second. Layla spotted the boat nearing the river Styx. She could make it, she could get out of here okay. But she would have to leave Bird, and Kill.

"LAYLA!" Killian was desperate now, turning to face her with both desperation and frustration. How could she let his sacrifice go to waste?

"You will not leave this place girl." The Kharon warned. They dipped their face to come to eye level with Killian. "Your sacrifice was admirable, but you can not believe that we would just let her go, would you?"

Killian did something neither of them expected.

He removed his hand from his stomach and grabbed a tight hold onto its beak. The Kharon screeched and struggled, fighting to regain its control but Kill held on tightly, pulling with the very last of his strength. When he yowled in pain and cut the beak straight off from its mask, the creature made a noise Layla was sure she would never hear again. It was inhuman, not of this place.

She couldn't see what Killian saw, she was too far away from its face to finally see what was beneath the mask. The herbs from the beak scattered to the floor, and the Kharon bent down to retrieve them. Layla glimpsed only its mouth, which was as rotted as the rest of it. The wrinkly, paper-thin skin and its long tiny, sharp teeth that chattered as the air hit it. It croaked, and she noticed the hesitating waver they had in their step. The atmosphere was killing it. Without its herbs, this thing will not survive. Even the tendrils that surrounded it shivered in displeasure, disappearing from the sides of the

Kharon as it writhed in pain. She found grim satisfaction in that.

Layla only had a few moments, she scrambled up on her feet, using the last of her own strength, and hobbled to the boat. When she was in it, she could see Killian staring at her, a deep emotion flickering across his face, but she couldn't decipher it. Everything had happened far too fast.

"I'm sorry!" She sobbed, wanting so badly to take him with her, but knowing neither of them had the strength to do so. Killian dipped his head in understanding, watching as the Kharon took its last breaths of this world and collapsed onto the bones below it.

"Whatever you do Layla, don't look back. Leave this place and forget everything about it. LEAVE. Don't look back!"

"I promise," she said, knowing he couldn't hear her but feeling the finality of it settling in her chest. Layla climbed into the boat and pushed herself into the water. The souls lapped at her boat, reaching over the edge and rocking it as they tried to retrieve her. Layla closed her eyes and let the river take her, its magic dragging her along the stream. She had done it. No matter the turn of events, she would make it out of this place and into the next, whatever that meant for her.

She was far enough downstream when she opened her eyes again. Time worked weirdly in this place, taking long stretches of hours, or mere minutes. You never knew what you would find when you opened your eyes again. Layla panted, trying so hard to finally keep her promise to Killian, it was the least that she owed him, but that was not in her nature. Layla was a product of her upbringing, and while she might not have been deserving of the same fate as Killian, she was not the person that deserved Bird either. So she did the one thing that she said she would not do, she looked. The goodwill in her disappeared once more, leaving her with the same hollowness she felt in the land of the living, except this time, she understood the consequences.

Layla turned around only once, a mistake she knew would haunt her for the rest of her existence, wherever that may be. Killian kneeled beside the fallen Kharon, dooming himself to a fate worse than he deserved. She watched him die, she watched as the last breath crossed his lips and his eyes glazed over. A fitting end for a murderer, but not for the man who saved her life. The draw to him was gone, he was no longer the center. She settled onto the boat, rocking side to side, wiping at her face, and wondering what sort of person deserved the life she lived. The horrors she's faced. The hurt she caused, and the hurt she took in return. Did they ever make it out okay, did they ever find the peace they longed for, for so long?

Or did they all have the same fate as she?

PART SEVEN
BUTTERFLY WINGS

"We are effectively destroying ourselves by violence masquerading as love."

- Dave Laing

I

He loved bugs. Some people were fascinated by marine life, some by the domestic animals that we coerce into loving us. Norman was fascinated by insects.

"C'mere, you tiny thing," he whispered, reaching a delicate hand into the net he'd fastened to the side of a tree in the nearby woods, grasping for the flying creature inside of it. Norman smiled, his deep brown curls were pulled back into a tightly rolled bun and his skin was glistening from the sweat that beaded down his face. His skinny arms pulled out nothing but air. Norman touched his face with his empty hand, wiping away the dirt and grime from his cheek.

"Fuck you," he panted, his words sharp. His harsh tone sliced through the quiet serenity of the woods. His face no longer glistened from the sun, his curls looked messier than they did tidy, thrown back in haste. Oh, what a mere turn of phrase can do to omnipresent onlookers.

Norman shook his head and reached into the net again, leaning so far in that he might have crushed the thing. When his hand surfaced once more, his smile widened significantly. Within his grasp was a tiny butterfly, its golden wings struggling to move between his fingers. "You're not going anywhere," he said so sweet that it was almost menacing, taking a hold of each wing and stroking them gently. A branch snapped to his right, causing him to almost let go of the creature. Norman turned in the direction of the noise with his teeth bared; the chipped, yellow bones stunk of a day's worth of meals. With nothing significant catching his attention, he returned his gaze, looking at the butterfly with a wild expression.

His finger flicked the wing, watching it flutter hopelessly against his palm, and in one swift movement, his fingers grasped one side of the wing and tore it clean off its body. The creature didn't scream, it didn't make any sound at all. Norman continued stroking the detached wing, letting its velvet skin fill his body with endorphins. He let go, watching it flutter to the ground, and then he did the same to the other wing. The butterfly was long dead before he finished his careful dissection. He needed to be full, and one butterfly was not enough; especially one with dull paper wings, not interesting enough to take home with him. Disgruntled by the crash of his high, Norman turned away from his death net and walked down the path that led him here, heading deeper and deeper within the forest rather than escaping it.

His feet were bare and he wore very little clothing, save for a brown tunic that hung to his mid-thigh. Norman knew where he was going, each step tickling his soles as he passed through a particularly leafy undergrowth, heading toward a creek where he could hop from rock to rock. Each one was more slippery than the last, but he gripped each stone with agile toes. Norman looked down at the river, his expression vacant. There were no insects this close to the water, and he doubted he would find any more as he walked home. He wouldn't be surprised if they avoided him on purpose. It was a disappointment, although not uncommon for this season, either. Fall hung in the air and he could see every inhale and exhale of his breath. Norman was quite lucky with his catch today. His fingertips rubbed against one another as if he could still feel the soft, delicate wings between them.

The river was winding, but shallow enough that he could brave the coldness of it and walk through the water despite the season, stopping every few moments to skip a rock or take a long-deserved drink. It was only about half an hour or so before he came across his home, which to the wandering eye would look like nothing. Norman stared at the large cave-like entrance dug out into the hill saddling up close to the river. There was lush greenery hanging off the front and covering the entrance, but nothing else besides the rocks and the water surrounding it. It was his hole and his home. Eroded by years of water wear, it was tiny and at some points uncomfortable, but it was the best he could do. Norman looked from side to side, careful not to make a sound as he approached his domain.

He was not afraid of intruders. The people here would not come to his cave, not unless he wanted it, and Norman hadn't needed to bring someone here in a long time. In fact, since he'd discovered the versatile capabilities of his trap and the delicious side effects of his insect, he didn't seek out human companionship any longer. All he needed was his butterflies. Or moths, or beetles. He was content with all types of insects. Norman felt his way around the shrubbery, feeling for any sort of disturbance in the moss. He would need to retire soon or he would be forced to move around in the darkness, something he hadn't particularly liked. Norman wasn't afraid of the dark, but of the things that danced between the trees, that whispered in his ears, that nipped at his skin with sharp teeth. The forest was his until the night set, the darkness only came out to play at night. He wasn't afraid of the dark, but he was especially afraid of the things that woke up when the sun dipped below the horizon.

He was lucky he left the trap when he had, or he'd have been wandering the path alone with no light and only a vague recollection of the direction to his hole by the river. Norman parted the curtain and maneuvered inside. His cave was something of a work of art. Across the dirt walls, he positioned the carcasses of various flying creatures. Some were fresh as a blooming flower, others were dry and flaking off. He gazed upon his work, pride bursting from his chest. He created that. In front of him was a soft pile of fall leaves, meant to keep him comfortable as he slept. He had an empty container of water that he'd fill tomorrow from the river, and a small pile of other natural materials over at the other end. The only thing that was uncommon was a tiny camping lantern, and exactly 6 batteries lying on the ground, covered in dirt.

Norman picked up the lantern and flipped it over, flicking the switch to 'on' and releasing his breath as his small cavern lit up. The machine blinked several times before it illuminated the entire space. He let out another sigh of relief. His cave was safer this way, filled with that orange lantern glow. The tendrils outside couldn't get to him here, and so he sat down cross-legged and closed his eyes. He was aware of every sound and every movement that happened just outside his haven. The darkness was out in full force tonight, lapping at the edges of his light source, desperately waiting for its life to run out. Norman kept his lantern on all night, and he had only 6 more batteries left. It would last him another few days at most, and only if he kept them from the worst of the rain.

He reached over to the hill of twigs and branches, grabbing a pine cone he'd collected a few days prior. Although they weren't his favorite, he would have to get used to the rough texture as the forest eased into winter. Norman peeled a sharp thorn from its petal and lifted the pine cone to his mouth. He took a hesitant bite, wincing as the sharpness of the bark splintered against his tongue. The texture was rough and hard and it moved unpleasantly inside his mouth. Norman swallowed, resisting the urge to gag. For once, *she* was quiet in his head, the woman that never left. *She* dug a way into his brain when he had slept, and now there was where *she* stayed. Norman wiped his mouth and threw the pinecone against the side of the cave. He didn't think this was going to be so hard.

Norman created his life in the woods two months ago. His survival instincts were still new and untested, but they grew every day. Even though he had been forced to leave his home just several weeks prior, he knew he'd been different for far longer than that.

He pulled his knees close to his chest and wrapped his arms around himself, moving back and forth in a rocking motion that kept him awake. He hardly slept at all, but it was for the best. His family never believed him when he talked about the shadows. They took him to doctors and counselors, took him wherever they could just to get rid of him, even if it seemed like they knew something. So he banished himself to this place in the woods, no more than a twenty-minute walk from where he used to live. He couldn't live there any longer, couldn't be what he was and subject everyone else he knew to it. The darkness took him as its prisoner, and he needed to let them go before they were caught in it, too. Norman wasn't a bad person, he just did very bad things. He could never let them know that he was so close. Sometimes, when he was feeling lonely, Norman would walk toward the loud cars that echoed in the distance. It always seemed so peaceful out here in the woods, but in no time at all, you were met with blinding fluorescent street lamps and the comfort of a white picket-fenced, suburban home. They were two different worlds, separated by such a short distance.

He would stand, just mere yards away from his home of the past, and when he looked into the windows and saw the dark sadness in his mother's eyes, he would turn around and leave. The mother he looked for in the window could never know the extent of what he'd become. Norman shook violently, pinching the soft spot where his arm met his elbow to keep himself awake. As the hours dragged on, he shut his eyes only a few times. The overwhelming whispers woke up once more to play, dancing along the perimeters of his safety and threatening his resolve. As morning came crashing in and the last of his powered lantern flickered in its drained form, Norman let the tears come. They were wet and slimy, traveling along his face as though there was no other vessel for it to release from. His eyes were bloodshot, and not even sidelong glances to his winged collection could rest his weary soul.

2

"*Wake up,*" she spoke to him then, and his head flung back in shock. The voices were unrelenting, tugging from behind a wall in his brain. It hadn't always been like this. Once, Norman might have told you he could remember what it was like before he heard the whispers in his ears. Now, it was all-consuming, and he didn't know how to live without them. Norman had fallen asleep in the night, after all, his chest laid flat against the hard earth and legs pushed out towards the inner cave. He scrambled farther back into the hole, knowing that the darkness couldn't catch him here, not now in the sunlight. Timidly, Norman pushed off the ground, his muscles stiff from another night of little sleep and tense positioning.

"*What shall we kill today?*" She said, her voice smooth like milk chocolate. It dripped down his throat, a bubbled heat, and a new sensation of want. She was his muse, his desires, and his nightmares. Norman didn't know her name, or where she came from. All he knew was that he needed to keep her satiated. Mostly, she hungered for blood. Norman didn't want to love her, but the ache he felt for her never ceased to exist. She was some part of him, even if he hadn't had the pleasure of seeing her in the flesh. He wanted to love her in the way she needed, he just never imagined she would make him feel the things he hated to feel. God, she was the center of his universe

"I don't want to kill anymore," he whined, pushing himself up from the floor and through the brush entrance, making his way to the path along the riverbed that he became so used to. Norman could almost see his footprints sunken into the mud, that was how often his journeys on this path occurred. He could feel her trying to wrestle her way up to the forefront of his mind. Although he let her sit idly most days, he would rue the day she sought to overpower him completely. His mind was his own, but his resistance was weakening with each passing second. She was ready to pounce, like a jungle cat awaiting its prey. His words were meaningless as each foot was placed in front of the other. Norman took the path back to his trap, where he wished for a winged creature to have fallen prey.

She paced back and forth in his head impatiently. She had long lost the desire to watch him dissect his insects. She wished for larger prey, something with more insides to turn outwards. Norman resisted, fear bubbling inside him. He had done a lot of bad things, but he could never do *that* bad thing. He would flick his lantern on each night and keep his eyes wide open so long it hurt, if only to escape the torture of what those tendrils might make him do. She had control of his thoughts, but he didn't want to know what they could do with his body if they caught hold of him.

"*We are here to kill,*" she hissed, scratching his insides with her razor-sharp nails. "*I do not want tiny things. Give me a human, give me something worthy of killing. Bring me something,*"

She begged for it, knocking hard with everything she had along the insides of his head.

"My love," he whispered in return, just low enough that one might not be able to hear him. He looked back and forth, to the passerby it must have looked as if he was talking to himself. He was grateful that no one else ever walked this path. She quieted down, and Norman was aware of the time bomb that seemed to sit right behind his temples. He had no power over her, he could not placate her.

"*Think of all the good we can do Nor,*" she said sweetly, flashing him images of a body within his sight line, blood pooling around his toes. His body tensed at the imagery. No matter how disgusted by it he was, Norman could not deny the satisfaction that ran through him, the desire. He walked quicker to his trap. He tried to stay focused, concentrating on the velvet touch of moth wings. Norman thought about the tearing sound that filled him with so much gratification that he wanted to start sprinting towards it. He needed the life, the soul that sat inside that little body. He wanted to be the one that took it away.

"*That's better,*" she purred, caressing each devastating thought and spinning it round and round through his head. It was all he could think about. Norman moved blinded through the woods, losing control of his own vision. When he reached his trap, his heart fell to his stomach. The net had torn, its loose ends swinging in the breeze. He ran to it, feeling the rip and a primal growl came up through his core. It echoed in the distance. His prey gone, Norman looked frantically for another insect, something that would take the edge off of this terrible ache. They had all scurried away in the distance, hiding out from the cold that fell over them.

The sun was high in the sky but Norman felt as though the shadows were everywhere. She paced through his thoughts, scratching the inside wall of his mind until it was raw. This was not uncommon, but today her nails were sharper, her frustration raging louder.

"Why today?" He pleaded, grabbing hold of the trunk of a nearby tree and digging his hands deep into the bark. He could feel the sting in his fingertips and watched as his nail beds turned a ruby red. Norman pushed harder because no physical pain could compare to what *she* was doing inside his head. His blood ran down his hands, dripping onto the fall foliage and staining the earth red. "Why?" He roared. Norman could hear his voice echoing throughout the woods, hitting each tree with a force large enough to knock them over. Was it him or were the trees swaying?

"*Your rage is delicious,*" he could hear her inside his head, smacking her lips and tasting the anger that filled him to the top. Norman shook his head aggressively. "It's going to be today," she said, with an awful cackle that made his skin prickle. Norman couldn't ask it out loud again, because he knew she would never tell him. The woman, the jungle cat inside his head would never tell him why she chose him, or why the darkness wanted him. His path was set in motion, though. Even if he truly wanted to stop it there was no use, because he could feel his restraint weakening. They would have him soon.

Without saying anything, Norman tore his gaze away from the net and the tree and twisted his body to walk away. It was far too early to go back to his hole, the sun hadn't even passed midday yet, but Norman walked across the path once more. His steps were heavy on the ground, eyes scanning the periphery. He paid no attention to the riverbed. He paid no attention to the slippery rocks. Norman didn't pay attention to anything, save for the roughness of the ground on his bare feet. The undergrowth picked at his heels and he could feel the calluses harden to the touch.

When the branch snapped, Norman didn't look at it. The overwhelming thoughts in his head rid him of all sensibility. Norman always played it safe and looked both ways to keep himself protected. This time the woman won. If he hadn't heard the small gasp come from behind him, he might have ignored the noise completely.

"Nor?" A small murmur came from behind him. He knew the voice instantly, and he could hear himself screaming before it even left his mouth. She couldn't be here, he made sure she would never know he was out here.

"You have to leave, Sirce," he said urgently. He needed to get rid of her before *she* knew Sirce was here. *She* would make him do something he would regret, and if he was going to snap, he would never want that to hurt her. His sister. Norman could see the hurt in her eyes. She was still so young, only ten years old and she had no place being here. Sirce had big doe-like eyes that stared at him in horror, and he watched as she took him in from head to toe. It was different seeing her out here in the woods instead of through the window of their home. She looked just as sad, but more vulnerable here. These woods were a dangerous place for her.

"I don't want to leave," she demanded, her small voice strong, but wavering. It hurt Norman to hear it, but he scowled at her anyway.

"Sirce," he said, more urgently still. "You need to go. It's not safe for you here."

"Come home," she said, ignoring him. "Come home." Her foot stomped hard on the ground in defiance. Despite that, Norman saw the shivers run up her spine.

"I can't. Sirce I can't be there. I would hurt you and I could never do that. Don't you see?" His fingers rubbed together, and

Norman tried to remember the calm that he felt when stroking the butterfly wing.

"You wouldn't hurt me," she said confidently. She took a step towards him, and Norman took an equal step back. He didn't fall backward, but he did step on a branch, causing it to snap in half and stagger back another step or two. The crack hit the air like a stick of dynamite and he winced as he heard *her* awaken once more. He always thought of it as if she slept and woke, but it was more like she disappeared into the darkness. Norman wasn't entirely sure what was there inside his head, but when she left, she could be gone for minutes, hours, or days. Never for too long though, she always came back to him. *She* was here now, looking at Sirce with predatory eyes.

Norman waved his hands in front of Sirce, trying to direct his gaze from her to the ground. He could hear Sirce start to hyperventilate, and Norman needed to get away from her as soon as possible before she...

"*This is it,*" she said. Her voice was gentle but powerful. There was a sudden urge in him to take a step forwards, and despite his best intentions, he watched his foot follow her lead.

Sirce looked innocent there with her eyes wide and her hands shaking. A piece of paper he hadn't noticed she was holding fell to the ground. A doe in the headlights and much too far away from home.

"*Don't you love me? You can do it Norman. I believe in you,*" she whispered, eager to dirty their hands. Norman shook his head, but his feet betrayed him. Norman kept taking steps forward until he halved the distance between him and his sister. With all the restraint in the world, he stopped, hearing the hiss of his inner voice. Norman leaned over, putting his hands on his thighs and dipping his head. He could hear Sirce start crying.

"Leave," he panted, his head was between his knees, he leaned so far over he was afraid he might collapse.

"*Now! Do it Now!*" She screamed inside his head, grabbing hold of his hands and twisting them towards the knife he kept hidden in the folds of his underwear under his tunic. Sirce looked at him, shock in her expression.

"I won't hurt her!" he yowled, startling his sister. She took quick steps back, falling over on her butt and crying out in shock. Norman moved towards her inch by inch. His vision blurred and he could feel nothing but rage deep in his chest, he couldn't remember who it was he didn't want to hurt.

He couldn't see his sister anymore, just a vague shape that needed to be eliminated.

Norman ran down the river with the water splashing behind him. He stumbled a few steps and his knees scratched against the rocks below. She had grown quiet since he left. Norman knew he was going to be punished and even though it was quiet here in the woods, save for his heavy breathing and scurried footsteps, he prepared for it to be the calm before this storm. He couldn't kill Sirce, she was his sister. It wouldn't matter to *her* though, she was going to kill him. Would it be worth it? He wasn't even halfway to his home before the rain hit. Norman looked up, feeling the large drops of rain hit his face. It didn't stop his feet from moving, though. The cave came into view, and he ran towards it at a speed he couldn't ever remember hitting.

"*What do you think you're doing?*" She was back, and she hissed harshly in his ear. Norman whined, crawling through the brush and past the wall of butterfly wings when he reached his home. Not even those would help him now. He moved to the far back and grabbed hold of his knees, bringing them in as far as he could. He didn't know what he was going to do, because he couldn't escape her.

"I can't do it," Norman wailed, rocking against the hard rock walls. His eyes were shut so tight, but she surrounded him. He couldn't get away. Norman removed his arms from his knees and pressed them harshly against his ear. "I couldn't kill her."

"*But you must!*" she roared, rocking the inside of his head so hard that he was afraid it might explode from the pressure building up inside of him. He could feel her pushing him to return to where he'd left Sirce, all alone in the woods. She would be cold and wet from the rain, and he ached at the thought of his sister being unable to defend herself out here. But she was safer without him near, without *her* trying to make him harm his sister.

"I can't kill my sister!" Norman was weak. The woman pushed hard against his skull, rattling his insides, so hard that he couldn't help but sob. He had a brother, once; a mother, and a father at times too. He couldn't abandon his youngest sister.

"*It's too late, Nor, dearie,*" she cooed, "*It's okay. Let us take you. We'll take care of you.*"

"I'm a monster," He whispered. He could feel her nod. It wasn't menacing like he would have thought it would be. It was more understanding, sincere sympathy for the regret washing through him.

"*We're all monsters. But monsters have to protect one another, right?*" She almost sounded human. If he didn't know any better he would have believed her. Norman felt himself nod, though he wasn't sure if the movement was his will entirely. He cried against the darkness, feeling the tendrils of darkness nip at his heels. The flashlight was nowhere nearby, and even if it was, he wasn't sure he could find the strength to keep it going. He was too tired to continue on, to fight against what they were trying to make him. Darkness flew over the sky, but it was much too early for it to come. It was time, Norman thought. They were going to take him now.

The river swallowed the inside of his cave, creeping closer and closer to him until it washed away the batteries. Even if he could fight back, there was no way to shine a light against the darkness any longer. Norman felt himself give in. It might have been the dumbest thing he'd ever done, but he couldn't remember the last time he felt this free.

"*Go to sleep now, Norman*," she whispered against his ears. He was already almost there, but the permission to submit to what was before him was too tempting not to take. He sighed big and deep, drowning in the tears that smeared across his face. He was falling asleep, and he didn't know how to stop what was coming, because it wouldn't be good.

"Goodnight, Lessa," he sighed. He had never called her that before, never knew the name to place on the devilish voice in his head. But it came to him then, and the world finally made sense.

"*Goodnight, Norman,*" She said, cackling as he drifted off into oblivion. She didn't sound human anymore.

3

She woke up disoriented. It was worse in this body, this tiny human body that didn't know how to comprehend the darkness around them. She was sick of their glazed vision, and of the slow reflexes. She was sick of entertaining this weak human boy. Lessa lived in his head for too long, never strong enough to take hold until yesterday. She still felt weak, and as she lifted the white dangling arms before her, the same ones who had torn off butterfly wings for months, she scowled in disgust. At least he had a knife. That was more than enough to do what needed to be done.

Lessa moved away from the cave, turning to look back at it with disdain smothered across her features. She glided across the floor, her feet now dangling in the air as she moved through the boy's memories, landing on a house that frequented Norman's dreams. She didn't care for this house in particular, or the people inside of it, save for one she met long ago. It was the one he went to most often, and the one he dreamed about, and so, it was the one she would go to. Lessa was a creature from the underworld, a creature that craved death. Norman's mind was so malleable, so open for her to settle in. She remembered crawling through his ear canal as a dark, slithering tendril while he slept. She remembered his shock when he found her, hiding in the dark corners of his mind. He didn't try pushing her away. He craved attention, and so it was easy to make him believe that she loved him. Or that he loved her. She force-fed him beautiful visions of what he could be, and what he could do.

It was a shame he didn't kill for her. Lessa was starved of the feeling for so long, and feeding him euphoria when a thought so dark and sickly sweet entered his mind. When he turned to insects, Lessa was intrigued. She had never met a human so capable of corruption, someone who wanted so badly to be whatever someone else needed him to be. It was delicious.

She stood in front of the back windows, where she'd seen him wander so many times. It was light out and the sun blistered down on her skin. Lessa hissed at the rays, so different from the darkness that she craved. She yearned for the tendrils of other dark souls, waiting until after the sun dipped to come out and play, all without bodies as she had. She was one of them too. Through the window sat the girl, the same one Norman had run from yesterday. Lessa smiled, the tips reaching the points of her eyes. She raised a hand tentatively and knocked on the window. What a way to finish what she started.

"Norman!" the shocked voice came from the other side of the window pane. Lessa cocked her head, raising her eyebrows encouragingly. Humans were so naive. The girl rushed to the window, undoing the latches that held it together, and lifted it up. She could see the girl's tiny frame and could feel the blood pumping through her veins. The desire to snap her neck was overwhelming. Lessa licked her lips in anticipation.

"Why didn't you come through the front door?" Sirce asked quietly, nervous. She could tell something was off, but her brother stood before her, and how could anything be wrong with that?

"I can't be seen here, and I can't stay. You know that," Lessa chided. Sirce thought of that for a minute and nodded.

"You decided to come to visit then," she said happily. Whatever tension she must have felt, she waved it away. What a simple human being Sirce was. She turned her back, walking towards the door and shutting it slowly, creating the privacy they so desperately wanted. When Sirce turned back around, Lessa was there, knife in hand and slimy glaze over her eyes.

"...Norman?" Sirce asked, her voice wavering. Lessa raised her hand, Norman's hand, watching happily as the knife glistened under the fluorescent light. She didn't answer, instead, she simply smiled.

PART EIGHT
THE GLORY

"People's lives are forever controlled by two emotions: fear and greed."

- Robert T. Kiyosaki

I
GRAYSON

When Grayson was little, he used to love to dream. Even when he was a baby, there wasn't a moment he'd been difficult to put down, despite being so young and restless. He reveled in being able to close his eyes and feel relief leaving this world. When he would dream, Grayson made sure he would be away for as long as humanly possible. This world was too dark for him to live in, and anything else to live in for that matter, but even the lure of dreams could not compete against the aversion he had to them now. As a grown adult, Grayson desperately avoided sleeping like he avoided the plague. Even with the evils he was faced with in the land of the living, he couldn't imagine closing his eyes again for more than a second. Each time he did he was greeted with the same horror, one that was made worse by the realization that it wasn't just a nightmare, but a memory.

He was just a child again, on a boat in the middle of the ocean. Grayson wasn't really supposed to be on it. In fact, his father would be absolutely furious with him if he'd found out. But, Grayson always loved the sea, and when his father had his crew ready up *The Grace*, he'd sneaked onto the lower deck and hid away between boxes before they could sail away without him. He wasn't sure where he was going, but he didn't care, as long as he could smell the salty air of the ocean and feel the wind lift him up under his bare arms.

Grayson loved the ocean almost as much as dreams and his father. The two often spent time out on the water together, fishing, sailing, and crabbing. It wasn't a place for everyone, but it was a place for them. Grayson stayed between the boxes under the ship for longer than he could keep track, falling asleep several times and rocking gently with the water and the voices above. It was a few hours before he opened his eyes again and could remember it, and when he did he almost forgot that he was on a boat in the first place.

Grayson heaved in a big breath and shook his head awake when he realized his father and his crew hadn't made much noise in just over half an hour. In fact, he couldn't remember the last time he heard them speak, period. He was tiny and agile, especially as a young boy, and as he got his lanky body out from behind the boxes and up the steps to the deck he brought a slender hand to his face to wipe at his eyes. When Grayson opened his eyes and time stopped completely.

There are many things boys this young should not be looking at, and at a moment like this, Grayson knew this was one of them. Even as he watched himself in this dream, even as he knew it was happening, even as he begged the gods for this nightmare to go away, he couldn't stop it. Blood was everywhere, the ruby red gleaming against the wood in the bright moonlight. Grayson looked around, shock and terror crossing his features. It wasn't just the blood, although that should have been enough. As the thick, sticky stuff soaked into the boat's wood, it was the accompanying bodies around the deck that did him in. Grayson moved swiftly for a ten-year-old, eyes wide as he looked around.

The entire crew, the ones that he had known since birth were on the floor, heads twisted at terrible angles. It was dramatic, almost as if it was a show. Everybody that littered the deck was spotless, clean of blood though it surrounded them. If Grayson had known any better, this could have been just a grand trick, a way for his father to get back at him for sneaking onto the ship. It sounded like something the old man might do.

"Gra-a-a-ay?" He heard a croaking voice up near the front mast. Grayson moved, sifting through the blood and the bodies until he saw his father. He was not an old man, only about twenty years older than Grayson, but he wore age like weights. The creases crinkled at his eyes, his muscles were toned but heavy with exhaustion. Death was hovering in the air, the smell of salt and blood lingering in his nostrils.

"Papa!" He squealed, his voice high. Grayson ran to his father's side, leaning near him. His father was too clean, save for two small, red pinpricks freckled on his neck. "Who did this to you?" He was too far gone to be saved, even if he wasn't a young child that could do nothing about it. Grayson would be the only one getting off of this boat alive, and that was if he could bring this boat back to shore.

His father gasped, and although Grayson wanted so badly for him to say something, he couldn't help but look out towards the ocean.

2
GRAYSON

He woke up with a start, swinging his arms in either direction and widening his eyes to take in any available light within the room. It was heavy with silent darkness, save for a sliver of sun peeking in from behind his curtains to his right. Sweat gleamed on his forehead and Grayson lifted his hand to wipe at it, trying to calm the panic that was threatening to overwhelm him.

He'd grown up since his time on that boat, fifteen years ago. He was twenty-five now and wearing the manhood proudly. He was tall and filled out, every bit the fisherman his father was. Long tendrils of hair hung on his face, sticking to his skin from the perspiration. His face was clean-shaven, but just after a night's worth of sleep, you could see the hairs on his chin casting that five o'clock shadow Livvy loved so much. Grayson turned his head, looking towards the spot next to him at the thought of his wife.

She was not there, her side of the bed messy, but not showing the familiar indent that he'd expected. She didn't sleep in bed with him for long if she did at all.

The panic seemed to set in again but he took large, deep breaths to lower his heart rate. Grayson needed to think things through rationally. It wasn't like he hadn't been through this yesterday, two weeks ago, hell from the moment fifteen years ago when he was actually on that boat. He knew he tossed and turned at night, that the nightmares weren't his reality. Knew that she left more often than once, sometimes after the damage had already been done. Once he woke up to his sheets stained with her blood. He curled into the duvet further, wincing at the memory. What seemed like a physical manifestation of his darkest nightmare had become his reality that day. Ever since, he'd answered her every beck and call.

Not like he wouldn't have anyway. Livvy was far too good for him, and someone his father would have loved. She was a woman glorious, with rough, unfinished edges. Undeniably beautiful, with a dimpled smile and a round body that squished as he touched her. She was the center. While she was a treat to look at, her features were secondary to the roughness of her hands.

You could tell a lot about a person by their hands.

Hers were calloused from years of hard work themselves. She had not lived an easy life, and it was when he touched her hands that he knew he would marry her. It took a lot of work and patience to be with him, he knew, and Livvy handled it with grace. She would get her hands dirty when needed, and Grayson had a lot of filthy closets to sort through.

"Liv!" he called, his voice pitching as if he was out of breath. He didn't hear a response from her, so, he took another deep breath before pushing himself from the bed and exiting their bedroom. The panic subsided the closer he got to the kitchen. Smoke wafted from the stove and she was swaying her thick hips to the tune of her own song.

He stared at her, mesmerized.

The fear subsided to something no larger than a nickel, hiding in the deepest corners of his brain until it could crawl back out tonight. Grayson moved swiftly towards her, wrapping his arms around her middle and bringing his mouth to kiss the spot on the back of her neck that she loved so much. He could feel her soften, hear the 'mmm' that escaped her throat She tilted her head back and smiled at him.

"Good morning," she said lazily, flicking her eyes back down what she was whisking.

"Where did you go last night?" There was a somberness to his voice, but she refused to acknowledge it. He loved this woman.

"It didn't get bad until early this morning, I promise," she reached up to caress his face, "I left just after the sun rose, to make breakfast." She was lying, the bed sheets looked too unruffled for her to have left that late into the morning, but he didn't push it. Livvy was always trying to help him get over his fear of the night.

"Are you going out onto the boat today?" She asked, maneuvering from him and plopping a plate of eggs and toast on their tiny kitchen table. Grayson smiled lightly and sat. There wasn't a lot on the plate, a carefully rationed egg and a slim piece of toast cut in half. He couldn't even remember if they had enough to buy margarine at the market the other day, either. They couldn't afford much, but they lived a quiet, quaint life on the sea. It was the same house he grew up in, which probably didn't help the nightmares, but it was rent-free; anyway they could cut the cost of bills. Grayson wished he could have given her the life she deserved, but there wasn't much more that he could do.

"No." He said hesitantly. Truth be told, he hardly ever worked on the boat anymore. Grayson was a good liar, apparently. "I'm having the crew take her out on the water today to fish." He grunted as he shoveled food into his mouth, Livvy looking at him with pursed lips.

"And you? You have the day off then since you won't be out of the water?"

"No ma'am. Paperwork, trading. You know, the stuff that puts money in our pockets." He looked at her with a bemused expression. She rolled her eyes but smiled, and Grayson knew he was in the clear.

"That's grunt work. Not for the owner."

"They won't respect me if I don't do it every once in a while," he argued, "I need to make sure all our contacts are buying and not scaring the grunts into haggling lower than I would allow. I wouldn't put it past them, the sneaky bastards. And besides," Grayson stood up and kissed her on the cheek before walking towards their front door. "Trading means I won't be home late."

"I'm holding you to that," she growled, but there was a playfulness in her tone that made him chuckle. The sound was unfamiliar in his belly, especially while his throat was still hoarse from screaming in his dreams. "Be home before dinner."

"Your wish is my command," he replied, and left, still smiling.

He knew he wasn't his crew's favorite captain, they'd be delighted for a day out at sea without him. They didn't respect a captain who didn't like to be on his own boat. He had to command respect, and unfortunately, there weren't many ways to do it without violence, lies, and under-the-table work. Grayson led a shaky, but successful fishing crew that made decent coin and provided fish for the markets. In a world where people were afraid to go out at all, he and his crew didn't have much competition. He stole all the dead beats, the thieves and the liars, those with nothing left to lose, and put them on a boat.

So far, he hadn't seen a Life Drinker since the one that murdered his father and his crew when he was ten years old. Even then, he hadn't actually seen the bloody creature. The wicked thing killed them for sport, draining them of their blood and throwing it around the boat theatrically. The monster was toying with them, sending a message, and as Grayson looked around he saw no harpoons that could have done any damage to protect them. He knew his father was a smart man, and to go without weapons might have seemed like an insult. Why else would it meticulously clean each and every man on that boat, licking them clean as their blood leaked through the cracked wood around them? Of course, that was all speculation. One day, when he was less of a milksop he would go after it. That Drinker was his white whale and one day he would get his revenge. Until that day, Grayson worked on overcoming his fears, and that started by owning a fishery and going out to sea as his father did, sometimes. Today was not that day.

Grayson would not consider himself a lucky man, but with Livvy and the boat he'd renamed after he met her, he got by.

3
LIVVY

The minute the door shut behind her husband, Livvy threw her spatula against the wall. It made a very loud thud, and she glanced towards the door again in case he had heard it. She put both hands on the countertop and sighed. It was hard, lying to him. She did love him, of course she did. Livvy didn't marry him for this poor lifestyle, she didn't marry him for his nightmares. She loved that big man and the heart that nestled somewhere between the layers of his trauma. They had only been married for three years and weren't together for too long before that. She really did want to build a life around him, but not this broken, battered, and bruised version of Grayson she had come to know.

She heard a quiet knock on her window pane to her left. It was a very distinct pattern. One. Two. Three and Four. She hated the way her heartbeat quickened the moment she heard it. When the door opened for the second time that day, Livvy smiled. This was a different sort of smile than the one she gave Grayson and she could feel it. This one met the creases in her eyes, it lifted over her lips to show a row of dull white teeth.

Seeing Cecil's tight-cut blonde hair and sharp jawline would do that to just about anyone. It was the way he looked at *her* though, the way her name sounded in his mouth when he lay next to her in bed. Grayson never looked at her that way.

Livvy knew he loved her, too. In fact, Grayson *adored* her. He'd do whatever she asked like she had him wrapped around her finger, but he never looked at her as something to be desired- not like Cecil did. Gray wanted to sleep next to her, and Cecil wanted to *fuck* her.

"Hi, Liv," he said, voice rough with lust and satisfaction. He was confident, sauntering into this other man's house as if it was his own. Cecil wrapped his arms around her and lifted her onto her toes, licking his lips lightly before pressing them against the hollow of her throat. Livvy loved her neck kissed, and the way this man did it had no comparison.

She hated herself, the desire that rushed through her as his hands roamed her body. She couldn't remember when she started fantasizing about him. It might have been when he told her she looked pretty that one day- though she doubted he could remember when he did that. It could have been when he looked at her a certain way. Livvy couldn't explain it. Cecil was tall and bulky, with meat on his bones for her to grab onto. Sensitive too, despite the confidence he exuded. He was sickly sweet, like hard caramel that rots your back teeth.

"Stop," she protested, pushing him back some, though she couldn't stop the smile that stuck to her face. "Not here, in the open like this."

"You haven't left him yet?" Cecil pouted, whining like an animal. She shook her head fiercely.

"I can't. You know that." He took a step towards her and ran hands down her shoulders in comfort. He had that playfulness in his expression, one that Grayson never had. He was always tormented by something, Cecil never was. Livvy couldn't stop comparing them, not when they were so very different.

"Yeah, yeah sure. I get it," he trailed kisses down her face, her neck.

"I don't think you do," she panted. It was hard for Livvy to think straight. "I can't just leave him, it would break him."

"For as long as I've known him, Liv, he's *always* been broken. You leaving him wouldn't help or hurt. It would just *be*. Then we can stop sneaking around."

"You told me you were okay sneaking around,"

"Of course," that wicked smile returned and he turned her around, pressing his body against her back. She could feel her heaving breath betraying her. Livvy wasn't very good at hiding her excitement for his presence, she loved having Cecil around. "But that was before I *knew* you. Now I don't think I'd like to share. Please? Leave him Liv. You don't love him, you know. But you *could love me*."

She pushed away from him, pressing her hands to her flushed face and walking away. She rolled her neck and cracked it, trying to calm the breaths that left her. She was aroused, too much so. Cecil could get anything he wanted from her when he got her like this, and she needed her wits about her around him. She was sure she loved him, Grayson, that was. She fell for his bravery and loved the way he tried to find himself despite the horrors that plagued him every night. Livvy was there for every nightmare, every meltdown. She showed up for Grayson every day. Maybe it was that she didn't like him any longer. You could love someone and not like them. She wasn't sure where she was heading until she bumped into the corner of her vanity. Livvy looked into the mirror and winced. Several bruises were yellowing near her collarbone, and she could feel the pain tingling in her shoulders and waist. How could Grayson look at these and not feel ashamed? She felt Cecil following her, this time he didn't get so close he could touch her. He looked pained, searching her body for more of those swollen patches of skin where Grayson hit her. Not on purpose, never on purpose, but she found it hard to sleep in the same bed anymore and fall asleep peacefully.

"You can't stay with someone that hurts you that bad," he commented. It wasn't malicious, in fact, he sounded almost as if he was begging her. Livvy bit her lip.

"He doesn't hit me," she wanted to protect him because it wasn't fair to him. Nothing about this was fair for Grayson.

"The welts on your body tell a different story. I know it's not on purpose, believe me I *know*," There was a delicate pain in his features. She hated hurting him just as much as the prospect of hurting Gray. "You wouldn't have to hide your body for me. Those delicious curves could get some sun."

He was right. Her porcelain skin would frizzle in the sunlight. She used to be tan and used to have that sun-kissed glow before she met Grayson. But now, her arms didn't see outside of a long-sleeved sweater. She was roasting half the time, but the rush of wind that came with the ocean was enough of an excuse to wear them.

"It's unfair to drag him along like this," he whispered gently.

"I don't know what to do," she admitted. Cecil was right, it was unfair to both of them to continue doing this. There was something about the idea of leaving Grayson that physically pained her, though. He must have seen it too because he deflated.

"Look," he said, turning her around and looking at her. Her eyes were the color of moldavite, and looking into them made him wobble on his feet. "You need to get him his courage back. You need to show him what it's like to stand on his own. Livvy you can't feel guilty staying with a broken man."

"Why does it always have to be on me? I didn't sign up for this,"

"Yes, you did. You signed up for it when you married him," he watched as her face fell. Livvy knew that he was right, but she didn't know how to make it better. It was hard to admit regret when it was so difficult to find it in the first place.

"So then tell me what to do, Cecil, tell me how to fix this. How do we show him what it's like to be whole? I'll do anything. He deserves that feeling, not me. He deserves everything. Once he has that I can let go. I can free myself, and I can free him. That doesn't make me a terrible person does it?" Cecil almost didn't answer her and for that, Livvy was grateful. She didn't want him to lie to her. His mouth stretched uncomfortably, but she reached out to touch his shoulder. "What do I need to do, Cecil?"

It was there on the tip of his tongue, she could almost taste the words as if she kissed him again.

"You need to convince him to go after his white whale."

4
GRAYSON

She never wanted to go out with him to the harbor, but today she did. Grayson smiled at the thought. This was progress in their marriage. After accidentally smacking her in the face this morning after his nightmare, he wasn't sure if it would be a good day or a bad day. She dressed in sunshine yellow, his favorite color on her, and when he asked if she wanted to join, fully expecting her to say no, he was pleasantly surprised. Livvy was too forgiving of him, he thought often, and it was hard to not want to try to talk her out of it. They walked in silence from their home to the water, Grayson watching her hair as it whipped behind her in the ocean breeze. It reminded him of their early days. She used to come to the port with him often, enjoying the smell of sea salt and the sounds of the waves crashing into the dock. It was a beautiful type of sensory overload that he knew she enjoyed almost as much as he did. Grayson would never have been able to marry someone who hated the sea. It was too much a part of him.

"What are you thinking about?" He asked her, reaching for her hand and squeezing it lightly as they walked. She didn't turn to look at him or respond, it was as if she didn't hear him at all over the wind. Eventually, she sighed, letting a slight gasp escape her lips. He loved looking at her.

"Do you think you're getting better?" she asked quietly. He sucked in a breath. He was the one that was quiet for a spell, now. They arrived at the port, which was bustling with traders. People traded fish, supplies, gems, and secrets. Grayson was fluent in them all, and his heart rate picked up as they got into the thick of it. Livvy seemed to liven up too, and the air between her question and his answer disappeared as they descended into the crowd. She hung back while he did his business, Grayson was much better at trading than any of his crew, especially when he was alone. He was great at bartering and found himself excited and riled up when he was negotiating. This harbor and its travelers thrived here.

Every once in a while he smiled as his eyes met Livvy's. She enjoyed it, too. Her arms were casually filled with her own spoils. Flowers, a new ring she must have gotten from the Cecil boy whose mother owned the gem stand. His eyes narrowed at that, she knew they didn't have enough coin to afford new jewelry. She must have batted those pretty eyelashes at him. Livvy could get almost anything she wanted by looking at someone and smiling. It was how she got him, too. He'd secured a good trade deal on their next outing, pending them actually getting lucky with fish, and rushed over to her to give her a quick kiss on the cheek.

"I need one more deal, and it's with Graybeard over there. He nodded his head towards the grumpy old man that would probably milk him for all he's worth. "Got somewhere you can be for about ten minutes?"

"Of course, Gray," she smiled and turned away, walking quickly back over to the gem tent. Women and their jewelry. She always liked to have the prettiest things around her arm, including him. Grayson wished he could give her more than what the trades afforded them. They didn't make bad money, especially here where fish was such a hot commodity. Running a boat was expensive though, and a lot of what he earned went back into maintenance. He tore his gaze away from his wife and walked over to Graybeard, who believe it or not, hated being called that.

"Hey old man," he said instead, which didn't sound much better, but he grunted in response. He used to be a part of a crew, but now he was the old man that traded in lessons. He was supposed to be on the boat the night that his father and his crew died, and Grayson couldn't help but hold resentment towards him. The old man shouldn't be here alive, much like Gray. The kinship didn't help his own self-loathing.

"Grayson," he said, his voice rough with age. "I haven't seen you around in a while. Given up on lessons?"

"Just busy with business," Gray replied, furrowing his brows.

"You haven't gone out to sea lately. I watched your boys dock *The Grace*, the other day, but didn't see you come off with them."

"It's called *The Livvy* now," he huffed.

"Those boys you got, you know they steal from you," he ignored Grayson and looked out at the water. *The Livvy* was rough looking but she was a great ship. Her masts were straight and tall and her wood, though chipped, was oiled and kept up with. "Their pockets are full of the smell of fish by the time they've transferred it all to bigger coolers."

"I know that," he didn't actually. It wasn't a surprise, though. Grayson knew what he was getting into when he hired a bunch of criminals to help man his ship, he would have to keep a tighter leash on them. It would mean no more trips on their own, at least for a little while. He would need to go out onto the water, a thought that made goosebumps rise on his skin. “Thanks though,” he supplied. It would hurt him to be on this old man’s bad side, and he did appreciate the secrets, after all. Graybeard nodded.

“What’re you trading today, boy?” he asked, cutting right to it. Grayson was grateful, the less time he could spend with him the better.

“More lessons,” he said. There was a threat in Grayson’s voice, he knew Graybeard didn’t like teaching him, it triggered some trauma response out of him, too; but there was no better teacher on the island about the subject of Life Drinkers.

“You still on about those bloodsuckers? We haven’t seen one since that night, boy. If I were you I’d forget about them.”

“I can’t really do that when I’m a deep sea fisherman,” Gray laughed, but it sounded fake. The old man nodded in understanding.

“S’pose you’re right. I would tell ‘ya to find a different trade if I weren’t so selfish. But I need the fish so I won’t tell you to stop. Ain’t nobody stupid enough to go out to sea anymore besides you and that misfit crew you put together.”

“It makes me indispensable,” Grayson said.

“It makes you indispensable and *stupid*.” He corrected.

“So are you going to teach me or not?” Grayson rolled his eyes and bit the inside of his cheek so he wouldn’t say something dumb. Graybeard looked at him for a long moment before nodding.

“Sure. Same deal? Bloodsucker lessons for your fish?”

“Same deal my father had with you when he was alive,” Grayson confirmed. They shook on it. Satisfied with the outcome, Grayson turned to look for Livvy. As much as he loved the harbor and its people, he wanted to go home and be with his wife. He started walking away, making it only a few steps before Graybeard called out to him.

"It's pretty lucky you got off that ship you know." Gray winced. He didn't like reliving the memory. "If you keep up what you're doing, the Life Drinker will come to find you, too."

Grayson turned around, angry and flustered. The red crept up his cheeks as he hissed. "It was lucky that you weren't on that ship when they went night fishing." He retorted. "If you had, you wouldn't be here either."

"Boy, that wasn't luck. I was *smart*. Your father got his crew all hell-bent on finding the creature and killing it for some vendetta he had. He didn't take you that night because he knew he could die. I wasn't going to sit around and die a death I knew could be prevented."

He talked a lot about this, how Grayson's dad went on a fool's mission to kill the bloodsucker. His father was the most calculated man he knew. Even with lessons from Graybeard - who really didn't ever give them proof of his credentials other than what his father vouched for- he wouldn't make such a reckless decision based on revenge.

"You don't know what you're talking about old man," Grayson was done with this conversation. He turned around and walked away. Graybeard didn't say much after that, turning back to polish his hook and scratch at his beard.

"Finished?" Grayson came up behind Livvy and kissed her on the back of her neck like he knew she liked it. His eyes flicked up, finding Cecil. Livvy stiffened at his touch.

"Yes dear," she said breathlessly.

"Thanks for keeping her company," he said gently to the old woman, Cecil's mother, running the tent and pulling on Livvy's hand. "I'm ready to go home." She obliged him.

The walk back from the harbor was his favorite part. She had a large bouquet of flowers under her arm and a small loaf of homemade bread in the same hand. Her other hand was laced through his as they walked.

"I'm sorry I didn't answer your question," he said without thinking. Livvy stuttered as she walked, but kept her face forward.

"How do you mean?" She asked, hair whipping behind her once more.

"I don't think I'm better. And talking to that old man never helps."

"So why do you keep trading with him?"

"Because my father did, and because I keep thinking those Life Drinker lessons will help me, somehow."

"They won't if you keep skipping out on the boat trips," She was being candid with him, good. He liked her best when she didn't beat around the bush. Grayson stopped, halting her as well.

"I don't suppose I know what you're asking me to do," he said, frowning. She looked resigned as if what he said annoyed her. Livvy never made it seem like his triggers bothered her. She was his biggest supporter. What was making her come out with it now?

"Look. I know you're hurting. Lord knows I've known you were hurting since the day I met you, and I've been here through it all, don't forget that. But you won't get better. You take lessons about the Life Drinkers, but you don't do anything with them. It's like you're content living in fear."

He stepped back from her, hurt crossing his expression. She really thought he *wanted* to feel this way all the time?

"And what would you have me do? Go searching for the creature? Kill it? You think that would help me sleep at night?"

"It couldn't hurt." She murmured to herself. His frown

deepened. If Graybeard's comments weren't enough to frustrate him, hers were worse. Graybeard called him a fool for not stopping the fishing. Livvy was calling him a fool for not fishing enough. He was sick of others telling him what to do, he was the only person that would get to decide how he felt.

"What do you want from me?" He asked again, exasperated. It was his fault for bringing the conversation around again, but he couldn't stop now. It bothered him to know she was growing unhappy with their arrangement.

"I want you to be a man," she said at last. "I want you to stare fear in the face and conquer it. I want you to seek glory and not complacency."

"So you want me to die," he concluded, crossing his arms. 'You would rather be married to a dead man."

"It's better than being married to a coward."

They stared at each other, eyes hardened and postures rigid with tension. Grayson didn't know she had been harboring those feelings for so long. She looked unyielding in her expression. Gray deflated, and let go of her hand. He started walking in the direction of their home again, there was no winning this conversation.

Livvy shook her head and the sympathy flushed her face.

"I'm sorry, Gray." She said, and Grayson felt that she meant it. "I don't want you dead, you know that. But we can't keep living this way. I'd rather you go after the creature to prove to yourself that you aren't owned by it any longer. I want you to come home a hero. Maybe then we could be happy, and raise children. You could be here for your child and teach them. I want that for us."

He stopped walking again and turned to her. Softness met her eyes, and he smiled. Of course, she wanted him to show her that he was the man her child would need. He was silly for thinking otherwise. Of course, there was an ulterior motive for this conversation, there always was with Livvy.

"You want me to go find the creature so you can be confident in me being a father?" He asked, curiously. Her face grew cherry red and she looked towards the floor, embarrassed.

"I want you to do whatever *you* think will help you get over your fear, so you can father my child."

He thought about that for a long moment. Grayson had wanted someone to make this choice for him for a long time. He could never convince himself to go after the thing on his own, he needed the push. He knew he could count on Livvy doing that for him. It was what made him fall in love with her, it was what made him choose her. He would tell her tomorrow, maybe.

She would be sad, of course. He knew Livvy didn't want him to take her seriously when she said to go after the creature. But she was right, it might have been the only way to prove Graybeard wrong, to prove to himself that he wasn't a fool. He would go after the creature, he would kill it as his father had failed to. Grayson had the advantage, he had a crew that had nothing to fear, and a wife at home who would be rooting for him. That was more than he could say for his father.

"You're quiet," Livvy said.

"I'm just thinking," he replied. Grayson would come back to her, and he would fuck her with every ounce of love he had. She would bare his children, and they would carry on his name. It was the only way he could see moving forward. It was blinding, how this thought now controlled his every decision. It would take him a week of preparation, and a few days to wrangle his crew to agree. They would, they each had nothing left to lose, either. He would tell them of the glory, of the fame they would come home to. No one would have to work for scraps again.

He had her to thank for it all, and Grayson was now fueled by anticipation. She turned to him and smiled. This was his destiny.

He could feel it.

5
LIVVY

Grayson turned to her and waved. He had a stupid smile on his face that made her smile, too. It was contagious. Livvy kicked the ground with her boot. He only looked happy when he was walking away from her, and it pissed her off. She had to live here with the sad, broken Gray for almost as long as she's been alive, and he gets to walk away with a smile. He used her, used her kindness, her open heart. Livvy wasn't a great person by any means, but she was too good to be used. The smile disappeared from her face quickly, but he had already sailed too far out at sea to notice.

Cecil came up behind her and put a hand on her shoulder. She shrugged away from him.

"He's sailing away, probably to die, and you're putting your hands on me? What the hell is wrong with you?"

"Liv, he only turned around for a second. He's not even looking anymore, see?" His long, muscled arms reached over her shoulder and pointed towards *The Livvy* drifting off into the distance. She shoved his hand away, frustrated. Livvy grabbed for her dress and lifted it, walking away in a huff. Cecil followed her, turning his back on her husband and the boat sailing away. It felt like she was walking away from her destiny.

"What is your problem?" He asked. Cecil's brows furrowed in frustration. "We won, don't you see? He's left out to sea, we've convinced him of his confidence. He'll come back a hero-"

"We've sent him out to *die*, Cecil!" she hissed. Heads turned towards them and he looked around them uncomfortably. "You think this is about winning? I am not a prize to be won. I sent my husband out to sea, and I will never see him again."

"I thought that was what you wanted?" He argued. "To be with me, to be rid of the man that made you miserable, who *hurt* you all of these years."

"I'm allowed to *mourn*, Cecil. He was my husband. *Is* my husband. That will not change until he has returned."

"So you're saying we still can't be together? He could be gone for months or years! He might not come back at all!"

"What I'm saying," she narrowed her eyes and looked at him. She was beautiful when she did this, fierce and powerful. This was the woman that was sick of being forgotten. This was the woman who put the needs of herself before everyone else. "Is that I am allowed time to suffer the consequences of my decisions. I have killed my husband, I have no intention of ever seeing him again. And yes, I will have you, because as much as your words anger me my body lusts for you. I am greedy, Cecil. I want everything, and I will get everything. I will have you, and I will be rid of my husband. I will have people pitying me, I will have condolences I do not deserve. And I am happy about that, I am happy for the life we will build and the passion we will experience," Livvy squeezed his shoulder in reassurance. His muscles relaxed instantly at the touch. Her body responded well to his. She melted, unabashedly aware of the looks others shot their way. “But I am allowed to be sad. I am allowed to mourn the life I thought I would have.”

“Okay,” he said, his breath releasing and his eyes finding hers. He smiled lightly, one she did not return but it didn’t bother him. They had all the time in the world. “I understand.”

Livvy looked back out towards the water. She hoped it would be an easy death. Grayson lived a hard life, one she would not wish on anyone in return. He did not deserve what she and Cecil had put on him, it was one of the many things that he did not deserve. His boat was nothing but a black spot in the expanse of the sea now, and the rest of the crowd that had gathered for his departure had dispersed. Cecil was wary to put his hands on her again, at least out on the dock where many could see them, so he whispered in her ear instead.

“So what do now?” Livvy leaned her head back, taking in one last gasp of salty sea air, and letting the last of it leave her lungs.

“We go home.” She said in return, a smile crawling onto her face. A sultry look passed her features, one that Cecil found hard to miss. The tension in his muscles returned, but not in apprehension. This time he tensed in anticipation, he loved when that look passed her features. He loved the way her jewel-toned eyes gleamed when she thought of them, together. “I think I’d like you in my bed as soon as I am able.”

“You need someone to warm the bed, to console you?” He teased.

“A mourning widow has her needs too, Cecil.” Livvy turned and walked away, her quick pace making him skip in pleasure.

She traced lazy circles on his bare chest, the bed a mess of sheets and tangled limbs. Cecil was quick to move in, quick to warm the space next to her. It was the first time she slept in her own bed for longer than a few hours, and it felt incredible. Grayson's recent trades before he departed had given them enough money to last a few months, and so they were left undisturbed in her home until Cecil would have to find work. Before *she* would have to find work, too. At first, she had visitors, those that checked in. Livvy played the role of the weeping love well, and sometimes Cecil was afraid that she had changed her mind. Livvy wanted so badly sometimes to be the worried wife they saw in her, but she couldn't. She was happier here, with Cecil. After she shut the door, carrying in pans of gifted baked goods, she would throw them onto the counter and return to bed with him. Livvy enjoyed not being afraid to sleep. When she would wake up next to this beautiful man, who loved her and kissed her as if she was the love of his life, she almost started to believe that she deserved it.

"Good morning, my love," he said, moving to position himself on top of her, kissing her long and deep. She missed this, too. Missed feeling like someone lusted after her, like she was desirable. She swept her tongue against his and felt him harden above her as he groaned into her mouth.

"Morning," she whispered into him. He kissed her again, wrapping his lips around hers and sucking her teeth lightly.

"What are we doing today?" She smiled. It was a game they had been playing. She knew the answer he expected, the answer he craved. Livvy would not disappoint him.

"I think I'd like to stay in bed," she said, stretching out beneath him, grabbing the sheets as he left a trail of kisses down her bare chest.

"I think I'd like to do the same."

It had been like this for two weeks now. Sometimes Livvy wondered how Grayson was doing. Maybe he would surprise them all and slay the Drinker. Maybe the life stealer was already dead. She never listened to the rumors about the night his father was murdered or asked him to relive it. Gray had so many demons as it was, and every moment he was not sleeping she wished to take him away from that memory that plagued him. What she did know, that it was a massacre, that Gray had only left the ship alive because he was hidden below deck, led her to believe that he would not come back to them. She hoped he wasn't the same coward now that he was back then.

The Drinker wanted its revenge as much as Grayson did, if not more. It was hard not to think about him when Cecil was on top of her like this. It was hard not to compare them. Grayson loved her hard as if he had something to prove. He would pin her hands behind her back and ram into her so hard that she would cry out in pain. It was a difficult love, but one that kept her there. Cecil was a different kind of person to be with. He made love to her gently, asking permission and allowing her to make the choice. It was always about her with him, and she felt powerful. Livvy shut her eyes. Cecil kissed her eyelids gently.

A wave of passion struck her and she wrapped her legs around him- she wanted that power *now*. Cecil buckled from desire, driving himself against her without hesitation. The sheets splayed about them and he slid his hands down her body. Cecil worshiped her. When they were close to finishing, when he had driven her to the point of madness, a knock sounded at her door. Her moan was cut off by a violent smashing of their lips, and Cecil groaned quietly as she stopped rocking against him.

Livvy placed her hands against his chest, pushing him off

of her. She raised a finger to her lips to shush him and he nodded, tossing his head back in unresolved frustration. She watched as his hands trailed down his torso to below the V at his hips and averted her gaze before she could decide to avoid the knock. It came again, louder this time and she moved quickly. Livvy wrapped a sheet around her, smoothing out her hair so that it might have looked as if she had just woken, which was not entirely untrue.

When she walked over to the door she breathed in deeply one last time, letting the rest of her arousal leak from her before she opened it a sliver. A man with a very official-looking suit was standing there, face solemn but amusement in his eyes. He raised his eyebrows, and Livvy knew he was not a dumb man. He knew exactly what it was that radiated from her, sex, love, happiness. He did not comment on it, instead, he gathered the papers in his hands and cleared his throat.

"Are you Mrs. Flint?" he asked curiously. He wished it was her, she thought. He wanted so badly to witness her cheating on her husband, and he was right. She smiled at him, a sweet, pretty smile that confirmed his suspicions.

"I am." She said confidently. Livvy adjusted her sheet so that he couldn't see the hard points of her nipples, though she caught as his gaze drifted for half a second. "How can I help you?" she pressed.

The man looked uncomfortable, coughing again into the crook of his elbow. He shifted his weight, and a look of pity swept over him. Livvy was not surprised at the words that left him next, because they were the ones she had been expecting for two weeks now.

"I regret to inform you that we got words from the Isles yesterday. It seems a ship was found at sea. Torn to shreds, as if from a storm, though none were projected within the last week. We're unsure how long it was at sea, you know how slow post travels from the Isles to us. Mrs. Flint, did your husband go out on the water within the last month?" He couldn't help but look behind her, into the house where he no doubt heard her and Cecil yowling like animals a moment before. She closed the door a bit more, stepped outside with him, and nodded.

"He did, he and his crew left two weeks ago." The man shook his head and frowned at her, judging. Infidelity was not uncommon here, but for strait-laced men like him, she could tell he was uncomfortable with the idea. Maybe he knew Grayson personally. He did a lot of trades down in the harbor. Maybe he felt a personal attachment to her dead husband, and that was why he judged her so harshly.

"I'm so sorry, miss. Their boat was found, and no bodies were found on it. It was as if they disappeared. Lost at sea, I would expect. He will not be coming home."

Livvy looked down, feeling the tears threatening to break. She was a terrible person, crying about the death of Grayson when she had Cecil naked in her bed, hot and sweaty from taking him over, and over again. She crossed her legs at the thought.

"And so he's dead?" She asked. Livvy couldn't help the relief that left her next breath. A weight had been lifted off her shoulders, one that weighed her down for many years before this.

"I'm afraid so. I can bring you bits of the ship to prove it was theirs if needed. The team cut the name of the boat from the wood, *The Livvy*. Does that name ring a bell?" She nodded again, it was the only validation she needed.

"Would you like to come down to my office and-"

"I would not like to do anything but mourn my husband now," she said confidently. The tears flowed freely down her face, and she went to open the door again.

"Mrs. Flint I really think you should-"

"Please leave me alone. I will compose myself and sign paperwork tomorrow," he looked at her wide-eyed, clearly unable to rationalize what it was she would be going back inside to do, "Please," She said again. He relented, frowning but bowing regardless.

"As you wish, here's my card. I will see you tomorrow, Mrs. Flint." Livvy flushed red and took his card, quickly walking inside and slamming the door in his face. She pressed her naked back flush against the door, dry heaving. She couldn't breathe. Cecil had not come out to bother her, and so she went to see him instead, composing herself and wiping the last of the tears before she entered the bedroom. He was in the same position she left him in, stroking himself long and slow, begging himself not to finish before she could return. Her eyes bulged, and he stared into them with deep satisfaction at her response.

"Is it done?" He asked, his voice rough and sultry. She couldn't stop looking at him. Livvy nodded her head curtly, and he smiled.

"Sorry for your loss,"

"No, you're not."

"No, I'm not." He confirmed. His hand squeezed once and Cecil's eyes closed. A guttural moan left his mouth and Livvy took a step closer to him. Everything about this felt wrong, but she was a greedy woman. Livvy wanted Cecil at this moment, she wanted every single piece of him. "Come mourn with me," he said, and she obliged.

Livvy went to bed with a smile on her face and climbed on top of him. The power she felt surge through her was intoxicating. She was drunk on it. She slid onto him and they rocked together, a mixture of pleasure, regret, and abandon.

Greedy women got what they wanted.

6
GRAYSON

He wasn't an idiot, although she would probably paint him out to be that way after he died. Livvy was everything he ever needed in a partner on the outside, even though he knew their marriage was broken for so long. *He* was broken for so long. She was good for him while he still lived, at least that much will still be true even after the devil gets them. There was nothing about her that he regretted, not a single moment. Grayson took hold of the wheel and turned it slightly, changing the direction they were sailing. His crew was down along the lower deck, and he could hear their murmurs as he sailed. They might have been regretting their own decisions, the ones that led them to this moment on the ship even if he didn't regret his. They wouldn't say a word, though. It must have been the crazy in his eyes. Livvy wanted *him* to do *this.* Even if it was for her own personal, selfish gains- of course, he'd seen the abandoned articles of clothing in their home, and the way Cecil came up behind her with a dangerous familiarity as he sailed away- it felt good that she had chosen this path for him. Fitting, for him to have an end like this.

Grayson tilted his head back and smiled with his eyes shut. He always will love the sea and the dangers inside of it. The sea knew him, better than he knew himself.

"Captain, what's the plan?" Someone yelled up at him. One eye opened lazily, he hadn't thought that far ahead. Truly the only plan was only to find the Life Drinker, the thing that killed his father, but there wasn't much thought put into it other than that. If he was out at sea on *The Livvy*, the Drinker will find him. The creature would recognize its enemy. When he renamed *The Grace* many years ago, a part of him felt like he was betraying his father. But it was odd having a ship named after himself. It was hard too, seeing the chipped name painted on the boat where his father and his crew died that night. His mother passed on when he was very young, and after his father was murdered, there was only so much a ten-year-old could do to manage the pain. So he painted over it. She went nameless for a long time, but after he met Livvy when he was nineteen, he knew that was the woman that he would marry. It only took a few days after their first date for him to paint her name across his ship. She's been named ever since.

"Sail until we can't see land anymore," he called back warily. They wouldn't like that answer. The crew felt wary of going out as far as they did when they were fishing. They've already been out on the water for a few hours, and after another without stopping they will have been out much farther than they had before. Not having a destination made his skin prickle with anxiety. Grayson knew it would be ten times worse with the pack of misfits he'd brought with them. They all knew what they were getting themselves into.

"...that's it?" Grayson laughed.

"Yeah, that's it." He hopped down from the wheel and trotted down the stairs to the deck. He patted the man he'd spoken to on the shoulder, who only looked at him with a frightened expression. He knew his answer didn't strike encouragement, but he also knew it would be worse to lie to them.

"C'mon, this is about the glory of the kill. This is about us getting what we've earned. We should be sparking encouragement, not fear."

"We don't have a plan," he protested.

"We have *me*. And you forget that I've trained for this." A few sparring lessons each week and dozens of research hours barely felt or counted as training but he couldn't let any of them get cold feet. Grayson was a fisherman, and not the sort to call himself a Drinker slayer. They were in this now though, whether they wanted to be or not. This far out at sea, they had even less of a choice. The man seemed to recognize the crossroads, too, because he grimaced in return and nodded. It was a nod that accepted death if it came, and Grayson had to look away.

"Fine. You're sure the Drinker will know where we are at?"

"He lives in the ocean. We are in his ocean. *He will know*," he squeezed the man's shoulder once and let go, walking in the direction of the rest of the crew. "What are the rest up to? Preparing?"

He dipped his head. "They are finished. There's only so much you can do with aconite-laced harpoons on a ship as small as this one. No offense." It actually made Grayson smile.

"None taken. So where are they?"

"They're praying, captain."

"Praying? Praying for what?"

The man shuffled on his feet uncomfortably. He didn't want to answer, but Grayson knew. He knew the minute he stepped on his boat that they wouldn't walk away. Grayson had decided he wasn't doing this for them, he wasn't doing it for Livvy, either. He would be doing it for himself. Everything he had done had been for himself. He went on the boat when he was ten years old for the feel of the wind, he kept the fishing business for the money. He kept Livvy for his comfort. Almost worst of it all, though, Grayson kept the men on his boat to die for the glory. Gray was a selfish man. He felt like the world owed him as it slighted him and that he was deserving of so much more. At the expense of others, even. He was not a good man, he was just as bad as his father. The man looked at him and narrowed his eyes.

"They're praying they don't die today, captain." They stared at each other for what seemed like hours but passed like mere minutes.

"Yeah, I know," Grayson replied. He tried really hard to smile, but nothing would come.

"There are no secrets that time does not reveal."
- Jean Racine

I

There weren't many things that Ansen liked about being behind a bar. It was dirty, the owners never paid him on time. Even if they did it would barely cover the charge of his rent, and nobody tipped enough to make it worth a dime. It was a shitty, run-down dive bar off the highway in the middle of nowhere, you could look out onto the road and see nothing but wheat fields and livestock for miles.

He fucking hated it there.

People often asked why he stayed, and for a long time, Ansen couldn't give them a straight answer. It wasn't the girls-they weren't much fun after one drink too many. Ansen might have looked the part, but he wasn't much of a drinker himself either. Just frequent cigarette breaks if it was slow enough to be allowed.

He stayed year after year, because of the anonymity of it. There was something thrilling about being a body behind the bar that people hardly noticed. If you ever had the chance to look at Ansel, a tall, rough man with gray in his beard and wrinkles at his ocean-colored eyes, face rested in a permanent scowl, you'd stay far from him. When he was behind the bar though, Ansen seemed to no longer exist. It was like he was a shadow, nothing but a small moment in the lives of travelers and regulars alike. He liked it that way. And that was why he stayed.

People didn't pay him any mind when he was behind a bar. He wasn't an unsavory bartender, they certainly had their fair share of those here. Thankfully, he was good enough to pick up the Friday shifts alone. He was quicker than any of the others combined, and after pulling on the arm of the owners, they agreed that he made them enough money to warrant solo shifts. Fridays were good, people were binging after a shitty work week, so he was busy. Being just another body meant people would talk. Ansen knew more about the people in this city than he knew how to count to ten. There was an unlimited supply of secrets in their little pocket of nowhere, and he was the keeper of them.

Ansen took a heavy inhale of smoke, letting the fog fill his lungs, occupying every last bit of space. He'd grown fond of the taste- 20+ years of the habit will do that to you. It coated his gums like a glaze of wax, and he swiped his tongue across his mouth to grab the ashy taste as it traveled down his throat. There was almost something of a bitter afterthought, just enough to encourage another puff of the wrapped tobacco. More than the taste was how it made him feel. The buzz kept him rooted firmly to the ground, loosening his muscles. He only got 15 minutes. Any more than that and the customers would be walking behind the bar themselves, and if he wanted to keep the boss off his ass he needed to keep them in line. Ansen flicked the bud to the ground, stomping on the remains with the scuff of his worn boots.

He shook out his shirt and walked back into the bar, smelling like smoke and sweat. It fits, in a place like this. Fluorescent lights ricocheted off the spirits sitting along the back wall, and Ansen washed his hands at the sink. When he turned around his eyes grazed the room before him. There were far more regulars in tonight than usual, which made him roll his eyes. His regulars were less likely to tip well- they weren't the rich sort of folk, or the most generous, but he would walk out of here with a handful of spare change, which was better than nothing. At least the travelers passing through felt sorry enough to put an extra few dollars out there for him. He wasn't used to many travelers, not on a Friday night. If they were smart, they'd stay clear of this shitty middle of nowhere after dark.

His gaze hovered for a moment before spotting two women sitting at the end of his bar. They were out of place here, and he had half a mind to ask them if they were lost. They were new faces, or at least new to him, not the regulars he'd come to know. One was a pale-faced soccer mom with blonde hair that hung at bob length around her chin. She wore an olive-colored button-down blouse that made her look almost sickly, and although he couldn't see her bottoms from the other side of the counter he was convinced it was far too uppity for a place like this. Ansen only looked at her for half a second before turning to her partner, and that was because she was far more interesting to look at.

She had long black hair pulled back in a high knot, but he could tell that the length would run past her hips if she let it down. She was also dressed too nicely for this place, a form-fitting red dress that clung to each curve of her body. She was beautiful in every sense of the word and he couldn't stop looking at her.

"Can I help you?" she said, her voice a few octaves higher than he thought possible. It caught him off guard, and he took a step back and shook his head. Her predatory gaze followed the grays of his stringy hair, and for a moment it looked like she was staring into his soul. It was unlike anything he felt before. Even after the shake of his head, he couldn't help but stare as his eyes came level with hers again. "I said, can I help you?" the question in her voice was gone, replaced by an irritation that he couldn't ignore. Ansen could hear her friend laughing quietly behind a used napkin to her face. The bar was loud, and most might have missed the small exchange, but he could feel the red creeping up onto the roundness of his cheeks anyway. He straightened and put on his best smile. The last thing he needed was two women reporting him to the boss for being a creep. So much for being the anonymous man behind the bar.

"You two don't belong here." He said gruffly, too transfixed by her to recognize the words coming out of his mouth. She looked affronted. He knew it was the wrong thing to say, and it was a mistake he was not used to making. But that girl, it was like he had seen her before. There was something oddly familiar about her, and it wasn't the after-effects of the cigarette buzz. It was impossible because surely Ansen would have remembered a face like that before. He couldn't place it, not in this life anyway.

"I suppose we should take our business elsewhere. Somewhere with better hospitality, I might say." He furrowed his brows, shaking his head again. Was he going to continue to embarrass himself in front of these beautiful women? Ansen pulled back, dared to take his eyes off of hers, and glamoured himself in his usual barkeep persona. Without looking at her directly, he turned his attention back to the friend with raised eyebrows and a curious expression. He placed two fresh black napkins in front of them and laid his hands on the bar counter.

"I didn't mean anything by it. Just, look around you," He waved his fingers around for emphasis. "We don't usually catch your types wandering this bar this late in the evening." They both looked at each other and laughed. He was relieved, at least he didn't seem to be going the route of a report.

"Honey you don't know the trouble we can get into," The woman in the red dress said, winking. Her friend smacked her shoulder lightly, and they were both in a fit of laughs again. Ansen smiled, at ease behind his safety net of a counter. He had no doubt that these two could get into trouble fairly easily if they wanted to, looking like that and all. Ansen would be lying if he said he didn't want to watch every bit of that train wreck as if it was his favorite sitcom. He would fade into the background again just as he always did and watch, eyes open and mouth shut.

"What'll you be having tonight?" He asked, cocking his head slightly to the side. "I don't have a menu or anything, but we have most of the fruity stuff. I can make almost anything." They looked at him unamused. Tapping her fingers against the wood, the friend twisted her mouth into a small pout.

"What do you have on tap?" she asked. Ansen widened his eyes. He was shocked but tried to smooth his face so they wouldn't notice. He pointed to the beer tap along the back wall and watched closely as she squinted her eyes at the labels. He tried desperately to not look at her, the woman in the red dress that didn't allow him to think straight.

"Blue Moon." She decided, clicking her tongue to get his attention. Ansen nodded wordlessly. He dared to look, promising himself he wasn't going to lose it in front of them again- he had the rest of the bar he had to run tonight. She looked back at him, a wicked glint in her eyes. Ansen felt like he would melt under her gaze.

"Jack and Coke," She said, and Ansen had to refrain from spitting all over himself. He looked at her in surprise, and she only smirked. "Heavy on the Jack, not so much the Coke."

He nodded, albeit reluctantly, and turned to prepare their drinks. Ansen knew a lot about the secrets of this small town in the middle of nowhere. But these two, he didn't know a thing about them.

He was determined to figure them out.

2

3 DAYS LATER

Ansen hadn't been able to get them out of his head. Every time he stepped into the bar his eyes glanced immediately to the far end, almost hoping he could spot the two beautiful women that infiltrated his thoughts and wouldn't leave. It was Monday afternoon and the bar was empty, much to his dismay. He wasn't shocked, but it was frustrating regardless. Hell, he wasn't even supposed to be here today. He hated grabbing shifts from other people, specifically on days like today, preferring to work the weekends instead. Ansen took a clean rag and started wiping down the countertops, nodding to a couple who already looked too drunk. Mondays were slow, people returned to their terrible jobs, trying to forget the night of regret they spent here. All that was left were drunks and deadbeats. He scowled, rubbing hard at the wooden bar tops until he heard the crack of the wood.

He'd only been here for half an hour before he couldn't wait any longer. He needed a cigarette to calm his nerves. Ansen had never been an anxious person, but remembering the woman in the red dress had his veins pumping with adrenaline. They didn't speak to him after their initial interaction for the rest of the night, so it was crazy for them to have such an effect on him. Ansen shook his head and pushed out from behind the bar. Nobody would miss him for fifteen minutes.

The cool air did in fact help calm his nerves, just slightly. The breeze tickled his chin underneath his beard and he stuffed his hand in his pocket. It was too cold for him to be out here with no jacket, the October air nipping at his ankles, threatening to freeze him the first moment it got. Time passed so quickly here in the middle of nowhere, and Fall sneaked up on them all. Ansen retrieved his shaky hand, holding a long, thin cigarette and his newest lighter. He'd never been the nervous type, but you wouldn't believe him if you saw his hands. They shook violently as he tried bringing it to his lips.

"Fuck!" Ansen cursed to himself, leaning over and placing his hands on both of his knees. He needed to calm down. It had been far longer than fifteen minutes, and at least ten of those were spent in that same position. Ansen checked his watch, threw his cigarette to the ground with vigor and frustration, and left it behind, rotting on the gravel.

If you saw Ansen as he was now, you wouldn't expect him to be a man of much. He reveled in his routine, the bar shift sprinkled with too many smoke breaks and a lonely drive home in his denim-colored pickup truck. Even his home wasn't much. He lived in a trailer not far off from the bar itself, and the inside was bare to the bone save for an old coffee maker and semi-decent sheets that he used to cover himself at night in his bed. He didn't like being at home and so he didn't spend much time there, opting instead to take too many work shifts, despite his revulsion to them. It would have been different if he had any family, but honestly, there wasn't much that was interesting about Ansen. He hadn't spoken to his father for many years, with no likelihood of that changing now in his old age, and his mother passed away long ago. He preferred being alone, anyway.

"There he is!" The drunk man yelled when he entered the bar once more and washed his hands at the sink. Ansen tried to ignore him, but the man waved his arms around and he could almost hear the sloshing of alcohol in his belly. "Another one, old man! I've been waiting for y-hic-ooouuuu." Ansen turned to him, eyebrows raised. He wasn't entertained by sloppy Drinkers, especially this early in the evening.

"I think you're cut off, chap." He said instead, returning to avoiding eye contact and keeping his back to the man instead. It was much easier to focus on his anxious breathing if he pretended as if no one existed there.

"Hey, fuck you!" He started screaming now, making an absolute fool of himself and Ansen found himself truly contemplating if he could live without hitting the man. He'd never felt this sort of rage before and had to take a physical step back and shake his head to rid himself of the thought. Violence would get him fired, and this man wasn't worth this job. He squeezed both his hands together into small fists, pumping and releasing pressure, trying to calm himself down. He was close to yelling something back that he would regret later, but the bell dinged and everyone's eyes snapped towards the door. Ansen lost his breath, and let his hands fall to his sides. His shaking stopped and he felt suddenly at ease, even if his head was warning him that it was the wrong reaction to have. Even if the drunk man across the bar looked as if he wanted to murder him.

It had to have been the same woman from the other day, though not in the same tight red dress. She had the same golden features about her, and Ansen found himself once again taken aback by how breathtaking she was. He wasn't the only one. It was so quiet you could hear a pin drop. If she knew the effect she had on people (how could she not?) she didn't seem to notice it. Instead, she took the same spot she did the night before, at the opposite end of the bar, and he felt his eyes follow her naturally to it. It was like no one sat there before her. That was her spot, even if it was only the second time he'd ever seen her.

"I think he said you're cut off," she said, finally turning to them and that tricky smile returned. They all just blinked at her. How loud had they been? Surely there was no way she could hear them from just outside the door. Ansen moved towards her in a protective movement, sure that the drunk man would transfer his anger to her instead. God forbid this woman ever be harmed in his bar. There was no need after all, though. The man sat back in his seat, his lips quivering as if he had no other choice than to listen to what she said. He hung his head, and it was like that for so long that Ansen thought he'd fallen asleep or was in a trance. After a few moments, the man stood up from his chair, mumbled a quiet apology to Ansen, and stumbled out the doors. Normally he would have worried about how the old man would get home, but he didn't think about that now. He didn't quite care if this man made it home okay or not.

He turned his attention to the woman and every worry faded away again. Ansen moved quickly to place a fresh, clean napkin in front of her and tried hard not to look nervous doing it.

"Thanks," he mumbled, embarrassed that he hadn't handled the situation better on his own. She shook her head, smiling at him almost shyly.

"Don't mention it," she replied, voice high enough to capture a dog's attention. It always threw him off, but he found that it didn't phase him as it had the other day, and he moved quickly to grab a clean glass.

"Jack and Coke?" he asked hesitantly. She nodded and Ansen blushed lightly before turning to grab the Jack Daniel's. When had he ever been the blushing type? With his back turned to her he felt much braver, and while he liked being the invisible body behind the bar, he found that he wanted to know so much more about her, and that required asking questions he couldn't get information for just by listening in on conversations. He wanted to know her, and he wanted her to know him in return.

"It surprises me that this is your drink," he said conversationally, topping off the glass with his soda gun and placing it on the napkin. She shrugged.

"Me too. Actually, the first time I had it was three days ago. Shocked me too when I ordered it. I guess I wanted to look seasoned in front of Ness."

"Your friend from the other night," he supplied and she confirmed with a small nod of her head.

"It was silly, but turns out I actually like it. Or maybe it was just the way you made it." She made him feel so comfortable, Ansen almost frowned when he thought about how nervous he'd been earlier. There was no anxiety when she was around, only a deep, settling calm. She changed the air around them, and even the creaks in the old walls had quieted because she was here. He watched as she took a long drink, and followed it as it ran down her throat.

"What's your name?" He asked suddenly, the words falling out of his mouth too quickly. He didn't have time to stop it. She didn't seem offended, instead, she tapped her fingers against her drink. He could tell she was trying to decide whether giving him her name was a smart choice or not. Ansen almost took it back, almost told her not to worry about it, but he was too curious, too hungry to let go of this opportunity to know who she was. It might be the last time he'd ever get to see her and he was eager to put a name to the woman that was stealing his attention, even when she wasn't here.

"Don't tell him your name," the two of them turned to see who he now knew was Ness, walking towards them. She looked angrier than she had the other night, her movements were sharper and more forceful. Ness glared at him and the mystery woman gave him a sheepish, apologetic smile.

"Luara." She said, ignoring Ness, who looked at her in annoyance. She looked like she wanted to say something, before turning to him and scowling.

"Blue Moon." She said, short but definitely not sweet. Ansen refrained from rolling his eyes and grabbed for another clean glass. Good thing too, he hadn't noticed that his bar was fuller as the clock neared 6.

"I don't know why you gave him your name," he heard Ness whisper to Luara. Ansen almost smiled, he could picture her face clearly, even if he wasn't looking directly at her.

"He's just the barkeep," he heard her say. With those words, he instantly deflated. Of course, she wouldn't feel the same pull to him that he had for her. Ansen thought about her constantly, and she only thought of him when she was here. He was just the barkeep. Ignoring her stare as he placed the clean, perfectly poured beer in front of Ness, Ansen moved away from them and tended to the others at the bar top.

He was off his game. Inconsistent pours and using wrong glasses, Ansen had never felt so embarrassed. He couldn't keep his ears or eyes off of them, those two at the end of the bar. Ansen pretended hard not to listen, but he couldn't help but try to listen in, it wasn't a smart move, he was spilling things all over the place.

"Shit!" he whispered, shaking his hands free from another overpour. Looking apologetically at the patron receiving his wet glass, Ansen wiped the counter around it and moved until he was far enough away that he could breathe again without being scowled at. What he wanted more than anything was a smoke, but he wouldn't leave, not when Luara was here.

"He's cheating," he heard Ness hiss through her teeth. Ansen frowned and cocked his head towards them.

"I'm sure it's just paranoia, his job requires him to work late right?" Luara tried to soothe her friend, but there was no use. Even Ansen didn't believe the tone in her voice, though he felt a pang of affection for her thought and empathy. He caught the feeling this was a conversation they'd had before, and by the way, Ness shifted in her chair, he felt like it wasn't one she was finished with. Not this time, anyway, she was seething with displeasure. Waves of frustration rolled off of her, palpable.

"I'm telling you, this time I'm sure of it. There are receipts for places I didn't even know existed. There's no reason he should be home this late, not this much."

Luara put her hands on her friend's shoulders, which had started rising and falling as Ness panicked. Ansen wanted to join them, but stayed far enough away, wiping a clean rag on wet glass instead. "Ness, no offense, but you've played this game before. We tried catching him, and it wasn't cheating."

Ness slammed her empty glass on the counter. The entire room went silent and Ansen could have sworn he heard another crack in the wood. Sooner or later this bar was going to fall apart around them. He snapped his neck to them and Luara looked stunned, hands up in the air in retreat. It was that movement that made Ansen take several steps forward.

"I'm not crazy!" Ness shouted, and Ansen went to grab her hands. She recognized it at the last second and took a large step back from him.

"Don't you fucking touch me," she snarled at him. Ansen frowned. It took him a second before he lowered his gaze. He looked towards the empty glass instead.

"Can I get you another Blue Moon? On me?" He asked tentatively. Ness looked at him bewildered, the tension in the air dying quickly. He watched as her lip quivered and tears threatened to break on her face, before nodding. Ansen gave her a wary smile and grabbed for the glass. It was only a moment, but he'd broken up his fair share of bar fights, and Ansen knew how to fix the room.

"Go wipe your face in the bathroom," Luara said quietly, rubbing her hand along Ness' arms, "It'll be here when you get back." Ness nodded reluctantly and walked away.

"Thank you," Luara said, sighing and tapping her fingernails along the edge of her Jack, which had run dangerously close to empty. He didn't want to offer her another one.

"You're welcome, figured I'd owe you one," Ansen replied smiling tentatively, setting a brand new full glass next to her. "I was afraid she was going to hurt herself, or you." Luara rolled her shoulders uncomfortably.

"She thinks her husband is cheating on her and I don't know what to tell her to convince her otherwise. Last month she came up with this crazy plan to...catch him doing it. She went to his work and had me trail him for a solid fifteen hours. Which of course I did for her, I'd be a shitty friend if I didn't..." She rattled on, and while he didn't necessarily agree with her there was no way in hell he was going to stop her. The secrets were pouring out of her like a broken water dam and Ansen was looking forward to soaking up every last one. He wanted whatever taste of her he could get.

Luara stopped when she noticed his eyes glaze over, but instead of looking angry, her lips pulled down into a small pout and her eyebrows did this strange little wiggle as if they didn't know what to do on her face.

"I'm sorry, you don't need to know my whole life," she apologized. Ansen was too quick to shake his head.

"No no, I mean, please don't apologize. You'd be surprised about the things I hear behind the bar. You know, people are looser when they get drunk. Not that you're drunk or anything...or loose. I didn't mean that." He was never a stumbler, and yet here he was, making a fool of himself in front of her. It was as if he had never spoken real words before. Thankfully, she only seemed to smile. She knew the effect she had on people, she had to. She had a smile that would melt anyone she met.

"It's okay, I know what you mean," she laughed lightly. They sat in silence together for a long while, until the rest of the bar seemed to forget about Ness' outburst and went back to business as usual.

"Do you need to go check on your friend?" He asked, his eyes trailing up towards the direction of the restrooms. It had been long enough, and while Ansen didn't know enough about the time women spent in the bathroom, he had the faintest idea that it had been too long. Luara shook her head.

"No, she'll join us when she's ready."

Ansen twisted his fingers in his beard, pulling on the strands lightly.

Where did you guys come from? He wondered to himself. He hadn't realized he said the actual words out loud until he heard her laugh again.

"You ask a lot of questions for a bartender," she mused, and he noticed that she distinctly didn't answer his question.

"It's my bar, I know all of the people that come through it."

"Except us."

"Yes, except you, it seems. Why is that?"

"Maybe because we aren't worth knowing."

"I doubt that very much." Ansen was close to her now, eyes narrowed and staring into her soul. How could someone like her not be worth knowing? He couldn't fathom a world without Luara in it. Now that he knew she existed...he had to figure her out. He could tell she was about to say something, but noticed Ness walking back towards them, eyes puffy and face a blotchy shade of red.

"Are you ready to go, Lu?" She asked, hiccuping. Ansen looked down at the untouched cup of beer, smiling sheepishly and pulling it back towards him. Luara tilted up her chin in affirmation. Ansen felt his body retreat inward as the realization hit him. They would be leaving, and it was possible they would never see each other again. He tried hard to keep from grabbing at her hands, from pulling her close to him and never letting her leave his sights. But she wasn't his to keep.

They paid their tabs and both turned to walk away. Before pushing through the door, he smiled as Luara turned to wave goodbye. As if he deserved that sort of farewell, as if they were friends.

"What was your name, bartender?" She asked.

"Ansen." He whispered. He almost repeated himself, but she must have heard him because she laughed again.

"Until next time, Ansen," she cooed, and he watched as she and Ness left, the door swinging as they walked away from it. He took a swig of Blue Moon, refraining from spitting it out - no matter how awful the taste.

There would be a next time.

Ansen almost fell over right there in the bar.

3
2 DAYS LATER

It felt like a week, but it had only been two days since he'd seen her last. This obsession was growing unhealthy. Ansen couldn't picture anyone but her, no matter where he was at. She was there in his dreams when he slept, and she was there when he woke up in the mornings, even if it wasn't physical. He was going a little stir-crazy, it had been less than a week and Luara was already destroying him thought by thought.

Ansen couldn't even smoke anymore. The calming nicotine no longer had any effect on his heart and the way it seemed to beat out of his chest a mile a minute. His hand shook violently whenever he reached for his pocket and he decided it wasn't even worth trying anymore. The effects of the withdrawal were already heavy upon him. He'd tried quitting before, but it was never like this. Ansen lifted his hands to his face, wiping away the sweat from his brow. His body was soaking, especially in the heater that was the bar back. They were lucky he even made it to work today. He was constantly dizzy, his nausea keeping him up most of the night anyway. Ansen stumbled into the bar, and those that didn't know him might have thought he was already drunk. He was, but not in the way they would think. He was drunk on Luara.

It had been a few hours, but he knew she would be here. Ansen didn't know how he knew she would be, it wasn't like he had any definitive proof, but he knew- it was a sixth sense. When she walked through the doors he couldn't even find it in him to be surprised. His eyes gazed upwards, and while he felt the tug on his heart, like an invisible line of string tying them together, he didn't want his heart to skip around in his chest anymore. It hurt to look at her, hurt to think about her. She hadn't said more than a few words to him, but she had done *something* to him. It was the only explanation, Ansen had never felt like this.

She looked half hazard. Two days had passed but it seemed like many more than that. Her hair was disheveled, and he could tell she already had a few drinks in her before coming here. Ansen took a hesitant step forward and dropped his hands from the station where he was washing dishes. Despite what his mind feared, his heart wouldn't listen to it. He had to remember that he was a body behind the bar, nothing more. Luara took her usual spot at the bar top, not even caring to wave him over. She seemed as drained as he was. Ansen entertained the idea that they had done this to each other, but that was only wishful thinking. She looked nothing like the person he remembered.

"Long night?" He asked, sliding her the same glass she had used days prior. Luara nodded.

"Long fucking week," she sighed. His eye widened in surprise. Luara had always seemed so...put together. This was unlike her. Ansen wanted to milk it for all that it was worth. It had only been two days but it felt like an eternity. *It had been a week.*

"Ness coming tonight?"

"Yeah, the bitch. She kept going on about how she was 'gonna- hic!- kill him. Kept rambling on how she was going to run him over with her car."

"So she caught him, then? Cheating, I mean." Ansen turned around to find a wet rag and set about wiping down the counters, lost in thought.

"No," she scoffed, annoyed. He raised an eyebrow at her. "She says she knows he did it, but she just can't prove it. I say she's close to a trip to crazy town."

"You two must be good friends," Would she be able to see through his dry humor? Ansen sucked in a large breath, exhaling when he heard her cough out a laugh in relief

"You could say so. Can I tell you something, Ansen?"

He was shocked she actually remembered his name. Ansen stopped wiping the counter, which had only really been the same spot he'd been circling over and over again. He didn't need to ask what, just look at her in that way. When his eyes met hers he felt the fire overwhelm him. This was why he couldn't smoke anymore, this was why he couldn't stop thinking about her. Her gaze was all-consuming. She could ask him to do anything and Ansen probably would have done it. He desperately hoped she would be gentle with him, because she could tear him limb from limb if she wanted to, with just a look.

"Do you believe in bad people?"

The question caught him off guard. Ansen stopped what he was doing and faced her fully. He felt a weird tug between them.

"It depends on what you mean by bad people." He

conceded finally. Bad was a spectrum, ranging from something as insignificant as a white lie or a 50-cent stolen candy to a dark evil he truly believed only a few experienced in their lifetime. Was Ansen a bad person?

He had been arrested several times in his youth, though he felt those years were long past him now. Seven years he'd served, and the rotten traffic cone color still gave him terrible flashbacks of times he'd rather not relive. Had he not listened to his brother, had he not stolen that car, or stole that money...

Ansen was a different person now. He worked at the bar and kept his mouth shut. He was a good listener and a great keeper of secrets. Would she consider a changed man to still be bad? Or could you ever rid yourself of the bad seed that takes root inside of you?

Luara looked at him, her lip pushed out into a small pout as if she was thinking of how to respond. She opened her mouth once or twice, but the breath escaped and she closed her mouth once more, content to stare at him a while longer.

"I suppose what I mean," she said finally, "Is...do you think evil is something people become? Or do you think it's something people are?"

Ansen pondered it for a second. His skin soaked in her words and he felt his pores open up to her voice. What did he believe?

"Do you want my honest answer?" He asked. Luara nodded her head fervently.

"I think-" he was interrupted by a slurry voice that yelped from the bar doors. He spotted Ness waddling towards them. She had been drinking too, he noted, though he wondered if they had been drinking together, too.

"There you are, biiiiiitch." Ness drawled, saddling up close to them. Her breath reeked of alcohol. Ansen could smell it from where he was, he might have taken a step back if Luara wasn't there. He wasn't sure he could stand so far away from her orbit. Luara gave him an apologetic glance that he didn't return and mouthed 'I'm sorry' to him. As if it was her fault this stupid girl had ruined their moment. Ansen shook his head and returned to wiping down the countertops- far more aggressively than he'd done earlier.

Ansen didn't speak to them much the rest of the night, but he caught important parts of their conversations when their pitch heightened. They were looser tonight than they had been before but Ansen wasn't surprised. Those that had never seen them before would have just seen two drunk girls making fools of themselves. Ansen had seen their journey this week, however, and he couldn't help but worry. Gone were the tightly dressed, well-mannered women he'd seen that first night several days ago. These two were a new breed, born of paranoia and toxicity in their relationship that made him want to take them far away from each other. They fed one another. It would not end well for them, Ansen thought.

He'd done the responsible thing and stopped serving them after one or two more glasses. They were both very tipsy, and he would make sure they called a cab before leaving, but they weren't too rowdy. Not nearly as bad as some of the people that walk through this bar.

"I think you're right, he has to be," he heard Luara moan. Just the sound of her voice made him turn his head, but he didn't engage. Ansen wanted to be the man behind the bar. He ached to see her, hated hearing the distraught tone in her voice. But he was just a body behind the protective wood.

"I always knew Evra was a piece of shit," Ness complained.

She had her hand on Luara's shoulder and looked dead in her eyes. Luara's gaze was wild, unsure of herself. It was a person Ansen wasn't sure he'd ever seen before.

"I'm sorry I didn't believe you, Ness," she sobbed into her collarbone. Ness pulled her close into a hug. Ansen grunted in frustration, he couldn't hear what she was saying between the sobs and wanted nothing more than to pull her away from Ness' embrace.

"It's not your fault men are assholes," she tried to soothe her, but Ansen knew better. She was stroking the fire.

"We can't trust them."

"I told you they'd do this."

"I trusted him with my life."

"I gave him his child."

"They abandoned us"

Ansen glanced over, worry wrought in his expression. It had grown late in the evening, and all others left the comforts of the bar and back to their homes. He was surprised Luara and Ness stayed this long, surely they should have been long gone by now. They spoke in hurried, rushed whispers now, their previous woes were almost forgotten.

Their faces did change, and ones that used to hold worry and dismay now held full, intentional focus. Ansen finished cleaning, opting to do the barest minimum of what was expected. He felt drawn to them again, and as expected, he leaned over the bar in front of them. His lips twitched in disapproval, and the accompanying glare that came from Ness made him even surer of his decision to interrupt their illicit murmurs to one another.

"Do you need me to call a cab?" He asked softly, looking only to Luara but meaning both. Ness shook her head fiercely.

"You don't close the bar for another half hour. You can't kick us out," she snarled. Ansen frowned in return.

"I can refuse to serve you," he said, a simple, snarky smile tugging at his lip.

4

"Let's get out of here," Ness hissed lowly. She didn't trust him, didn't believe him to be just the body behind the bar, not as Lu did. Ansen cared too much, he was too invested, and he broke the most important rule. Ansen watched as Luara's head shook wildly in both directions. Although he wanted so badly for her to be away from Ness, who seemed to be in a world of crazy he didn't want to touch, he couldn't send her away when the look on her face sent a shrill up his spine.

"I don't want to leave. I don't want to go home," his heart broke at the hurt that echoed through her voice. Something felt off, and the crack in her calm facade receded, if only for a moment. He narrowed his eyes and watched as Ness glanced between them uneasily.

"I didn't mean you had to go." He said, frowning. Ansen's fingers tapped quickly against the countertop. It felt smooth to the touch, and while it used to calm his nerves, not even the familiar feel of the bar top was enough to soothe his rattled soul.

"All I meant was to find you a cab if you were too indisposed. You two are welcome to stay as long as it pleases you."

Luara's eyes were empty bulbs, glazed over. Ansen was too afraid to turn back to Ness, who was surely cataloging every movement he made. He put up his hands in retreat.

"Look," she said, leaning forward on the bar. He could feel her breath on his lips she had leaned so close. It wasn't a pleasant sensation. Ness smiled, but it was something sort of wicked. There was an evil that hid there, something he saw in Luara too, but more aggressive. It felt more like something that was hiding inside of him. Ansen's hands shook violently, but no one looked at them.

"We don't need help. Not from a bar keep." Saliva landed on his lips, and he tried hard not to wince from the insult.

"So stay out of our way. None of this concerns you," Luara looked distraught, and Ness turned away from Ansen and physically stepped between them.

He took several staggering steps back, his mouth open in disbelief.

"I uh-" Ansen stammered, he stepped back into the back bar, knocking over several glasses. They watched as the glass shattered as they touched the floor on contact. It ricocheted off the tile, the sound deafening. Several pieces dug into the palms of his hands as Ansen fell backward onto the floor. He could hear Luara's gasp and Ness' sad attempts at muffled laughter. Ansen's face flushed, his cheeks tinting a cherry red. He ran a blood-stained finger through his gray beard, leaving ruby marks as he combed through it, another nervous tick that'd come about because of her. He ignored them as he turned over, intent on never leaving this position again as embarrassment rushed through his veins. His fingers toggled a piece of sharp glass, turning it over in his hand and grabbing for a small waste bin and gently placing it in there.

"I think we need to do it, Lu," he heard Ness whisper. They were so far gone now, so intoxicated by fear, adrenaline, and alcohol. Their whispers were more like car horns, but with an empty bar, he let them continue. Ansen narrowed his eyes as he continued selecting the larger shards of glass

"What do you mean-" Luara started, but Ansen could hear Ness shush her. There was a long pause afterward and he stilled completely. Two pairs of eyes burned holes into his back and he tried desperately to disappear.

"What do you mean?" Lu's whisper was far quieter than how she started, but nowhere near a quiet voice.

"We need to do it. We need to show them what happens when they're unfaithful. Men can't keep doing it to us, Luara. They can't keep hurting us like this," Ansen's heart cracked again, and he waited in the looming silence, trying not to guess her response. The silence stretched into long minutes.

"What do we do, Ness? Tell me what we do?"

Ansen rose from his knees, grunting at the soreness that radiated from the bone. The two women watched as he grabbed the bin and moved it to the other side of the bar. They must have thought he couldn't hear them. There was no way she'd have said it otherwise and he was anticipating the words, almost prophetic. Ansen's insides curled in on each other as if he knew what she was going to say before she uttered the words aloud. This is what it was like for a man like him. This was what it was like to be a body behind a bar.

"We kill them, Lu. We kill them."

Ansen pulled a cigarette from his back pocket, flicking it with his fingers before settling it between his index and middle finger.

"Mind if I smoke?" He laughed, the sound deep and fulfilling. He must have spooked them, had they forgotten he was there? Ness cleared her throat and Luara squeaked.

"Isn't that like...illegal?" Ness scoffed. He had the audacity to give her a look, a look that told her he knew all of her secrets. Ness' lips pinched into a tight line.

"Do you mind?" He asked again. They both shook their heads. Ansen snapped his lighter and watched it delightfully flicker a tiny orange flame. He stared at it intently, wanting the flame to burn his fingertips but coming up unsatisfied.

"You're crazy," Luara whispered, and he caught her vehemently shaking her head again. The length of her hair twisted around her. She looked feral more than posh, a very different girl than the one he'd met only just under a week ago.

"We could do it, I know we can," Ness insisted.

"I have a child, I have a life."

"You have the spawn of a lying, cheating husband. They are not worth your goodness, Luara. We are victims and this is our only way out. Can't you see that?"

"Can we go back to when we thought it was *your* husband that was cheating?" She whined. Ness looked at her with an annoyed cocked eyebrow. Silence surrounded them.

Ansen took a deep inhale, letting the smoke fill up his lungs. It was less satisfying than it used to be, but he wasn't surprised, not with her in the room. He breathed in and out evenly, even though his body was electrifying. Tiny spasms of lightning rushed through his veins, connecting him and Luara together. It was like she was the sun and he would forever orbit around her. In such a short span she became the center of Ansen's universe.

"I don't know if I could," she whimpered in reply, finally. As if they were talking about a minor inconvenience, not a life-changing decision. As if they were thinking about something that needed a decision at all. He could see her expression from here, even as he let out another breath of sour smoke. They must have known that he could hear them. He was never truly invisible, as much as he wanted to be in this moment.

Ness let out an angry sigh. Ansen sensed her foot tapping against the wood panels, the tap tap tap louder than the stillness of the room. The silence that sat between them all was deafening.

"You couldn't do it," he let out. Both their necks snapped towards him. Ness dared to laugh. He was breaking all the rules.

"Stay the fuck out of it," she said. She didn't dismiss him, though, instead taking a daring step forward. Ansen threw his bud to the ground, setting the ash with a stomp of his foot.

"I should call the cops you know. Two drunk women talking about murder." Ansen laughed, the smile not reaching his eyes. Ness' face went pale, and her body rigid. "You two are obviously out of your league. Don't play with fire, or you'll get burned."

"As you said," she drawled, "we're two drunk girls. Cops won't give a fuck."

"These walls listen. Don't go around saying things you don't mean. The bar has a way of making things happen."

"You mean, like ghosts?"

"I mean," Ansen bit down hard, grinding his teeth together in frustration. His hands curled up into small fists that rested in front of him. He leaned over. "That joking or not, don't say shit like that. I should report the two of you. And trust me, I don't want to do that." Ansen's gaze flicked to Luara's perfect, round cheeks. His hand lifted to his face, breaking their contact by closing his eyes and leaning into his palm. He took another long, steadying breath.

"Do you think we should be victims?" He heard her ask. Ansen hadn't expected to hear Luara. Just the sound of her voice sent a shiver down his spine. He ground his teeth harder into each other. It was a miracle he was still able to stand here without looking at her for so long, it was a miracle she was still here with someone like Ness, someone like him.

"No. I think those pathetic excuses for men should get what the fucking Devil has coming for them. I want them to rot in the deepest parts of hell for the damage they've done to you."

"I think you've done worse."

It wasn't an insult. He could hear the timidness in her voice as she said it. It came out as more of a question. She wanted to know the darkest parts of him too. Were all men this way? No, Ansen didn't think so. Luara didn't think so either, that was the reason for her question anyway.

"I have," he confirmed, nodding her way. "But I have also atoned for those sins." A prick tickled his elbow, and he frowned.

"Currently am, I mean."

A flash of darkness crossed Luara's features. He wasn't sure if he had actually caught it, or if it was just a trick of the light. Something inside him gurgled in amusement. Like called to like. There was no lie, he was currently atoning for those sins, although unfortunately, he could never be rid of them completely. "To answer your question, yes, I do think there is an evil that exists in people. I think they are born with it inside of them, and I don't think there's truly a way out of it." Fear penetrated his joints, causing him to lose balance and stumble off to the side. Ness looked at him with only suspicion, and Luara's eyes were petrified. He saw the wheels turn, and discovered the moment where she understood. While Ness continued to watch him with almost hazy eyes, Lu was sharp. She knew the implications of his answer, and it wasn't an answer she wanted to hear.

"So what do you suppose we do?" Ness snapped. Her eyes glazed in that disoriented way, one he'd seen often. This was the face of a person too far gone, the alcohol poisoning her system. She would remember very little of this tomorrow, and what she did remember would be as far away as a distant memory, impossible to grasp. Ansen huffed and ignored her, opting to open his eyes fully to take Luara in again. He thought for a moment longer, the desperate feeling of wanting another cigarette making him smack his tongue against the roof of his mouth. His hands fidgeted. Just her looking at him made him twitch and squirm.

They were drunk, Ansen had to remind himself. They wouldn't remember any of this in the morning. He could feel the darkness sinking through his skin and infiltrating his veins. It was like a coat of black tar sticking to the walls of his core. They weighed him down. Like called to like, and when it heard her siren song, it latched itself onto Ansen quick and with sure feet.

"Poison I heard was the best method," he laughed, joking, trying to shake the feeling away. She continued to look at him curiously, careful to not let her emotions show, "Antifreeze is the easiest. Hard to prove, hard to detect," Ansen shrugged his shoulders, the laugh really building inside of him now, "But you want quickest? Best to run them over with a car. I saw that truck you drive, Ness. That'll shut them up, it's bigger than mine."

Ansen's cackles echoed in the room, clashing with the

silence but neither of them said a word. The demons inside him roared in delight, relishing the darkness that clouded his thoughts. He had beaten this, he thought. Ansen ignored this part of himself for many years now, even as the tendrils seemed to coil around his heart and suffocate him. It tightened harder. He might not have wanted to be this man anymore, but the darkness would never fully let him go. It would hold him tightly until his dying breath; there was an evil inside of him, try as he might forget it. Ansen cleared his throat, letting the croaking laugh fade.

"Once I heard of a man who was killed by his wife," they leaned forward, fully intent on soaking in every single word he spoke, "In his sleep, she injected aconite underneath his tongue, weird, right?" He scrunched his nose up in emphasis, "Pumped him full of the stuff and he overdosed in his sleep. No mark to be found on the body. It's a paralytic, too. Even if he woke up, nothing he could do, really. Not smart in the end, though. She was just growing the stuff in her garden, people like to call it Wolfsbane. Cops knew exactly what to look for, and who."

They stared at him in horror, but not the type he expected. This was a calculated sort of horror.

"I'm kidding, obviously." He said, red creeping up his cheeks again. He suppressed it and shoved the tendrils back down his throat and into the pit of his stomach. Ansen tipped his head in their direction, questioning. "You don't know a joke when you hear one?"

The quip seemed to snap them out of their trance. Ness laughed uncertainly and Luara stared at him intently. It was a bizarre phenomenon to watch their roles reverse. Her stare frightened him some because mirrored in her were the same things he saw in him; and while that might have been cause for some celebration, he couldn't find it in himself to appreciate the kinship. There was a darkness in her that scared him. It could and would make her do some terrible, awful things. He wouldn't be able to stop her, not when the demons danced inside of him, too. Ansen wanted to smile but his muscles wouldn't let him. There was a green tint in her eyes that made him flinch. It seemed so familiar, as every other part of her did. Had she always had green eyes?

"I think it's time for us to go, Lu," Ness said, snapping them all out of their trance. The silence should have only lasted a few moments, seconds at most, but it felt like hours. Luara shook her head.

"No, I don't think I want to go," she said. They both looked at her in shock. Her lip quivered, and as quick as anything she was in front of him. Ansen thought she was going to kiss him until her hands caught at his throat.

"Lu what are you doing?" Ness shouted, grabbing for her and pulling her off of him. Ansen rubbed his throat, where a solid red mark from her hands stamped across his skin. There was a steely look in his eyes, but he hadn't so much as lifted a finger in her direction. He never would.

"Lu, let's fucking go," she hissed under her breath, pulling her out, dragging her to the door and up into the truck. He didn't move, just stood there rubbing at his throat as he heard the door shut and the engine roar to life.

The only thing he could think about was the cruel, wicked look in her eyes. She knew him at that moment, saw deep into his soul. She knew him, and she hated him.

She would come back, he was sure of it.

5
3 WEEKS LATER

Ansen was wiping another glass. It was his fortieth today, he'd been counting. The night was slow, the town was spooked. Things were happening here, and so close to home. No wonder no one wanted to come back. He knew it was them, those two beautiful women with terrible intentions. They had spoken about it just a few weeks ago, and he didn't turn them in. Did that make him a bad person? He laughed, setting the glass off to the side and grabbing for another. Forty-one. He was already a bad person, but this might have made it worse. They were drunk, but the world didn't know how dangerous a woman could be after a few drinks and a surge of confidence. They could have done anything in the world that they wanted to, and he knew that. Maybe there was a part of him that wanted it to happen.

The bastard had it coming to him. It's what happened when you cheated on your wife, the one that bore your child. The one you promised to take care of until death. He didn't take care of her, and he paid greatly for it. Ansen looked up at the door, wanting to see them walk in through them. He was sure they'd return, even after she'd accosted him with those beautiful, delicate little hands. Instinctively his hand lifted to his neck, feeling the spot where those hands wrapped around his skin. It was arousing, he could feel the tug of his pants and shifted uncomfortably on the balls of his feet. It was habitual, each glance at the door was met with disappointment. Up until yesterday when he'd watched the news, he wasn't sure they were even real. Ansen wished it had been a dream, that might have been easier than living in a world where Luara existed and he was not near her.

He hadn't been one to turn on the TV and actually watch it in the bar. Some of the bartenders spent their whole shifts looking up at that stupid box of pictures, but not him. Ansen found that it distracted from his pours, and damn if he wasn't the best bartender in that building because of his aversion to it. Now, his eyes were glued to the screen. He was surprised he even caught it, maybe it was because it was something he was already looking out for. In his soul, he knew what would come next. Why did he need television when he had his own soap opera here in the bar?

"Man killed. Ran over by a truck and almost unrecognizable," he heard someone say to his right. Ansen's head snapped towards him and shook his head to rid himself of the haze that clouded his brain.

"I'm sorry?" he said, placing a new napkin in front of him and taking his empty glass. "Another?" he added as a bit of an afterthought. Yikes, he was losing his touch.

The man pointed to the television like Ansen hadn't already been watching it all day. He was an older man, in his late sixties with a full beard like his own. His breath smelled like cigarettes too. It made him hungry for one, even if he hadn't had one in over three weeks. He just couldn't anymore.

They didn't give him what he needed, Luara was the only one that could do that now.

"A man was run over, right here in town. Do you always have this many crazies?"

"Must be new around here," he joked, tapping on the napkin. The man nodded at the empty glass, and Ansen went ahead to refill it.

"You could say that," he replied, coughing. He had that raspy old man voice, sounding just like his father did before he died. It was comforting, of some sort. "I came from a small, small town a few hours from here. This place...it's too big. Too metropolitan for me." Ansen laughed again and set the newly full glass in front of him. His voice tapered when he realized the man wasn't joking.

"You think...this...is metropolitan?"

"Boy, where I come from, we call you city folk. We don't have people running their neighbors over with trucks. We're not barbarians." Ansen nodded, silently. There would be no use arguing with him, anyway. He glanced back up to the screen instead. They came back to it every so often. It was labeled as a hit and run, the most they were able to tell anyone was that the body was mangled so much he was almost unrecognizable. They found his teeth, and that was it. Damn girls were reckless. He didn't know they would take him seriously. Despite not doing it himself, Ansen felt a large amount of responsibility for that man's lost life.

"It doesn't happen often, sir," he said, wiping down the counter. The old man nodded.

"Doesn't happen at all, where I'm from," he mumbled in reply, "And it doesn't look like they're any closer to finding the murderers." Ansen's shoulders shuddered. He shook his head and raised an eyebrow at the old man.

"No, no it doesn't," he sighed.

The door burst open, and Ansen's heart skipped a beat. He didn't know how he knew it was them, but he did. Bumps raised on his arms and chills shivered up his spine. He looked towards the door and smiled.

He knew they would have come sooner or later, and here they were.

They weren't the same women that walked into that bar the first time. Ness and Luara had a saunter before, but now they half dragged themselves to his counter. He looked at Ness first, although not because he wanted to. His eyes desperately wanted to find Luara, but Ness was obviously the more beat up of the two. They both looked like they had been through hell and back, but Ness looked like she was dead to the world. Ansen wondered how she was able to get here because there was no way in hell that she drove herself on her own. Her eyes were glassed over with a gray coloring, her face looked far more zombie than it usually did. It was yellowing, flaked with dead skin and he would have sworn he saw dried blood around her hairline. Even the muscles were drooping, hanging low into a permanent frown. The wrinkles worried into her forehead as she sat at the countertop. He watched as she moved with agonizing slowness, pulling out the chair and heaving her heavy body onto it.

It was harder than he wanted it to be to tear his gaze from Ness and onto Luara. His body was aching, his muscles tensing in frustration. His mind wasn't letting his body move, wasn't letting his eyes travel to the woman that he wanted to see, needed to see. He knew he would have to look eventually. Ansen wanted to soak in every piece of ugliness from Ness, to remind himself that she could never look as bad as that. Luara could never look dead.

Then he looked. He could feel his body contracting inward. She didn't look half as awful as Ness did, but that didn't mean she looked great. Done was the woman in the red dress, the one with the long, beautifully shining onyx hair. The green in her eyes dulled to a chartreuse, not quite the emerald that he loved looking at so much. Her face wasn't yellowed, but more of a charred terracotta. Her once beautiful freckled, sun-kissed face was haunted by a dark, looming cloud. She wasn't dead, not like Ness, but she was not confident like he knew her to be. She wasn't Luara.

"Ladies," he said quietly, watching Luara take the seat next to her friend. She had sluggish motions, moving into the chair as if her life depended on it. They both nodded in his direction. Ansen didn't move to place napkins in front of them. He didn't move to grab them drinks, not as he might have a few days ago. No respectable bartender in the nation would let them drink, not the way they looked.

"Are you going to serve us or what, Ansen?" He was surprised to hear Ness screaming at him from across the bar. Ansen raised his eyebrow in her direction, beckoning more from her.

"You don't seem to be in the shape to drink, tonight," He replied. Luara hissed at him as if she were a cat. The sound made him stop and tilt his head.

"Get her a fucking drink," she snarled, curling her lip up at him, "She deserves that much."

"You two look like you got into some trouble tonight," The old man looked up at them, and smiled. He wanted to tell him not to push it, to ignore that they existed, but Ansen couldn't speak, he could only look at her. He prayed the unstable look in their eyes wouldn't pull the pin here. To his surprise, they ignored the old man. Instead, they looked at him, glaring. Ansen set to work like a well-oiled machine. He grabbed two glasses, two that he saves specifically for them. He filled them to the brim and shoved the glasses in front of them. It was stupid, filling them up with more alcohol, but he knew it was the only way that they would stay. Ansen guessed they weren't there because of him, but it felt nice to pretend. He wasn't the glue that kept them together, there was no glue. Maybe that was why they were falling apart.

"What are you doing after work tonight, Annnsen?" Ness smiled and giggled. The giggling was unbecoming of her. It was so different than the permanent scowl that sat there every other day.

"I'm shocked you remembered my name," he murmured back, almost too quiet for either of them to hear. Luara smirked. She was too exhausted to move. He could tell just by looking at her face, even if she wanted to talk she couldn't.

"What did you guys do tonight?" He asked warily. They looked at each other instantly. A lot can be said between eyes. The tension in the bar increased, and even the old man in the corner shifted uncomfortably in his seat. Ness and Luara stared at one another with anxious but determined faces.

"We were here," Luara said confidently, eyes flicking to him. She was lying. He would have known if she was here. He orbited around her presence, every hair on his body knew when she was around. The green flecks in her eyes were trying to tell him something dangerous, but he wasn't listening.

"Ma'am, I've been sitting here all day. Surely I'd have seen two knockouts like yourselves," the older man was joking, you could see the crinkles pull at the corners of his eyes. He smiled in their direction, kind and gentle and every bit the middle of nowhere kind of person you would expect. "Looks like you two have seen better days, though. I bet there was another bar in the area you might be confusing this one with."

Ness narrowed her eyes at him and spat on the floor next to her. The gurgle in her throat was not a sound that was pleasant to hear. "Just because your old eyes can't see doesn't mean we were lying," she growled.

"I never said you were a liar," he replied. He must not have picked up on the social queues. He continued shuffling in his seat, feeling the heat and the stiff air, not realizing that it came from these two women, who were very obviously lying, "Just that a place like this ain't the sort of place you'd find two women like yourselves. Didn't you know there was a murder here today? You two should be home, safe with your husbands."

They laughed. It was a gross, ugly sound. Luara cackled and he could see the life breathe back into her again. It would have been nice, had he not seen the sinister behind the smile. She looked like she wanted to rip his head straight off his body, snapping the neck and tearing the skin until it was rolling on the floor next to them. She looked like a predator and everyone in this room would be her prey if she wished it.

"Ansen," Luara turned her head towards him. He stopped with a glass in his hands, threatening to fall from his grip and shatter against the ground below them. He didn't want to nod, he didn't want to give her the satisfaction even if his body was trying to move towards her. "Ansen," she said again. Reluctantly his eyes found hers.

"Ansen, we were here all day, okay?" He found himself nodding, even though he hated himself for it. She smiled again.

"Good," Ness grabbed her shoulder and shook it lightly. It was a gentle movement, the caress of someone you loved, someone you trusted with your life. Luara leaned into the touch and nodded once more.

"It's time to go, Luara." She whispered in her ear. They both looked at Ansen and he watched Ness bite her lip as if she wanted to say more.

"Be safe out there, girls! Watch for trucks!" The old man called. His voice snapped them all out of it.

They hurried out of the bar quickly, and Ansen waited for Luara to turn her head back, to look at him and beg him to come with, but was met with nothing but disappointment.

"What was that about?" Questioned the old man. "You really have some oddities here in this part of town."

"Don't think you're coming back?" he let out a loose breath. The old man's presence made him on edge, made him acutely aware of the wrongness that settled in the air around them. He shook his head and ran his hand through his beard, the movement convinced him to run out from behind the counter and towards the door, not even waiting for the man's reply. Ansen reached out his hand and pushed the door open. He'd waited too long, the little blue pickup truck he'd identified as Ness' was backing out of the parking lot and moving onto the road. Ansen put his hands to his head and tipped his neck back. He was hyperventilating, not knowing what they were doing, what they had done. He wanted to hurl out everything in his stomach. Those two were dangerous, and maybe Ansen was the only one left alive that knew that.

It was hard to miss the new tires that rolled out, attached to her old truck as they drove off. Lazy, sloppy. Someone would find out if *he* did. Ansen couldn't have been the only one that guessed. They were shiny and new, not yet stained with dirt roads or rough gravel. Ansen hiccuped as he breathed in a large gulp of country air, before going back inside. It was in the hands of God, or something darker. He couldn't protect them, not from themselves.

When he kicked the ground below him and touched his

forehead to the worn counter he groaned. The old man tapped his fingers, sending vibrations through the wood.

"Probably not," he answered at last. It was as if he didn't even notice Ansen running after them. His eyes were trained forward, his fingers making that insufferable tapping sound. "You got odd women like that, killers and the like. If I were you I'd get the hell out of this place."

"I can't," Ansen whined, lifting his hand from the counter and wiping at his face with his hands. The old man seemed to nod in understanding. As if he knew the sort of hell Ansen had been through these last few weeks. He couldn't stop feeling like he would never see them again. It was better this way, better for him, but the throb was unbearable. He could never leave this place, even if he wanted to.

"I get that. I loved someone once. Didn't do much good for me. Doesn't look like it's doing much good for you either, son."

"You don't know the half of it," a big sigh escaped him, the ache in his heart pounding so unbearably hard in his chest. The man tapped his empty glass again. Seemed like just a minute ago when he'd poured him a new one. He went to grab it from him.

"Another, please. And do me a favor, boy," Ansen looked up at him.

"Pour yourself a glass, too."

6
5 MONTHS LATER

Time seemed to move in slow motion. Before too long, five months had passed, and it felt like only a microsecond. It was as if Ansen just blinked, and years were taken off his life. He felt old as if he'd aged ten years. He even cut down his beard and shaved it to the 5 o'clock stubble you'd see right now because he wore the aging badly. Even with half the hair taken off his face he still looked like death. 5 months ago was the last time he saw them, he should have been relieved. Ansen knew not knowing Ness and Luara was in his best interest. He couldn't stop thinking about them, though. They never did find out who killed that man and didn't air him again on national television after that day. Ansen couldn't stop thinking about him. He might have been a bad man, what sort of man cheated on his wife? Did that mean he needed to be killed for it?

Ansen spent hours agonizing about those women and what that man could have done to deserve to die. To be run over by his wife in a truck, no less. He'd have hated going out that way, too. Ansen shook his head and swept, letting the broom head collect dust that'd been sitting on the floor for days now. He'd secluded himself to a far corner, content on letting the newest bartender tend to the patrons at the bar. A few months ago, he would have fought her for the spot and made her sweep. He was a changed man, now. Pouring liquor didn't have the appeal it once did, he never felt the itch to be at the bar any longer. It was as if his body knew Luara would never be in it again, and so he didn't want to be in it either.

She was cute, too. Only about ten years younger than he was. Ansen could have sworn she'd given him the side eye too. A smile here and there. Maybe he should give it a real shot. Just having the thought made his stomach curl. She didn't have the same sharpness to her, she was all round, in her cheeks and in her heart. She was safe. Ansen wondered often where his sharp girl went, and whether or not she thought of him too. That one was trouble wherever she went, and not just because of the influence of her friend, although that definitely didn't help. The love was still there, but he pretended to dull it around the edges. There was no use pining after someone he didn't know even existed anymore.

"Ansen?" the voice called from behind the bar. He lifted his head and found her smile, allowing the butterflies to make their way through his stomach. The accompanying urge to vomit came in right behind it, but he swallowed it down as he approached the bar and dragged his hand on the counter as he circled in.

"I forgot how to make this for that gentleman over there," she pointed her hand to a patron at the far end of the bar, "Can you help me?"

Ansen wanted to remind her about the recipe cards that were sitting next to the well, but she knew that. He also knew that they had gone over this particular drink several times over because he was the one who trained her. There was something under the request, and by the way she put her hand on his shoulder and winked as she smiled, he knew what it was that she wanted. If only he could give it to her.

"Yeah, of course," he said, despite his stomach's protests. When the door opened, he felt no urge to look up. He'd lost that impulse three months in, tired of the disappointment he felt when it wasn't *her* walking through them. Ansen was too busy trying to teach the new tender how to make the drink, he wasn't bothered enough to remember her name. She was so... poor at it. Not a great hire, but there were no standards left in this bar anymore. Even the boss knew it. The minute Ansen decided to stop trying, the worse the drinks got, the dirtier the bar became, and the less money they made. He jumped off of the Friday schedule, now opting for the day shifts where the amount of work was half what it should be. He'd dragged his regulars out of bed too. The last Ansen heard, they'd switched to day drinking since his shifts changed, Friday nights were not what they once were.

Soon he'd get the hell out of this place. Lord knew he needed to, and Ansen was close, too. Not looking at the door was part of the battle. Soon he'll stop looking for her in every girl he comes across, he'll stop comparing every laugh, the way people spoke his name- like it was a secret and not something to be warmed by instead. He was so close to moving on from this place and from Luara. He could be out of this dump before the end of the year if he kept it up.

"Go help them down at the end," he whispered against her neck even as the churn of his belly made him woozy. Ansen danced on the soles of his feet, waiting out the feeling. He nodded towards the new customer taking a seat opposite them and smiled as the girl shuffled in embarrassment, the goose-bumps rising on her arms. She giggled and nodded, dragging her nail lightly down his hand. "Remember, the boss is here today so be on your best behavior." She walked away without confirmation, and his smile turned down into an exhausted frown. Ansen turned to refill a few beers from the tap, shaking his head. He might not even have a few months, things have gotten so bad that even the boss was losing faith in his abilities. He knew he was only here to oversee training. Maybe fire him, while he was here, it wasn't often the boss stepped foot in his own bar.

When the young bartender tapped him on the shoulder, Ansen gave her a low grunt in reply.

"They're asking for you," she said, annoyance plastered across her features. Ansen smirked and raised his eyebrows.

"Who?" he asked, skeptical. He'd come across a few regulars who refuse to be served by anyone else but him. They would get used to it, by the time he left. They would have no other choice.

"That girl over there. She won't let me even pour her a beer. I'm not an idiot," he had no reply, just a disgruntled sigh as he lifted his head, tossed the wet rag into the sanitation bucket, and turned around. It was a good thing he set aside the glass before he turned around or else it might have shattered across the floor. He stared right into her sea glass eyes and froze. Ansen's entire body was rigid, and he was afraid he might not ever be able to move again. Luara was the last person he ever expected to see again, here, at the bar. She was in a seat he hadn't ever seen her sit at, and everything just felt wrong.

"Luara," he whispered and walked purposefully towards her. He could see the obvious slump in the new girl's shoulder as he left her to tend to the rest of the bar, but his eyes were there for no one but Luara.

"Hey, barkeep," she said, smiling. It didn't quite reach her eyes. She looked different, but he knew 5 months would do that to you. She didn't look quite as rough as she had the day she and Ness had walked in for the last time, but that wasn't to say that she looked good. She cleaned herself up and chopped off her hair so that it sat just above her shoulders. Her shirt was baggy and her posture was less confident than it was when he met her. Luara seemed to shrink in on herself. She didn't look as beat up, but she did look exhausted, almost as much as he felt.

"What happened to you?" He asked. This felt familiar, and maybe it was because there was a very obvious lack of a presence from Ness or because of the new vibe she carried around with her but he felt more confident than he ever had in her orbit.

"Ansen!" the annoying pitch of his trainee echoed through the air. He had a very visible wince. Lu looked like she wanted to laugh at him. He refused to look at her.

"Yes?"

"Did you want to help me with a few drinks?" A sigh escaped him. Now Luara did laugh at him. He forgot how beautiful that sound was.

"Grab the recipe cards. You won't have me around all the time, and you learn more when you do it without a babysitter." She didn't say anything in return, instead, she grumbled and turned her back on him. Good riddance. He was right, she would learn better when she was making things on her own. It had been five months. Five months, and he was close to being over her; but then she walked through those doors and it was like those months hadn't passed at all. How had she walked into this building without him knowing, or caring? Ansen didn't know how that happened, but it physically hurt him to think he could ever not love her.

"She likes you," Lu mused, and he would be lying if he said he couldn't hear the frustration in her voice too, no matter how small it seemed.

"Yeah," he agreed. What was the point of hiding it? "But I don't even know her name," she pushed her lips out and pouted. There was no way she felt bad for the girl, but at least she was pretending, "So, it's been a while, is your friend coming?"

She recoiled at the mention of Ness, shaking her head so hard he was afraid it would leave her body. "No, she's not."

"What happened?"

"You know, I forgot how nosy you were," she teased, albeit halfheartedly. Ansen let it drop.

"You know, she was sleeping with my husband." Every time she opened her mouth he looked at her. He must have looked confused because the floodgates opened up.

"You would think, after twenty years of friendship, your best friend wouldn't be sleeping with your husband? Piece of shit, both of them."

"Fuck, Luara, I'm so sorry. I didn't know. I knew you both were worried, how did you find out?"

Lu threw her head back and laughed. The sound was so loud that everyone in the bar looked at them, but she didn't seem to notice.

"Found them in my bed. The bed we christened our marriage in. The bed we conceived in. The bed my five-year-old crawls into when they've had a bad dream." She didn't sound hurt, or confused. She knew exactly what she was saying, but she sounded like she didn't care. He wanted to ask about her child, wanted to curse that man for giving her the gift of life, and then betraying her.

"Don't feel bad for me," she said, tears welling from the corners of her eyes from the hysterics her laughs had her in. He had a panic on his face, and he had nothing to say to the admission. "I slept with hers."

"I'm sorry?"

"Told the shit head about their infidelity and he told me to take off my pants. So I let him."

"I don't understand," his brows creased at the center.

"Oh, I think you understand me perfectly, you just don't want to. Yeah I know, call me a whore, call me whatever it is you want to call me, Ansen, but I slept with him. And then I killed him."

Ansen felt like he was going to drop to the floor. He had nothing to say to her, and the way her voice dropped into a hushed whisper, he knew she wasn't done. There were so many things she needed to get off her chest, and he was the body behind the bar.

"I stabbed him," she mumbled, "well, sliced his throat, more accurately," Luara laughed, "Ness, you see, she was already planning to kill the man- who never actually cheated on her if you were wondering- so really I was doing her a favor."

He didn't want to ask her but, he couldn't just let her say it without asking. "Did you...her...did?" Ansen stuttered.

"Did I kill her? No. I didn't. It was funny, actually. I walked in on her sleeping with my husband. She walked in on me killing hers."

There was too much going on at once, too much information to process. Luara let her head hang in her hands. Ansen walked out from around the bar near her, but she raised a hand and pushed him away from her.

"Don't," Luara said, "I didn't kill her, I said. She saw me, screamed at me, which...I get. And then she told me she wasn't the only one, and then she left. Skipped town. She probably won't turn up again, if I know her." She lifted her finger to shush him as if Ansen had a word to say otherwise. "I know you're probably thinking I didn't know her at all right now, but

I promise I knew her better than most. I won't have to worry about seeing her face again.

"Luara," He said firmly, loudly. Heads turned their way, but he didn't care if they watched.

"What, Ansen?"

"Luara, didn't she kill her husband with her truck five months ago?" Her face dropped. He'd never seen her this way before. She looked confused, she looked so much like a stranger at that moment that Ansen wasn't convinced she was the person he wished for every day of his life since she disappeared.

"I...uh, I got to go. It was nice seeing you, Ansen," Luara tried to get up, and wobbled on her heels. She looked both ways like a rabid dog might. Ansen looked at her warily, arms out to steady her but she shoved him away.

"No." She snarled. That feral look was in her eyes, but it wasn't the composed feral he'd been intrigued by. This was a feral that was let loose, and a feral Ansen couldn't let out. He needed to keep her caged, like an animal.

There was the crazy, the deep dark, and evil that he saw in himself. It was manifested in her. It was like the tendrils crawled away from him and into her. He looked at her, and her eyes looked wild, and when she got up Ansen was afraid to touch her.

7

"Don't go!" Ansen pleaded. He dropped onto his knees, hands praying towards her, someone close to royalty, or a god, or something. Luara stared at him in return, void of emotion. He thought she was good, that she was different. Luara was turning out to be just as bad as the rest of them, just as bad as him. She smacked his hands away and he winced as they fell to his sides. "Please don't go. I can help you. We can leave, get away together."

"You don't know what you're saying," she hissed at him. From this angle, she looked dirty and rugged. She had dirt smeared across her face and her hair, which was normally so beautifully long and shiny, glistening with sweat and grime. Like she hadn't washed it in several days. Ansen wouldn't be surprised if she hadn't. How hadn't he noticed it before? She came in looking fine, she didn't come in looking like this.

"You're not who I remember you to be," his voice was pained, desperate. Ansen wanted to cling to what he remembered of her. Not this person who he barely recognized. It had been months since he'd seen her properly, but there was no way 5 months could change this much about a person.

"You barely knew me to begin with, barkeep," she laughed. The sound was dry and painful sounding as it emitted from her throat. "It's been five months, I thought you'd have gotten over it by now." She was being callous, downright cruel. No, this was an entirely different Luara than the one that asked for his name several months ago. Ansen rolled to his knees. The pain was sharp and his eyes twitched from the hurt, but he pressed on. It didn't matter that there were others staring at them. It didn't matter that the boss would be coming around the corner any minute, wondering why the hell he was on the floor, begging this woman to stay.

This woman who he didn't know at all.

"I know," Ansen admitted. She scoffed and shrugged her shoulders as her laugh echoed through the room again. "But you felt it too. I know you had to. It's why you kept coming back. You felt drawn to me too, I know it. Like calls to like." He had to distract her and keep her from leaving the bar. He could help her when she was safe inside the bar.

"I kept coming back for the shitty beer," Lu's mouth moved to a smirk. He could hear several coughs and side comments made by passersby. None were very pleasant. They must think of him to be a beggar, a loser.

"Luara, I love you. You can't go," and there it was. It sort of slipped out, a whisper in a crowded room. She stared at him dead in the face. Ansen winced, waiting for the laugh to come. That her gross, cruel snarl would pierce him deeper than if she had stabbed him with that knife he saw poking out of her pocket. Nothing came. Instead, her leg came out from under her and kicked him in the kneecaps. He stumbled, but solid, Ansen was always the strong sort. Even if he had never felt more defeated than he did now, kneeling in front of her, he would be a pillar of strength. One of the many things he was good for, was what his past had built out of him.

"You don't even know me, keep," she spat at him, physically spat at him. Her saliva was warm and sticky, and he felt it as it splashed against his face. Ansen let it sit there, marking him, his hands still praying up at her. "You don't know who I am, you didn't know who I was. You don't know who the fuck I'm going to be. So I suggest that you get your pathetic ass off the ground and get back behind the bar. You're good for nothing but pouring crappy beer and harassing women. Like all men do. I don't have to answer to you."

The whispers around them grew louder. He felt several hands reach out to touch his shoulders and help him up, but he pushed them away. He didn't want help, not from them. They might surround them, but in their bubble, it was only him and Luara.

"I can help you," he said.

"I don't need your help."

"Luara. Please. Listen to me. I can help you."

It must have been the way he said it. Like his voice or tone, or simply the inflection of certain words that made her stop. Her eyes glazed over and she cocked her head, taking in his desperation. Lu lowered her foot and looked at him curiously. Her green eyes sparkled with newfound interest. Did she understand what it was he was trying to say?

"How can you help me, Ansen?" The darkness that clouded her voice was now gone, replaced by the familiar purr he was so used to. He missed that voice. The sound of it immediately put him at ease, whether he wanted to or not. Ansen could feel his muscles relaxing, his stiff shoulders loosening. She made him this way, and she would be the death of him.

"I don't think it's something I should say so publicly, dear," he threw the insult back at her. If he wasn't mistaken, he could see the tiny wince in the crinkles of her eyes. Luara hid it quickly.

"Well, since you begged so nicely," her hand stretched out towards him, a beacon of hope. He wasn't sure he wanted to do what he was about to do, but this might have been the only way to talk some sense into her. He hadn't seen her in so long, and if she were to leave and never come back...Ansen wasn't sure what he would do. He would go to the ends of the Earth for this woman. His hand connected with hers, and he allowed her to pull him up from the ground. "Let's go somewhere more private, shall we?" she whispered in his ear. It was velvet smooth and seductive, and he was positive she could have said anything to him at that moment and he would have let her take him. Ansen nodded clumsily.

"Boss, I'm checking out for a bit!" He called over his shoulder. Who knew if the boss actually heard him? The trainee looked at him helplessly. She had to stay, she needed to be on her own to learn anything. Ansen was spoken for. But while Luara was in this building no more drinks would be made. Maybe not ever again if he had his way. If he was lucky enough, he might leave with her and never return either, just two shadowed souls born of darkness.

They walked through the doors of the bar and he led her to a worn awning, passed the clouds of smoke and the bikers that loitered near the entrance. Her hand was far too warm in his, almost hot to the touch. It was like she was boiling from the inside.

She wrapped her hands around his waist, digging her nails into his soft flesh. Ansen gasped as she stuck her tongue down his throat, exploring the inside of his mouth as she kissed him long and deep. His body melted before her, catching fire. Just as soon as she latched onto him like a leech, she let go. Ansen took a step back, dazed.

"Help me kill my husband," she breathed, and he could still feel her against his mouth. He only nodded. "That thing you said, about the aconite. How did you know that? Does that really work? Where, how, when?"

"Slow down, Lu," He smiled, despite the wrongness that settled in his stomach.

"No," she hissed, "I will not slow down. My cheating husband cheated with my cheating friend. And now the cheating friend is missing. Dead, probably. Hell, if Ness were here I'd kill her again myself. She deserves it anyway." Her eyes glazed over again with that fire he saw when she came in. This girl was dangerous, and it was hot. But there was something a bit frightening about it, too.

"That's a lot of killing you have to do," Ansen ran his fingers through his stubble, missing his beard and shifting back from one foot to another in apprehension. He watched her furrow her brow. It was like she was thinking really hard, like she wasn't quite all there. There was a bit of that crazy again in her expression, and he was afraid to push her any further. He'd seen that face before, it was almost like a mirror of his own.

"Don't patronize me," she said. "You promised me you would help."

"I didn't promise anything."

"You said you would help." The fire was almost tangible, licking the top layer of her skin. He was worried that he would burn if he touched her.

"I-" will he help her? Was it that easy for him to fall back on his past? The tendrils that avoided him for so long manifested before his eyes. He could tell she saw them too, the way her eyes flickered in recognition. She wasn't afraid, in fact, Ansen could have sworn the tension was looser in her shoulders when she saw them. Luara didn't turn her head, didn't so much as take another step towards the tendrils that wrapped around them, devouring their darkness.

He needed to lie to her. "I will." He conceded, drawing near her. She lifted her chin and looked at him with those doe eyes, green and opal. He could never say no to her. The smile that drew on her face made him hot with bother. It was the only way he could keep her at bay.

"It's the only way," she hummed. Ansen felt himself nodding. Of course, it was the right thing to do. He couldn't let her do it alone. He couldn't leave her. They deserved it. He had to admit, it was fun playing in the dark again. "But my dear Ansen, no one can know."

"I won't tell," he breathed. It would be the best promise he ever made.

"I know," Her face lit up, all devilish and cruel. Ansen could have sworn he'd seen her before, that they had crossed paths at some point in their life. "You're just the body behind the bar. "

2 Days Later

"A woman was poisoned in her home last night, foul play suspected. If anyone has any information regarding this cruel attack, please contact us at the number listed below. While the husband is not deemed as a suspect at this time, no more can be said. As Channel 5 gets more news, we will keep you updated." That was it. The entirety of her life boiled down to this moment, just five seconds across the screen before they moved on to something they deemed more important. Nothing was more important than her, and yet, she was only the 'woman that was poisoned'.

They'd never get the full story. They wouldn't know about Ness or the infidelity. He was probably the only person left that cared about all of that. He didn't even know if they would host a funeral for her. Ansen stared at the screen, memorizing the face of the husband that killed her. He might have had an alibi, he might have gotten away with it, but he did it. There was no doubt in his mind that this man was the one that killed Luara.

Ansen slammed the glass he'd been holding. He was supposed to meet her today. He was supposed to go to Luara and they were going to do it together. Now she was gone. Poisoned in her sleep, like she didn't matter at all. The glass left his hands and shattered across the floor. Heads turned but he didn't care.

He wanted to die, and that's what it seemed like he was going to do. His back slid across the bar back and his bottom hit the floor.

So much for being a nobody. He broke all the rules, he fell for her, and now he was going to pay for every second of it. So much for being just another body in this place.

Fuck this city, fuck this world, and fuck this terrible, dirty bar.

PART TEN
OTHER MONSTERS

"Hell is empty and all the devils are here."
- William Shakespeare

I

Day 101

Icarus looked towards the sky, an unresting purple hue falling over the distance. While he'd looked out towards that horizon before, it was today that he'd frowned. There was nothing he could see in the distance past the terrible color. At first, it might have been beautiful, like she was, but no longer. The purple now fueled the hatred, the oranges and reds now wrapping around his bones and crushing them to dust. Every time he saw it, he wanted to die. For a time, he pretended the ache in his chest was gone, that this place didn't take away everything Icarus was and had been. Now it was impossible to ignore. He was only skin and bones, but just barely so.

The fact was, he already was dead. As dead as they come. People dreamed of hell and told stories about the fiery pits and the darkness that followed each soul on their travels through it, but none of them knew how it truly was until they died.

Everyone would come to hell and they would all call it something different. It was hell, it was the underworld, it was purgatory or inferno. It didn't matter how good you were or how pure your life was. Hell was terrible. It was cruel, but not because of the external pain you suffered. Hell was limbo. There was nothing but loneliness and heartache. Hell was where you would never feel anything ever again.

Sometimes he thought eternity was too long a sentence for his crimes, no matter how many there were. There were many, each deliciously more awful than the next. Had she given Icarus another chance at life, there was hardly a doubt that he would screw it up again. More often than not, the reason for his damning was because of *her*. She was the succubus that destroyed him time and time again. Icarus should have known, there was no person that could have been as beautiful as she was, it was more than the mortal world was able to create on its own.

Despite all of that, this half-life he now lived was the worst sort of torture. Icarus hated her. It didn't matter how much he *thought* he loved her, he couldn't stand to look her in her eyes. She was not who he wanted her to be, no matter that their faces were identical. She was not his, not who he thought he had loved. To survive here, however, he needed to hold onto a moment, any moment, and his moment will always be at the center of the universe. With her.

Icarus let her believe it too, let her wander this Earth, waking each day for nothing but a single dance. As he agonized in this eternity, he would not let her do the same. It was a terrible game to play, to both hate and adore someone so completely. So, as if it was like any other day, he dressed in his suit. There was a blue tint to it, though it wasn't as bright a blue as he usually liked. There was something about the color that made him queasy, but it was the only thing he had.

This man who didn't deserve this story appeared on the side of the road, as he always did day in and day out. Icarus walked the unknown city, watching as its people stared at him with their soulless, empty eyes. There was something familiar about them, as there was with the suit, and try as he might forget it, the memory haunted him. People often forgot their memories. They remembered very slim fragments, and the brain would toss the rest. People didn't remember events, they remembered feelings. Icarus remembered every feeling, and that was what ripped his soul out of his chest.

He knew he was beautiful, with a sharp jawline and a crisp suit jacket that settled itself comfortably around his body. He was toned, allowing his quick steps to be graceful, but powerful. If you were mistaken he would have looked like he was in charge of this place, and certainly not the victim. Like each day before this one, he knew where he was going. It was an odd pull, almost like tendrils that followed him wherever he went. He couldn't remember when he first met them; they were sentient, moving in and out between the darkness and pushing him closer and closer to the center of this universe like they had every day. At one point they were just there, and the man couldn't even remember being frightened of them. They were lifelong companions and he could not reach far back enough to know a day without them.

When he saw her in the clearing, he smiled without even meaning to. It was muscle memory. Icarus felt his muscles twitch in anticipation, his body always responding to hers. They were two halves of a whole. She was everything he wanted, and when she stood there with her hands by her sides and her eyes closed he remembered the feeling of love making a home in the deep cavern where his heart had been. It was always this way, and he couldn't stop the way his heart pounded when he saw her. The problem wasn't getting here, it was always easy to follow the tendrils as they guided him to her day after day. The problem wasn't getting the chance to see her as he remembered her.

The problem was when she opened her eyes.

They were hollow pits, and the longer he stared at them, the deeper he seemed to drown. Each night they were different, filing through a variety of tortures that made fear boil up inside of him. Tonight she had chosen something special. Inside the sockets were rows and rows of sharp tiny teeth that seemed to go so far back that it didn't make sense. He knew if he tried to look she could swallow him whole. The man didn't want to take another step forward. This was another level of hell he could not handle. Yet, the tendrils pushed harder, wrapping themselves around his legs and dragging each foot in front of the other despite his reluctance. When she saw him, she smiled wide, unaware of the tiny matching teeth that littered her mouth, too.

Was it that she couldn't remember anything? Was it really *her* that continued to haunt that body so? Icarus took hesitantly forced steps to the center of the universe, and she held out her hand. Their fingers touched and he felt the fire once more. The room spun as he took her into his arms, closing his eyes from the horror of her face. Icarus could tell she didn't feel a thing, didn't recognize the despair on his face as he twirled her round and round. The fire licked his arms, burning what was left of his mortal flesh. He could have sworn there were patches missing, but when he looked he still appeared whole. It was another piece of the hell he was given, he was sure. With a steady three count, he danced with her into the night, trying desperately to ignore the pain that throbbed in his soul.

As the sun disappeared the man closed his eyes tight, wishing for it to come back up and release him from this nightmare. That fire tickled the core of his bones. She was never fazed by the heat, but it burned him up from the inside. The man resisted the urge to scream, using this dance to remember the life he used to live when he was above ground. There wasn't much that he could remember, save the last twenty-four hours of his ticking clock.

2

He forced himself to open his eyes after what seemed like hours and she was staring at him. Icarus had done this before, and remembered every moment that would pass each night. Tonight was different, though. Luci never looked at him the way she was now. It had been over a hundred days and she never once stared at him with the horrific pleasure that graced her features. The teeth in her sockets chattered, causing the rise of goosebumps across his skin. She stopped them mid-twirl and his breath hitched. The dance never stopped. All one hundred days of dances before this and not once had they stopped before the hazy glow reappeared in the sky.

Icarus looked around in fear. The bodies were gone, their familiar grey gazes nonexistent in this world. This time he felt completely alone, and very much in danger. The tendrils, sensing his fear and urge to run, tightened their grip on him. He was all alone in his desire to leave. Luci stepped away timidly, confident in a way he was unfamiliar with. He so wished he could do the same, had the dark shadows not rooted him to the very spot he stood, mid-twirl. She cocked her head slightly, the razor-sharp teeth clamping down once, twice, three times. Icarus flinched every time her teeth collided, making an awful sound that would follow him into tomorrow. If there was going to be a tomorrow.

"Do you not like them?" Luci asked, and although it sounded sweet, her voice dripped like vinegar. Icarus didn't even know what to say to her. They had never spoken, not once in a hundred days. She cackled an evil sound that echoed through this unnamed city. It sounded nothing like the woman that he loved once. Icarus continued to avert his eyes from her, searching the buildings for a face, any face that might have been able to help him. He was alone. Alone with *her*. Could he speak at all? He'd never tried, never had a need to in this world with no company. The man opened his mouth slightly, letting a little breath release. His throat ached as if it had breathed in a lungful of smoke. It was dry and scratched with each attempt. Icarus coughed once, and Luci laughed. She wasn't who he remembered her to be.

Gone was the girl in his dreams, the one that kissed him goodnight and made him breakfast in bed. Gone was the girl he loved. He had doomed her to this afterlife, forcing her to endure a life where she couldn't remember their world. He once thought that there were two people living inside of her, but maybe it was that there was only ever one, the other overtaken long ago. This monster that stood before him clicked her tongue, causing him to betray his determination and focus on her instead of the buildings in the distance. Her teeth rattled like a snake, morphing before his eyes like a trick of the light.

Looks were deceptive, but even limbo wasn't that good at tricking its victims into believing any of it was real. He supposed that was the purpose, was it not? Icarus couldn't believe that the dangers on her face were real. What was worse than having to live in your dreams but knowing they weren't the fantasy you wanted? He had forgotten she said anything at all, wanting so badly to ignore her. With the way she stared at him, her head tilted so far to the right that he thought it might fall off her shoulders, causing a shiver deep in his core. The man was afraid of what might happen if he didn't answer in feeble words.

"You are not her," Icarus said with finality. The delivery was less than ideal, his lungs failed to have it come out coherently, opting for a gargled cough instead. It wasn't so much an answer to her question as it was a test to see if she had taken his voice away in this place too... and if he could speak at all. She only smiled that knowing grin again, showing her teeth purposefully. His voice held not the confidence that he once had, but the shriveled squeak of a child.

"I could be if you would just let go," Luci answered, practically skipping to the other side of the clearing. It was lightning fast, and if he had blinked he would have missed it completely. He watched her bend down to pick a large white rose from a bush tracing the perimeter. Had that bush always been there? Within a flash she returned to his side, far too fast for the mortal he fell in love with. If he was confused about who was in front of him before, he wasn't now. She caressed the side of his face, her nails stretching into thick, curved talons. It cut a small thin line across his cheek and the man flinched, scared that it might be more if he didn't play his cards right. Even that movement seemed too familiar, but he couldn't place why. She smiled again, those shiny sharp teeth glittering in the moonlight. He just needed to wait it out until sunrise. That was when she would disappear and he would have a reprieve again.

"I don't need her anymore," his voice heightened at the end, betraying his nerves. He did, he needed her like the sun needed the moon, like the body needed a heart. She lifted her claws, extending them to his neck and dragging them alongside his collarbone.

"Your wife or me?" She cooed. The man didn't know what to say. He had never been married before. He had died when he was twenty-four. He didn't so much have a ring on his finger before he was underground.

"I don-, you se-, I don't know who you're talking about," he settled on. It was true, there was nothing that Icarus could grasp from his old life that would help him understand what she was saying. Was it possible that she might have had the wrong person? Was he pulled into this world by mistake? Had she spent the whole of her life-ruining him when there was someone else that was supposed to be in his place?

"I think you're lying, Icarus," she hissed. Hearing his name from her mouth was like flipping a switch. Memories flooded through him, each one more bright and colorful than the next. Icarus felt himself hunch over from the overwhelming amount of information flying across his screen of vision. She cracked her neck, a terrible crunching sound that hardly seemed to faze her. When his eyes snapped back to hers, he glared. Names were powerful things. How would he have known that just a matter of his given name would give him the memories he was desperate for, for so long?

"I do not lie to you, Lucifer."

3

"I miss when you called me Luci," she sighed, cradling the words against her chest. It was the first time he had said her name since he died. Hearing her chop it in that high innocent voice snapped something within him. He raised his chin to meet her grin with a fire in his own eyes. It was less intimidating than hers, but it was more feeling than he felt in the one hundred days he was trapped here.

"I do not call a monster by its pet name," he said sharply. It was a mistake.

Icarus felt a raging pain slice across his chest. He gripped his hands against it and fell to his knees, gasping for breath. The cut was deep enough to be fatal. Blood was everywhere, his bones white as the moonlight if anyone looked in. He felt his insides fall out and scatter across the ground in front of them. Icarus tried to hold everything together with both of his strong hands, but it was no use. The crimson bled through the dull blueness of his suit, staining it beyond repair. The sight was one to behold, one that he might have remembered before. The memory seemed to evade him.

"Do you not know who I am?" she roared. The sound echoed in and out of the buildings of the unnamed city. Icarus could feel the ground quiver in anticipation. He looked up and the fire was gone from his eyes. While he was sitting with his insides wrapped around his arms, there wasn't much fire left in him. He begged her once before to take away the memories and take away all feelings. She granted him the latter with one condition. He would feel pain, for as long as he was here. Unfortunately for Icarus, he was sentenced to eternity, and so that meant he would forever feel. The pain was unbearable, and as he lay on his side, clutching his knees to his chest and sobbing dry heaves, Luci smiled. She snapped her fingers, which now were the form of beautiful, soft, and almost tourmaline-colored hands, and at once the pain was gone. Icarus looked down to find the wound no longer there. In its place was a long, ugly-looking purple scar, and the memory of pain. He winced as he looked at it.

"Get up," she growled, kicking him with a hard thump. Icarus had no option but to obey. It was an excruciating sight to behold, and he groaned in agony as his body resisted the movements. His muscles stiff, and Icarus faced Luci with a sadness ringing through him. This was the first time he'd spoken to her like this since she placed him here. He would not make that mistake again. Icarus thought he learned a long time ago that it was pointless to anger her. Here in her world, he had no voice at all, really.

"I thought you learned," she sighed, lengthening it as if it was only an inconvenience to her. She lifted her nails to her mouth and started biting them. It was a nasty habit, one that he remembered inhabiting that body when it was still living. He stared at her, open-mouthed, reveling in the memories. It had been too long since he could remember, and while it flooded his mind like a restless tidal wave, it also filled him with a feeling close to relief. Luci stared back, catching her finger in her mouth and cutting it clean off.

Icarus shook his head in shock, widening his eyes and reaching to rub them with his own hands. He lurched after he made the movement and tried to grab at his chest again instead, forgetting momentarily that the wound was now only a scar. His suit fell to either side of him, hanging only by the threads off his arms. Luci laughed, flicking her wrists and revealing her hand back to perfect health. Icarus removed his fingers from the scar and draped them on either side of his body. He looked pitiful, on his knees in front of Lucifer herself, with tears staining his pink cheeks.

"What do you want from me?" he whimpered, letting go of a held-in breath and feeling the silent tears trail down his face. "Why now?"

Luci started walking around him, circling him like a shark in the water. She was much more frightening than sharks, though, and Icarus didn't dare speak again.

"I don't have much time, Icarus. I have other lives to torture, other people to kill. You know I have a hard, busy job."

She was just toying with him, of course. He knew the Devil could be anywhere she wanted. She could be everywhere and nowhere at once. Luci stopped right in front of him, cupping his face in her delicate hands. They were hands that had killed people. They were the same hands that killed him.

"Do you remember the first time you saw me, Icarus? I remember the love in your eyes. Yes, you loved me. You loved me immediately, I could see it."

He loved that body more than he loved breathing. But back then it wasn't Lucifer. It was Lucinda, the daughter of a butcher boy and a seamstress. She was poor and lived paycheck to paycheck. He fell in love with her mind and her wit. The girl, the monster, the Devil standing in front of him now was not her. It never would have been her. Even before that though, it felt to Icarus that he had known her many times over. The daughter of a butcher was not the first time he stared into those emerald green eyes.

"Icarus, do you ever wonder why we met? I could think of a few reasons."

"I thought you had other lives to slay. Why won't you leave me to this Hell you've given me?"

"You think this is Hell?" Luci scoffed, rolling her eyes and dragging a reformed claw up and down her arm. The talon didn't pierce her hard skin. It made a screeching sound like nails on a chalkboard. "You should be praising me for my generosity."

She held out her hand once more, and this time Icarus took it. She wove her fingers through his and pulled him along. It was at this moment that he realized he hadn't felt the presence of the tendrils. It felt lonely without the shadows. They were persistent, yes, but they kept him safe. It was a sense of security when they wrapped themselves around him. Without them, this world felt more...dangerous. She pulled him along the street, one he'd never been on before. It was odd that Icarus had lived here and took no roads but the only one he knew. He looked around, perturbed by the monotony of it all. Each building was various shades of grey. The shadows danced in the dark corners and Icarus heard whispers coming from the walls. They were chanting something but he couldn't quite make it out. It was more unsettling than walking hand in hand with the Devil.

"Why did you choose this?" He whispered. He was no longer angry at her. The more he walked with her in this unnamed city, the easier it was to see clearly. There were many wrongs Icarus did in his life, there were decisions and pain he needed to atone for. Remembering his twenty-four years of existence made him see that maybe she was giving him an easy out. Luci's duties were to damn the damnable. If there was no cut-and-dry definition, he would fit that description.

"You don't remember, my dear," she said, amusement filling the holes in her voice again. "But we were here once. You told me about your parents here. You told me you wanted to move here. So it was my decision to place you in a world I created that resembled it. You see, I only have so much at my disposal. I'm sorry it wasn't a complete copy."

She said many things that made little sense. He was so sure that he could remember everything from his past life, so why was it he couldn't remember this place? She looked at him with a smile. If he wasn't as smart as he was it might have looked like it was meant to be sweet. Icarus knew better, though. This smile was threatening. He would have to watch what he said or he would find himself keeled over again with another scar to show for it.

"I don't remember," he said finally. Icarus didn't look right at her. Instead, he focused his gaze out towards the buildings as they walked. They ran on for miles, but past that he couldn't see much else. He wondered if this place would continue as long as they wanted it to. If Luci was creating this place as they walked, she could take him wherever she wanted.

"Of course you don't," she huffed. She sounded annoyed by that fact but resigned all the same. "You won't remember unless I will it. And I am in no place to will it just yet. You have more torture in your years to come." There was something in her voice that was off. It sounded like bitterness, but he wasn't sure. Icarus raised his eyebrows.

"You seem angry about that," he commented.

"Do I?" she hummed. Her fingers tightened around his hand and he winced from the pain. The claws were long gone but in their place was a strength he didn't expect from her.

"You do. It seems like you want me to know. Why won't you tell me?" Icarus pressed. It seemed surreal that just a moment before he had been dancing in this torturous loop, and now he was speaking with the person who damned him to it. Although he was conversing with the she-devil, he didn't want it to end. The break from the loop was something he had wished for a thousand times over for. He would not ruin this. While he may pay for it later, Icarus was in no place to deny himself this one day that wasn't completely heart-wrenching.

Luci *tsk*-ed her tongue, chastising him. "I am no fool, Icarus. I know when I am being tricked. I will not tell you, my personal feelings aside. There is nothing in it for me. You see, as the creator of this place, if something does not benefit me then why would I do it?"

"Then tell me about it," he pleaded. He didn't know this Lucifer, the one that destroyed worlds and collected the souls of the damned. He only knew Luci. He wanted to know what made her this way. "Can you show me your true face? It hurts to look at hers." He tried to avoid her face if at all possible, but Luci didn't seem to mind. He could feel her shaking her head fiercely.

"Oh no, puppet. That face is reserved for someone very specific tonight, and you are not on that date." She slowed their pace, stopping at nearby floral arrangements and statues that seemed to populate out of nowhere. Icarus trained his eyes to stay forward. "And I quite like this one, don't you?"

"Why did you have to bring her here too?" His voice was growing hoarse. It was from lack of use and Icarus swallowed hard to try and moisten his airways.

"She was no better than you, Icarus," Luci said, stopping and turning to face him once more. When she looked at him the way she did, he found it hard not to look into those eyes of hers. The rows and rows of teeth filled the sockets and never ended. She put a finger under his chin and forced him to look up. The teeth were gone, replaced by a light green color that reminded him of a moss-covered cave near his home when he was living. There was relief in the breath that he loosed, and Luci laughed, all-knowing. "She was just as wrong, just as much a bad seed. Unfortunately, her association with you would have brought her here anyway. You just sped along the process." The she-devil looked away from him then, for reasons he couldn't seem to decipher.

"And why me? Why did you take me when you did?" Luci's eyes widened in surprise. She was as much taken back at the question as he was. Her face flicked back to him.

"Well, of course, you don't know that either."

"And you won't tell me." Icarus' voice was soft but definite. He wouldn't talk in circles anymore with her. If Luci needed to be somewhere, she would leave. She wanted to be here, and that want was what frightened Icarus the most.

"No," she sighed. Icarus tried pulling his hand away but she wouldn't let him. The strength behind that hold reminded him again of his shadow tendrils. "Not unless you wanted to hear the whole story."

"Would it help me at all?" he asked. Luci pondered that thought for a moment. She tilted her head, letting a tongue as quick as a snake fork out between her lips.

"Maybe. But probably not. Although now that I think of it... it might help *me*. And isn't that the point of this place, puppet?"

He shifted on both feet uncomfortably. His desire to know the truth outweighed his fear of this place being any worse than what it already was. He was so terribly frightened of what this conversation would mean for years to come. Would she subject him again to the dance with an unknowing girl? He wasn't sure he would be able to bear it for much longer. She moved her fingers across her throat, humming in satisfaction as the nails raked tiny pink lines across her skin.

“Okay, I’ve decided,” she said loudly. The entire world shook then as if shivering from the proclamation of her decision. Icarus followed suit. When the Devil made a decision, he knew nothing good was going to come out of it. Unfortunately, now that he was the center of her attention, he knew no good was going to come to him because of it.

4

After over a hundred days of walking and dancing, Icarus felt an unsettling wave of relief wash over him. Before them, at the snap of her fingertips, was a bench. It was so unlike this place, an anomaly in the darkness that radiated off of his little piece of the universe. Icarus shifted his weight forward, scowling as he so often did. Whatever he did, he couldn't let Lucifer see the content on his face. She could, and would, take that from him in a heartbeat. She lived to watch him suffer, and for the first time since he died, he wasn't suffering. It was the calm before the storm. Icarus looked at her, awaiting her next move patiently. He had gotten on the ride and there was no leaving until she ended it.

"Icarus dear, what is it that you remember?" she asked him. His mouth curled into a cruel, wicked grin. It didn't quite meet the tips of her eyes.

"Why do you ask me that?" he sneered, wincing as he caught himself. "You know what it is I remember." Luci laughed, another loud, boisterous sound. It was the first time he'd heard her laugh like that in a long time. It almost made him miss it, long for another one.

"It would be more fun this way." Luci's voice was soft and aloof once more. Icarus was lucky she hadn't taken offense at his outburst. She loved playing with him. He might have believed she actually loved him too if she continued talking as she was. It was a preposterous idea because the she-devil had never known love. She has damned herself, and damnation rarely rewards love.

"I remember dying." Icarus hated returning to that place. He never wanted to remember what it was like to take that last bit of breath, of the ache in his chest when his heart stopped beating. But what did he hate more than death itself? The horror that was leaving his body. While painless in practice, the repercussions of his decisions were the most heartbreaking of all.

Icarus remembered dying, but he also remembered Luci, and not the one sitting before him, the one with the body that this monster stole sobbing over his breathless body. The sight was ingrained in his vision forever. Icarus remembered the funeral, where only a handful of people paid their respects. He remembered the last moments as if they were the worst he'd had on earth. And Icarus never did live the life that those in Olympus or in Heaven or whatever it was that was up there would deem worthy. But he didn't want to talk about all of that with Luci. She knew what it was he remembered, and her purpose was only to dig the knife deeper into his chest.

"Ah yes, your death in this life was one I spent a long time planning. Not that I needed to do much anyway, you were so hell-bent on getting down here yourself. Had I not intervened, you might have just died on your own a few years later. Icarus you were never destined for a long life. Just many." He looked up into those piercing blue eyes, so sharp that they cut him.

"I don't understand what you mean," he said at last. Icarus ran his hand across the pebbled surface of the bench, catching each groove in his fingertips. The movement soothed him.

"Well, first you must tell me what else you remember, puppet." Her lips curled upwards for her tongue to flicker out again. He could just make out the teeth behind those red inflamed lips.

He tried harder to remember if only to appease her. She would not rest until he answered this trivial question. Icarus opened his mouth to speak, and then stopped. Luci's smile widened. He tried once more, coming up with no words other than a cough that sent him hunched over with a pain in his chest again. It wasn't only the words he couldn't come up with, however. It was the memories. Where he thought he stored millions of tiny strands of memories, he was now coming up empty. It wasn't like his bank had been stolen from him, it was as if it was never full, to begin with. There was no trace of the memories Icarus thought he knew. He looked at her wildly.

"Ah, I see," Luci tapped her knee. Her gaze was all-knowing and it made Icarus weak with frustration. She placed her hand on his temple and tapped once, gently, "You don't remember, do you? That's a shame. I just needed to make sure."

"You knew."

"Of course I knew, puppet," she sighed. "I was the one that took them from you. But I had to be sure you weren't trying to trick me. It would be awfully dumb of you to do that, you know."

"Stop talking in circles Lucifer," he growled. His contentment made him loose with words, causing him to misstep. Lucifer frowned.

"Then stop pretending to know better, mortal," she hissed in return. Luci snapped her fingers. The bench below him shattered, and crumbled into pieces before it disintegrated into thin air. Icarus fell, his tailbone screaming in pain from the hard ground below. He looked up to see Luci still sitting there, hovering over thin air. Instead of getting up, he stayed where he was. The moment of contentment was gone, back was the egregious agony that bounced around inside his body, happy to be back home where it thought it belonged.

"I suppose enough is enough," Luci smacked her lips and lifted Icarus from the ground. He felt the shadows again, coiling around his body and moving him without his consent. Closer he drifted towards his former love until he was on his knees in front of her once more. Lucifer bent over so her mouth was close enough to his ear. He was frightened that she would bite it off, which was in character for her.

"I want you to remember," and she kissed his forehead. Icarus gasped, and everything went black.

5

Icarus thought he remembered everything. How naive of him to think that he did as he walked down the road of that unnamed city, towards the center of the universe. He knew nothing. He crawled away from Luci, heaving heavy sobs as he inched backward. He knew. He now knew the true meaning of everything.

"I know you!" he screamed, the ducts empty and no more tears to cry. His breath rose his chest up and down and he gagged from the oxygen he was no longer breathing in. Lucifer stared at him with newfound interest.

"Had I known you would be this tortured, I would have done this a long time ago," she purred. He tried to escape, but with another snap of her fingers, she was in front of him instantaneously. Her green eyes were gone, replaced again by the Corinthian-style sockets, teeth chattering in anticipation. Icarus' sobs were louder than was appropriate. Each intake of breath flashed another memory. They came one after another, each life filling him up to the tip before pouring out again. How could one body and one mind know so many different kinds of lies and lives?

"What do you remember now, puppet?" Luci's voice turned from the sweet innocence she had portrayed to a dark, sinister growl. Icarus could no longer be fazed by it because she was no longer the person that frightened him the most. The thing he was most afraid of wasn't the Devil; it was himself. Icarus lived a thousand lives, and each was shorter and more awful than the last. He remembered the drugs, he remembered the blood, he remembered every single bad thing he had done in every single life he lived.

"You remember everything now, don't you?" She looked at him, baring her teeth and snapping them so close to his face that he thought she was going to bite his nose clean off.

"I remember," he whispered.

"And what do you want me to do now?" Her question seemed like a trick, but he looked into her eyes earnestly. He knew exactly what it was he had done, and he deserved every moment of this.

"I want you to kill me," Icarus said in resignation. He lowered himself to his knees and dipped his head, bowing to her, giving her access to his neck. It was silly in retrospect, Luci could have killed him any way she wanted to, anywhere. He was vulnerable every day in this world. Bowing to her was almost like an insult. Lucifer scowled deeper, raising her claw up in the air. Icarus waited for the swing, for her to put him out of his misery forever but it never came. Instead, Luci's razor-sharp nails swung down and the air hissed near his ears.

"You fool. You sorry, pitiful fool," her voice was near his ear now, the hot breath burning his skin. It was so hot Icarus could smell the burnt tips of his lobes. "Death would be too easy a punishment for what you did, puppet. I plan on keeping you here for a very, very long time." Icarus let out a sharp gasp and a sob, crawling into himself and rocking back and forth. Luci frowned, sitting down again on a bench in thin air. She stuck a nail in her mouth and chewed delicately. "Now get up. You're embarrassing yourself."

Icarus wiped his eyes and sat up once more. His face beet red, his eyes bloodshot. He looked at her with sadness in his expression. "Why can't you let me go?"

Luci laughed and shoved a foot in his side, digging in deep. "Do not question me, child." She tapped her chin and contemplated. The seconds turned to minutes, and Icarus felt it run into hours. He looked at her now with newfound recognition. The silence was a blessing of sorts. Because when he looked at her, Icarus was able to see her in every single life they had lived together. They always did find each other in the end. It was like it was destiny, two awful halves, part of the same whole.

"Are we soulmates?" he asked, hesitantly. That was the only thing he could come up with that wasn't too crazy to say out loud. To say that his love was destined for the Devil was outrageous, but it was the only thing he could come up with that could help bring meaning to the pull that led them together time after time. He should have watched his tongue, but Luci was not angry with him. It seemed, now that he knew their true history, she didn't have a plan for what came next. It should have been killing him, dying a true death, and not like the others he had died before. But he knew Lucifer and knew how much it pained her to let him leave without an ounce of consequence. Death really was more than he deserved.

"I don't think so," she said finally. He relaxed his shoulders and turned to face her. The face he saw was more like the Luci he remembered. She really was beautiful. Dark black curls circled her hair, and the green jaguar-like eyes lit up, especially in this moonlight. Her dress, simple but magnificent, draped across her body and dangled below her feet. It looked like she was gliding on air. The wind picked up then, ruffling through her hair, but he didn't feel cold. The elements never paid attention to him, only to her.

"Then why is it that you've found me in every life I've ever lived?" He thought he must've known the answer, but hearing her say it out loud would comfort him. Even if it wasn't the answer he wanted to hear.

"I found you on my own," she admitted. "I was sent to kill you in every life, and so I did. It was my job, and nothing more."

"But you're the one who makes the jobs, so surely it wasn't something that was forced upon you." She got up swiftly, walking away from him. In another world, in a world where he did not remember, Icarus would have run far away in the opposite direction. In this world though, he knew, and so he had to follow her until his heart stopped beating. He wasn't sure if she wanted him to follow, as she glided far past the path they had set for themselves. The world morphed around her, the place where the bench might have been disappeared into the shadows, leaving a hole of black behind them. Icarus skipped forward, fearful that the darkness might take him, too.

He walked behind her, careful to keep a safe distance of three feet. The world did change the further they went into it, buildings crumbled to dust, the wind scattering their remains. In their place rose large pine trees. The scent was captivating; fresh minty pine and rough upturned dirt. This place, like the one before, was familiar in feeling but he couldn't place the memory. The strange Deja Vu knocked the breath out of him. Luci stopped by a riverbed. He could hear faint howls of car horns not too far off, though the forest surrounded them on either side. She bent to her knees, staring at her reflection in the water.

"I don't make jobs," she said finally. It had been so long

since she last spoke that it took Icarus a second to remember what they were talking about. He stared at her quietly, waiting for her to go on.

"Sometimes things just need to be done. I don't create the work, I only execute it. I am forever cast as the villain of every story, and most times I don't remember what that story is."

"I don't understand," there were a lot of things that he couldn't understand, but this one seemed important. So he wanted to try, for her.

"Of course you don't."

"So you mean to tell me that you're not the villain?" She smiled at that, and he let out another breath of relief. There was a dangerous line that he walked on, and Icarus crossed it more than he probably should have. There was an uncomfortable heave of her chest as if she was spasming. Icarus moved forward subconsciously, reaching a hand out to help her before he realized that she was laughing.

"Oh, puppet, I am no fool. Of course, I am a villain. There is not one that takes my place and is not. We've all done very wrong things, mine sometimes worse than the others. But I am not the only villain, and I think people seem to forget that."

He certainly did. He thought she was tormenting his soul for no reason at all. Now knowing, it was hard to not feel pity for her. How lonely must it have been down here? Especially being the only one to know that there were other monsters walking around you... her life was a punishment on its own.

"Not everyone forgets," she said, splashing the water with a hooked finger. The fish underneath all scattered. "Each being's version is slightly different. Your punishment just so happened to have been your forgotten memories." He watched her shrug as if it was no big deal at all. Icarus clenched his fists. "I find you in each of your lives because I can't seem to let you go."

There wasn't much he thought he could say as a suitable reply. Icarus' mouth hung open, parted lips chapped from the dry air. He felt the sudden urge to take giant gulps of it to cleanse the ache in his throat. "Are you ready to tell me the truth now, Lucifer? The whole truth?" He rubbed his fingertips together in anticipation. In some way or another, this felt as if they were close to the end. Their chapter was closing, and maybe Luci noticed it too because she looked up from the water and faced him. Her face was vacant, her eyes wandering across his features. He watched her swallow, and pat the floor beside her near the riverbed.

"Come sit next to me, Icarus."

6

"Do you remember your first life?" she asked him as if it was a perfectly normal question to ask someone. He looked out towards the trees across the river, his feet sliding under the cool water.

"I remember every life," he said, shaking his head to clear it. He did, somehow, remember all the various lives he'd endured above ground. All the while staying here in his dances. At one point he would have told you that it was impossible to be in two places at once, but now, he knew anything was possible, at least here. The memories jumbled in his head, each bleeding into another. He couldn't tell where one stopped and another began. "But no, not the first."

She contemplated that for a moment, bringing her nails to her mouth to bite on again. Luci nodded as if she knew. She was content with him not knowing, and he could tell by the look on her face that she wouldn't tell him any more than what she thought he needed to know.

"Do you remember me?" There was a shy timidness to her that he'd never seen before. Lucifer narrowed her eyes when she registered the shock in his and turned away towards the water. Icarus thought for a moment. It was a silly question, because of course he could remember her. She was always there, in one form or another. Always the most beautiful person in the room. She constantly took the breath right out of him, as she did now. It wasn't just beauty that devoured him, though. It was her wit and her brain, it was the dangerous edge that she had wherever she went, drawing him to her. Icarus thought there might have been more to it, there was no way she had been the one finding him on her own. There was this magical draw, like an invisible string that tied them together, a way they would always find each other. It was also why Icarus thought they might have been soul mates; things like this never happened because of chance alone. But no, they were both too twisted to have deserved that much. Maybe they were each other's reckoning instead, cursed to love, only to hurt.

She could have changed the hurt part, he thought.

"Of course I remember you," he said instead, sounding only slightly offended. "You had always been the one to kill me, after all."

"Only a few times!" she hissed, chomping her teeth together so hard it made his chatter. A Devil who doesn't take credit for what she was built to do. How interesting.

"Enough for it to matter," Icarus scoffed, taking off the remains of his ripped suit and tossing it into the water. His bare chest was toned and scarred, a tribute to whatever hells he faced before coming down here. The irony was not lost on him. "Each death I remember being attributed to you to some degree. Whether it was love, loss, lust, or a combination of the three. Somehow you were always the reason."

She kicked the water, spraying a nearby tree. They watched together as the water dripped downwards. She didn't say anything again for a long while. If they continued sitting like this, it would be like he wasn't sitting next to Lucifer at all, not the devil that tortured all those lives every day she walked among us. It was more like talking to Luci, or whatever else she wanted her name to be. "Why the different names, Luci? Why not just stick with Lucinda?" he added, almost like an afterthought. He could have sworn he saw her smile.

"I said my real name to you, once. Lucifer, not Lucinda," she admitted. Her eyes glazed over as she relived the memory. "Our first life together, actually. I remember you weren't paying much attention to it when I said it, we were...in the middle of something else that took your attention instead."

Icarus could feel the deep red blush that brushed across his cheeks. She didn't pay attention to it. "I remember I said it, and you looked at me as if you thought I was joking. Lucinda was the only thing I could come up with at the time, not even Lucifer, my own name. Over the years it just became a game I liked to play. You wouldn't remember anyway, so what did it matter? At least I was able to be someone else for a little bit." Icarus thought he might have heard a tinge of resentment in her tone. It was so bizarre, seeing her this way when only moments before she was slicing his chest right open.

"You're right though," she continued, and Icarus's face flicked to hers. He was so sure she was going to ignore his latest revelation, but here she was, surprising him yet again. "I was always there. Believe it or not, Icarus, I didn't want you to die, not that first time, anyway. But then it happened, and then it kept happening. I didn't know how to stop it."

His eyebrows furrowed together. There was no possible way he was going to feel bad for her. So why did his heart lurch? "I can't help but want to challenge that statement," he wondered out loud. Luci growled, her fingertips now digging holes in the soft earth. The world seemed to rumble around them as she did it. "We're past lying, aren't we?" He grabbed for her hand, hissing as the heat radiating off her skin blistered his palm at the touch. Luci's frown turned upwards. He could almost hear her laugh again.

"I hate it when you're right. Let's not try for a third time, okay?" Her fingertips didn't cool, and Icarus moved his hand away. He could sense her frustration. "You do remember your first life, in fact. You just don't know it as your first."

"Whi-"

"I'm not going to tell you which one and don't you dare interrupt me again." Her voice took that dangerous tone that he knew so well. He snapped his mouth shut and let her continue. "But there was a first time, and I would say, our first dance with each other really did screw up our lives, didn't it? I do blame you, for most of it anyway. You started this," Lucifer waved her arms around her as if she meant he had created Hell itself.

"I was mortal once if you could believe it. And when we met I was infatuated with you. Of course, you weren't Icarus then. You were quite smitten with me, too. You weren't as afraid of me as you are now. Or, maybe you were. I couldn't say for certain."

Icarus couldn't imagine not being terrified of her. If she was any bit as beautiful then as she was now, he probably would have followed her anywhere. Would he make it, if he took off now? Probably not. Icarus wouldn't doubt that she would follow him to the ends of the Earth, but for vastly different reasons. Ones that would come to a more violent end, more than likely.

"You betrayed me once, Icarus. It broke my heart, tore me apart and I wasn't sure how I was going to get over it. I didn't know what I was going to do. But then I decided I wasn't going to get over it. I was going to get revenge. I wasn't innocent, not by any means and I knew that." Luci laughed. It was as if it was an old joke that they both shared. It made Icarus angry. He clenched his fists and whirled on her to find that she was no longer there sitting next to him.

Luci had appeared on the other side of the river, picking up a large rock and skipping it down the river. It shouldn't have worked, not as it would have in an open body of water. But Icarus watched as it did in fact skip in the water, creating ripples across the surface. The rocks glided along the shape of the river bend, following the path of the stream. It was a beautiful sort of magic to watch.

"How dare you say it was me?" he roared. His voice reverberated throughout the forest, bouncing off of the tree trunks. She looked at him, eyes red, a predatory gleam to them. She could pounce across the water in one leap if she wanted to tear him apart. Icarus could see she was close to it, too. Her nails on either hand elongated and she bent her knees to jump across. It didn't stop Icarus from screaming at her though. He let out his rage then, and as he vocalized it he could feel the relief leave his body. All the air was leaving his balloon, and it was the first time in a long time that he felt like he had any sliver of control again.

"Luci, I'm sorry if I ever did anything to hurt you. I know I did the wrong things. And I'm so so terribly sorry. But you've trapped me here for eternity, surely nothing I've done could have warranted that?"

Luci let out a guttural sound that made his insides boil. "The worst of what I've done cannot outweigh the wrong of what you are. And sometimes, people apologize not because they regret what they did, but for themselves," she said. Again he was struck by the sadness that radiated through her.

"So tell me how to fix it," he pleaded. At that moment, Icarus would do almost anything to take that look off her face.

She was quiet for a long moment. He was starting to get

used to these lapses in conversation and started enjoying the quiet peace that surrounded them when they didn't talk.

"There is one way," she said finally. Icarus didn't look up at her. Instead, he dipped his head deeper into his chest. "Tell me, dear puppet. Do you really want to leave this place?"

7

"Don't take me back to that world. I don't deserve it." Icarus stood up, wiped his hands on his pants, and turned to walk away from her. She caught up easily, galloping alongside him like a gazelle.

"I don't think I could do that, not in your current body, or your current memories. If I did, you would be a new person, and we would inevitably find each other again. And it would be a vicious cycle. Trust me, I hate it almost as much as you do, but I do my job well."

"So then, what do you suggest?" He put his hands in his pockets, feigning nonchalance.

"Icarus, do you know the story of the Devil?"

They walked slowly. She grabbed for his hands like he remembered they had done a million times before in a million different bodies. "To become a Devil, you must meet one."

He didn't want to answer her, because all of this was crazier than what his mind could comprehend. How does one meet a Devil, as if there were more than one? He squeezed her hand gently, ignoring the black flames that crawled up his arm. Now that they were holding hands the heat didn't seem as unbearable. It was a dull ache that pulsed in his veins, a reminder that there were worse things to come, but he wasn't quite there yet.

"I'm not sure if I'm supposed to answer that, or if it's just rhetoric," he admitted out loud. She laughed. He would never get over the sound of Lucifer's laugh.

"It is not a real question, but it is a real statement. It's as real as the bench you sat on, the river I skipped rocks at, and the place you danced with me."

"It doesn't feel real at all, then, if that's the only criteria." He laughed now too, for the first time in the last hundred years or so. The sound was warm but raspy.

"It's surprisingly easy, believe it or not," she said, ignoring him. "I was told you need to be at your absolute worst. You need to be so sad that it breaks you. You need to be in a position where you're willing to do anything to make it stop."

He could only think of so many times that he'd been in that spot. It seemed too easy.

"I know you think you've seen that place. A lot of people do. But not many ever truly feel that kind of loneliness. And those that do, do not walk the mortal realms on their own for very long."

"I can only assume that you were there because of me. You've said as much."

"Naturally," she said, her voice one octave higher than it usually was. "I called out to a power that would help me, one that would take away the pain but leave me living and breathing. I didn't want to die, you see. Even at my very worst, I didn't want to die."

"And did something answer your call?" Icarus' breaths were low and steady. It was all he could do to keep from interrupting, but he knew he had to hear this out. To hear her out. They were running out of time. Her eyes darkened. Icarus had a flash of Deja Vu, he'd seen this look before. In another dance probably. They were deep black holes, and the further he looked into them, the deeper he was sucked in. There was such sadness in those eyes and it made him writhe in pain.

"Something came to me that night," she said. The world fell around them, engulfing them in the same blackness that matched her eyes. The concrete crumbled before them, and they fell together into the shadows. He could barely see her, the glow of fresh Devil tears streaming down her face. "It's not a long story, really. He came to me, and asked me what it was I desired most. You must see, Icarus, it was a terrible mistake. I didn't know what it was he would do, or what he *could* do."

"He was so handsome, rugged like you but much larger. There was a stockiness to him that scared me. You were always so polished; he was not. I told him I needed to punish someone, that I wanted to hurt you just as badly as you hurt me. I thought he was a big guy, that he might find you and rough you up a little bit. I don't know what I was thinking."

She trailed off, and Icarus looked off into the darkness. He could barely make up the scene in his head. Devils were not what they appeared to be, so he was unsure that he would have been able to pick him out from a crowd. He could feel himself clenching his fists, wishing for some sort of release. He wanted to know everything, and he wanted to know nothing at all.

"When he asked me if I wanted to die, well, you know my answer. Because I really didn't. I was a glutton for punishment. I'd have rather withered away in my sadness forever than cease to exist. What does that say about me?" He assumed her pause was not meant for him to answer, but rather, to reach out to her. He refused to do either.

"He told me he would take me to his home, and show me a way to get back at you. I was so young then, and when a handsome man told me he would solve all my problems, I believed him."

"You wouldn't have liked his version of this place." She turned to him now. Icarus snapped out of his trance and ignored that look. He could feel her gaze on his face, but he refused to look. Not until she decided his fate, not until she finished her story. "It was dark, but in a much more menacing way. Large stalagmites and fire everywhere. It was where you mortals got the depiction of Hell, I think. But I wasn't frightened. How could I be when this man only offered to help me?"

"He told me I had two choices. That I could die and forget all the bad things I had done and had been done to me, or I could take his helm."

"Take his helm?" Icarus asked, his voice disappearing in the darkness the minute he said it.

"He wanted me to become the Devil."

Icarus' face distorted into one of horror. His eyebrows raised and his mouth hung slightly open. His blue eyes raged, and if you looked closely you might have been able to see the little fires in them, too. "That's why you are here," he surmised. He watched her shrug as if it was no big deal at all. Lucifer nodded.

"He seemed too eager to give it to me. I should have known better, but as I said, I was naive. To be fair, he did give me everything I asked for. I won't traumatize you with the details."

Icarus whirled on her, "What do you mean you're not going to give me the rest?!"

"It's not important to our story, Icarus. You see?"

He did not in fact, see. Lucifer snapped her fingers, bringing them back to the center of the universe. It looked different than it had before. Icarus was sure it was the same place, but it transformed, becoming a part of every single life he lived on Earth. He spotted moments, he spotted landmarks, and he watched as the pieces of his life fit into place around them. And there, at the center of the universe in that tiny gazebo, was a large door. It was hanging slightly ajar and had a strange light emitted from it. With no streetlights, it was the only thing lighting the entire city.

They glided over to the open door together with their hands entwined. It felt comfortable like they'd done it a thousand times before that. Icarus felt a large, nervous knot in his stomach with each and every step. Not a sound could be heard in this city with no name.

"I will give you the same choice I was given," she said as they neared it. There was a heaviness settling around them, waiting for a pin to drop. He realized then that this was indeed the last day he would have here. It would be the beginning or the end, and he wasn't sure he was ready for either. Icarus looked up at her, tugging lightly on their hands to disconnect. Luci held on tighter, not allowing their fingertips to part. He couldn't say that he didn't like it, just a little bit.

"I will warn you that neither of these choices are ones that I want for you. But this isn't about want, Icarus. It's about need. We've come too far and now we can't go back."

"Stop dancing around it, Lucifer, and tell me what needs to happen."

She fumbled with her words. "I'm sorry, I've never done this. I don't quite know what to do." She let go of his hand then, shaking her head. When she looked up at him, her eyes were no longer the same shade of beautiful green. When he looked at her, he could see the fire in their pits, the red flame dancing in those two black sockets.

"Tell me," her voice was deeper now, more menacing, "do you want to stay in this loop forever?" He looked at her with a vacant expression. He could see no hint of a joke in her expression, but the question seemed to be mocking him. He wanted to say as much but kept his lips tightly together. Icarus knew better than to answer without knowing his options. The fire in Luci's eyes burned brightly, and he couldn't let his guard slip, despite her warm hand and soft expressions. She was still the Devil, and the Devil was known for tricks. She hummed, clicking her tongue in disapproval at his silence. Icarus smirked slightly, though it looked more like a twitch in his lip.

"You're no fun," she teased, finally releasing her grip on his hand. "The other option is not much better."

"Out with it, Lucifer!" Icarus said, exasperated. He was tired of these games. She looked at him with a furrowed brow and hissed.

"Fine!" she spat. The kind Lucifer was gone once more, replaced by the she-devil that haunted his dreams. "The choice, if you so make it, is to continue in this loop as you are. Nothing must change, outside of your memories being wiped once more. It seems a relief almost, right? You go back to our dances, never knowing more than your most recent life and death. I would say this is forgiving." She tapped her thumb against her elbows, crossing her arms and staring at the door in front of them.

"The second choice, if you make it," he rolled his eyes at her pandering, "is to take the helm. Become the Devil and remember everything, but escape the loop. Escape me."

He narrowed his eyes. Surely this must have been a mistake? "I don't understand what it is you want."

"It's not about what I want. The choice is yours, just as it was mine. I will not persuade you one way or the other."

"But surely there is one that you prefer?"

She shrugged, her slender shoulders moving gracefully. In fact, Luci looked quite bored. "I don't understand why that is what you're concerned about. Surely anyone would kill to be in your position, right? To thwart the Devil, or to forget their past sins. You are a winner either way, at least how I see it."

Icarus couldn't seem to see it the same. These were not wins, but losses. However, considering the lives he *had* lived, this was far more than he deserved. It could have been a trick, she would never admit it even if it wasn't. The choice was his, after all. He looked towards the door, sitting ominously in its luminous glow.

"And the choice is mine, and mine alone?"

"Completely," she purred.

He wasn't sure he believed her, but there was nothing more he could do at this moment other than make the choice. Icarus hung his head and closed his eyes. His lives blew past his vision, playing out like a movie on a screen. He watched as his sins counted, one after another. Every time he thought he might have taken a proper path, Luci was there to steer him away again. He was sure he was right, they were meant for one another. In some sick way, destiny played them like fools. They stood there together for what seemed to be hours, but down here it might have only been seconds, minutes. She waited for him patiently, and only on occasion could Icarus hear her teeth grind together.

Before too long, the sun started to set once more. Icarus had forgotten that there was a sun at all. He looked out at it, hating the way the purples met against the oranges. The colors bled into one another, each holding their own, and he could only laugh at the defiance there. The two were opposites, mashing together to create a sight so beautiful, but there was a danger that lurked there too. The sunset meant that night was coming, and he knew nothing good ever happened after dark. Icarus couldn't help but despise it. Was there ever really a choice? There was a much thinner line between sin and virtue than most would ever realize. He walked that line every day, and now he was going to pay the price for those crimes. There were so many of them. There really was no decision to make at all. When he looked at Lucifer again, she looked more radiant than she ever had before. He could see her true light, shining bright from within her. She was the Devil, but maybe he was already one too. She read the look on his face, tapping her chin with a long fingernail.

"I'm surprised," she said. "And honestly, a bit disappointed." She wouldn't elaborate. Icarus was too afraid to say it out loud. Luci sighed and beckoned him over to her. There was a finality about this moment, and it made him sad. They had played this game for far too long. It was bittersweet watching it finally comes to an end. But if there was one thing Icarus was good at, it was finding her again. For better or worse, he knew they would play this dance again, in whatever capacity this decision allowed them to.

"We've already had one hundred dances together," she said, lips curling up in a smile. There was no sincerity in that smile, no love housed behind her eyes any longer. He wondered briefly if any of that had been real at all. As he stared at her, the draw between them seemed to intensify. The invisible line that held them together shined brighter and brighter until he couldn't look at it any longer. If Icarus tried to cut it, he was sure it would not budge. Lucifer held out her hand, and he took it without hesitation. Together they walked towards the door, which opened as they neared. He didn't look at it, instead opting to look at her face one last time.

It was beautiful, and Icarus could see at that moment all of the masks she wore. She was Lessa, and she was Lola, and she was Lorena. Luci had become Layla, and Livvy, Lindin, and Lena. He watched each life and dance play out before him before she morphed into the face that started it all. She was Luara, and she looked up at him with a fierceness that made his heart beat out of his chest. A woman hell-bent on exacting her revenge.

If this was the last time he would ever look at her, he was glad it was like this. Clarity washed over his features. The decision felt too easy now, the evil that crossed her eyes acting as the catalyst for this next series of lifespans ahead of him.

"What's one more dance together?" Luci winked at him.

Icarus smiled in return. It was a cruel, wicked smile, one he had learned from her in her infinite lifetimes. The existence of being hunted by Lucifer had prepared him for becoming the Devil as she had been for so long.

Icarus took her hand, and they descended through the door and into the darkness together one final time.

PLAYLIST

- **Lose It** - Oh Wonder
- **Helena** - My Chemical Romance
- **Simmer** - Hayley Williams
- **all the good girls go to hell** - Billie Eilish
- **Hurt** - Nine Inch Nails
- **Wings of a Butterfly** - HIM
- **Killer In The Mirror** - Set It Off
- **no body, no crime** - Taylor Swift
- **The Drug In Me Is Reimagined** - Falling In Reverse
- **It's All Over** - Three Days Grace
- **The Haunting** - Set It Off
- **A Little Bit Off** - Five Finger Death Punch
- **Dance Macabre** - Ghost

Acknowledgments

Writing a book is hard. Publishing a book is harder. No, not hard, it's excruciating and exhausting and I don't know how I did it. I cried, I laughed, I lost and I won. I learned so much about myself and the world around me writing and publishing this book, and there are entirely too many people who have helped me get to this point that it is near impossible to name them all.

Sincerest thanks are to be given to my editor, Alexis Aumagamanaia (@littlelionslibrary), who made sure the words you just read were the best that they could be. When I told you I wanted to do this, you told me, "We can make that happen," and I don't think you know how much that impacted me. So thank you, from the bottom of my heart. I am in love with every word on every page and that is largely thanks to you.

My absolute thanks and adoration to the family I created at Barnes & Noble. I have the coolest job in the world, and it's amazing to see all sides of the industry I love so much. You all help fuel my passion.

To all of the individuals who read a portion or the entirety of this manuscript, your input was invaluable and it'll take me a long time to finish up all of those thank you letters. You were integral to the development of this story.

To my very special friend, Delta Gowen. I don't know if you remember this, but that night at the Paramount was the night I wrote the first 1,400 words of this manuscript. Back then it was only to pass the time, and I remember making you read it at 8 pm because I was so proud of it. Who would have thought this is where it would end up? Thank you for being that forever sort of friend, no matter how far apart. I feel really good about the fact that you're the first person to have ever read a piece of this.

It wouldn't be like me if I didn't include my parents, who push me every step of the way and who constantly encourage me to try new things. I know I try a lot of things. Some work, some don't, and I'm so lucky to have you cheering for me through every endeavor. Extended gratitude to my grandmother, Julie Pollard, who inspired me to believe that anything was possible because she paved the way for me to do so.

And because he would kill me if I didn't mention him, to my husband, Gabriel, who, let's face it, had to work overtime in our home while I was writing this. I love you lots and I appreciate what you do. And yes, credit goes to you for that one story...you know the one.

Lastly, I wanted to thank you, reader. To have you read the words I put to paper is humbling. I never thought what I had to say was important enough, so to see you here is a joy I can't express loudly enough.

ABOUT THE AUTHOR

Cassandra Celia (she/they) is a Maryland bookseller, turned author. She writes gothic, horror, and paranormal fiction, such as her debut, STARS AND OTHER MONSTERS, and her latest release, THE ELRIC UNDOING. Cassandra obsesses over stories with love, death, ambiguous endings, and everything in between. In her books, she takes inspiration from dark, haunting art and media, and she absolutely loves writing about angry, scorned women.

Stay up to date by visiting her website, www.cassandracelia.carrd.co.

facebook.com/cassthebookseller
instagram.com/authorcassandracelia
tiktok.com/@authorcassandracelia

www.ingramcontent.com/pod-product-compliance
Lightning Source LLC
Chambersburg PA
CBHW030603310726
48979CB00003B/559
* 9 7 9 8 9 8 5 8 6 5 9 2 9 *